Treat yourself this Christmas to two novels
from bestselling authors

Cathy Gillen
THACKER

"Cathy Gillen Thacker gifts readers with a
charming story in *Baby's First Christmas*..."
—*Romantic Times*

"With a flair for fun, Cathy Gillen Thacker
delivers sheer enjoyment..."
—*Romantic Times*

and

Leigh
MICHAELS

"Leigh Michaels eases us into the holiday season
with *The Unlikely Santa*... Ms. Michaels weaves an
enchanting tale overflowing with lovable characters,
a charming plot and joyous emotion."
—*Romantic Times*

"Michaels...has a knack for creating likable
characters with whom it's quite pleasant to
spend a couple of hours..."
—*All About Romance*

CATHY GILLEN THACKER

is a full-time wife, mother and author who began typing stories for her own amusement during "naptime" when her children were toddlers. Twenty years and more than sixty published novels later, Cathy is almost as well-known for her witty romantic comedies and warm family stories as she is for her triple-layer brownies, her ability to get grass stains and red clay out of almost anything and her knack for knowing what her three grown and nearly grown children are up to almost before they do! Cathy's books have made numerous appearances on bestseller lists and are now published in seventeen languages and thirty-five countries around the world.

LEIGH MICHAELS

has always been a writer, composing dreadful poetry when she was just four years old and dictating it to her long-suffering older sister. She started writing romance in her teens and burned six full manuscripts before submitting her work to a publisher. Now, with more than seventy novels to her credit, she also teaches romance writing seminars at universities, writers' conferences and on the Internet. Leigh loves to hear from readers. You may contact her at: P.O. Box 935, Ottumwa, Iowa 52501, USA or visit her Web site: leigh@leighmichaels.com.

Cathy Gillen THACKER

Leigh MICHAELS

TEMPORARY Santa

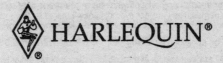

HARLEQUIN®

TORONTO • NEW YORK • LONDON
AMSTERDAM • PARIS • SYDNEY • HAMBURG
STOCKHOLM • ATHENS • TOKYO • MILAN • MADRID
PRAGUE • WARSAW • BUDAPEST • AUCKLAND

ISBN 0-373-23017-6

TEMPORARY SANTA

Copyright © 2003 by Harlequin Books S.A.

The publisher acknowledges the copyright holders of the individual works as follows:

BABY'S FIRST CHRISTMAS
Copyright © 1998 by Cathy Gillen Thacker
THE UNLIKELY SANTA
Copyright © 1995 by Leigh Michaels

Visit us at www.eHarlequin.com

Printed in U.S.A.

CONTENTS

BABY'S FIRST CHRISTMAS

Cathy Gillen Thacker

Chapter One

Kate Montgomery's younger sister, Lindy, charged into the workroom at Gourmet Gifts To Go and slammed her crammed bookbag down between the stacks of Thanksgiving gift baskets and decorative Christmas sleighs still waiting to be filled. "He's here," she announced.

Kate looked up from the home-delivery order form emblazoned with the logo of her Chapel Hill, North Carolina, store. Although she and her twenty-six-year-old sister looked alike—they had the same pale blond hair and light green eyes—they remained as different as night and day. Lindy, who couldn't get enough of school, was currently finishing up her PhD in mathematics. Whereas Kate had had all she could bear of classroom education after just four years of college.

"Who's here?" Kate asked casually.

Lindy slipped off her UNC windbreaker with the sweatshirt lining. "That guy with the really sexy voice who keeps calling you for an appointment and won't say why. He's cu-u-u-te, Kate. You ought to go talk to him. After all," Lindy said to Kate, a matchmaker's sparkle in her eyes, "he might not be selling anything."

That'll be the day, Kate thought, her lips curving upward wryly as she added tins of smoked salmon and chocolate truffles to a gift basket already filled with goodies. "That's what you said about the last half-dozen," Kate reminded her sister patiently as she carefully fit in individual packets of raspberry-flavored cappuccino and fruit snack mix. "And I ended up listening to two life insurance salesmen ready to write policies on my baby in utero, a peddler of encyclopedias ready to educate my child via audiotape, a beachfront property time-share Realtor who wanted me to have a vacation home to take my baby to, a financial analyst who wanted to plan my baby's college fund for him or her and—last but not least—a person who just knew, because I was pregnant, that I'd be needing to turn in my beloved Saturn sedan for a station wagon ASAP."

Always quick to help out, Lindy cut off a length of blue satin ribbon and tied it around the handle of the wicker basket Kate was filling. "How do you figure all these guys know you're pregnant?" she asked, pausing to make sure the bow was tied just so.

"And single? I don't know." Kate slid off the stool and straightened, one hand on her aching back. Today was one of those days she just couldn't seem to get comfortable. She'd been having a lot of them lately. Though never had she felt this sort of aching, insistent pressure in her thighs, too. She smiled at Lindy, who was not only her only sibling but her closest friend. She strode past the Santa cookie tins and golden-mesh gift totes that were sold year-round. "But I guess I do need to go talk to this guy before he interferes with any of my regular customers.''

Lindy cupped a hand around her mouth and used the low singsong voice they'd adapted when both were starry-eyed teenagers, ''Be nice now. He really is cute.''

Kate rolled her eyes at the blatant matchmaking. Suddenly, everyone—including her strongest ally—wanted her to get married again, but she knew there was no way that was going to happen. One disastrous marriage was enough. She was ready for motherhood. And nothing else. Meantime, there was this nuisance to be dealt with, afternoon deliveries to be made, a quick dinner with her mother and one final Lamaze class to attend. And all in the five hours before nine o'clock, her self-imposed bedtime these days.

Taking a deep breath, Kate tucked the satiny ends of her pale blond bob behind her ears, smoothed the lines of her black velvet maternity jumper and white satin blouse and breezed into the shop where Dulcie, the store's assistant manager, and Jeff, another part-time employee and premed student, were busy chatting it up with a well-dressed man in his early thirties. Her glance sweeping past the window display promoting upcoming holidays and events—namely Thanksgiving, semester exams and Christmas—Kate focused on the center of activity.

Darn it all if her younger sister wasn't right, she thought, amused despite herself as she glided gracefully between the rows of elegant gift baskets and gourmet treats. The persistent man of mystery was cute. Devastatingly so, even in profile. His dark sable brown hair was windblown and shiny clean, his ruggedly handsome face clean-shaven and, she noted as she neared, scented with a deliciously spicy aftershave. Tall and fit, he was dressed in khaki slacks, a pale blue shirt and tie and a navy sport coat that made the most of his broad, imposing shoulders.

"Here Kate is now!" Dulcie said, and beamed at her introduction.

The attractive stranger turned to her, enfolding her hand in the warm, strong palm of his. "I'm Dr. Michael Sloane. I work over at the medical center."

And, Kate thought, alarmed, he wanted to talk to her in person and wouldn't say why. As her next thought came with frightening speed, Kate's hand flew to her swollen tummy and hovered there protectively. "The baby," she said breathlessly. "Is there—"

"There's nothing wrong with the baby." Michael Sloane paused. His sensually chiseled lips thinned and he looked her over from head to toe before his sable brown eyes lasered in on hers with disarming intimacy. "Is there some place we could talk privately?"

If ever there was a person who looked like he'd been tapped to deliver bad news, it was Michael Sloane. Kate swallowed. "This is serious, isn't it?" she asked softly.

"It's—" He stopped abruptly. Took her arm firmly but gently. "Before we continue, we need to be somewhere you can sit down."

As MICHAEL had half expected, Kate dug in her heels and refused to budge. "Anything you want to sell me, you can sell me right here," she told him stubbornly.

No doubt about it, Michael Sloane thought as he studied the five-foot-six-inch blond dynamo, the woman was every bit as memorable and feisty as the guys at the lab had said she was. In general, Michael had never really cared for short hair on women, but Kate's silky pale blond bob suited her perfectly, even at this late stage of her pregnancy. Her face was heart-shaped and pretty, her features delicate, feminine and perfectly proportioned. Her light green eyes were framed with twin sets of thick blond eyelashes and delicate brows, her skin fair, her full lips and delicate cheeks a natural shell pink.

"I told you before, Ms. Montgomery," he said, aware the bizarre circumstances he found himself in left him no choice but to be darned mysterious over the phone as he'd tried to get an appointment with her. Only to be cut off as soon as she found he wasn't willing to disclose the very delicate nature of what he wanted to discuss with her over the phone for fear she'd be so upset she'd cut and run. "I'm not selling insurance," he told her dryly. Although, as he took in her sexy, feminine build, he half wished he was.

"Then what, pray tell, are you selling?" Kate asked, pushing the hair from her heart-shaped face. "Opportunity?"

More like bad news, Michael thought, as he inhaled the intoxicating smell of her tuberose-and-jasmine perfume. Really bad news, at least as far as single mother-to-be Kate Montgomery was likely to think. Still, this was no discussion to be having while she was on her feet in the middle of the shop.

The door opened. A group of customers walked in.

Dulcie and Jeff went to wait on them, and Kate led Michael into the back of the immaculately kept store. On one side of a narrow hallway was a workroom and storage area. On the other were a lounge, office and bathroom. Kate led him into the small but cozy office decorated in shades of pale mossy green and cream.

Hoping fervently she wouldn't scream, faint or cry uncontrollably when he told her the news, he gestured toward the sofa opposite her desk and suggested mildly, "Perhaps you'd like to sit down."

Kate shook her head and kept her eyes on his. "I'd prefer to stand," she said.

And, Michael thought, she'd prefer him to leave— immediately—judging from the expression on her face. "All right," he said reluctantly, knowing he was going to have to blurt it out. "We'll do it your way. As I said earlier, my name is Dr. Michael Sloane." Michael reached into his coat pocket and produced several pieces of identification for her perusal. "I'm an emergency room physician at the medical center in Chapel Hill."

Kate studied the ID in her hand without comment, then carefully handed it all back.

"I'm here because I have something to tell you about your baby's biological father."

Kate paled and backed up until her hips were resting against the edge of her desk. She folded her arms in front of her swollen tummy in a protective gesture. "You couldn't possibly know anything about that," she said stiffly, beginning to look all the more perturbed with his uninvited presence.

"That's where you're wrong." Michael paused, knowing however he said this, whenever he said this, it was likely to be a tremendous shock. He sat on the sofa opposite her and clasped his hands between his spread knees. "I know everything there is to know about him."

Kate's beautiful eyes turned stormy as she circled

her desk and carefully lowered herself into the up-holstered swivel chair behind it. "Then you also know he's chosen to be anonymous," she said tightly, as pink swept into her high, delicately chiseled cheeks.

"I know the person you selected to father your baby felt that way," Michael corrected.

Kate's green eyes did not waver from his. "So if you will kindly leave," Kate continued.

Michael shook his head in mute disagreement. "Not before I tell you what I came here to say."

Kate's chest rose and fell beneath her white satin blouse and black velvet jumper. "And that is…"

There was no easy way to say this. Michael swallowed. "I'm your baby's father."

LONG, INCREDULOUS SECONDS ticked past. Kate shot to her feet. So did he. "That's impossible," Kate said flatly at last as she stormed around her desk to confront him.

His feelings rigidly in check, Michael towered over her. "How do you figure that?" he asked softly, studying her from head to toe.

"Because!" Kate flushed at the way he was looking her over. "You're not at all what I ordered," she told him hotly.

No surprise there, Michael thought. He hadn't ordered this, either. But it had happened. And like it or not, this delectable-looking blond with the fiercely independent nature was bearing his child. "What did you order, then?" he asked curiously, determined to rescue them both from this mess whether she wanted his help or not.

Kate flushed and gave him a self-conscious look

that spoke volumes about her comfort zone with men. "Someone of medium height and build—a maximum of five-ten, one hundred and eighty pounds."

Michael struggled to keep his mind on the conversation rather than the slender and supple—yet very pregnant and feminine—body beneath her black velvet jumper. He had never realized a pregnant woman could turn him on like this. "And I'm six feet two inches tall and two hundred pounds."

Her lips curved wryly as she folded her arms beneath the soft swell of her breasts and admitted, "Not to mention way too athletic and solidly built."

His glance roved the incredible softness of her hair and face before returning to the sparkling intelligence of her light green eyes. "Don't tell me you're one who thinks brains and athletic talent are traits that are mutually exclusive?" he teased.

"You said it, not me," Kate replied, just as humorously. "Although now that you mention it—" she turned to give him an appraising glance that heated his blood "—you do look like someone who played a lot of ball."

"Baseball, and you're right, I did, all through elementary, junior high and high school. I was also on the honor rolls and a member of Phi Beta Kappa." Neither of which was any big deal to him. Nor, he felt, should it be to her.

"See, that's another thing." Kate breezed past him and headed for the workroom, where a dozen or so gift baskets were lined up, waiting to be delivered. She fished a set of keys off a hook, picked up a basket filled with wine and cheese and headed for the exit, her hips sashaying lightly. "I didn't want anyone who was too smart."

Admiring her composure in the face of such a potential catastrophe, Michael held the door as she slipped past him.

"I didn't want my child to be called a nerd by the other kids. Furthermore," Kate confided petulantly as she slid the key in the lock and opened the back of the full-size powder blue Gourmet Gifts To Go delivery van, "I wanted the father I selected to have blond hair, fair skin and blue eyes." She slid the basket onto the carpeted floor of the van, then straightened, leaned against the door and looked at him. "Not sable brown hair and eyes to match."

Unable to help himself, Michael laughed. "This is the first time those traits have ever been held against me!"

"I'm not holding them against you!" Kate pivoted on her heel and headed into the building at a clip. "I'm just using them to point out the fact that the lab couldn't possibly have mixed up your sperm with the sperm of the man I selected." She lifted two more baskets-to-go into her arms and watched as Michael pitched in and did the same. "You're just too far off from what I wanted," she explained logically.

Michael helped put all four of the baskets in the van. He slid them all the way forward behind the captain-style driver and passenger seats. Straightening, he turned to her. He'd known this would be as hard for her—if not more difficult—than it had been for him. But it had happened, and like it or not, they had to deal with it.

"Except for the social security numbers," he told her softly, looking at her and wishing like hell there were some way to fix all this without hurting her or the baby or him. "There, the father you selected and

I were only one digit off, Kate. The last two numbers of my number were five, three. His were five, four.'' Seeing she was about to stave off the truth and protest again, he touched a finger to her lips, reveling in the satiny softness as he effectively and quickly silenced what she was about to say.

"And yes," he continued as another thrill shot through him, "they did indeed mix up the vials, because his sperm is still in the deep freeze, perfectly intact, not a drop missing." Aware his finger and her lips were both heating, he dropped his finger from her lips. His frown deepening, he finished, "Mine, on the other hand, is all gone, and the experiment I agreed to participate in has not yet been done."

Kate suddenly felt as if the wind had been knocked out of her. Her heart pounding, she leaned against the open door of the van. She looked as shaken as he'd felt when he'd first done the detective work and confirmed for himself what had happened. "Is that how you found out there'd been a mistake?" she asked, aghast. "The lab called you?"

Michael nodded grimly. "They asked me to come down and donate some sperm for the experiment on ways to improve genetic testing. I said I already had, months ago. They said I hadn't. Obviously something had happened, so an investigation was done."

Kate gulped. Finally, it was beginning to sink in. "If this is a joke, Dr. Sloane," she said, swaying slightly, "it is definitely not funny."

Michael put out a hand to steady her. He guided her to a sitting position in the back of the van. "Believe me, I didn't think it was funny when I found out about it, either," he said grimly as he knelt in front of her. In fact, it still seemed like a nightmare from which he'd never wake up. But it had happened, and had to be faced.

Michael took her hand in his and clasped it firmly. "Look, I figured you wouldn't want to just take my word for all this."

"You're right about that much," Kate said hotly. She pushed his hand away and leaped to her feet.

"So I brought proof," Michael said.

Ten phone calls later, Kate finally appeared satisfied he was telling her the truth. Once again, they squared off in her private office.

"The question is," Michael said, as he stared into her flushed face, "now that we know what happened, what are we going to do about this?"

THOUGH IT HAD been a shock, Kate had had time to think about it, and she knew what she had to do. Play her cards to the hilt. "Why should we do anything?" she asked with a great deal more serenity than she felt. "We could sue the clinic, but what would that bring us, except more unhappiness. We're just going to have to deal with the situation as it exists."

Michael blinked, stunned by her casual assertion. "I beg your pardon?"

Kate palmed her chest. "You didn't plan for this baby. On the other hand, I did." In her opinion, that gave her vastly superior rights.

Michael's eyes darkened as he closed the distance between them. "Be that as it may, this is still my child, too," he stated.

"I know that." Kate smiled. Feeling as though she had a tiger by the tail, she planted both hands on her hips. "But you don't have to feel beholden to either of us."

"I want to be involved," Michael insisted.

"You feel that way now..." she said.

"I'll feel that way forever," Michael corrected, as his expressive brows lowered like thunderclouds over his eyes.

Kate shrugged, aware the aching pressure in her thighs, which had been there all day, was increasing—maybe because of the amount of time she'd spent on her feet, pacing back and forth, as she talked to Michael about their situation. "We'll see," she replied cryptically.

"What's that supposed to mean?" he demanded.

Kate stomped closer, not stopping until she and Michael were toe to toe. She angled her head at him, wishing he weren't so tall, so fit or so unerringly handsome and masculine. "It means once the novelty wears off, you could lose interest in this baby and in me," she said mildly.

He flashed her a crocodile grin. "I don't think so."

His soft voice sent another whisper of sensual awareness spiraling through her. Feeling as though she couldn't breathe, Kate drew a deep—albeit shaky—breath and continued to study him like a problem she had no choice but to solve immediately. In the meantime, she still had her afternoon deliveries to do, a scheduled dinner with her mother and one last Lamaze class to attend.

"Look," she said finally, "if you still feel the same way in a couple of weeks, we'll sit down and talk." She was being vague, hoping against hope that time would take care of everything.

"And work something out?" Michael pressed.

Kate didn't want to do anything like that, but she knew—out of fairness—that she had to consider his position, too. "I'll try to do what's right for all of us, as soon as I figure out what that is," she promised sincerely. "Meanwhile, if you'll excuse me, I have seventeen deliveries to make."

Michael caught her wrist in his hand and held her in place.

"I still want to help you," he insisted.

The skin of his palm felt like hot silk around her wrist. "Everyone does," she replied.

His grip gentled. "What do you mean?"

Kate shrugged. "Since I became pregnant, all sorts of people have seen fit to counsel me on the wisdom of my decision to be a single parent and raise this child alone. People who wouldn't dream of telling me what brand of mustard to buy have no qualms at all about telling me I need a husband in a hurry."

Michael smiled in understanding, his hold on her becoming more intimate before he reluctantly released her altogether. "But you don't see it that way," he guessed softly.

Kate sighed and—a hand to her aching back—leaned against the edge of her desk. In a continuing effort to get comfortable, she crossed her ankles in front of her and clasped the edge of the desk on either side of her. "It'd be nice if every child in this world could have a mother and a father who loved each other desperately, a ton of siblings and live in a house with a white picket fence. But that doesn't always happen."

Michael pushed the edges of his sport coat back and braced his hands on his waist. "Still, whenever possible," he repeated, his kind brown eyes locking with hers, "I think a baby should have a mommy and a daddy."

Kate, who'd done an awful lot of thinking about this very subject before becoming pregnant, stubbornly refused to concede the same. She angled her chin at him, determined to let him know, along with everyone else, that she could handle this. "I think every child needs lots of love, security and a sense of family. My child—" not *our* child "—will have all that and more," she stated.

"What about my child?" Michael asked, his expression determined.

Kate looked away evasively, and her lips tightened mutinously. "When *you* plan for a child, then *you* can also plan the environment in which you will bring him or her up."

Michael did a double take. "Surely you're not intending to cut me out of our baby's life entirely?"

Kate's shoulders stiffened as she—once again—found herself in the unenviable position of having to defend herself. "I'm sure there will come a time, when our child is much older, that some explanation will be in order," she asserted.

Michael placed a palm on the desk on either side of her and towered over her, "And until then?"

Kate planted a hand on his chest and pushed him away. Standing, she breezed past him haughtily. "Until then I suggest you think about it as much as you would've had your genes merely been guinea pigs in a genetics experiment."

He caught hold of her shoulders and turned her to face him. "I'm afraid that's not going to work," he said tightly, staking his claim on their baby—and, by default, her.

"It will work," Kate insisted, inhaling the spicy, masculine scent of aftershave clinging to his freshly shaven jaw. "As long as you want it to work." Wanting it to work was key. She headed for the front of the shop, where she informed Dulcie, Jeff and Lindy she was leaving to do her deliveries.

Michael watched her gather the turquoise duffel packed with her Lamaze stuff, the keys to the van, her cell phone, clipboard of addresses, area street maps and purse. He followed her out the back door to the van.

"I know this child exists," he said, as Kate—who wished she could do something about the unprecedented aching in her thighs, which seemed to get worse with every passing second—unlocked the driver's door and tossed in her gear.

"I'm going to want to know he or she is okay," Michael continued stubbornly as the two of them continued to be buffeted by the brisk November air.

Feeling about as graceful as a whale on roller skates, Kate levered herself up and into the driver's seat and fit the key in the ignition. "Then I'll send you progress reports, okay?"

Michael stood between her and the door, preventing her from closing it. "No. It's not okay." His voice lowered a notch as his eyes held hers in a manner that let her know he wasn't about to be dissuaded. "I'm going to need—I'm going to want—a hell of a lot more than that."

Kate drew an exasperated breath as she reached behind her and drew her seat belt across her chest. "Look, just because I'm carrying your child—by accident, I might add—does not mean you need to be involved in my life, too."

Michael regarded her grimly. "If we're going to have a child together—even by accident—we need to get to know each other. The only way for us to do that is for us to spend time together.''

She considered that notion for a moment, finding it oddly—engagingly attractive, then discarded it.

Rolling her eyes, she claimed facetiously, ''Next you'll be proposing marriage—''

Michael shook his head. ''Not at this stage.''

Kate breathed a sigh of relief. ''Thank heaven for small miracles,'' she said dryly, as Michael leaned into the cab of the van.

''Although, now that you bring it up, maybe it's not such a bad idea,'' he replied, unwilling, it seemed, to throw out any possibility whatsoever that would bring him closer to the child she was about to bear, ''should we eventually find we can get along.''

He was an attractive man. There was even, it seemed, a purely physical chemistry between them, as evidenced by the way she tingled whenever, wherever, he touched her, but the rest was just plain nuts. She studied his face. ''You're serious,'' she whispered, able to feel for the first time how much he wanted this child in his life, in his heart.

''Very.''

Silence fell between them, more awkward than before.

The situation was amazing. Incredible. Unprecedented. And so very complicated. Kate had no idea what to do. She only knew she felt simultaneously threatened and oddly comforted, cossetted, by his presence.

Michael swore softly and ran a hand through his wind-tossed hair. ''Look, I don't want to make your life any harder, but this is my child—the only child I may ever have—and I want to be a part of his or her life, too. A big part.'' Noting she was beginning to shiver in the increasingly cool afternoon air, he circled the front of the van and climbed into the passenger's seat. He swiveled to face her, all the love he felt for their unborn child in his eyes. ''If you were in my place, you'd feel the same way.''

True, Kate thought, as they stared at each other in contemplative silence. Suddenly she knew—as much as she might want him to—he wasn't going to back off. If she didn't want to end up in court, fighting for custody of her child before he or she was even born, she was going to have to cooperate with Michael Sloane. Or at least put up the pretense of doing so until he realized this was more commitment than he really wanted over the long haul. ''What exactly are you suggesting?'' she asked calmly as she shut the driver door and switched on the ignition.

''Only what's fair,'' Michael said as she turned on the heater. ''That starting now, you let me be a part of our child's life in every way. Including the birth.''

Kate's knees turned to jelly as she thought about the implied intimacy of that. ''You want to be in the delivery room?'' she asked in a low, trembling voice as she splayed a hand across her chest.

''I am a doctor.''

But not my doctor, Kate thought. And the thought of being disrobed in front of him, for any reason, made her heart beat all the harder. Ignoring the tingles of awareness ghosting over her skin, she frowned and glanced at her watch. ''I'm going to have to think about this.''

Michael looked as though he had expected that. ''It'll have to be fast,'' he warned. ''If the guys at the

lab were correct about the date of your artificial insemination, you've only got a day or so.''

As if she needed reminding about that! Kate
shrugged. ''The baby could be late.''

''Or early.''

Swallowing around the sudden dryness in her
throat, Kate glanced at her watch again. ''I really do
need to go.''

Michael frowned at the list of addresses on the clipboard and the rows of gift baskets in the back of the
van. ''You're going to make all these deliveries yourself?''

Kate nodded. ''I always do the late afternoon deliveries. Dulcie does the ones first thing in the morning. Jeff takes care of the ones at noon.'' She paused.
''I like this part of the business, too. It's fun, seeing
the expression of delight on the customers' faces
when they receive a gift from my shop. And I enjoy
the change of pace after being in the shop all day.''

''Let me help you. You drive. I'll carry the baskets
up to the door. It'll go twice as fast that way. Then
maybe the two of us can go to dinner and finish re-
solving all this.''

Kate had to admit she could use the help. Because
of her talk with him, she was running a good hour
behind schedule for deliveries. ''It's going to take me
several hours,'' she warned. ''And I have to go out
in the country to do the rural deliveries.''

''Then you really shouldn't be out there alone. Not
this close to delivering. What if something happened?''

''Then I'd call for help on my cell phone,'' she
told him calmly, knowing first babies were generally
notoriously slow in arriving. And she had yet to suffer

her first real contraction. Nevertheless, he had a point. She didn't want to put her baby in danger. And she had been feeling a little achy and tired all day. Maybe it was best if she accepted his help and let him tag along with her. It would give her a chance to show him she could handle work and a baby and subtly persuade him he didn't want to be a father as much as he thought he did. If she were successful, it would be well worth the additional time she spent with him.

While she drove, Kate told him about the preparations she had made for the baby, going into detail about the nursery she had prepared, the type of crib and changing table and rocking chair she'd selected and the extensive layette of baby clothes. Michael was interested and impressed. Nevertheless, by the time they had gotten halfway through the list of deliveries, Kate felt oddly trembly and exhausted. When he offered to do some of the driving, too, she agreed with barely a murmur of dissent.

"You feeling okay?" Michael asked as he got behind the wheel and steered the delivery van onto the lonely country road.

"Sure," Kate fibbed with a lot more assurance than she felt, then abruptly doubled over with a sharp cry of pain.

"What is it?" Michael asked, alarmed.

Kate clutched her tummy all the harder. "Guess."

Chapter Two

"You're in labor," Michael proclaimed, surprised to discover that beneath the usual physician's calm he was feeling the initial panic all first-time fathers felt.

Kate groaned and sank even farther into her seat. Breathing through the contraction—which appeared to last about thirty seconds—she put her hands on the edges of the upholstery and gripped it until her knuckles turned white. "It would certainly appear so, yes." Kate pushed the words through a row of even white teeth. Delicate beads of perspiration dotted her upper lip.

She seemed awfully uncomfortable for a very first contraction, Michael thought. Unless... Oh, no. "Was this your first contraction?" he asked.

"I—" Kate gasped between panting breaths that told him another contraction was starting, just seconds after the conclusion of the first. "Suppose." No sooner had she spoken than she let out a sharp little cry.

"What do you mean you suppose?" Michael demanded. Figuring the rest of the delivery baskets could wait, he turned the van in the direction of Chapel Hill.

"I've felt a little funny all day," Kate confessed as she grabbed a tissue from her purse and pressed it to the dampness at the back of her neck.

"Funny how?"

"I've had this pressure—this sort of aching—in my thighs, like I overdid it exercising or something."

"But no actual contractions until just now."

"Right."

"And you're sure what you felt just now was an actual contraction?" Michael persisted.

"Oh, yeah. Definitely."

The important thing here was to stay calm. "When did the funny feeling—the pressure—start in your legs?"

"This morning, when I got up."

Which meant, Michael thought, she'd likely been in the very early stages of labor all day. "I noticed you rubbing your back in the shop. Was your back aching all day?"

"Yes, but that's been the case off and on for several weeks now, so I didn't think anything of it. But—" Kate caught her breath as the cramping in her lower abdomen intensified. "It's never been this bad," she said with tears in her eyes.

Michael reached over and squeezed her hand. "Hang in there," he said.

"I'm trying." Kate waited until the worst of it had passed, then, still panting, reached behind her and grabbed the duffel bag she took to her Lamaze class. Inside were clean workout clothes, a blanket to stretch out on, a pillow, an unopened bottle of mineral water and a stopwatch.

"Try breathing in through your nose and slowly breathing out through your mouth," he said as the next contraction gripped her without warning. "That's it," he said, as Kate gasped again and hit the start button on her stopwatch. "Take deep, slow breaths, just the way they taught you in Lamaze class. That's it, Kate. Again. And yet again—"

At long last, the pain subsided. As it did, Kate released a long, ragged breath. And suddenly became aware—as did Michael—that she was drenched with sweat. From the looks of it, Michael thought, as she turned the temperature control knob to cool, this was going to be one hard and fast—maybe too fast—labor.

"How long was the contraction?" Michael asked as Kate's color slowly returned to normal and he continued to drive in the direction of the hospital at a safe, steady pace.

Kate glanced at her stopwatch. "Three minutes and fourteen seconds." She seemed surprised as she contemplated that, murmuring, "No wonder it felt like an eternity!"

"Okay, let's time between contractions now," Michael said. "Then we'll call your doctor."

Kate reset the stopwatch and absently rubbed her tummy. Five seconds, ten seconds, fifteen, Michael noted with relief. All blissfully free of pain. Beginning to relax, she lay against the seat. Without warning, Kate's teeth began to chatter. A shiver spiraled through her slender shoulders. Kate gasped as another contraction gripped her. She turned alternately red then white. "Do you know your OB's number?" he asked calmly.

Still fighting the contraction gripping her, Kate pulled the cell phone out of her purse. "Dr. Amanda Gantor. Just punch one," she panted.

Michael did as directed and was patched through. He explained what the situation was, then listened as he received instructions. "Right. Yes. We'll be there as soon as we can." He hung up as Kate's contraction finally came to a halt.

"Let me guess," she drawled, still panting from the strength of her last contraction. "Dr. Gantor wants me to go straight to the hospital."

"Right. She'll alert labor and delivery and the emergency room and meet you at the hospital."

Kate nodded, letting him know she'd heard. "Good thing you're driving." She gasped, leaned forward and clasped her tummy as yet another contraction gripped her. She whimpered. "I don't think I could drive and endure this kind of pain, too."

"Do you have a labor coach?"

"My baby sister, Lindy. She's a teaching assistant at UNC. She's teaching a class right now." Kate shifted in an effort to get more comfortable and found, as Michael had figured would be the case, that it was hopeless. "You met her at the shop."

"Ah, yes, the one who said I was cu-u-u-te."

"You heard that?" She slanted him an inquiring glance as she continued to shift restlessly.

Michael zoomed past a trailer park, a deserted country church and a farm. "I think she may have meant me to," he confided, in an attempt to divert Kate's attention from the pain. He smiled at her. "I had the feeling she would have liked nothing better than to set the two of us up."

Kate nodded, humorously conceding this was so. "And that was before she knew who you were or what your connection to me was—is," Kate groaned.

"You think this will up the stakes?" Michael

paused at a four-way intersection, then seeing it was safe, continued on.

"As far as Lindy is concerned, heck, yes. She's an incurable romantic." Kate picked up her bottle of water, ripped off the plastic seal and cap and took a tiny drink.

Michael slanted her another glance. "But not you."

"Nope. Not anymore." Kate handed him the bottled water. "I am a very practical woman."

Michael also took a small swig. "Good for you."

Kate capped the water, grimaced and began to pant as she was hit with yet another labor pain. "I guess it's lucky you're a doctor so you know about Lamaze." Kate stuffed her belongings into her Lamaze bag. "You can coach me through it until we get to the hospital and Lindy and a nurse take over." Thirty seconds. Forty-five. Sixty. Seventy-five.

"No problem," Michael retorted as they passed a road sign that said, Chapel Hill, twenty-four miles. "I could coach you through the Bradley and Gamper methods, too. But my real talent—" noting her contraction was continuing some two and half minutes after it began, he reached over to give her hand a comforting squeeze "—is in catching babies."

Kate forced a weak smile and let herself take comfort from his touch, even as the pain increased. "With or without a mitt?" she asked, panting.

"Without." He winked at her playfully. "Though I imagine it could be done either way."

"That's it," Kate gasped, looking as if it was taking everything she had to resist the urge to scream with the pain. "Keep the banter coming," she advised.

Michael nodded at her bright red cheeks. "You hurting a lot?"

Kate concentrated on her breathing. "Oh, let's just say it feels like an eighteen-wheeler truck is inside me roaring to get out."

"Hang on. We're less than twenty minutes from the medical center."

"Oh, no." Kate raised her hips off the captain's seat.

"What?" Michael was beginning to look as panicked as she felt.

"Oh, no-no-no-no," Kate wailed in distress.

"What's going on, Kate?"

She leaned back and gripped his forearm, hard. "I feel the baby coming."

"That's natural."

Kate shook her head vigorously. She was trembling. "No. You don't understand. The baby's starting to come out of me, Michael. I can feel it. I can feel the—baby's head!"

Michael guided the Gourmet Gifts To Go van into the first safe place he saw, the dirt road entrance to a farmer's field. He put the van in park, switched on the hazard lights and set the emergency brake but kept the motor running, the air on. "I'm coming around," he said.

He got out of the van, circled the front and opened her door. "I'm going to hit the recline button on your seat, take your seat belt off and lay you back." He put his hands beneath her shoulders and hips, leaned in and scooted her back and up. "I'm going to have to take a look."

She turned her head from him as he eased the hem

of her jumper up and did what was necessary with clinical care.

"Well?" Kate asked when he'd assessed the situation.

"You're right," Michael said grimly. "There's no time to spare. We've got to get you to the back of the van. Put your arm around my neck. That's it." He slid one arm beneath her knees, the other beneath her shoulders, then swept her effortlessly into his strong arms and carried her to the back. He opened the door and laid Kate gently on the carpeted floor of the van, pushing aside the gift baskets.

Perspiration streamed down her face. He went to get her Lamaze gear and shut the door. Kate struggled against the pain that was gripping her nonstop. "I'm going to have the baby here and now, in the back of my delivery van, aren't I?" she panted as one contraction slipped into another.

Michael climbed in beside her and shut the rear door so there'd be no draft on her or the baby. "Looks like it, yes." His expression all business, he lifted her hips and slid the blanket from her Lamaze bag beneath her.

"I can't believe this," she moaned. "First the mix-up at the sperm bank and now this!"

Michael knelt beside her and quickly divested her of her shoes, stockings and panties. "Maybe it's just a Murphy's law kind of year for us." Swiftly, he checked on the position of the baby.

"Not for me." Kate shook her head as he pushed the hem of her jumper high enough to allow him to work yet left it low enough to afford her some modesty. "I plan things out meticulously. Always have, always will, only to have everything suddenly go awry now in such a big way.'' Kate groaned help-lessly and tightened her hands into fists.

"If there's one thing you can count on in this life, it's that nothing ever goes according to plan any-way.'' Working rapidly, Michael ripped into one of the undelivered gift baskets and extracted a bottle of wine. "Besides,'' he continued, working to give her as much confidence as possible as he splashed his hands and then the birth area with germ-killing al-cohol, "it's been my experience that the best things in life are unplanned.''

"Well, you being the father of my baby and my going into labor now are the two absolute exceptions to the rule,'' Kate muttered cantankerously. "As far as I'm concerned, the screw-ups stop here,'' she said, looking panic-stricken as another contraction gripped her. She grabbed his arm. "I have to push.''

"Not yet, Kate.'' Knowing he had to have some-thing to cut the cord with, Michael plucked a silver-plated serving knife from the gift basket and sterilized that, too. "We don't want the baby's head to pop out too suddenly.''

"But you can see it?'' Still holding tightly to his arm, Kate struggled against another gripping contrac-tion.

"The very top of it, yes.'' He put a hand on her abdomen, another on her thinning perineum. "I want you to pant or blow while I apply a counter pressure here to help the baby's head come out gently and gradually.'' Working with her to guide the baby into the world, he said gently, "That's it, Kate, nice and slow. You're doing great. Keep panting,'' Michael said as the baby's head began to emerge. Just a little at first, and then, several contractions later, all the way.

"There. Okay," he said victoriously, glad all was okay so far. "The head's out, and as soon as I get the baby's mouth and nose clear—" Michael stroked downward on the baby's nose, cheeks and throat "—he's going to test his lungs for us." Michael and Kate both grinned as the baby let out a choking, startled cry.

Knowing there was no time to lose, Michael continued to kneel between her thighs, both hands supporting the baby's head, one above, one beneath. "Okay, Kate, I want you to push now." Again, he supported and guided the slippery, squirming infant. "We've got one shoulder out," Michael said, using gentle continued traction. "Now two. And here he comes." Laughing exultantly, Michael lifted the kicking, screaming, healthy pink baby and placed him where she could hold onto him.

"We've got a boy, Kate. A beautiful baby boy. And he's not too pleased about this," Michael continued as he swiftly clamped the cord three inches from the baby's abdomen. He cut the cord and carefully wrapped their squirming baby boy in Kate's soft cotton workout pants.

"We'll make it up to him," Kate promised thickly as tears of joy streamed down her face. Laughing and crying simultaneously, Kate held their baby close to her heart. "Oh, Michael, he's just perfect, isn't he?" Kate whispered, looking as overwhelmed with the joy of the experience as he was.

Michael nodded. "He sure is," he said thickly, aware of the love and pride welling inside him even as he checked their newborn son's heart rate and respiration and did a routine medical assessment of the infant's condition. "And he looks as healthy and strong as they come," Michael said, as he touched the baby's face, then Kate's.

Kate caught Michael's hand and kissed the back of it. "Thank you," she said gratefully. "Thank you for being here."

Michael swallowed around the rising lump of emotion in his throat. "My pleasure." Heaven knew there was no other place he would have wanted to be at this moment than with Kate and their baby.

She grimaced as another pain hit her.

Michael coaxed her through the spasms until the afterbirth appeared. "Okay, we've got the placenta out." Michael wrapped the placenta up, too, made both Kate and the baby as comfortable as he could, then retrieved the cell phone. "I think it's time we called Dr. Gantor and the hospital, too."

As IT TURNED OUT, there was a fire station with an ambulance some fifteen minutes away from them. Deciding the sooner they got the two of them to the hospital the better, Michael drove Kate and the baby to a midpoint, then helped the EMS personnel transfer Kate and the baby to the stretcher and the waiting ambulance.

Realizing he was planning to follow them in the van, Kate reached out to grab him. "Stay with us," she urged quietly. Incredible as it was under the circumstances, the two of them had bonded during the birth, and she didn't want to lose that bond any more than she wanted to ride the rest of the way to the hospital alone.

Michael nodded. "Just let me close up the van," he told her huskily.

By the time he got back, the EMS workers had started an IV in Kate's arm. "So what are you going to name the baby?" the EMS worker asked.

Good question, Kate thought, looking at Michael, knowing this involved him, too. So much had changed in such a short time. "I was thinking about Timothy for a first name," she told Michael quietly as he sat on the bench beside her.

"That's nice."

"And for a middle name?" the EMS worker prodded as he filled out the paperwork on Kate, and Michael continued to watch Kate and the baby.

"Initially, I was thinking about naming him after my grandfather," Kate said softly, "but now I don't know. I think maybe his middle name should be Michael. Timothy Michael Sloane-Montgomery. Or Montgomery-Sloane. What do you think?"

Michael's eyes darkened as myriad emotions crossed his face. "I think nothing would make me happier."

"If I didn't know better, I'd think something was going on between you two," the EMS worker teased.

Michael and Kate flushed simultaneously.

"Whoa," the EMS worker said.

Exactly, Kate thought, as heat crept into her face. When word of this got out, people were going to think she and Michael had made this baby the old-fashioned way. And to tell the truth, they'd shared so much intimacy in such a short time, it almost felt as if they had. Except she didn't even know how he kissed. Might—because of circumstances—never know.

Michael looked at the EMS worker. "If you

wouldn't mind moving up front with your partner—" he nodded at Kate and the baby "—maybe we could have a moment alone?"

"Sure." Knowing Michael was a physician from the Chapel Hill emergency room, the EMS worker easily granted the request. "No problem. Take all the time you need." He smiled at the happy trio, his glance resting on the blissfully sleeping baby nestled in Kate's arms. "I'll just radio the hospital and let them know both mother and baby are doing fine."

Michael waited until the EMS worker was out of earshot then turned to Kate. He knelt beside her and took her hand in his. "Kate, this is a big step." He searched her eyes. "Are you sure?"

Kate nodded. "Yes. If you hadn't been there to bring my—to bring our—baby into the world—" Well, she didn't even want to think about what might have happened. "Michael, I owe you so much," she said softly, meaning it. "Timmy and I both do."

It was swiftly apparent gratitude was not what he wanted from her, but it would do for now. "I'm the one who owes you, Kate," Michael told her softly. "Not just for now." Again, he looked at their sleeping newborn son and released a wistful sigh. "But for a lifetime."

Thinking about it, Kate knew he was right. Through Timmy—and fate—she and Michael were going to be connected forever.

"IT'S ALL OVER the hospital," Kate told Michael an hour later, after she and Timmy had been settled into a private room in the maternity ward.

"No kidding," Michael drawled, even as he marveled at how pretty and together Kate looked after all she'd been through. "It's bigger news than the original virgin birth."

Kate sighed, her full breasts rising and falling beneath the soft cotton of her hospital gown. Her lips thinned to a soft, rosy line. "I don't know how I'm going to tell my parents."

Michael paced to the Plexiglas bassinet beside Kate, where their baby slept. Because she had requested the rooming-in arrangement, Timmy would be with her as much as possible during her stay in the hospital. Reassured their son was undisturbed by their low voices, Michael edged to Kate. He could imagine how difficult it was going to be for her to tell her parents about the mix-up at the fertility clinic. He hadn't told his parents, yet, either.

Sliding his hands in the pockets of his trousers, he brought her quickly up to speed about her family. "They've both been called, by the way."

"What?" Her expression incredulous and upset, Kate rose halfway off her hospital bed.

"When you registered for the birth, you listed both your parents as next of kin, but there were two phone numbers, your father's law office and your mother's home. The emergency room nurse asked me who she should call. I didn't know, so the clerk called both."

"Oh, no." Kate covered her face with her hand. "Did they reach both my parents?" She looked at him from between spread fingers.

Michael nodded, wondering what the big deal was. "They're on the way to the hospital as we speak."

"Oh, no," Kate moaned again, looking even more distressed.

"Something wrong?"

Kate nodded vigorously. "The two of them can't be in the same room together."

Kate's sister, Lindy, who had been called to come to the hospital, walked in. Kate looked at her, distressed, and swiftly explained. "You have to do something."

Evidently agreeing with Kate's assessment of the situation completely, Lindy sprang into action. "I'll head off Dad downstairs in the lobby. Meanwhile, when Mother gets here, you do your best to make her visit as snappy as possible. And then I'll bring Dad up when the coast is clear."

"What's going on?" Michael asked curiously, figuring if he was going to land in the middle of some familial calamity, he should know the reason for it.

"My parents separated last summer, at my mother's insistence, shortly after I told them I was pregnant with Timmy. My mother said she just needed some time and space to herself, but that doesn't make any sense." Kate shook her head and sighed. "I never thought either of my parents would have a mid-life crisis, and that goes double for my mom, who made the family her whole career."

"Any chance she's suffering from the empty nest syndrome now that you're having a child of your own and your younger sister's about ready to graduate?" Michael asked kindly. He'd seen it in other families.

Kate looked perplexed. "My dad and Lindy think so, but I'm not sure it's quite that simple. Unlike my dad and me, my mother has always been ruled by her emotions. And right now her emotions are running at an all-time high. Add to that the fact my dad's protesting her petition for divorce and feeling pretty hurt and angry. My mom is being really stubborn and closemouthed about whatever it is that is going on with her and—well, you can just imagine how awkward it is when they do see each other. Right now, it's stretching it for them to say a civil word to each other. Suffice it to say—'' Kate paused to draw a ragged breath ''—I don't want them up here together.''

''Too late,'' a pale but elegant-looking blonde in a tailored suit said as she swept into the room, a well-dressed man in a business suit and Kate's sister, Lindy, fast on their heels.

''Mom—Dad.'' Kate flushed scarlet as Michael looked at Kate's parents and took in the unmistakably stiff body language of a couple at war.

Kate's younger sister lifted her hands in a helpless gesture. ''I tried, but neither was willing to let the other go first.''

''There are some things parents should do together,'' Kate's mother said.

''This is still one of them,'' her father agreed.

''Hello, Kate.'' Kate's mother bent to kiss her, her deep and abiding affection for her daughter evident. ''Congratulations, darling.''

''Thanks, Mom.'' Kate's voice was muffled against her mother's silvery blond coif.

She headed for the bassinet to look at her new grandson. ''He is so darling,'' she murmured proudly.

Kate's father hugged Kate, too, then approached the bassinet from the other side. He regarded his new grandson with affection, finally murmuring, ''He looks a lot like you did at that age, Kate.''

Kate beamed. ''You think so?''

Her father nodded. ''Absolutely.'' Straightening, her father turned to Michael. He extended his hand.

"I'm Ted Montgomery. This is my wi—this is Kate's mother, Carolyn Montgomery, her sister, Lindy. And you must be Michael Sloane—the doctor who helped deliver Kate's baby."

"Right." Michael shook her father's hand, not sure this was the time to get into the details.

Ted gave him a look of sincere gratitude. "We're very lucky you came along when you did."

"I'm not so sure about that, if everything I just heard from the head nurse is true," Carolyn said. She looked at Kate, then Michael. Her gaze zeroing in on him suspiciously, she asked in a low tone, "Is it true? Are you the father of Kate's child?"

SILENCE REBOUNDED in the room. Even Lindy looked completely, thoroughly shocked. "I can explain," Kate said, flushing.

"I think you'd better." Kate's father sat on the window ledge while her mother continued to pace, her high heels making a staccato sound on the polished linoleum floor while Kate filled them in on the mix-up at the lab.

"I just found out about it myself," Michael told them.

"And he told me," Kate added.

"I see." Kate's father looked grim.

No doubt he was thinking about all the legal and familial complications. Her mother looked upset, too. Whereas her matchmaking sister looked intrigued. "Michael and I have already talked about it. Everything's going to be fine," Kate hastened to reassure them.

Again, her parents exchanged uneasy glances that needed no verbal delineation, then her dad looked at

Michael. It was obvious, divorce or no, he was speaking for both of them. "I assume that means you're going to be reasonable about this."

Michael nodded gallantly. "I wouldn't think of behaving any other way. I'm not here to make trouble for Kate or little Timmy."

Kate's dad regarded Michael gravely. "I'm glad to hear that."

Knowing her dad was just getting warmed up, Kate said quickly, "I'm pretty tired." She looked at her parents, knowing at a time like this they were hard-pressed to deny her anything. "Maybe you could come back tomorrow. One of you in the afternoon and one of you in the evening?"

Her parents looked at each other, the tension that had been there earlier resurfacing. "I'll take the afternoon," her mother volunteered.

"I'll take the evening," her father said.

"In the meantime is there anything you need for me to bring you?" Kate's mother asked.

Kate shook her head and fought the sadness that threatened to overwhelm her. She wished her parents would drop this foolishness and get back together. "No, I'm fine. Thanks."

"How about your suitcase, with your nightgown and robe?" Carolyn persisted.

"I've already promised Kate that I would go get it," Lindy said.

"All right, darling." Kate's mother patted her shoulder gently.

"Call us if you need anything," her dad said.

Her parents kissed her and left, walking far apart as if they were strangers. Lindy hugged Kate, promised to return with the suitcase and followed them out the door.

Michael stood. "I'll go, too."

"No." Kate reached out and caught his hand before he could depart. "I need to talk to you a minute, Michael." She tugged him closer until he sat on the edge of her bed. "I'm sorry my father grilled you that way." Kate shook her head in mounting exasperation, already knowing what Michael didn't, that this was just the beginning of her father's involvement in the situation. "Sometimes he can be such a lawyer." Making mountains out of molehills.

Michael grinned, understanding and accepting her father's protective behavior. "That's okay," he said gently. "In his place, I probably would have behaved much the same way. And speaking of reactions—your mother didn't say much."

Kate made a face and predicted dryly, "Which is another curious thing. Before the separation from my dad, she would've lectured me soundly and told me she knew this cockeyed plan of mine to have a child via artificial insemination would lead to trouble. Since she left my dad, she tells me to go for everything and grab as much gusto from this life as I can."

That did sound like a mid-life crisis, Michael thought, as he playfully nudged her thigh with his and attempted to lighten the mood and get Kate's mind off family problems she was unable to do anything about. "Hey, Timmy's no trouble," he teased with a wink. "In fact, as far as newborn babies go, he's a little angel."

Kate made a comical face at him, then chided dryly, "That wasn't what I meant, and you know it, Dr. Sloane."

Michael bestowed on her a sexy grin and covered her hand with his. "Ah. You think I'm trouble, then."

In a certain, very sexy way, maybe he was, Kate thought a tad wistfully. And suddenly that didn't seem like such a bad thing. Kate found after all the months alone she was in the mood for a little trouble of the romantic variety, as long as it didn't unnecessarily complicate her life. Smiling, she said, "I think the situation we're in is trouble."

Michael shrugged his broad shoulders. "It is sticky, I'll grant you that," he said in a low, serious voice. "It doesn't mean we can't handle it. So far, after we both weathered the initial shock, we've proven that we can handle it just fine."

His confidence—his willingness to conquer this challenge—was contagious. It lifted her spirits immediately. Unfortunately, Kate knew there were even rockier roads ahead. And she knew for certain that in the few short hours she'd known Michael, her life had changed. She wanted the chance to see where the future would lead.

Still holding his eyes, she drew a bolstering breath. "The nurse asked me earlier to fill out information for Timmy's birth certificate. She left the forms in the drawer. You should probably have a look at them, too."

Michael looked at her thoughtfully as he retrieved the papers.

"I didn't know how we should fill them out," Kate told him as he perused the sheets. "So I'll just come right out and ask." Kate brought herself up short. She took a deep breath, aware her hands were trembling. "Do you want your name on Timmy's birth certificate? Do you want to be legally known as his father?"

Chapter Three

Michael hadn't known what to expect when he had tracked Kate down, but never in his wildest dreams had he imagined he would be so attracted to her, physically and otherwise, or be on hand to single-handedly bring their baby into the world in the back of a powder-blue delivery van. But all that had happened, and it had changed him—and probably Kate, too—forever. Just as the step they were about to take would change all their lives forever, too.

"I think it's important for a lot of reasons that his birth certificate state the whole truth. So the answer is, yes, Kate," he told her softly, "I do." In fact, if the truth be known, he was now hoping for much more than that.

Kate looked into his eyes. Abruptly, she looked as overcome with emotion as he. It had been, Michael thought, one hell of an eventful day. "Then the truth it will be," she echoed softly.

In the bassinet, Timmy squirmed beneath the white flannel blanket he'd been swaddled in and, his cherubic face pinkening, started to whimper. Michael and Kate turned in time to see his dark lashes flutter open to reveal a pair of big baby-blue eyes.

Michael smiled, amazed at the depth of the affection already welling inside him as he contemplated their newborn baby boy. "Looks like our son is waking up."

Kate grinned, as eager to get more thoroughly acquainted with their baby as he was. "He's probably hungry," she stated, as a pink flush crept into her cheeks. Her glance cut briefly to Michael. "I haven't breast-fed him yet."

And, Michael knew, that was supposed to be done within the first five or six hours after birth. As soon as both baby and mother—who were usually exhausted from the birth—were up to it. Glad he was going to be around to witness this, too, Michael asked, "Do you want me to bring him to you?"

Kate pushed the button that raised the head of her bed until she was sitting up. Her green eyes glittered with excitement as she tucked the gently curving ends of her silky blond bob behind her ears. She shot him a grateful glance that made her seem—in his eyes, anyway—all the more angelically beautiful. "If you wouldn't mind."

Timmy's eyes widened as Michael slid one hand beneath his head and neck, the other beneath his back and legs, and lifted him from the bassinet. Michael grinned as Timmy stopped crying immediately and blinked at him.

"Hey, there," Michael teased in way of greeting. "Remember me? I brought you into the world." Timmy cooed and gurgled in response as Michael lowered him gently and put him in Kate's arms.

Kate stroked the straight, downy soft hair on Timmy's head as Timmy regarded her with unabashed delight. "I think he does recognize you, Michael."

Michael studied his son's cherubic face, deciding Ted Montgomery was right—Timmy did have Kate's chin. And nose. And eyes. Along with his daddy's dark, straight hair. "I think he knows your voice, too," Michael said.

"Probably." Kate chuckled. "I've done nothing but talk and sing and read to him for the last nine months."

Somehow, Michael thought, as he went to get a diaper from the corner of the bassinet, that didn't surprise him. He had known from the first Kate was going to be one devoted mother.

He brought the diaper back and watched as Kate unwrapped the white flannel blanket. They changed him together, marveling over his tiny perfect form, as Timmy squirmed. Deciding to reswaddle him after he'd been fed, Kate lifted Timmy toward her. Abruptly, she looked unsure how to proceed. "I've never done this before."

"And you're feeling self-conscious and would like some help," Michael guessed, finding that perfectly understandable. He touched her shoulder compassionately, then volunteered, "I'll go see if I can round up a nurse."

When he returned—alone—a scant minute and a half later, Kate had lowered one shoulder of her gown, draped the white cotton diaper over one shoulder and was cuddling a loudly protesting Timmy to her breast. Trying not to think how beautiful and sexy Kate looked, Michael shoved his hands in his pockets and announced as he neared, "They're really swamped. Every baby on the floor has decided he or she is hungry *now*. They said maybe ten minutes.''

''I tried but I can't get him to nurse.'' Kate looked at Michael helplessly.

Knowing that wasn't unusual for first-time mothers and their babies, Michael shut the door to her room to insure their privacy and crossed to her side. ''Let's see what we can do to get you more comfortable,'' he told Kate gently, repeating what he had learned over the years as both a physician and an uncle.

''For the first few feedings, lying on your side may work best,'' Michael told her with a reassuring smile. ''So, the first thing we're going to need to do is get you situated.''

Michael took a loudly squalling Timmy from Kate and cradled him against his chest. With his free hand he pressed the button that would lower the head of her bed. And then helped Kate—who was still moving a little stiffly after the delivery—into a reclining position. ''And then pull your arm out of your gown entirely so you'll have more freedom of movement,'' he said.

''Right.'' Kate flushed crimson.

''Okay.'' Michael helped her free her arm while still maintaining her modesty as best as he could. ''Can you shift onto your left side?'' Keeping his actions as clinical as possible, he helped her do so. ''Good. Let's put this pillow beneath you.'' He moved it longwise, so it cushioned her from head to breast. ''And we'll put your left arm up, like this, so you can rest your head on your upraised arm. And move this cloth aside.'' Keeping his mind resolutely on the task at hand, he gently exposed her breast. ''Now we'll get Timmy in here—'' Michael placed

Timmy on his side, facing Kate, and brought the infant as close as possible to his mother "—and try again."

Still crying and clueless about what to do next, the newborn turned away and wailed even louder. "See?" Kate cried, distressed, her whole body tensing at her son's rejection.

Figuring the sooner mother and son connected, the better, Michael looked at Kate, asking to simply show her—through touch—what needed to be done. "May I?"

Flushing and looking a little shy, Kate nodded. Michael covered her hand with his and lifted her nipple toward Timmy's lips. He touched the top of Timmy's bow-shaped lips with the tip of Kate's breast, then the bottom lip, then the top again, repeating the motion gently until Timmy's mouth opened. Michael continued to help her as he explained, "Once Timmy's mouth is open, place your nipple in the center so he can latch on."

Kate's gaze was fastened on both breast and baby. "He's not doing it," she said, obviously disappointed this was proving to be so difficult for both of them.

"Then let's try it again," Michael said, aware how silky and warm her skin felt beneath his fingers. "Upper lip. Lower." Michael smiled as Timmy's crying quieted and progress was made. "See, he's starting to root around a bit. Yeah," Michael said victoriously, as Timmy's cheeks moved in and out in a clumsy attempt to nurse, "there he goes."

"He's nursing!" Kate said as Timmy stopped wailing and latched onto her breast with all his might.

"Darned if he isn't," Michael said proudly, feeling as contented and happy as Kate was that this first hurdle with their son had been climbed. "Now there are a few more things to watch out for," Michael cautioned. He paused, wary of interfering too much. "If you want me to show you…"

Kate nodded and shot Michael a grateful glance. "Please," she said, eager to learn. "Starting with how long I should nurse him."

Michael repeated what the lactation nurse would tell Kate later. "For today, no more than five minutes on each breast. You can go ten minutes on each breast tomorrow. After that it'll be fifteen."

"How often will I nurse?" Kate asked, as she stroked the downy soft hair on the back of Timmy's head.

A wave of almost unbearable tenderness moving through him, Michael advised, "Once your milk comes in, you'll probably need to nurse him every three or four hours."

Again, their eyes met. "What else should I know?" Kate asked Michael softly.

I'm drawn to you, and would be even if you hadn't just unexpectedly borne me a son, Michael thought. Knowing, however, this was not the time or place for such a confession, Michael turned his attention to his nursing son. Briefly, he explained how to position Timmy to insure he had plenty of room to breathe while nursing, then said, "Make sure Timmy has a hold on the areola as well as the nipple—sucking on just the nipple will leave him hungry. And be sure he isn't sucking on his own lip or tongue while he nurses."

Her self-consciousness temporarily forgotten, Kate continued to nurse. She looked so beautiful and angelic it made his heart ache.

She bent to kiss the top of Timmy's head, then asked curiously, "What happens if he does any of those things?"

"If he starts sucking on his lower lip, you can simply work it free with your fingertip while he continues to nurse. Otherwise, break the suction and start over again." Michael continued to watch her another long moment, then glanced at his watch. "Ready to switch sides?"

Kate nodded.

Timmy protested at the interruption, but only half as vigorously as before. "This isn't as hard as I thought it would be," Kate murmured. Michael noted she was beginning to look and act as completely exhausted and drowsy as their infant son.

"And it'll get easier every time," Michael assured her.

Kate grinned. "How do you know?"

"I've got four sisters." Michael pulled a chair up beside the bed, turned it backward and straddled it. "They all have kids, and all of them nursed. It was hard for all of them in the beginning. Even for Winnie, who's an obstetrics nurse by profession. But my mom, who's also a nurse, coached them through it, on the phone and in person. So I know the drill—and then some."

"Plus you have experience as a doctor."

"Right again."

In contented silence, they watched the baby nurse at her breast. "I think he's falling asleep," Kate noted, yawning.

Michael picked up Timmy's tiny fist and kissed the back of it. "Poor fella. He's probably all tuckered out." Just like his mother, Michael thought. "Want

me to put him in his bassinet?'' he asked, when
Timmy's jaw went slack.

Kate yawned. ''I think you'd better,'' she said
drowsily.

Michael lifted him away from her. He wrapped
Timmy in the white flannel blanket and settled him
on his side in the Plexiglas crib. By the time he turned
to Kate, she was just as he'd left her, fast asleep. His
heart going out to her, Michael slipped her arm into
her gown and tucked the covers around her.

''Timmy wasn't the only miracle today,'' he murmured. Knowing she needed her sleep, he gently
touched her cheek. Wishing he could kiss her, he
slipped from the room.

''You're looking chipper this morning,'' Lindy said
as she came in at ten o'clock the next morning with
a brimming shopping bag in one hand, a coffee and
bake shop bag in the other.

Kate knew that was true. ''Maybe because I feel
almost human again,'' she said. She'd had a long, hot
shower and shampoo and changed into her own robe
and slippers. Sitting up in bed, she was smoothing the
silky blond ends of her hair with a cordless curling
iron. She shot Lindy a grateful glance. ''Thanks for
bringing my stuff over last night, by the way.'' It
would be a treat to face Michael Sloane in something
other than maternity clothes or a hospital gown. ''I
don't remember you coming in.''

Lindy opened the decaf cappuccino she'd brought
for Kate and put it on the bed tray. ''That's because
you were sound asleep, and I didn't want to wake
you.''

Kate nodded, grateful for the extra sleep. "I only woke to feed Timmy."

Opening her coffee, Lindy kicked off her shoes and settled in, cross-legged, at the foot of Kate's hospital bed. "Why isn't he still in here with you, by the way?"

"He will be later. Right now he's down in the nursery, getting his own bath. They're going to keep him there for a while." She had to force herself to remain calm as she took a sip of cappuccino and admitted, "He's being circumcised this morning."

Lindy groaned in sympathy.

Kate nodded. "Yeah, I know," she commiserated with her sister. "It sounds like it hurts to me, too, but Michael and Timmy's pediatrician swear he won't feel any discomfort. They're going to use a local anesthetic, and Michael will be with him the whole time the procedure is done. And," Kate sighed, "in the long run, it's supposed to be better, healthwise, so we're going to stick with tradition and have it done."

Lindy pulled two light and flaky Danishes out of the bag. "This was a joint decision?"

Finding she was famished, Kate accepted one of the flaky buns. "Uh-huh." The only surprise was how good it had felt, sharing that decision with Michael. What she'd thought would turn into an utter disaster had instead turned into something good.

Lindy took another sip of coffee. "I stopped by the nursery on my way to the room, and I have to tell you, I saw the name on Timmy's bassinet." Lindy leveled a warning look at Kate. "I don't know what Mom will say, but Dad is going to flip when he sees it."

Kate had figured as much. It didn't change anything.

"It's one thing to be grateful," Lindy said sternly, for once being more sensible than hopelessly romantic. "It's another to link lives with him this swiftly."

"I know. If it had been anyone else coming into the shop yesterday, telling me something like that, I probably would have panicked and felt the need to get a whole team of lawyers immediately. But it was Michael, and he was so…reasonable in the light of such a complete and utter disaster."

"Not to mention the fact he later delivered your baby and got you both to the hospital."

Kate recalled how kind and wonderful and good Michael had been as he coached her through childbirth and showed her how to nurse. "And that experience brought us together very quickly," Kate explained. It had also left them feeling unbearably close, despite the fact they were virtual strangers to each other.

She shrugged. "I don't know. I really can't explain why I trust him as much as I do, I just do." And somehow she knew, in her heart, that was not going to change. Even if her romantic past was telling her to proceed a lot more cautiously.

Lindy studied her. "Maybe you don't have to explain it, maybe you just need to go with your instincts."

Unfortunately, Kate thought, as she watched Lindy retrieve the shopping bag with a Thanksgiving turkey and a popular area mall insignia on the front of it, her instincts regarding the people closest to her had failed her more than once. But she didn't need to think about that now.

"What have you got there?" she inquired.

Lindy beamed. "Gifts, of course, for you and the baby, from your employees at the shop. And a sample gift catalogue from Dulcie. She said you need to check this over and make sure it's the way you want it because you need to give the printer final approval by Friday if you want the catalogues in the mail before Thanksgiving. And she also said to tell you they finished the deliveries that were supposed to be done last night, and retrieved the van, which was still in perfect shape."

Kate thought about the upcoming holidays. Though she had planned well for the season and her very brief maternity leave, as she thought about Thanksgiving, which was roughly two weeks away, and Christmas, which was another six, she felt a little daunted. "How are things at the shop this morning, by the way?" she asked curiously.

"Busy. Can you believe you had fifty more orders for semester exam care baskets in yesterday's mail alone? Sending out brochures to the parents of students was a great idea."

Kate did some rapid calculations. "This brings the shop total to well over a thousand."

"Dulcie thinks that given the increase in holiday business and your being out on maternity leave, you may want to hire some more seasonal help."

Kate nodded. "Absolutely. I'll call the newspaper and get an ad put in immediately."

"Someone else could do that for you, you know," Lindy chided. "You just had a baby."

Kate grinned at her baby sister's protectiveness. "As well as a great night's sleep. I feel fine. Really. In fact, I'm raring to go home."

Lindy frowned. Her green eyes grew troubled. "Just don't push too hard, okay?"

"I agree with you there." Michael pushed the Plexiglas bassinet into the room. He picked up Timmy, who was wide awake and wrapped in a blanket, and put him into Kate's arms. "New mothers need a lot of rest."

Lindy sighed contentedly at her new nephew. "He is so precious," Lindy enthused while Kate held her baby close and glanced at Michael questioningly.

"The circumcision is done. He didn't cry at all."

Kate breathed a sigh of relief.

Lindy rose reluctantly. "Well, I better get going or I will never get that doctorate in mathematics."

"Kate said you were a teaching assistant at Chapel Hill."

Lindy nodded happily. "It's a family tradition, haven't you heard?" Lindy grinned as she bent to kiss Timmy's cheek. "My mom and dad both went there. So did Kate."

"So did I," Michael said. "For undergrad and med school, which makes it even better." Before either woman could say anything, he held up a staying palm. "Wait here a second."

He left and came back carrying a white teddy bear with a powder-blue felt shirt emblazoned with the Carolina logo and a huge bouquet of flowers. "For you." He handed the flowers to Kate. "And for Timmy." He took the flowers, put them on the bureau, and put the teddy next to Kate.

"Nice," Lindy said.

"Very nice," Kate agreed as Timmy studied the teddy bear with wide baby-blue eyes.

"I'll talk to you later." Lindy gave Kate a one-shouldered hug and was off.

Kate and Michael looked at each other. Kate found herself wishing he could stay. "Do you have to work today?" Kate asked.

He nodded reluctantly. "I've got the noon-to-midnight shift in the emergency room downstairs. I'll leave my beeper number here for you." He handed her a card with the number scrawled on the back. "If you need me, don't hesitate to give me a buzz. And I'll be up to check on you and Timmy on my breaks. That is—" he hesitated "—if it's okay."

It's more than okay, Kate thought. "I want you to be close to your son." She wanted Timmy to have a dad. She wanted him to have Michael in his life. Not just for now, but for all the years he was growing up.

Without warning, Michael closed the distance between them all the way. He took her face in his hands and lowered his mouth to hers. Kate closed her eyes, anticipating the touch of his lips, the sweet soulfulness of a kiss that had been brewing for what now seemed a lifetime, and that was when they heard a pair of rapid footsteps screech to a halt and a very adult gasp of surprise behind them.

Reacting as if they'd been hit by a live wire, Kate and Michael broke apart and glanced automatically in the direction of the intrusion. A flush of embarrassment heating her cheeks, Kate looked at the fifty-something couple standing there. She'd never seen either of them before, but they looked familiar to her nevertheless. The woman had a head of thick, straight sable brown hair—like Michael's—and was wearing a slim denim dress, cardigan sweater and flat shoes. The man had cropped salt-and-pepper hair. He was wearing a casual tweed sport coat, coordinating shirt and tie and slacks and had an air of gentleness about him.

"When we heard," the woman began softly, pressing a hand to her heart.

"We didn't believe it," the man said for her.

"Michael!" The attractive woman propped her hands on her hips and demanded, "Why didn't you tell us?"

IF THIS WASN'T a disaster in the making, Michael didn't know what was.

"We didn't even know you were dating this young woman!" Michael's dad said.

That was because Michael had felt they had enough complications with just Kate's family in the picture at the moment. But there was no helping it now. He strode forward amiably and brought his parents into the room.

"Mom, Dad, I'd like you to meet Kate Montgomery and our son, Timmy. Kate, my mom, Ginny, and my dad, Hugh."

Kate greeted them both graciously. "Pleased to meet you."

"The feeling is mutual, believe me," Hugh said gently, smiling at Kate and the baby before turning to his son. "Michael, I'm still waiting for an explanation."

"First, I want to know how you found out about this." Michael gestured his parents to chairs and shut the door behind them.

His mother looked hurt. "You aren't the only one from Hickory who works at this hospital, remember? Tina Delaney is a nurse in oncology. She heard it from someone in radiology, who heard it from someone in the ER. She called her parents last night and told them, and they called to congratulate us." Ginny flushed, looking both embarrassed and incensed. "And of course we had no idea what they were talking about, so we called the ER this morning to talk to you and were told you were with your new son, and they weren't yet sure if you were coming in today or not."

Michael swore silently, though he could hardly blame the emergency room staff, who had no idea of his decision to delay telling his family.

Hugh shot Michael a glance riddled with disappointment. "Why didn't you tell us?" he demanded sternly. "We waited all last night for a call."

Noting Kate was looking pretty embarrassed and uncomfortable, Michael put his arm around Kate's shoulders. "I wanted everything to be worked out first," he told his parents. Briefly, Michael related finding out about the mix-up at the lab and the ordeal of Kate giving birth to their baby in the Gourmet Gifts To Go delivery van before the two of them had been given a chance to deal with the situation. "I didn't want to call you until we knew how we were going to work all this out."

Michael's parents sat facing them in stunned silence. A knock sounded on the door. But at least, Michael realized, they were no longer angry with him for what they would have seen as highly irresponsible behavior.

"I didn't really want to tell you anything unless I was going to be a part of the baby's life," Michael said as he went to open the door.

"And are you going to be part of Timmy's life?"

Ginny Sloane asked her son point-blank, looking as if she were unable to think about the alternative.

"That's what we'd like to know," Kate's father said, as her parents unexpectedly walked in, one after the other, and joined the group.

FOR A MOMENT, silence reigned. Then introductions were made all around and Kate's father took the floor. "Look, I know having a baby is a very emotional and exciting time in a person's life." Ted sent Carolyn a poignant look that spoke volumes about how much his daughters' births had meant to him before turning to Kate and Michael. "And there is nothing more romantic than bringing that first baby into the world. But I feel the two of you are acting way too swiftly and emotionally for your own good." He opened his briefcase.

"And to that end, it's necessary for you both to protect your own interests, in a legal sense. So I've taken the liberty of having papers drawn up at my law firm this morning."

Afraid Timmy, who had fallen asleep in her arms, would feel her distress if she continued to hold him, Kate gently leaned over and put him in the bassinet.

"This is a letter of agreement stating that Kate relinquishes all claims of financial support for herself and her son," Ted continued as if this were the most logical thing in the world for them to be doing. "And though she clearly acknowledges Michael Sloane is— inadvertently—the father of her child," he said with lawyerly ease, "Kate makes no demands on him, custodial or otherwise, as a parent, now or at any time in the future. In return, Michael will relinquish any and all rights to ever sue for custody of Timmy or make financial claims on Kate's business or personal holdings.''

Kate stared at her father, aware he couldn't have done more to extinguish the flame of attraction between her and Michael had he thrown a bucket of ice water on them. Which was, she realized belatedly, clearly his intent. "I can't believe you did this," Kate gasped indignantly, feeling hurt and angry beyond measure.

"Nor can I," Ginny Sloane murmured, looking distraught as she lay a hand across her heart.

"I second that," Kate's mother said, staring at her estranged husband as if she'd never seen him before.

Ted held his ground. "You'll all be grateful to me in the long run for taking care to protect both Kate and Michael from future legal action."

"I think if these two kids should be talking anything, they should be talking marriage," Hugh Sloane said, "if only for a short while, for appearance's sake. Who knows?" Michael's dad continued optimistically. "Maybe things would work out."

For the past few hours, Kate had thought their future was ripe with possibilities—romantic and otherwise—too. But now, seeing the dissent among their families and her warring parents, she was less sure.

"At least then," Ginny Sloane concurred as she looked at Michael and Kate, "you'd be able to tell Timmy you two gave it a shot." Ginny shrugged. "If it didn't work, it didn't work." But clearly, Kate thought, the hope was that it would work.

But she couldn't force Michael into that. Any more than she would want anyone to force her into marriage because of something someone else decided. And having this baby had been all her idea. Michael had had no part of it until yesterday. "We're not getting married just because of the baby," Kate told Michael's parents firmly.

"Agreed," Michael said, backing her up. "There'd have to be a lot more between Kate and I for us to even consider taking that step."

Not surprisingly, Kate noted, her parents looked abruptly relieved. "Then you won't mind signing this document for Kate's peace of mind, will you?" Ted asked, stepping forward.

Kate's heart pounded as she watched Michael accept the legal documents from her dad.

"Sure I'll sign them if it'll make you feel better," Michael said, grimly flipping to the last page and scrawling his name. "It's true, anyway." He finished writing with quick, angry strokes of the pen. "I have no intention of suing Kate, on any level, at any time now or in the future."

Looking visibly relieved he'd bullied one person into doing what he wanted, Kate's dad turned to her. "Honey?" he asked cordially. "Don't you owe Michael the same peace of mind?"

Kate had to admit she didn't want Michael to think she would ever come after him for financial support. Oh, hell. "Why not?" Kate muttered grimly, taking the pen from her dad. "I don't have any intention of slapping him with a paternity suit, either." Never mind asking him for money!

"If you'll just witness the signatures..." Ted Montgomery turned first to his wife, then the Sloanes. Everyone signed on the dotted line. Finished, her dad put the papers away. "I'm glad we have that all worked out," he said happily. "Now, about this business of the baby's last name—"

Kate and Michael exchanged looks. On that, they were firm. "There's no discussion," Kate said resolutely, accepting the hand of support Michael offered her. "The name stays," she announced as she and Michael tightly entwined fingers. "It's Timothy Michael Montgomery-Sloane, hyphenated. He has two parents. He is going to carry both our last names. It will avoid confusion in the future."

Michael added, "Kate and I didn't create this situation, but we're going to do our darnedest to make the best of it."

"Good for you," Hugh Sloane said, sending his son an approving glance.

"Well, Kate's probably tired," Ginny Sloane said, rising to her feet.

"You can come back and see your grandson any time," Kate told Michael's parents, meaning it.

His parents smiled. "Thank you," Hugh said.

"And you come and see us, too," Ginny added.

"I will," Kate promised, meaning it, too. Michael's parents seemed like really nice people. She wanted to get to know them a lot better.

Michael glanced at his parents. "I'll walk you to the elevators," Michael said.

As soon as Michael and his parents had left, Kate's parents turned to each other, and silence reigned. It was an acutely uncomfortable moment for all of them.

Michael walked in. He looked handsome and relaxed in blue scrubs and a white lab coat. "Everything okay in here?" He looked at her folks, then Kate.

Kate nodded and forced a smile. "We were just talking." *Or trying to.*

Kate's mother turned to Kate and pressed a hand

to her sternum. Kate noted there were shadows of fatigue beneath her eyes. But maybe that was par for the course. Between her parents' separation and Kate's suddenly so much more complicated situation, her mother probably hadn't slept much the night before.

"When are you and Timmy going to be released from the hospital?" Carolyn asked.

"Tomorrow morning, if all goes well," Kate said.

"Call us and let us know about the time, then. Your mother—or I—will be by to take you and the baby home," her dad said.

"That won't be necessary," Kate fibbed, hoping Michael would forgive her the brief but very necessary duplicity. "The arrangements have already been made." Kate looked at Michael, silently begging him to play along with her. She didn't want to be caught between her parents. She didn't want to be accused of taking sides. Or be in a position where she had to choose one parent over the other. "Michael's taking us home."

"But you two hardly know each other!" Ted murmured, upset, while her mother looked hurt and disappointed.

Again, Kate refused to choose between the two. "High time that changed, don't you think?" she countered glibly, feeling her inherent stubbornness kick in as she continued to lose herself in the brown depths of Michael's eyes. "After all," Kate turned slowly to her parents "—Michael is Timmy's father."

Ted's lips thinned. "Fine, Kate. But you're still going to need assistance the first few days. So just tell your mom and I what time, and in what order, you want us each to come and stay with you and Timmy.''

Kate felt so backed into a corner she didn't even stop to think. She drew a bracing breath and blurted the first way out that came to mind. ''Thanks, Mom, Dad, but Michael's offered to do that, too.''

Chapter Four

For one excruciatingly long moment, silence reigned in the cramped hospital room. Michael noted Kate's parents were clearly as stunned as he felt by their daughter's announcement. Then all eyes turned to him. "That's very kind of you to offer," Carolyn Montgomery said.

"But not at all necessary," Ted Montgomery added protectively.

Kate looked at Michael, silently beseeching him to rescue her from the turmoil of her parents' impending divorce.

More than happy to help her out, he turned to her folks. "Kate and I prefer it this way," he said simply.

"And to tell you the truth," Kate continued, her slender shoulders sagging slightly, "I'm a little worn out by all the company today."

Carolyn's expression softened with motherly concern as she picked up her coat and slipped it over her arm. "Of course."

"I'll call you tomorrow, as soon as Timmy and I get home and get settled," Kate promised.

"Call me, too," Ted instructed his daughter protectively as he leaned forward to kiss the top of her head. "If I'm in court, just have my secretary take a message."

Kate nodded, her relief evident as her parents said goodbye to them both and departed one after another.

"Oh, wait." Kate looked at the chair her mother had just vacated. "Mom forgot her purse."

"I'll take it to her and be right back." Michael sprinted out the door. As he rounded the corner, he saw the elevator doors shut. Carolyn was headed toward him when suddenly she paled, swayed unsteadily and put a hand on the wall next to her.

His pulse picking up, Michael swiftly closed the distance between them. "Are you okay?"

"Yes." Carolyn trembled. "I'm just a little light-headed."

Michael slipped a hand beneath her elbow and helped her across the corridor and into the lounge. He eased her into a chair and knelt in front of her. "Better?"

Carolyn took a deep breath, nodded. Tears glistened in her eyes as she pressed three fingers to her sternum and kept them there. "Don't tell Kate."

"Has this happened before?"

"Yes." Carolyn drew another shaky breath. "But it always goes away after a moment."

"What about the pain in your chest?" Michael asked, having been a doctor too long not to notice. "Has that been recurring, too?"

Carolyn blinked in surprise. "How did you know about that?"

Michael nodded at the telltale pressure she was exerting on her breastbone with her hand. "You didn't answer my question."

Carolyn pushed to her feet. Abruptly, she looked a

lot steadier, despite the perspiration dotting her brow and upper lip. "It always goes away, too. I just shouldn't have eaten this morning before I came over here." Looking as if she were angered by his attention, Carolyn brushed by him tensely.

Michael followed her and handed her the purse she'd forgotten not once, but twice. "Maybe you should have that checked out," Michael suggested.

"There's no need," Carolyn said smoothly. "I know what it is." She was not, however, going to reveal it to him. Her light green eyes—so like Kate's—lasered in on his. "I meant what I said. I don't want anyone else to know about this—and that goes double for everyone in my family."

"I'll keep your confidence," Michael promised reluctantly. That didn't mean he wouldn't try to keep an eye on things, or try to discover a little more about what was going on. If Kate's mother had a medical problem, she needed to see a physician.

"Everything okay?" Kate asked as he entered her hospital room several minutes later.

Already feeling guilty about keeping a secret from Kate, Michael nodded. "I caught up with her."

Kate's relief was palpable. "Thanks for taking Mom her purse. And thanks even more for playing along with me when I said I'd made prior arrangements with you to take Timmy and me home from the hospital tomorrow."

Michael crossed his arms and braced one shoulder—and the bulk of his weight—against the wall. It was one thing to be in a tough spot, as he now was with Kate's mother. It was another to be used as a pawn in a family chess game. He looked her straight in the eye and announced softly, meaningfully, "I wasn't playing, Kate."

Twin spots of pink color brightened Kate's high cheekbones. Her fingers pleated the folded edge of the soft cotton blanket spread across her lap. "I know you weren't, Michael." She swallowed and said with a sort of edgy affability, "I'm just saying you don't have to take me and the baby home. I'm perfectly capable of taking a cab. It's no big deal."

But it was a big deal, Michael thought. This was his son they were talking about. Their son. And his trip home from the hospital should be an event, a moment of happiness and celebration, at least for the three of them.

"I'm aware of that," he told her cordially, as a hot, restless feeling filled his soul, "but I want to do it."

Kate swallowed and continued looking at him as if she didn't know quite how to handle that pronouncement or him. Finally, she looked away. Abruptly, Michael's heart went out to her. Through no fault of their own, Kate had been through a lot in the last few days. They both had. And now she was being pressured by her father. And her mother—unbeknownst to Kate—might be ill.

Acting on instinct, Michael pushed away from the wall and crossed to her side. As he stood looking at her, he could see the faint shadows of exhaustion beneath her light green eyes, the intriguing ivory softness of her skin. Her lower lip, soft and pink and bare, was trembling slightly.

Knowing she needed to realize he had no intention of hurting her, he sat beside her and took her hands in his.

"Look," he said gently, "I don't pretend to know what the right thing is in a situation like this. I don't think anyone does."

A weary breath soughed between Kate's lips. "And yet…" She trembled all the more as he continued to hold her hands in his. "You're suggesting…"

Michael tightened his hands over hers reassuringly, doing his best to imbue her with his strength. "That we take it one day at a time, at least until we figure out how to handle this situation in the long run."

Michael knew Kate liked to plan, but for him, taking things day by day and not worrying too much about the future was always best.

"Meaning?" Kate prodded.

Michael stood. Suddenly he was restless, and as anxious as she was. Which in turn told him the sooner they worked things out between them, the better. And to that end, he might as well be blunt. Still wanting like hell to protect her—to protect them all—he regarded her directly. "Should we parent Timmy separately?"

Kate paled and went back to pleating the blanket with her slender fingers. "I want to be fair to you."

Michael studied the sexy disarray of her blond hair. She'd lifted the sections closest to her face toward her crown and caught them there with a butterfly clip, but her straight silky bangs brushed the top of her brows and the remaining chin-length ends formed a bell-shaped curve against the graceful lines of her neck. Even when she wasn't trying to be sexy in the least, he noted dispassionately, she was.

With effort, he forced his mind to the conversation. "I want to be fair to you, too," he told her honestly. And that meant not acting on the considerable attraction he felt for her, at least until they worked everything out. Then, all bets were off.

Kate bit her lip, sighed and looked at him. As she studied him and his intentions, her shoulders began to relax and a small smile spread across her face. "I guess it would be better for Timmy if you and I worked as a team. Heaven knows we don't want him to feel as if he's in the middle of an emotional tug-of-war between us, like I've been with my parents, because that is just not easy."

Relief eased the tension in his tall frame. "I think it'd be best for us to parent him together, too."

"And it'd be easier for you to drive us tomorrow than for us to take a cab," she said finally.

"Absolutely," Michael agreed, glad they'd been able to come to terms about this much. "It'll be easier this way," Michael promised in a gruff voice. But even as he spoke, even as he continued to assure her it was no problem, he knew that wasn't quite the truth.

Nothing about this situation they found themselves in was going to be easy. In fact, truth be told, it only looked to get more complex and difficult with every day that passed. But he couldn't think about that now. Now, it was enough to get through each tricky situation as it came up. If that meant living life one moment at a time indefinitely, than so be it.

"I CAN'T BELIEVE Timmy didn't wake up when we moved him from the car to his crib," Kate murmured the following morning as she gently covered the sleeping infant with a soft yellow receiving blanket. She and Michael took one last look at Timmy, turned on the baby monitor, then exited the nursery, which had been decorated in a Winnie the Pooh motif.

Kate led the way past a guest room, a small bath and the master bedroom before heading down the stairs of her spacious town-home-style condominium to the living room. A sapphire-blue and white print sofa and two blue armchairs formed a conversation pit around the white Colonial-style fireplace. An armoire entertainment center held a television and stereo. Built-in bookshelves on either side of the fireplace displayed a variety of books, tapes, compact disks and magazines. A comfortable-looking desk and chair held a computer and printer, several notebooks and stacks of thick manila files. Beneath the cherrywood coffee table, a sapphire, navy, white and beige wool rug added warmth and a cozy feel.

To the rear was a well-equipped kitchen and beyond that a guest bath and a utility room on the left and a cozy breakfast nook on the right with bay windows overlooking a private deck and a small, fenced backyard.

Monetarily, at least, Kate lacked for nothing, Michael noted. There couldn't be a better place to bring up a child. And while that pleased him, it also left him feeling a bit unnecessary. It would have been easier, in some respects, had Kate—and their son sleeping so peacefully upstairs—needed his help a little more.

"He's probably all tuckered out from the excitement of leaving the hospital," Michael explained.

Kate paused by her telephone answering machine. Her pale blond brow furrowed as she saw the message sign flashing two.

Figuring she needed a little privacy to screen her

calls, Michael said, "I'll bring in the rest of your stuff while you check your messages."

Picking up the receiver, she smiled at him. "Thanks."

When Michael returned with her suitcase, Kate was standing at the bay windows overlooking her landscaped yard. One hand was propped on her hip. The other was rubbing the back of her neck. She looked tense and unhappy. It was all he could do to not take her in his arms and hold her close until the stiffness in her slender body melted away.

"Everything okay?" he asked.

"Yes." She lifted her sexy, long-lashed green eyes to his and sighed. "It was just my parents, checking in with me. I called them both back."

Michael studied her upturned face and wished for the hundredth time they'd met some other less problematic way. "And?" he prodded.

Kate lifted her slender shoulders in a shrug. "They're still worried about us, the whole situation."

Michael paused, aware this wasn't as much a surprise to him as it was to her. "More than you think they should be, obviously," he guessed, resisting the urge to smooth an errant strand of silky blond hair from her cheek.

Kate shrugged, and after following his gaze, tucked the gently curving ends of her blond bob behind her ears. "Nothing new there," she quipped lightly.

The last thing Michael wanted to do was cause problems between Kate and her loved ones. Doing what he could to restore the peace between Kate and her family, he pointed out matter-of-factly, "It's not surprising, given the circumstances, that your father wouldn't trust me or my motives entirely."

"It's more than that. Dad's always been practical to a fault and a stickler for getting things done the way they should be done. He's very driven and goal-oriented and can't rest until he knows every last detail of whatever case he's working on. And like me, he gets irritated when life does not go according to plan."

"Whereas your mom—"

"Has always been more of a free spirit, driven primarily by her emotions. She never cared what any of us accomplished in terms of school or work as long as we felt good about ourselves and were happy."

"From the way you describe them, it's surprising they got together."

"That's just it. They're complete opposites in some ways but a perfect match in others. Which was why it was so odd when Mom abruptly asked Dad for a divorce last summer. The whole time I was growing up, the family was everything to her. She loved everything about being a homemaker and a mother. She didn't have a career outside the home, but she was very active in the community and volunteered for a number of charities and had a great social life as well. Never once did she show any signs of being discontent with the way things were, even when we grew up and went off to college. Then suddenly, boom, she told my dad she was leaving him."

"He must have been shocked and upset."

"Very. Of course he also thought this was something that would soon pass, which was why he insisted she stay in the house where we'd grown up, and he did the gallant thing and moved into a hotel-apartment he could rent by the month. Only now they're both angry with each other. My mother because my father doesn't seem to take her desire to live an independent life seriously, and my father because he just doesn't understand why my mother's behaving the way she is. Not that any of us do.'' Kate sighed as she opened the refrigerator and brought out a jug of milk.

Michael wondered if Carolyn's symptoms had started before or after the separation from her husband. Maybe now was the time to do a little medical sleuthing. ''Divorce can be very stressful,'' he said casually. ''A lot of times people will get sick, start smoking again or lose or gain a lot of weight as a result.''

Kate poured herself a glass of milk, and when he nodded, poured him one, too. ''My parents gave up smoking years ago, but I know what you mean. When they first separated, my dad spent so much time running he developed shinsplints. And over the last six months, my mom's dropped about fifteen pounds. One minute, she's on a vegetarian diet, the next she's eating only champagne and caviar.'' Kate sighed and shook her head as she brought out a container of cookies. ''I can't figure it out. There are days when my mom acts like it's all going to end tomorrow.''

''Any particular reason she might feel that way?'' Michael asked, as they sat across the table from each other.

''Well, now that you mention it, just one. My mom is now the same age her mother was when she died.''

That was enough to jump start a life crisis, Michael thought. ''Your grandmother must've died young, then,'' he surmised.

Kate nodded. ''She was fifty. She had bone cancer and she suffered terribly, especially at the end. I was only ten when she died, but I still remember what a hard time it was for all of us." A mixture of grief and pain flashed across Kate's face. "Anyway, I hate to be the one to tell you this, but I very much expect them to continue hovering over us, monitoring the whole situation, each in his own way, if only so they don't have to dwell on their own problems now that the holiday season is upon us."

Michael did not find that surprising. If Kate were his daughter, he wouldn't want to see her hurt, either. And theirs was a situation rife with potential for heartache. "They probably don't want to see you hurt."

"They also feel guilty for not being able to talk me out of having a child on my own, via sperm bank."

"It was your decision to make."

"Yes, well, my parents don't exactly see it that way."

"I know what you mean." Kate shot him a curious glance, and he continued, figuring she needed to be forewarned, too. "I didn't tell my parents about the mix-up at the lab for fear they'd react just the way they did."

"You mean they gave you grief, too?" she asked.

"When I walked them out yesterday, they told me they thought it was a mistake for me to sign any papers at this time." Papers, they had not hesitated to remind him grimly, that could be used against him if he were later to change his mind about custody.

"But you did anyway."

Michael shrugged, knowing he'd had no choice but to do what he had the previous day. "No child should start out his life in the midst of a custody battle, or even the threat of one," Michael said meaningfully.

And if signing those papers had made Kate and or her parents relax even a little then it was a good thing. Whether Kate realized it or not, she was going to need a lot of help from him in the next few weeks, until she and the baby settled in. And he intended to be there for her.

"So what are your plans for the day?" he asked.

"I'm going to do a little paperwork while Timmy sleeps."

Michael arched a brow. "Sure you want to jump right back in like that?" he asked.

Kate's green eyes flashed with pique as she countered mildly, "What else should I be doing?"

Michael shrugged and tried not to think how good it felt to be sitting opposite her this way. "Sleeping— while Timmy sleeps." Whether she admitted it or not, she had to be tired after giving birth just two days ago.

"I'm fine. Besides..." She lifted the mug to her lips. Eyes on his, she smiled and said, "I never nap."

"Normally, neither do I." Michael munched on a cookie. "But you just had a baby, Kate."

Kate rolled her eyes in exasperation, then finished her milk. "Will you stop worrying? I feel great. I know what I'm doing."

So did most new mothers, until their adrenaline wore off and the lack of sleep caught up with them, Michael thought wryly. But he sensed this was one lesson Kate would have to learn on her own. Until then, he had his own work to do. And an important stop to make on the way to the ER.

MICHAEL HAD a little trouble finding a place to park—apparently a neighbor down the street was having a tag sale that had drawn quite a crowd—but he eventually found a spot a block and a half over and walked back.

Carolyn answered the door. Although it was nearly noon, she was wearing a luxurious white satin peignoir set and matching slippers. "Michael. I thought you'd still be over at Kate's!" Carolyn said, her surprise at finding him on her doorstep evident.

"I have to go back to work, but she has my beeper number if she needs me." Michael noted Carolyn's cheeks were pale and her eyes were slightly puffy, as if she'd been crying. He was glad he'd decided to go with his instincts and check up on Kate's mother before any more time elapsed. Aware they were standing in a draft, he asked kindly, "May I have a word with you?"

"Certainly." Every inch the gracious Southern lady, Carolyn led him through a vast front hall to a cozy sitting room at the rear of the redbrick Colonial-style home in an elegant, older section of Chapel Hill.

"I wanted to talk about yesterday," Michael continued as he took a seat on the cushioned wicker sofa Carolyn indicated.

Carolyn paced next to tall windows decorated with lacy white sheers and heavy velvet floor-to-ceiling drapes. Without warning, her skin was as white as the elegant peignoir set she was wearing. "I'm fine."

Michael's eyes fell on the stack of books spread out on the coffee table in front of him. He studied their titles surreptitiously, and their subject matter confirmed his hunch. "Is that why you're reading all these books on cancer?" Michael asked. Carolyn froze like a deer in headlights, and he continued gently, "Kate told me your mother died when she was your age."

Though clearly uncertain how to proceed, Carolyn could no longer hide her sadness. "That's how I know what's wrong with me. My mother's illness started the same way. Pain here." Carolyn indicated her breastbone. "Occasional bouts of light-headedness. Weight loss. An inability to sleep."

"When did it start?" Michael asked sympathetically.

Carolyn settled in an armchair opposite him. Michael noted she had clenched her fists until the knuckles turned white. "Late last summer."

"About the same time you separated from your husband," he guessed.

Tears welled in Carolyn's eyes. "My mother suffered horribly at the end. I won't put my family through that."

Michael couldn't blame her for wanting to protect her family. But this was not the way. "You said something yesterday about this pain happening after you eat. Is it only after you eat? Or does it happen at other times, too?"

Carolyn hesitated. "It's usually right after I eat, but not always."

Which meant, Michael thought, the pain she was feeling could be related to a problem with her digestive system. "There are many causes of chest pain. Many are treatable with medication or a change of diet. The only way to know for sure what's causing yours is to see a doctor."

Carolyn sighed. "I wouldn't know who to go to— our family doctor retired last year, and I don't like the man who took over his practice at all."

"No problem." Feet flat on the floor in front of him, Michael leaned forward, his hands clasped between his knees. "I've got an internist friend who's an excellent diagnostician. I could set something up for you."

Carolyn bit her lower lip. "And keep it quiet?"

"Absolutely," Michael promised. At least until they knew what was going on medically. Then he would encourage her to tell all to her family promptly.

At the other end of the house, a door opened and shut. "Carolyn?" A familiar male voice called as heavy footsteps sounded on the wood floors.

"Oh, my God, it's Ted!" Carolyn said. She vaulted from her chair, grabbed the books on the coffee table and shoved them in Michael's arms. "He can't find you here!" she whispered.

"Why not?" Michael asked, as Carolyn frantically hauled him to his feet.

"Because then he'll know there's something wrong with me, and I won't be able to keep him away no matter what I do or say! Now hide!" Carolyn ordered in a voice not to be denied. She put a hand to Michael's spine and shoved him behind the drapes. And not a second too soon, either, Michael thought grimly, as Ted entered the room.

"Carolyn! What are you doing in a negligee at this hour?" Ted sounded indignant while Michael was left to wonder how he'd gotten himself in this mess. "It's almost noon!"

Carolyn's low voice bristled. "I think the real question is what are you doing here and why didn't you ring the bell instead of using your key, like I asked," Carolyn retorted icily as her footsteps moved toward the other end of the sitting room.

Ted's footsteps followed. Michael flattened himself against the wall and tried not to move.

His voice sounding as if his back were to Michael, Ted continued. "Because our divorce isn't final yet, and as I've said on more than one occasion, Carolyn, if I have my way, it never will be."

"I'm not discussing that with you today, so if you have anything else to say, do so and get it over with," Carolyn told him haughtily.

Ted paused, then spoke in a slightly less aggravated tone. "I came over to talk to you about Kate and this Michael Sloane."

Michael swore silently to himself. Now he really didn't want to be here!

"I've seen the adoring way Kate looks at Michael," Ted growled worriedly.

Carolyn's voice rose emotionally. "Kate's a grown woman! She can have a crush on whoever she wants!"

Were they right? Michael wondered. Did Kate have a crush on him? Or was that wishful thinking on all their parts?

"Don't you care she could get terribly hurt here?" Ted demanded unhappily.

"I just want her to be happy," Carolyn countered, as she brushed by where Michael was standing. The move was far too close for comfort. She ushered Ted to the only way out of the sitting room. "Now you have to go!"

To Michael's relief, their voices receded. Dropped to a murmur. Finally, the front door shut and the lock turned. Carolyn hurried back, her slippers slapping against the wooden floor. "You can come out from behind the drapes now!"

Finally, Michael thought, more than a little irked to have been put in such a position. What if Kate's father had found him? He'd have had a hell of a time explaining why he was hiding. "That really was not necessary." Michael handed Carolyn's books to her.

"You let me be the judge of that!" Carolyn huffed, suddenly looking a lot healthier now that she had some color back in her cheeks. She drew a bolstering breath. "Now, about that internist friend of yours, Michael. You better call him before I change my mind."

FOR MICHAEL, the rest of the day passed slowly. Not for lack of patients. As usual, there was a steady stream of people waiting to be seen in the emergency room. He kept waiting—or maybe just hoping—for Kate to decide she needed a little help, or a shoulder to lean on, or even someone to share some happy news with. But she didn't call.

At midnight, as Michael signed himself out of the hospital at the end of his shift, he admitted he was more than a little disappointed. Maybe it was selfish or unrealistically optimistic, but he'd wanted Kate—and Timmy, too—to need him, or at least want him to be there with them, this first day home from the hospital, just a little bit.

He drove by Kate's condo on the way home. At midnight, he expected to see it dark and quiet, as most of the other units in the complex were. Instead, every light was blazing. Which in turn made him wonder if everything was okay.

Figuring it couldn't hurt to see, he parked in front of her condo and got out. Kate answered on the first bell. Clad in a robe and pajamas, she looked deliciously cuddly, drowsy and ready for bed.

Unfortunately for the obviously exhausted Kate, the baby in her arms looked ready for anything *but* a little shut-eye.

Michael grinned at his son, who—if he wasn't mistaken—was getting more adorable by the minute. "Hey, there, slugger," he said softly. Unable to resist, he took Timmy's tiny baby-soft hand in his. Inhaling the sweet baby scent of his skin, Michael kissed the back of Timmy's tiny fist. He looked at Kate. "I was hoping he'd be awake."

"Oh, he's awake, all right," Kate quipped dryly as she ushered Michael in. Her slipper-shod feet moving soundlessly across the wood-floored entryway, she led him into the living room. Her hips swaying provocatively beneath her thick terry-cloth robe, she paced back and forth, holding Timmy against her shoulder and patting him on the back all the while. Doing a swift about-face, she strode past Michael. "And he has been for the last six hours."

Realizing how long a time that was for a newborn baby, Michael did a double take. "You're kidding," he drawled.

"Nope." Kate shook her head in chagrin, looking every bit as proud as she was exasperated by their infant's refusal to stick to the prescribed schedule. "He slept all day, only waking to nurse." As she paced by once again, Timmy let out a tiny burp. "Then around dinnertime he woke up and has been awake ever since."

Michael studied Timmy's cherubic face and big baby-blue eyes. The feathery curls of dark hair atop his head were sable brown, like his own, and his skin had the same golden glow. But the shape of his face, the nose, the lively curious expression in his eyes, were all Kate's. "He looks happy." But then, Michael thought, what baby wouldn't be, snuggled so closely to Kate's warm, soft breasts?

Kate made a comical face and trod closer to Michael once again. She turned so Michael could better see into Timmy's face. "He is as long as I'm carrying him around, but the minute I put him down he lets out a wail that would wake the dead."

Michael grinned. Timmy was no fool. He knew a good setup when he found one. Right now Timmy had two parents who were completely nuts about him and had been from the very instant he was born. Not to mention a biological father who was, despite his fervent wish not to complicate things further, very attracted to his biological mother.

Michael offered, a great deal more casually than he felt, "As long as I'm here—need help?" He didn't want to think about how he'd feel if she refused.

Kate stifled a yawn with the back of her hand, even as she studied him. He knew what she was thinking. He had been working all day, too. And she'd said more than once she could do this alone. She was determined to prove it. Yet she had been at this pacing and soothing a long time. So long she looked, when she finally let her guard down just a little bit and faced him, as though she felt ready to drop.

Kate let out a tiny sigh and studied Michael hopefully. "You really wouldn't mind?"

Michael grinned from ear to ear as he held out his arms. "Are you kidding? I'd love to have another chance to hold him." He'd been wistfully thinking about it, wishing for it, all day. With the minimum amount of jostling, he accepted Timmy from Kate. "Did you get any rest?"

"No. None." Kate ran a hand through her hair. She sank onto the sofa, pajama-clad legs spread out wearily in front of her as Michael took up the pacing. Kate stretched her back, her hands clasped together, her arms unfurling high above her head. "When I wasn't taking care of Timmy I was telephoning suppliers, doing my books."

Michael watched her rub her eyes. "You couldn't get someone else to do any of that for you?" he asked, amazed, as Timmy cuddled contentedly, but unsleepily, against him.

"The buck stops here, as they say. Besides, this time of year they're busy enough at the shop as it is." Kate yawned again as she rolled to her feet. "Then my dad stopped by, and boy, was that a trip! He was practically hysterical. He thinks my mother's having an affair! Can you believe it?"

Oh, damn. "Where would he get an idea like that?" Michael asked casually.

"Apparently he went by to see my mother around lunchtime, unannounced. There was a tag sale going on at a neighbor's, and about a zillion cars, so he couldn't tell if anyone was visiting Mother specifically, but he's sure he interrupted something."

Michael put on his best poker face and asked mildly, "What made him think that?"

"Well, for one thing she was wearing this beautiful negligee in the middle of the day. And he said he saw the tocs of some guy's shoes behind the drapes! Can you believe that? My mother, having an affair!"

Actually, since he'd been the man in the shoes, Michael said to himself, and Carolyn had been behaving somewhat suspiciously in her efforts to hide her illness from her family, he could see how Ted had surmised what he had.

Determined to get them off this track, Michael said, "I don't care how things looked. I wouldn't jump to conclusions about your mother, Kate. And I'd advise your father not to do so, either."

Confusion turned Kate's eyes a darker green. "Look, I know it sounds crazy—I had a hard time believing it myself—but I know my father," she said emotionally, "and he would not make this up!"

Michael accepted that with a shrug. "Maybe your dad misinterpreted what he saw. Maybe there was a guy there but he was there for some other reason."

"Believe me, I'd like to think that way, but she was in a white satin peignoir set, Michael—her very best one—and it was noon! There had to be a reason for that."

Yes, Michael thought, there was. She was ill, she was too afraid of what she might find out to get medical help, and she was scared to death she was going to die. With all that going on, why not wear her very best peignoir? She probably was at the point where she'd begun to wonder what she was saving it for, the way some women who were dying started using their very best china every day.

Abruptly, Michael became aware of something warm against his shoulder emanating from the area of Timmy's diaper. He headed for the quilted diaper-changing pad Kate had spread on the middle cushion of the sofa. He laid Timmy down gently and began unsnapping his sleeper. "Look, all I'm saying is you shouldn't be mad at your mother."

Kate handed Michael a diaper and continued to

pace, getting more aggravated with every second that passed. Waving her arms at her sides, Kate fumed, "If this is why my mother left my dad—because there's another man in her life—I certainly will be mad at her! Marriage is sacred. When you make a promise to love and cherish and honor someone for life you should certainly do so. You don't walk! Even in the full-blown throes of a mid-life crisis! Furthermore, I don't care what reasons a spouse has for deceiving their loved one! It's wrong to lie, conceal or mislead a partner."

Michael grinned as he finished diapering Timmy. "Struck a nerve, have we?" he asked dryly.

Kate skidded to a halt at the other end of the sofa. "I'm sorry." She slipped her hands over the rounded back of the sofa. Her expression was abruptly sheepish, as if she just realized she'd been passionately lecturing the wrong person. "I'm just—I get angry and frustrated with myself when I don't see something like this coming," she confided quietly. "Plus—" she sighed wearily "—part of me thinks there is no way my mother would be cheating on my dad!"

Good for you, Michael thought. *Because she wouldn't.*

"The other half wonders how I could have been so out of touch with everything around me." Kate shook her head. "Their separation caught me completely off guard." She bit into the enticing softness of her lower lip. "I've never felt less close to my mother than I do right now." Her shoulders sagged as Michael exchanged Timmy's soggy clothes for a T-shirt and sleeper from the stack of extras on the coffee table beside him. "Plus—" Kate sat on the other side of

Timmy and looked at him, then at Michael "—my father is in a world of pain due to my mother's strange behavior." Kate shook her head ruefully. "And I don't know how to comfort him, or her, either." Kate stopped her tirade and rubbed the back of her neck. "I'm sorry." As she calmed down, her eyes turned a soft, muted green. "I really unloaded on you, didn't I?"

Michael finished dressing Timmy and lifted him into his arms. "It's okay," he told Kate honestly, even as he evaded her question. *I just wish I could confide in you in the same way.*

One thing was certain, Michael thought, Kate would not take the news well that she was being shut out of her mother's illness. And she'd be doubly unhappy if she knew Michael was keeping it from her, right along with Carolyn.

"Look, I'm sure it will all work out," Michael soothed.

Kate's brow drew together in a tight, worried frown. "I hope so," she sighed, looking suddenly unbearably weary. "I don't know how much more of this family stress I can take."

Deciding Kate needed a little TLC as much as their newborn son did, Michael stood and slid a steadying arm about her waist. "Why don't you catch a few Zs?" he suggested softly, tugging her to her feet. Hand on her spine, he turned her toward the staircase.

Kate's body tensed even as her feet carried her along in the direction Michael wanted her to go. "It's tempting, believe me."

Michael paused with her at the foot of the stairs. He looked at her, amazed at the tenderness she effortlessly engendered in him. "Then take me up on it,'' he advised her gently. He paused to kiss their newborn son's forehead. ''Timmy and I will be fine. If there's a problem, I'll call you.''

Kate paused, her hand on the varnished oak banister, her expression woeful. ''I can't believe I'm crying uncle so soon. I thought I was going to be Super Mom.''

Michael reassuringly patted her arm. ''You're not crying uncle. You're just responding to your body's urgent need for sleep.''

Without another word he escorted her up the stairs toward the master bedroom he'd seen that morning. He and Timmy walked her as far as the cozy queen-size bed. ''However, as long as a helping hand is needed,'' Michael teased with a playful wink, ''need tucking in?''

''I think I can handle it from here,'' she told him wryly, teasing him.

Michael grinned. You couldn't blame a guy for trying, and Kate Montgomery was one hell of a dish. ''Okay.'' Michael angled a thumb at himself and Timmy. ''Us guys will head back downstairs and see what we can find on television.''

Kate blinked rapidly. She seemed to be struggling to keep her eyes open, even as she tossed off her robe, slipped beneath the covers and positioned her head on the pillow. ''Lotsa luck this time of night.''

''I'm sure there's some infomercial just waiting to capture our attention. Besides, if one of those won't put Timmy to sleep, nothing will.''

Kate laughed softly, agreeing. ''Michael?'' She lifted her head slightly and looked at him steadily as an aura of coziness fell over the room. ''Thanks.''

He switched off the light, knowing this was, in fact,

only one of a thousand chivalrous errands he'd gladly do for her and Timmy. "Any time."

KATE WOKE to find the first beams of sunlight streaming in through her windows. The clock said it was almost seven. Swearing mentally and struggling to get her bearings, she flung off the covers, pushed herself upright and swung her feet over the side of the bed.

She had a fuzzy recollection of Michael bringing Timmy in to nurse. She didn't remember putting Timmy in his bed, but obviously she or Michael had, because he wasn't in here with her now.

Pushing groggily to her feet, she headed swiftly and silently for the adjacent nursery. Just as she had expected, Timmy was in his crib, fast asleep.

Michael was stretched out on the carpeted floor next to the crib, a pillow tucked beneath his head, and he was also sound asleep. Looking down at him, Kate was filled with both gratitude for all he had done for her and Timmy, and an overwhelming sense of tenderness that came from…she didn't know where. And there was something else, too, something she knew she didn't want to identify—something that made her melt a little inside whenever he was near her.

Kate headed back to the master bedroom suite and into the shower, where she quickly bathed and shampooed her hair. By the time she returned fifteen minutes later in an emerald green chenille tunic sweater and black slacks, looking and feeling immeasurably better, Timmy was awake, too. Big blue eyes wide open, he was lying on his back, looking around and waving his arms, his tiny sleeper-clad legs backpedaling in the air.

Knowing from experience it wouldn't be long before her infant son added a loud indignant cry to his bid for attention, Kate grabbed a clean diaper from the changing table and tiptoed toward the crib. There was no way to get to Timmy without going over Michael, so she stepped over his chest and into the narrow space between Michael and the crib.

Simultaneously, Michael shifted in his sleep and rolled toward her, draping a possessive arm around her ankles even as his chest contacted her legs. At the feel of him, so hard and warm and masculine, snuggled against her, it was all Kate could do not to groan.

Now what was she going to do?

Chapter Five

Michael snuggled against something warm and soft and definitely female. Either this was the best dream he'd ever had, he thought drowsily, inhaling the sweet, sexy scent of fragrant woman and just-washed clothing, or it was real, and the legs he'd wrapped himself around were...

Michael opened his eyes with a start. The legs were definitely sexy and definitely real and endless and slender, and they belonged to one Kate Montgomery. Who was, at this very moment, standing with her arms akimbo, looking down at him.

Michael flashed her a sheepish smile and reluctantly let go of her curvaceous calves. With an effort, he pushed himself to a sitting position. "Sorry. I was dreaming." Precisely what, he figured she'd rather not know. In his dreams, the two of them had been a lot more intimately acquainted.

Kate pushed the damp hair from her face and smiled at him. "I'm sorry I woke you. But I saw Timmy was awake and knew it was time to nurse him again. Do you know when he ate last?"

"Three-thirty this morning. Both of you fell asleep right after." It had been a beautiful sight, poignant and sexy all at once. The two of them cuddled together, Timmy's downy lashes shut, his baby-soft cheek resting against the silk of Kate's bare breast. Michael had been rigid with arousal as he lifted his sleeping son in his arms, returned him to his crib, then returned to button Kate's pajama top and draw the covers around her so she wouldn't chill. Even if she had woken, there would have been no kiss. It wasn't part of their bargain. But Michael had wanted to kiss her—and he still did.

With effort, Michael forced himself to curtail the passionate nature of his thoughts and, aware Kate was still watching him, he continued his recitation of the night's events. "I didn't know if I'd be able to hear him from the sofa downstairs, so I stretched out on the floor beside the crib. I only intended to sleep for a few minutes. Instead, it was—" Michael glanced at his watch, calculated "—about four hours."

Kate turned to survey him from head to toe. She guessed correctly how tired he was. "Now I'm really sorry I woke you." She put out a hand to help him up, and he pushed wearily to his feet.

"Why don't you take the bed in the guest room?" Kate suggested.

With every inch of him aching with fatigue, there was nothing Michael would have liked better. But the last thing he wanted to do was wear out his welcome before he even had a chance to really get to know her. He shook his head. "I don't want to impose—"

"Nonsense. I'm the one who imposed on you last night, when I drafted you for Timmy's all-night babysitter."

Michael locked eyes with Kate, wanting no mistake

made about this. "It was my pleasure," he said softly. "Honest."

With Timmy still looking contentedly at the Winnie the Pooh mobile above his head, Kate slid an arm about Michael's waist. "I'm glad you feel that way. It makes it easier for me to put you to bed in my guest room."

Michael groaned in protest.

Kate dismissed his protest with a cheerful smile. "You can thank me later, after you've had another four hours sleep." Not about to take no for an answer, any more than he had been the previous night, Kate propelled Michael out the door and into the next room. One arm still around his waist, she flipped back the covers and guided him to the edge of the bed. She rested both hands on his shoulders and looked deep into his eyes. "Just sleep, Michael," she breathed, pushing him onto the soft, fragrant sheets. "We'll talk later."

WHEN MICHAEL WOKE again, it was late afternoon. Kate was in the kitchen, peeling and chopping vegetables for a big pot of soup simmering on the stove. Timmy was dozing in a bassinet nearby. "I see our son is keeping to his usual schedule," Michael drawled.

"Yep. Sleep all day. Be up all night." Kate's eyes glinted with humor as she bustled about the kitchen with the ease of a woman who loved to cook. "You seem to be on the same schedule," she teased.

"Lucky thing," Michael said, as he looked at the blooming red and white poinsettias placed here and there on Kate's kitchen counter. Otherwise, he thought, he probably wouldn't be here. He gestured to the coffee on the warmer. "May I?"

Kate gave him a warm, welcoming smile. "Help yourself. Mugs are in the cabinet just above the coffeemaker. Sugar's on the table. Cream is in the refrigerator." Kate opened the oven door and withdrew a baking sheet of golden scones.

. "Thanks."

Michael inhaled the scents of soup, freshly brewed coffee and scones while Kate wielded a spatula like a pro, piling the raisin cinnamon biscuits onto a serving platter.

She glanced in his direction. "As long as we have a minute, I'd like to talk to you about something."

"Shoot."

Kate brought out napkins, forks, knives, two plates and a pot of whipped butter. "I realized this morning I couldn't do it all myself," she said as she set the platter of scones in front of him. Straightening, she braced one hand on her hip. "So I want to take you up on your offer of help." Kate paused to freshen his coffee, then poured a mug of her own. "Only I don't want to shuffle Timmy back and forth between our two places."

Michael couldn't blame her for that. Babies required bottles, diapers, clothes changes, blankets, bedding and an array of other things. Of those items, he currently had none, and it would be a hassle to continually pack them up and lug them back and forth every time he wanted to see Timmy or she wanted to take Timmy home.

He shrugged, willing to do whatever was necessary until he could put together a setup equal to hers. "I could come here," he offered genially.

Kate bit her lip. "Actually, I had in mind something more drastic. At least for the next six weeks." Briefly, her eyes roved his face, lingered, ever so hopefully, on his eyes. "I don't know how you're going to take it. So I'm just going to put it right out there and see." Kate squared her shoulders and leaned closer. "Michael, I want you to move in."

MOVE IN. Michael mulled the words over in his mind. It was so much more than what he had expected, and yet everything he could have wanted. To be here night and day, to kiss Timmy good-night and see him—be a dad to him—every day. She put up a hand before he could interrupt.

"I know what I'm suggesting is unexpected, not to mention unusual, but our whole situation is so unusual, and the bottom line is Timmy needs us both right now. The first six weeks of a child's life are so important. I mean, it's a crucial bonding time for both parent and child, not to mention Timmy's first Christmas ever! Not that you and Timmy couldn't bond any time or any place, but—"

Michael lifted a hand stop-sign fashion, too. "If I could get a word in edgewise," he drawled, grinning, "I'd tell you yes."

Kate blinked in amazement. Apparently, Michael thought, amused, she'd expected him to put up much more of an argument. "I'll do it as soon as you want as long as you let me pay half the living expenses while I'm here," he said.

Kate sipped her coffee and watched him demolish a scone and start on another. "How about this afternoon, then?"

"This afternoon would be fine." Aware his pulse

was jumping at both her nearness and the thought of all he had to do, Michael quaffed the rest of his coffee and pushed to his feet. "I need to go home and get a shower and shave and some clean clothes, anyway."

"Great." Kate stood along with him. She braced her hands on the edge of the table and regarded him cheerfully. "Should I expect you for dinner?"

Her warmth and hospitality made him smile. "Dinner sounds great, but you shouldn't be cooking an entire meal. You just got out of the hospital."

"Actually, I'm not." Kate smiled. "My sister, Lindy, is bringing something by, and I'm giving her half the soup and scones."

"In that case—" Michael glanced at his watch "—I could be back by around six."

Kate smiled with relief, apparently as glad the situation was all settled as he was. "I'll see you then."

"YOU'RE KIDDING, aren't you?" Lindy asked, half an hour later as she set her bags on the table. She regarded Kate with sisterly concern.

"I don't kid about Timmy."

Lindy began unpacking the food she'd brought for Kate's dinner—a chicken rice casserole, spinach salad and a loaf of crusty French bread. "Kate, you barely know Michael Sloane!"

And yet, Kate thought, she knew so much. He was a good man. Decent. Caring. Kind. The fact he also made her feel all hot and tingly inside whenever he so much as looked at her a certain way had nothing to do with it.

Kate drew a breath. "He's a good guy, Lindy."

Lindy frowned. "That's what you thought about Kirk."

Kate tensed at the mention of her ex-husband's name.

"I thought we had agreed we weren't going to talk about him," she reminded her younger sister stonily.

"And we wouldn't be if I didn't see you behaving just as impetuously with Michael as you did with Kirk," Lindy replied, just as fiercely.

"That was different," Kate defended herself. She knew she'd made a mistake there. "I married Kirk when my life was in flux."

"Just as it is now," Lindy said as she put the salad in the refrigerator.

Hanging on to her temper with considerable effort, Kate slid the chicken rice casserole into the oven. "Kirk was a user."

"For all you know, Michael Sloane is, too."

Kate frowned. There were times when her sister, who was woefully inexperienced in the romance department, came on every bit as protective as their ever cautious, ever legal-minded father. "Wait a minute here! I thought you were pushing me to see him!"

Lindy lounged against the kitchen counter and threw up her hands. "See him as in say hello, chat a little, maybe go on a date—or two or three or four. *Not* share your child with him and move in together!"

Kate drew a deep breath and tried to remain calm as she reminded herself her sister was just trying to protect her. "Thanks to a mix-up at the lab, Timmy is Michael's child," she said evenly.

"I know," Lindy said quietly as she poured herself some coffee and sank down in a chair. She propped her elbow on the table and rested her chin on her upturned palm. "Look," she said, exasperated, "it's only natural you'd want to lean on Michael since he's Timmy's father."

"You think that's what it is?" Kate asked, aghast at even the idea she could be so self-serving. "That I'm just looking for someone to lean on?"

Lindy reached across the table and gently touched the back of Kate's hand. "Not deliberately, no, of course not, but having a baby is a very romantic thing, Kate. It's only natural you'd want to share that with someone—if I were you, I would! But don't confuse the euphoria you and Michael both feel over the wonder of Timmy's birth with the kind of love you can build a lasting relationship on, because this is like any mathematical equation. And sooner or later the reality of the situation is going to come crashing back, as certainly as two plus two equals four. And you and Michael will have embarked on this arrangement with one another. And then what?"

Then what, indeed? Kate wondered, as she wrapped the promised scones for Lindy, and all sorts of daydreams and fantasies came to mind. "What are you saying?" Kate asked.

Lindy gave Kate a knowing look as Kate moved to the stove and ladled soup for Lindy to take back to her place. "Let's be practical here, Kate. The man is so drop-dead gorgeous he'd make a nun's heart pound. If he moves in here, he's going to be here at all hours of the night and day and sleeping in the bedroom next to yours. Heck, you may even see him working out or whatever it is he does to stay in such great shape. I mean, the possibilities for physical and emotional intimacy in such a situation are unlimited, even if the two of you didn't have a baby together!"

Kate paled as her hand flew to her throat. "Oh, no—"

Lindy blinked and regarded Kate suspiciously. "What?" she demanded.

"I didn't even think about that!" Kate snapped the lid shut on the soup container and clapped a hand to her forehead. "I've got a houseguest coming and I haven't dusted or vacuumed that room since I can remember when, or put out guest towels. Or taken certain feminine unmentionables from beneath the hall bathroom sink. I've got to get busy!"

Lindy looked at her and sighed. "You have got it bad, sister."

KATE WAS STILL tearing around as fast as her postpartum body could go when Michael returned at six, his personal belongings in tow.

Still mentally making plans about how best to square their arrangements and divide their time with Timmy, Kate held the door for Michael and waved him inside.

He'd showered and shaved and changed into a snowy white T-shirt, soft gray Carolina sweatshirt and jeans. He looked sexy and at ease.

Suitcase in one hand, hanging clothes in the other, he scooted past her just as the phone rang. Kate leaped to get it on the second ring, but it was too late. Timmy had already let out an indignant cry.

"Hello," Kate said, and listened. "Yes. Just a moment, please. Michael—" She handed him the receiver. "It's for you."

Michael set his suitcase down and took the portable phone while Kate hurried toward Timmy's bassinet in the kitchen.

Timmy was cranky and hungry, and he let her know it in no uncertain terms.

"Boy, you are wet!" Kate said, over Timmy's highly indignant wails, as she picked him up, and he immediately stopped his angry, staccato cry. Her breasts were leaking with the need to nurse him. But that was going to have to wait until she'd made him comfortable. He'd soaked through his sleeper, clear through to the sheet beneath him.

"We're going to have to change you from head to toe," she said to her infant son as she tiptoed past Michael, who was still on the phone.

"A complete workup, ASAP. And it needs to be done on the QT—the patient doesn't want friends or family to know." Michael paused, his shoulders tensing as she passed. He gave her a tight smile then turned and paced toward the window, avoiding her eyes all the while.

His back to Kate, he continued in a hushed, grim tone. "I'm hoping against it, but yeah, it could be very serious." He spouted a rash of medical terms Kate neither recognized nor understood. Getting the hint he wanted to be left alone to carry on his discussion in private, she mounted the stairs, his ultra-low, ultra-competent voice drifting after her.

"I'll give you the other information at the hospital tomorrow. Right. Thanks. I owe you for this one, buddy."

As Kate headed down the hall, she heard Michael sever the connection, then a moment later, he said, "Hi. It's Michael Sloane. The appointment is all set for tomorrow afternoon. Four-thirty. Dr. Saul Zimmerman." A pause. "Sorry about that," Michael said, as he joined her in the nursery seconds later. For some odd reason, Kate noted, he still looked a little uneasy about taking the call at her place. "I've been playing telephone tag with that doctor since yesterday afternoon."

"No problem," Kate said. What was a problem for her, however, was the ease with which he partook in a deception of said patient's family.

"What's wrong?" Michael asked as Kate gently laid Timmy on the changing table.

"What do you mean?" Kate asked evenly, preferring not to get into this.

"When I left here two hours ago, you were chipper as could be. Same when I came in. Now you look peeved." He regarded her silently for a moment. "So what is it? What's changed?" He positioned himself next to the changing table so she had no choice but to look at him, and waited.

Damn if he hadn't put her on the defensive already. Kate hated feeling so judgmental, but he had pricked a nerve, and they both knew it. "It's none of my business." Kate unsnapped Timmy's sleeper and eased him out of it one limb at a time.

Michael paused to help her gently extricate one of his feet. "Look, if this is going to work, we have to be straight with each other, even when it's uncomfortable."

As it was now, Kate thought, sighing. She plunged on recklessly. "I couldn't help it. I overheard part of your phone call just now."

It was Michael's turn to tense as Kate removed the soggy diaper and put it aside.

"You shouldn't keep information from a patient's family," Kate stated, remembering full well how it felt when Kirk had done the same to her.

"In principle," Michael said mildly as he handed her a disposable baby wipe, "I agree. But in this case there are extenuating circumstances, and it's the patient's wish."

Kate thought about the way she'd been systematically shut out of important events and decisions in her marriage. Kirk would have called those extenuating circumstances, too. But looking back on it, all she felt was bitter and sad. So much time and energy had been wasted.

"I see," she said, as she gently but thoroughly cleaned Timmy's diaper area. Finished, she slid a clean diaper under her son and lightly powdered his bottom. "Just out of curiosity, is this patient married?" She fastened the diaper and secured the tabs, then looked at Michael. "Does he or she have children?"

Michael edged closer, the sleeve of his sweatshirt brushing her arm. "Yes to both."

Kate frowned. In her opinion, that was even worse.

Anticipating her next move as easily as if they'd been a team for months instead of a few days, Michael handed her a clean T-shirt and sleeper from the stack. "Is this about me and the patient I'm trying to help, or something else?"

"Like what?" Kate asked, stalling.

Michael gave her a bluntly assessing look, and his sable brown eyes lasered in on hers. "Like something that happened to you."

Damn, he was perceptive, Kate thought. Ducking his searching glance, Kate settled into the rocker with baby Timmy.

Michael pulled up a footstool and sat in front of

her, the brisk, spicy scent of his cologne inundating them both. "Want to tell me about it?"

Kate draped a soft flannel blanket over her shoulder. "No," Kate replied, as she unbuttoned her blouse and settled Timmy for his dinner. When he was suckling hungrily, she looked at Michael, who was still waiting patiently for her to explain. "But maybe you're right, maybe I should." Nothing would be gained by them keeping secrets from each other. Heaven knew she didn't want another relationship with a man like her last.

Kate drew a deep, bracing breath. "First, for whatever reason, my mom seems to be going through a really rough time right now. Lindy, my dad and I all want to help her, but she won't let any of us in or talk to us about what is bothering her. And unlike the patient you were discussing just now, my mother's not sick. So, to think of any patient's family being deliberately shut out of the patient's life when they could potentially be there to help is something that upsets me on principle. Because it hurts to find out someone you love is hurting and not allowing anyone to help.

"Second—" Kate took a deep breath and plunged on. "It reminds me of my ex-husband, Kirk. He was always making these unilateral decisions about our life that should have involved me, and didn't."

"I have a hard time picturing you putting up with that."

"What can I say?" Kate lifted her shoulders in a helpless shrug. "I was very young—just out of college—and in love with the idea of being taken care of, protected, nurtured by a knight in shining armor. I was also pretty confused about what I wanted in life. It's not the kind of thing you ever want to admit, but for a while it was easier to let someone else take responsibility for everything good or bad that happened to me and just let myself be sort of carried along by the current. And for a while, anyway, even when I did find out what he'd done—''

At Michael's curious look, Kate elaborated. ''Like the time the car he had his eye on and wanted me to stop by and take a look at so I could give him my opinion had in reality already been purchased by him. Well, it seemed more of an annoyance than a reason to end the marriage, especially when he promised he wouldn't do anything like that again.''

''But he did,'' Michael guessed.

Kate nodded.

Michael frowned, his eyes darkening. ''He sounds like a real jerk.''

''And it only took me four years to force myself to see and accept the truth,'' Kate said dryly. Which in turn had left her feeling like there was some fundamental flaw in her.

Otherwise, she would have concluded much earlier that she was in a no-win situation that was never going to change.

Instead, she'd been clueless, preferring to keep her head buried in the sand, her heart cocooned by her self-imposed naïveté.

But no more, Kate thought. She had a new life now. A fresh start. And she was going to make sure she was never hurt like that again.

''But some good came out of it, as happens after most bad things.'' Kate forced a smile, taking comfort in the fact she was much stronger and wiser now. ''I promised myself I'd never again allow myself to be in a relationship where I'm that disconnected from what's really going on.'' She had promised herself she would never again be so hopelessly blind or put her trust and love in the wrong person. And it was a promise she meant to keep.

Meanwhile, Michael seemed to be doing battle with his own inner demons. What they were, Kate had no clue.

His expression gentling, Michael asked, ''What *do* you want in a relationship?''

Kate noticed Timmy starting to nod off. ''What everyone wants in a relationship, I guess. Love. Tenderness. Intimacy. The kind of closeness that's so real and tangible a couple doesn't even have to speak, where they can communicate everything on their minds and in their hearts with a single glance.'' The kind her parents had once had and could have again, if only they'd stop being so stubborn.

Michael grinned and leaned forward, his elbows on his knees. ''Guess if I want a chance with you,'' he teased, ''I better sign up for those ESP classes now.''

Kate waved her hand between them. ''Note, I did not say a wisecracking beau.''

Michael winked at her and replied, ''I'll keep that in mind.''

An easy silence fell between them. ''Looks like our baby boy is asleep,'' Michael said fondly.

Our baby boy. Kate's heart filled with tenderness at Michael's softly uttered words and the optimistic future they conveyed.

THE PEACE and quiet lasted through dinner. Then Timmy released two tiny whimpers. He followed that with a squall loud enough to wake the dead, letting them know he was ready for action once again.

"He's got a fine set of lungs, doesn't he?" Michael remarked, grinning, as they headed up to get him.

"That's an understatement if I ever heard one," Kate retorted dryly as they entered the nursery. She stood back, allowing Michael to lead the diaper brigade this time.

"Not just wet but dirty," he pronounced.

"It's bath time anyway," Kate said, grinning, as she began to gather everything they needed and Michael took care of diaper duty. "And I'm glad you're here, because it's going to be our first time ever to do this, since the nurses at the hospital bathed him yesterday before we left." And she was feeling more than a little apprehensive about giving Timmy his first ever sponge bath at home.

Finished cleaning Timmy up, Michael held onto his hands and made funny faces at their son. "I've never done it, either, but I'm sure it's not that hard."

"Right." Kate consulted the how-to book on baby care she'd been studying all afternoon. "We just need to keep him out of a draft, use tearless soap and luke-warm water, make sure we don't get the circumcision area or what's left of the umbilical cord wet and be careful to support his head and back at all times. There's only one problem...." Kate nervously bit her lower lip as Michael removed Timmy's sleeper and T-shirt and dropped them into the dirty clothes hamper. "What if Timmy doesn't like being bathed?" The book said some babies didn't.

"He will," Michael said confidently as he wrapped Timmy in a towel and held him against his chest.

"Are you saying that as a physician or a daddy?" Kate asked as she led the way to the master bathroom.

"Both." Looking like the proudest, happiest papa in the world, Michael continued to cradle Timmy close.

Kate spread several layers of towels on the bathroom counter next to the sink, then began to fill the basin with lukewarm water. "Why did you become a doctor, anyway?"

Michael walked Timmy back and forth. "I got drafted into helping out at the county hospital one summer when they were short of funds." He paused to kiss the top of Timmy's head. "I discovered it was very satisfying helping someone get well."

Kate shut off the water and rolled up her sleeves. "Why emergency medicine?"

"Several reasons. I'm good at sizing up a situation and quickly deciding what needs to be done. I like the excitement and fast pace. Families coming into the emergency room are often in the throes of a real crisis." Michael paused, then finished humbly, "I have a knack for dealing with them."

Kate could see that. He'd been wonderful with her when she delivered Timmy.

He smiled. "Ready to get started?"

Kate nodded. She tested the water with her elbow. "Feels nice and warm to me. See what you think."

Michael put Timmy down gently on the thick bed of toweling Kate had set up, and while she held their baby securely in place, he checked the water. "Feels good to me, too. Not too hot and not too cold."

Michael consulted the book Kate had propped open on the counter, then moistened two cotton balls and handed them to Kate. "We start with the eyes, wiping gently from the area closest to the nose outward. That's it.'' Michael watched as Kate gently washed Timmy's face and around his ears. ''Now for the shampoo.''

Still holding her son firmly but gently with one hand, Kate dampened Timmy's hair with a dripping washcloth while Michael opened the bottle of tear-free baby shampoo for Kate and poured a tiny amount into her damp hand. Using a football hold, she gently worked the sweet-smelling lather through his hair, then watched as Michael rinsed away the suds with a dripping washcloth.

Kate held Timmy, talking and soothing him all the while, as Michael soaped and rinsed his front. Michael held Timmy while Kate bathed his back. Together, they dried him thoroughly, applied alcohol to the umbilical area, antibiotic cream to the circumcision and then diapered and dressed him again in a baby blue sleeper with teddy bears embroidered on the front. The whole process took less than twenty minutes, and when they were finished, Timmy was as happy as could be and Kate and Michael were relieved it was over.

''That wasn't as hard as I thought it was going to be,'' Kate said as the three of them retired to the cozy nursery once more.

''What was not to like?'' Michael said, as he put the baby toiletries on the shelf next to the changing table. ''You were great with him.''

Kate looked at Michael shyly. She didn't know when she'd ever felt happier. ''So were you.'' In fact, he'd been incredible.

''I'm glad you think so,'' he said, every inch the

sexy, rugged male, "'cause I take this all very seriously."

Kate studied him. Not in a million years had she ever thought her decision to have a child would turn out this way. "It's important to you to be a good father, isn't it?"

He nodded. "My mom and dad have always been there for me. I want to be there for Timmy in the same way."

UNLIKE the previous night, Timmy was not awake all evening. He went to sleep at seven. Kate was ready for bed shortly thereafter. "Don't worry about the dinner dishes." Michael pointed Kate toward the bedroom. "I'll clean up down here. You just get some sleep."

Feeling guilty but knowing he was right—she had to sleep while she had the chance—Kate headed for bed. She fell asleep as soon as her head hit the pillow. And stayed that way, right along with her infant son, until nearly midnight, when two things woke her— the sound of Timmy stirring and an almost unbearable pain and tightness in her breasts.

Feeling groggy and disoriented, Kate swung her legs over the side of the bed, looked at her chest and gasped in dismay.

Chapter Six

"There's no reason for you to have to get up with Timmy tonight, since I'm the one who has to nurse him anyway," Kate had told Michael before she turned in.

So, when Michael heard Timmy and Kate stir simultaneously just after midnight, he reluctantly honored his agreement to Kate and stayed put.

And when soft, feminine footsteps flew down the hall to Timmy's room and a light flicked on in the hall, he turned onto his side away from the half open guest room door and any fantasy-inducing glimpses of a tousled, sexy, pajama-clad Kate, and waited for Timmy's cries to turn from hunger to contentment.

When that didn't happen, when—over the next minute or so—Timmy's cries grew louder, more indignant, and Kate exclaimed finally in sharp dismay, Michael knew the time for being a passive nighttime guest had passed. He vaulted to his feet and sprinted for the nursery clad in boxers and T-shirt.

Kate had turned the rocker so it faced away from the door. He could see the back of her head, the fact she had a squally, crying Timmy in her arms, and not much more.

"Kate?" He started to circle to face her.

Kate lifted her free hand in a firm gesture that told him to stop right where he was. "Everything's under control, Michael." Kate's voice was high-pitched, stressed.

It didn't look or sound like things were under control, Michael thought, catching a glimpse of Kate's flushed, red cheeks as she turned her head. "Why isn't Timmy nursing?"

"I, uh—it's just taking us a little while to get started." Kate shifted Timmy to her other breast, and he let out another loud, piercing wail. "I'm sure he'll be fine."

He didn't sound fine, Michael thought, and neither did Kate. Michael knew nursing mothers had to be relaxed to be successful, and that—like many new mothers—Kate was still a little shy about being around anyone while she was feeding the baby, even when she had a blanket covering her chest. "Do you want some help?" he asked gently.

"No!" Kate replied quickly. Too quickly, Michael thought. She paused and drew a stabilizing breath even as she waved him away.

Her back to Michael, Kate continued rocking Timmy. Eventually he quieted. Vigorous sucking sounds filled the room as Timmy again began to nurse. "Well, if you need me, I'll be in the next room," Michael said, feeling a little out of sorts because she wouldn't let him help.

"Thanks." Kate's voice was curt, dismissive.

Taking his cue from her, Michael exited the room and went back to bed. But when Timmy began to cry again five minutes later and Kate let out a second muffled gasp that sounded like she was in pain, Michael shot to his feet once again. He knew his presence might not be desired, but it sounded like Kate and his son needed his help, and he'd be damned if he'd stay away one minute longer.

MICHAEL BURST THROUGH the nursery door about the same time Kate had decided to swallow her pride and go to him for help, because heaven knew she didn't know what to do.

"What happened?" Michael demanded.

Kate held the edges of her pajama top as close together as her ballooning breasts would allow. As he circled in front of her she tilted her head. Just looking at him made her heart pound and her mouth go dry.

"If I were to guess," Kate said, doing her best to ignore her exceedingly painful breasts, "I'd say my milk came in."

Michael's gaze lowered to the engorged swelling she'd been trying to hide. His eyes widened and zeroed in on the imprint of her nipples straining against the fabric. "And then some," he drawled, noting no doubt that she'd almost doubled in size since they'd gone to bed for the night.

"No kidding," Kate quipped, blushing fiercely as she juggled a fussing Timmy to her other arm, then gave it up and handed him to Michael.

"I thought I'd gotten chesty during my pregnancy, but this!" She let out a grim laugh as she swept a hand down her body. "Look at me!" she complained, tears of humiliation welling behind her eyes. "I'm triple the size I was! Timmy can't seem to get a drop of milk out of me! Which is no wonder, since my breasts are hard as granite."

Timmy snuggled against Michael contentedly, his

tiny fist resting against the warmth of his daddy's bare, muscled chest. "And it hurts you when he tries," Michael guessed as silence once again fell over the room.

Kate nodded as she struggled to contain her frustration. She'd thought this mothering business was going to be so easy and serene. Instead, every time she turned around there seemed to be a problem of some sort.

"Well, Tim, looks like we've got our work cut out for us." Michael stroked the downy soft hair on Timmy's head. He surveyed the well-equipped nursery before turning to Kate and eyeing her absently. "Where's your breast pump?"

Kate wanted to die from the embarrassment of it all, but her discomfort forced her on. "In the top dresser drawer."

Michael gently lowered Timmy into the crib, settled him on his back and turned on the mobile. Entranced, Timmy stared at the whirling figures of Winnie the Pooh, Tigger, Christopher Robin and Eeyore.

His attitude confident and commanding, Michael plucked the pump out of the drawer and turned to Kate.

If he saw how reluctant she was, he ignored it. "We'll get your milk going in no time. Just come with me." Hand on her shoulder, he propelled her toward the bathroom. His hand dropped to her waist, lingered there for a moment as he scoped out the none-too-roomy quarters. His decision made, he patted the foot-and-a-half wedge of countertop between the his-and-hers basins. "Sit up here for a minute."

This is no big deal, Kate told herself firmly. *Michael is a doctor.* She watched as Michael took a hand towel from the cabinet, turned on the hot water and began to dampen the towel. "You're going to have to open your pajama top."

Kate's throat constricted as she caught the fresh, soapy scent of his skin. Like the situation wasn't intimate enough already without them both being in the small bathroom in their sleeping attire naked from the waist up?

Oblivious to the sensual nature of her thoughts, Michael wrung as much water from the steaming towel as possible, then unfurled it and folded it in half.

Flushing self-consciously at the way he was looking at her, Kate unbuttoned her pajama top the rest of the way. He put the towel across her breasts, molding it top to bottom. To Kate's relief, the heat and moisture combination was as instantly soothing as the firm but gentle pressure of his hands.

"Just hold that there," Michael murmured, as he turned to put the syringe-style breast pump together for her. He shot her a curious glance. "Have you tried to use this yet?"

Kate shook her head as his bare midriff nudged her pajama-covered thigh. "I meant to read the directions thoroughly but I didn't get around to it."

He edged closer, his body heat emanating through the cloth of her pajamas to her skin. His sable eyes were gentle as he looked at her. "How's the discomfort level?" he asked in a soft, serious voice. "Any better?"

Kate hedged, ignoring the new tingling behind her knees and the fluttery feeling in her tummy. "A little," she said.

Michael held out the assembled pump. "Do you think you can do this? Or do you want some help?"

Kate bit her lip. The truth was she hadn't a clue how to use the syringe. Timmy was quiet now, but his attention in the mobile above his crib was bound to fade any minute. When that happened, he'd wail to be fed, and she didn't think she could bear to hear him cry.

Kate sighed. "You may as well help," she said, telling herself it didn't matter if Michael touched what he had already seen. There was nothing sexual about the heat of his palms on her skin. No reason for her pulse to be jumping.

"You've seen everything anyway. In fact, if you add tonight to the mix, there isn't an inch of me you haven't seen."

Michael grinned at her testy remark but passed on the opportunity to counter with a facetious comment. He took the edge of the towel and folded it back to expose the swell of creamy white flesh and jutting rosy nipple on her left breast. His head bent, his expression intent, he fit the syringe pump over her breast and began to gently express her milk. "Tell me if it's too much," he said softly.

The pressure increased then lessened slightly as Kate's milk began to fill the syringe. One ounce, two, three. The pressure inside her built, like the slow, steady climb to orgasm.

"Did it stop hurting yet?" Michael asked.

Ignoring the pulsating need inside her warring with the desire to cover herself with her arms, Kate realized it had. She nodded.

"Okay." Michael smiled, pleased at the results. His eyes met hers. "Let's try the other side and see if we can't get the milk flowing there, too."

Minutes later, Michael and Kate had filled the storage cylinder on the pump with her milk. Kate was a lot more comfortable physically, and was once again able to nurse. By the time Timmy had finished, he was sound asleep. Gently, Michael took him from her arms and returned him to the crib. Kate pulled the edges of her pajama top together and stood, feeling as limp and exhausted as a wrung-out rag. She told herself the weakness in her knees had nothing to do with the warmth and gentleness of his touch, or the tender way his hands and eyes had moved over her skin.

If she felt like this now, what would she feel like if he were actually to make love to her? Kate wondered.

Pushing the forbidden thought away, she slipped out the door of the nursery and stumbled head-on into Michael. He put his hands out to catch her. For one long second, they were pressed together, chests, bellies and thighs. She felt the warmth and strength of his muscles and the hardness at the apex of his thighs just as surely as he felt the skittering of her pulse and the trembling weakness in her knees.

Still clinging to him, Kate let out a shuddering breath and looked up. Michael tightened his hands upon her waist and looked down. The next thing Kate knew, his head was lowering. His lips were on hers, and their mouths were fused in a hot, searing, incredibly passionate kiss that obliterated her defenses and took her breath away. She had known his mouth would be hot and firm and wonderful. What she hadn't anticipated was how quickly she would respond to the masterful pressure of his lips on hers, or that yearning would sweep through her in sweet, wild waves. She opened her mouth to the plundering invasion of his tongue and the sweet, sizzling nature of his kiss and knew, in that instant her life had changed forever.

MICHAEL HADN'T MEANT to kiss her. In fact, he had promised himself when he moved in that he wouldn't complicate matters unnecessarily. They'd focus on their baby, building a friendship without bringing passion into the mix. But that was a pledge easier made then kept, Michael thought as he coaxed her lips apart and made a deep, achingly sweet exploration of her mouth, especially when she melted at his slightest touch and looked at him the way she did, with such sweet, torturous need.

Kate might not know it, but she needed a man in her life. She needed him. And he wanted to be there for her, he thought, as she surrendered to his will and surged against him. He wanted to give her all the tenderness and love she'd so obviously been missing.

"Michael..." she whispered between deep, searching kisses.

"I know," he murmured against her lips, as her soft, flannel-covered breasts molded to the muscled contours of his chest and her sex cradled the rock-hard proof of his desire. He ran his hands down her spine. "I didn't expect it, either." But there was no pretending something extraordinary wasn't happening between them. In fact, it had been from the very first.

Kate put her hands on his chest. Abruptly, she returned to the reality of the situation. "Listen, Michael. I—we—"

"I know," Michael repeated softly, still holding her close. It took every bit of willpower he had to call a halt to the lusty embrace. "It's too soon for this."

Kate sagged against him in relief. "Exactly. It wasn't part of the plan."

And Kate, Michael knew, needed things to go according to plan. He threaded his hands through her hair, tilted her face to his and gently traced her cheekbone with his thumb. "Then we'll call it a night?"

Kate raked her teeth across her lower lip, which was pink and damp and swollen from the kiss they'd just shared. She blew out a shaky breath. "I think that would be wise."

Elated that she didn't seem to regret the kiss—just had wanted things to go no further until this became part of the plan, too—Michael slid his arm around her waist and walked her as far as her bedroom door. He bent to kiss her temple, then remembered what he had been en route to tell her in the first place. "I saved your extra milk for Timmy in the fridge and washed and sterilized the pump in case you want to use it later. And you're going to want to nurse Tim as frequently as possible the next few days until your milk supply sort of evens out."

Kate lingered in the portal, color sweeping into her cheeks as her eyes met his. "Thanks, for that, and everything you did for me tonight."

"I was glad to help."

Silence fell between them, rife with intimacy and unmistakable sexual energy. Michael knew if he didn't get out of there, he'd end up kissing her again, and he wasn't prepared to deal with the consequences of that. Instead, he bent and kissed her brow. "I guess we better try and get some sleep," he whispered, inhaling her soft, womanly scent. Meanwhile, he'd work on figuring out how to fit this into the plan, too. "Timmy'll be up again in no time."

"YOU'RE LOOKING chipper," Ted Montgomery observed early the next morning when he stopped by to check on Kate and the baby before heading to his law office.

If a bit bosomy, Kate thought. "I'm feeling pretty good," she said cheerfully, noting her dad seemed to be in a take-charge mood. But that, as she well knew, could be deceptive. "What about you?" she asked gently, remembering how upset he'd been the last time they'd chatted.

"I'm fine," he replied brusquely as he helped himself to a mug from the cupboard and poured himself some coffee. He hung his suit coat over the back of a chair and sat down at the kitchen table. "Listen, I wanted you to know I've done a little checking."

Kate got out another place setting for her dad. "On what?" Kate asked as she sat opposite Ted and poured raisin bran into a bowl. She hoped he hadn't done anything rash where her mother was concerned.

"Michael Sloane has an excellent reputation as a physician."

Like I didn't already know that, Kate thought, as she added milk to her cereal. "Dad, he delivered Timmy in the back of a delivery van. If that didn't prove his mettle, I don't know what would!"

"Maybe there's something you don't know."

Kate paused, the spoon halfway to her mouth. "And that is?"

"Apparently, it's a well-known fact at the hospital here in Chapel Hill that he's desperately wanted a child for several years."

And now, through an unexpected quirk of fate, Kate thought uneasily, he had one.

"Nevertheless," Ted continued, "from what the private investigator our law firm keeps on retainer has been able to discern, the mix-up at the lab does seem to be a genuine mistake, a one-in-a-million accident."

"Thanks for telling me," Kate said politely. *But I already know all that, Dad.*

"But that doesn't mean Michael Sloane couldn't still take advantage of you, even with your agreement," her father continued protectively as Kate munched on her cereal. "Because he could."

"Yes, he could," Kate said flatly. "But he won't. You know why? Because I won't let him," Kate stated stubbornly.

Her father continued to look worried even as he said, "That's good to hear."

Kate got up to bring the coffeepot to the table. She freshened both their mugs and added a generous dollop of skim milk and cinnamon to hers before sitting down again. "Speaking of personal situations, what about yours?" She searched her father's face. "Have you and Mom been able to work anything out yet?"

"Nothing has changed. She still wants to go ahead with the divorce. But I convinced her to wait until after the holidays to file the papers, primarily because there are still financial matters to be worked out between us."

Kate studied her father. She knew he still loved her mother desperately. "Are you sure you want to do this?"

He hesitated, his eyes troubled. Finally, he rubbed the back of his neck and said, "Of course I don't want to do this. No one wants to get divorced. But if Carolyn is seeing someone else—'' His voice cracked. ''If she's been cheating on me—'' He squared his shoulders beneath the starched fabric of his dove gray dress shirt. ''At least I've still got my pride.'' His jaw was set. ''I'd like to leave it that way.''

Kate pushed back her chair and regarded her father stoically. ''Dad, I thought about this a lot. And I am positive Mom is not having an affair with someone. If she were, I'd know!''

''Really? How?'' Ted queried sarcastically. He sat back and jerked loose the knot of his gray silk tie. ''Have you been looking for men's shoes beneath her drapes, too?''

''No, I don't need to, because I know the signs of infatuation! The giddiness, the flushed cheeks and sparkling eyes, the nonstop excitement.''

Kate knew firsthand what it was like to be unable to stop thinking about a man or to stop from fantasizing about what it would be like to really be with him, in the closest, most intimate way possible. In fact, she'd dreamed of nothing but making love to Michael, again and again, after she went back to her bed.

''If Mom has been anything lately,'' Kate told him firmly, ''she's been sort of pale and fatigued and depressed.''

His lips compressed unhappily. ''Not to mention stubborn and shortsighted.''

Kate sighed. ''That, too.''

Her dad shrugged and suggested with exaggerated amiability, ''Perhaps her conscience is finally getting to her.''

Kate regarded her father with mounting frustration. She knew he was hurt, but his stubbornness wasn't helping anything, nor was his considerable pride. "I wish you'd just talk to her and tell her what you suspect is going on. For all you know, there's a perfectly logical explanation for what you saw yesterday."

"Logical, my foot!" Ted muttered. He shook his head. "Honey, look, I know this is hard on you and Lindy both, but I promise you, you girls will adjust, and so will your mother and I."

How? Kate wondered, when her whole family was being torn apart for no real reason she could see, albeit very, very civilly.

"Kate," Michael called from upstairs.

Her dad looked at the clock, then at Kate in amazement. Oh, no, Kate thought, as her hand flew to her mouth. She'd been so wrapped up in her father's problems, she'd completely forgotten Michael was still upstairs.

"What is he doing here at this hour?" her father demanded, looking at the clock.

Good question. One Kate wished like heck she did not have to answer.

"Are you downstairs?" Michael asked.

"Yes!" Kate shouted frantically as she tried to phrase an explanation for Michael's presence that her very by-the-book father would accept.

Torn between her need to head off Michael and say something to her dad, she smiled tightly at Ted. "I know this looks bad, Dad—"

Ted instantly switched into concerned father mode. "And then some, considering it's barely seven in the morning. Just tell me one thing," Ted demanded. "Tell me he wasn't here all night."

Oh, perdition! Kate made a face and lifted a hand to the back of her neck in true mea culpa fashion.

"Kate!" her father reprimanded, incensed, when he came to the obvious conclusion.

"Dad, it's not what it seems." *That is, if you could bar that one long, very sexy kiss.*

"How are your breasts feeling this morning?" Michael asked from around the corner. He stopped dead in his tracks when he breezed into the kitchen and saw Ted. The two men sized each other up like soldiers about to engage in a battle.

Michael squared his shoulders and regarded her father cautiously and with the respect due someone his age. "Good morning, sir," he said.

"Dr. Sloane." Her father delivered the greeting like a death sentence.

The silence in the room was deafening.

"It isn't what it seems," Michael stated carefully.

His expression getting more foreboding by the second, her father folded his arms in front of him and continued to stare furiously at Michael. "So Kate said."

Michael looked at Kate. Wanting to help. Not wanting to say too much. Leaving the final decision up to her.

Kate stepped in quickly and picked up the ball. She carried her empty cereal bowl and spoon to the dishwasher. "He's just helping me out with the baby, Dad."

"I see." Ted's brows lowered like thunderclouds over his penetrating gaze. "And is he helping you out with your breasts, too?"

Kate flushed and told herself not to think about that kiss, not now. If she did, her dad would surely see it. Needing something to do, she poured Michael a mug of coffee and handed it to him, reacting only slightly when their hands touched. "My milk came in last night. I didn't expect it to hurt like that. Timmy couldn't seem to nurse, and I didn't know what to do, so Michael talked me through it."

Her father nodded and continued to study her with deep reserve and mounting disapproval. "Why didn't you call your own doctor?"

"Michael was here. With me in pain and Timmy crying and needing to be fed right then, it just made sense for him to help out."

"And then what? It also made sense for him to spend the night?" Ted accused with a lawyerly precision Kate could very well have done without.

Biting back a moan of despair, Kate folded her arms in front of her and looked at her dad. She really did not need this third degree. "Could we please not get into this now?" she asked tiredly.

Obviously, for her father, that was not an option.

He turned to Michael. "Did you or did you not spend the night here last night?" he demanded in a terse, forthright manner.

"Actually," Michael said as he lifted the coffee mug to his lips and sipped, "I moved in."

A CANNON could have gone off in the silence that fell, and no one would have moved an inch. Things were that tense. Not that Michael blamed Ted Montgomery one iota. If it had been his daughter here with a man he didn't know who had spent the night, Michael thought, he would have been ready to hit the ceiling, too. Which is why they had to clear things up, pronto. And if Kate wasn't going to do it, he would.

Michael took another gulp of coffee then set his

mug aside. "Kate asked me to move in for the next six weeks," Michael continued.

Kate groaned, sank down in a chair and buried her face in her hands. Michael took that as a sign she did not want her father to know this. But Michael wasn't in the habit of keeping secrets from the fathers of the women he was involved with, and he wasn't about to start now. He continued to look Ted straight in the eye. "She thought it would be a good chance for me to bond with Timmy and vice versa."

"Did you tell your mother about this?" Ted demanded of Kate.

Kate lifted her head and rolled her eyes. Her expression cautious, she said, "Not yet."

Ted picked up his suit coat from the back of the chair. His expression was grimly prophetic as he shrugged it on. "Well, she's going to have to know."

"Dad—"

"Don't 'Dad' me, Kate. And don't think we're finished discussing this, because we are not. Unfortunately, I have to get to court." Eyes glittering, he turned to Michael. "You hurt her or my grandson, and you will answer to me."

Michael nodded. He had expected as much, and would have thought less of Ted if he hadn't been upset.

FIGURING it was best if she hustled her father out of there as quickly as possible, Kate left Michael in the kitchen and walked her dad to the door. When she returned, Michael was studying the selection of breakfast cereals she had left out for him.

He turned and surveyed her long powder blue moleskin shirt with the shirttail hem and the trim black leggings beneath it before looking at the flushed contours of her face. "Did you get him to calm down any?" he asked softly as he helped himself to a bowl of Rice Chex.

"What do you think?" Kate sighed. She tossed the remains of her father's coffee into the sink, then put the mug in the dishwasher.

Michael grimaced. "I'm sorry."

"Why?" Kate poured herself a glass of juice.

"Your father seemed really disappointed in you."

Unfortunately, it wasn't the first time their wills had clashed big-time. Nor, given their equally strong wills, was it likely to be the last, Kate thought with weary resignation.

She shrugged, handed him a glass of juice and sat down. "The year I decided not to go to law school was worse," Kate told Michael as she sipped her juice. "He really wanted me to follow in his footsteps and join the law firm where he works. He was ecstatic when I was accepted at three great law schools." Kate drew a breath, remembering that very uncertain yet oddly euphoric time in her life. "We talked for hours over which I should choose, and I finally decided on Vanderbilt." Her mood clouded as she recollected. "When I bailed out at the last minute, I think I broke his heart. But I couldn't do it," Kate confessed as she looked deep into Michael's eyes. "It just wasn't right for me. I would have been miserable as a lawyer."

Michael reached out and covered her hand with his. "But he eventually forgave you for that."

"Yes." Kate let herself take strength from the tenderness in his grip. "But it took a while." She released a ragged sigh as tears of remembered misery clouded her eyes. She had hated not being able to talk to him and she didn't ever want to get to that point in her life again. So she was going to have to find a way to make her father understand that, as crazy as this plan of hers to bond Timmy and Michael together might seem, this was all for the best. "It wasn't so much anything he said, back then, or even today, as it was the look in his eyes."

Michael sighed and squeezed her hand. "I know what you mean," he told her empathetically. "I can't stand disappointing my parents, either."

Another silence fell between them. Michael looked at her intently. "I'm really sorry. I could shoot myself for what I said." He swore heatedly, sarcastically echoing his impetuous words, "How are your breasts feeling today?"

The same as last night, Kate thought. *All tingly whenever you're around.*

"It's okay," Kate said. Feeling herself flush, she pushed away from the table and began to busy herself wiping counters that did not need to be wiped. "You didn't know he was here."

Michael picked up his bowl and carried it to the sink. While Kate tried her darnedest not to think about the kiss they'd shared that had not been part of the plan, Michael rinsed his dishes and put them in the dishwasher. "Next time," he vowed passionately, as she turned her attention to wiping the table, too, "I'll make sure we're alone before I make any comments that could be misconstrued."

Finished, Kate turned and tossed the dishrag into the sink. She pivoted to face Michael. "He knows we're not sleeping together."

"Of course we're not. You just had a baby," Michael said bluntly as he braced his hands on his hips and continued to regard her matter-of-factly. "But that doesn't mean I don't intend to make love to you as soon as it is possible, and your father knows that, too."

As the meaning of his words sank in, Kate suddenly found it impossible to breathe, never mind frame a coherent thought. "Do you?" she gasped, aware her heart was suddenly pounding triple time and her knees had gone a little weak.

Michael blinked. "What?"

"Intend to make love to me?"

Chapter Seven

"Yes," Michael said simply, stepping closer until their bodies were a scant half-inch apart. "I do."

Kate sucked in a breath. They were standing so close she could feel the undulating waves of heat from his body. She tipped her head back but didn't move away. "You don't believe in sugarcoating your intentions, do you?"

Michael regarded her for a long, thoughtful moment. "I believe in dealing with things directly." His dark eyes glimmered with renewed passion as he leaned evocatively close. "We kissed last night, remember?"

"As if I could forget." Kate flushed, recalling the uninhibited way she had returned his embrace. Her reaction to him had definitely not been in the plan. "But one kiss doesn't mean the next step is making love."

"Then we'll plan to get there by degrees," he teased.

Kate didn't even have to try to imagine Michael's lips on her skin, his hands touching every inch of her and hers touching every inch of him.

Trying desperately to ignore how good he looked

with the morning sunlight gilding the handsome contours of his face, Kate folded her arms. "No wonder my father is furious with you," Kate said, her heart pounding at breakneck speed.

She looked up and saw something different in Michael's eyes, something she'd have one heck of a time reckoning with. She drew a halting breath and tried in vain to find some middle ground that would allow her to appease both Michael and her father simultaneously without sacrificing her emotional well-being in the process.

"Look, Michael," Kate said, deciding the last thing she needed was a resurgence of the romantic feelings she had for Michael. She backed up until her hips brushed against the kitchen counter. "Everything I said to you earlier is absolutely true. Timmy does need us both. This is a crucial bonding time. And I want Timmy to have everything possible, including a mommy and a daddy." *I just don't want you to think I'm part of the package, too, even if it is almost Christmas!*

"It's a crucial bonding time for us, too," Michael said firmly, folding his arms.

Kate dropped her gaze to the starched fabric of his dress shirt and the muscled contours of his chest before returning her gaze to his face. "What do you mean?"

His sexy grin was enough to light a thousand inner fires. "Babies bring people closer together."

Kate's heart flip-flopped in her chest. He was moving way too fast for her again. "Not that close," Kate reprimanded sternly, even as her knees turned to jelly.

His face split into a sexy grin as he closed the distance between them and shot a hand out to encircle her waist. "How do you know?" He tugged her closer.

Kate hitched in a gulp of air. "I'm not looking for romance here, Michael." *Not if it's because of Timmy. And I'm not looking for any more kisses, either.*

Their bodies were touching in one long, electric line. The warmth of the sunny kitchen was nothing compared to the heat of this man. His hands tightened possessively as he searched her face. "When I came to see you, neither was I."

"And now?" Kate gasped, forcing herself to ignore the romantic feelings welling inside her at an alarming rate.

Michael sifted his fingers through her hair, tilting her face to his and staring into her eyes. "I'm not going to make any bones about it. I'm interested in you, Kate."

Kate had been hurt in the past by not looking before leaping. She was determined not to let herself get swept away, or hurt, again.

"As the mother to your firstborn child?" she asked as her body continued to tremble.

"As a very new and very interesting woman in my life," Michael corrected her softly. His eyes darkened. He tilted his head to the side and lowered his lips to hers. "You have to know, Kate," he whispered in a deep, velvety voice as their breaths and wills meshed, "that I would have pursued you even if you hadn't had my baby."

He held her mouth under his as he inundated her with kisses and the comfortable warmth of his tall, strong body. Kate hadn't meant to respond so unabashedly, but as his lips coaxed hers apart, as his tongue swept into her mouth searching out every tender, aching, yearning spot, she found her blood bubbling with pent-up desire. Abruptly, not caring what the future held as long as she had this explosion of passion now, Kate succumbed to his advances and threw herself into his ardent embrace wholeheartedly.

She kissed him back with hunger and need, moaning as his hands moved sensuously through her hair, then moved lower in long, smooth strokes over her shoulders, down her spine, to her hips, then up to her breasts. His hands were on her breasts, caressing and soothing through her clothes, until her flesh grew hot and her nipples peaked. Tremors of desire swept through her as she stood on tiptoe, wreathing her arms about his neck and urging him closer still.

Knowing Kate still had her reservations about the wisdom of starting anything romantic with him, Michael hadn't meant to do this. But he'd felt her surrender, felt her softness pressing against him. There was no stopping with just one kiss. No pretending that something incredible wasn't happening between them. Instinct told him Kate hadn't been well loved in the past. If he had his way, he thought as he felt her shudder in his arms, that would change. Before the six weeks were up, he would convince her what they had was very special, and make love with her. Not once, but again and again and again…

But first, he thought, as he reluctantly let the passionate kiss draw slowly to a halt, she had to trust him. Trust this.

Just as his lips left hers, Timmy let out a piercing

cry. "Saved by the baby," Kate murmured humorously, in relief.

"For now," Michael said softly, kissing her cheek. But only for now.

AT NOON, knowing they were behind at the shop, Kate had Jeff bring over work so she could assemble gift baskets in her living room while caring for Timmy. And she was still at it around three that afternoon when her mother came in carrying two shopping bags full of gaily wrapped baby gifts.

Carolyn was wearing a gray wool pantsuit and a pale blue silk blouse that set off her silvery blond hair, but there were shadows beneath her blue eyes that even expensive makeup could not erase.

"Friends dropped these off at the house, and I knew you'd want to open them right away. And I also brought over two photo albums that I prepared for Timmy."

Kate flipped through them while her mother went over to the bassinet to check on the sleeping baby. There were tons of pictures dating back three generations, all of them from happier times. Kate's heart swelled as she studied them. "Mom, these are beautiful." She shook her head in awe and leaned over to give her mother a hug. "They must have taken hours to put together. Thank you so much."

"You're welcome, darling." Carolyn forced a smile. "I thought Timmy might like a little family history when he's older. I documented each photo so he'd know where he came from."

Kate stared at her mother. Carolyn was talking as though she would not be around to do so herself. "You'll be here to explain it all to him, Mom," Kate told her confidently.

"I hope so, I really do, but you never know." Carolyn lifted her slender shoulders in a shrug. "And in case I'm not..."

Was her father right? Kate wondered uncomfortably. Was her mom having an affair? Maybe thinking of running off with another man? Leaving her husband and daughters behind? Kate knew she hadn't been very supportive of her mother's need for some time and space to herself, but as she studied the unhappiness in her mother's eyes, guilt and remorse came flooding in. Suddenly, it was all very clear.

"I'm to blame for this, aren't I?" Kate pushed the hair from her face. "I've tried so hard not to get caught between you and Dad in this divorce that I've more or less pushed you both away." *And in the process maybe made leaving seem like a good idea.* "Mom, I need you—I will always need you both."

"I know that, honey." Carolyn patted her daughter's arm. "But I also know that one day you and Timmy and Lindy will have to go on without me and your father. And when that happens, you'll be fine."

Kate studied the sadness etched in her mother's profile and tried to figure out where this new pessimism came from. "Are you thinking about Grandma?" she asked. "The fact she was just your age when she died? Mom, *nothing* is going to happen to you. You and Dad will both be here with us for a very long time."

Her mother forced a cheerful smile, reminding Kate how sudden and unexpected her grandmother's illness had been. "I certainly hope so," Carolyn replied with breezy self-assurance. "I'd love to tell Timmy the story behind each and every one of these pictures when he gets a little older." Her mother paused and looked in the direction of the stairs leading to the second floor, as if she were concerned they were not alone, before she asked oh, so casually, "What about Michael Sloane? Is he still here?"

So, Dad told you, Kate thought, not at all surprised. "No," she said dryly, pleased the episode with her father that morning resulted in her parents talking again and being mutually concerned about something—in this case, her. "Michael's at the hospital—working."

"Oh." Carolyn's face fell as she studied the gift baskets Kate was in the process of assembling.

"Don't look so disappointed," Kate chided.

Carolyn lifted her chin. "I'm not. I'm just sorry I didn't have a chance to say hello."

Kate regarded her mother curiously. "Then you also know I asked him to move in for the next six weeks." Her mother nodded. "And you don't mind?" Kate asked, stunned.

A shadow passed over Carolyn's face before she shrugged and said, "Life's short, and while you're here, you've got to do what you've got to do. Besides, he's a very nice man," Carolyn said with what seemed a genuine smile. "A good man."

I think so, too. Kate sighed, relieved her decision was backed by someone else in the family. "I wish Lindy and Dad felt that way."

"They'll come around in time," Carolyn soothed.

Maybe, Kate thought. In the meantime… "Listen, why don't you stay and hang out with me this afternoon? I've got to keep putting together Thanksgiving baskets for the shop, but we could chat while I work. You could even help and spend some time with Timmy." It would be like old times, Kate thought wistfully, before her family was torn apart.

Carolyn's face fell. "Oh, honey, I'd like to—"

"But you have other plans," Kate guessed, unable to completely mask her disappointment.

"Yes."

It had been so long, Kate thought wistfully, since she and Carolyn had done any mother-daughter bonding. Months, really. And she missed it. "Couldn't you cancel?" Kate asked softly.

Her mother hedged. "I'd like to," she said finally, "but I can't leave the bridge club in the lurch. It wouldn't be fair."

Kate frowned as she walked her mother to the door. "I thought your bridge club met on Monday afternoons, right after lunch."

"They still do. What I have to do today is extra," her mother explained hurriedly.

"Could we do something tomorrow, then?" Kate asked.

Carolyn glanced at the clock on the wall. It read four-fifteen. "I...don't know. I may be busy then, too. I'll let you know." Carolyn kissed Kate's cheek before hugging her again. "I love you. You know that, don't you?" she said.

Kate nodded. "And I love you, too, Mom."

"I FELT SO GUILTY, Michael," Kate confessed as they shared a quick meal of Chinese take-out during his dinner break from the hospital. "I mean, here I am, passing judgment on my mother for everything she's done recently like the worst kind of nosy parker, and she just accepts the idea of you moving in with me, no questions asked, no lectures given."

Michael was glad they had one Montgomery family member in their corner. "You said your mother left

here at four-fifteen?'' he asked casually. He had yet
to hear how Carolyn's secret meeting with Saul Zimmerman had gone. This at least seemed to indicate
Carolyn had kept her appointment.

Kate nodded. ''She said she had to be somewhere.
Bridge club or something.''

Damn, Michael thought. He had been hoping Carolyn would have had a change of heart and told Kate.
Keeping a confidence for a patient was one thing. He
did it all the time in the course of his job. Keeping a
confidence for the mother of the woman he could very
well be falling in love with was something else entirely. Had there been any other way to get Carolyn
to seek the medical help she so clearly needed, he
wouldn't be in this position. But there hadn't been,
and he was, he reminded himself sternly, so he was
just going to have to deal with the uncomfortable situation until it was resolved—which, knowing Saul
Zimmerman's talents as a diagnostician, would be
very soon. Meanwhile, he'd have to hope Kate never
found out he'd kept something like this from her, because gut instinct told him she wouldn't take the news
very well at all.

''So how was the rest of your day?'' Michael
asked, studying the flushed contours of her pretty
face.

''You mean, aside from the six phone calls you
made here, checking on me and Timmy?'' Kate
teased as she helped herself to more moo goo gai pan.

Michael knew he'd overdone it in the concerned-
daddy department. He couldn't help it. Kate—and
Timmy—were all he'd thought about all day.

''I was worried you might still be feeling some
discomfort.''

Kate gave him a relaxed grin. "It's a lot better since I started nursing Timmy every couple of hours."

"Good." Silence fell between them. Michael could tell by looking at Kate that she didn't want him to go back to work any more than he did.

Michael sighed and swore softly. "I wish I didn't have to go back to the hospital. But with flu season in full swing, I've got no choice."

"I'm just glad you could swing by to see Timmy and me when you did." Taking the demands of his career in stride, Kate walked him to the door and lingered in the portal while he put his suit coat on. *This is what it would be like if she were my wife,* Michael thought.

"When will you be home tonight?"

"Midnight." He leaned forward to gently touch her face with his hand and kiss her brow. "I'll see you then."

MICHAEL HAD no sooner driven away than the phone rang.

Her face still tingling from the sweet caress of Michael's lips, Kate reached for the receiver. Much more of that, she thought, and she'd begin to feel like his wife.

"Hello."

"Hi." The sweet feminine voice came at her in a rush. "Is this Kate? This is Susan Sloane, Michael's sister. Listen, I know the situation is a little awkward and that Michael's working over at the ER today, but my three sisters and I have got a baby gift for Timmy, and we thought we'd bring it by and look in on him and meet you, too, if that's okay."

"Of course," Kate said, relishing the chance to meet more of Michael's family.

"Great." Relief tinged Susan's tone. "We could stop by in about twenty minutes, if that's okay."

"Sure," Kate said. "I'll give you directions."

Twenty minutes later, Kate's doorbell rang. Four beautiful women with sable brown hair and eyes stood on the threshold. They were wheeling a deluxe stroller, complete with padding, canopy and diaper bag rack. It was decorated with a bright red bow.

Kate spent the next half hour getting to know Susan, a hospital administrator, Rachel, a full-time mom, Meredith, the registered nurse, and Paula, a part-time real estate agent. They cooed over Timmy, who woke long enough to put on a show, stretching and yawning and waving his tiny fists, before falling back to sleep. However, they all waved off Kate's offer of tea. "Really," Paula replied, "we don't want to put you to any trouble."

"But, as you've probably guessed," Susan said, taking the lead, "our visit isn't exactly without an agenda." The four sisters exchanged a glance, then Susan plunged on. "We wanted to talk to you about Michael and this miracle baby the two of you have had."

Kate put up a hand in an effort to reassure them. "We've already agreed to share parenting duties from here on out."

The sisters released a mutual sigh of relief.

Meredith laid a hand across her throat. "That's so great to hear. Mom and Dad will be so pleased."

"Not that Michael's ever really disappointed them yet," Rachel added.

"The only time he ever came close was when he

and Val split up,'' Susan said. ''But they understood there were reasons for that.''

Paula agreed. ''Mom and Dad just want Michael to have a family of his own, too. Especially since Michael's wanted children for such a long time.''

''And he would have had them,'' Susan confided unhappily, ''if his first wife, Valerie, hadn't done such a number on him in that regard.''

''Not that he saw it coming.'' Meredith shook her head.

''No, after that mountain episode…well, let's just say he thought himself invincible,'' Rachel added. ''Val taught him the invalidity of that!''

''C'mon.'' Susan gave the others a censuring glance. ''If Michael's forgiven Val and made peace with her about that, so can we.''

Her curiosity piqued, Kate made a mental note to ask Michael about Val the first chance she got, then asked, ''What kind of brother was he when you were growing up?''

Susan smiled. ''In a word—protective. I don't know if it was because he was the only boy, but he was always rushing to our defenses.''

Kate could see that—Michael was very protective of her and Timmy, too, and had been from the first. It probably had something to do with the way he'd been reared. ''Michael said all four of you are married and have kids.''

The Sloane sisters exchanged enthusiastic nods. ''Mom and Dad have ten grandkids so far. Want to see pictures?''

''Absolutely,'' Kate said.

All four women brought out picture wallets from purses. As Kate perused them, she felt a little envious—the Sloane sisters and their families all looked so happy and content. Among them, still single and childless at age thirty-two, Michael was definitely the odd man out. And the sense of what he was missing had to be even sharper this time of year, Kate thought, as children were such an integral part of the Thanksgiving and Christmas holidays.

"We all get together for New Year's Eve, too," Susan said.

Paula added shyly, "I know the two of you aren't married, but maybe this year you and Timmy could come, too."

KATE WAS on the floor of her bedroom in a black Lycra leotard, matching tights and an oversize Santa's Workshop T-shirt, doing tummy crunches, when Michael came in that evening. He waved hello to her as he passed, went to peek in on Timmy, then returned to lounge in the door. "Getting back in shape?" he asked as he took off his coat and tie.

Kate nodded. *As well as waiting for you.* The visit from Michael's sisters had engendered so many questions, she barely knew where to start. "Timmy and I had company this evening."

"Really." His brown eyes alight with interest, Michael unbuttoned the first two buttons on his shirt. "Who?"

Kate rolled onto her side and began a series of scissor leg lifts meant to strengthen her inner thighs. "Your four sisters."

Michael paused in the act of rolling up his sleeves. Eyes widening in surprise, he pulled up a chair from the writing desk in the corner, turned it around and sank into it, straddling the seat. "All four at once?"

"Uh-huh." Kate rolled onto her other side and continued the leg lifts. She propped her head on her upraised hand. "It was fun. They brought this incredible stroller and a homemade baby quilt, showed me pictures of their families and invited Timmy and me to join you at the Sloane family get-together New Year's Eve."

"They have been busy," Michael commented dryly. "So what all did they tell you about me?" He seemed to think whatever they'd said was probably too much.

"Oh, a little of this, a little of that," Kate teased mischievously as she sat up and patted her face with a towel.

Michael kept his eyes on her as she reached for her water bottle and, sitting cross-legged on the floor, leaned against the foot of the bed. "Such as?"

Kate uncapped the bottle and drank deeply. Blotting her lips dry with the back of her hand, she said, "They made some references to a mountain episode that left you feeling invincible."

Michael winced and took the bottle of water when she offered it to him. He shook his head ruefully before putting his lips where hers had just been and taking a long, thirsty drink. "They're never going to let me live that down." He handed the water back.

Kate raised one knee and put the other leg straight out in front of her. She decided this was as good a time as any to gently lead the subject around to Val. But first, she wanted to know more about the infamous mountain episode. "What happened?" she asked softly.

"It's not that a big deal," he said reluctantly, looking away.

Kate reached up and caught his hand between hers. "Tell me anyway."

Without breaking their grip on each other, Michael swung himself off the chair and came down to sit on the floor next to her. "It happened when I was ten. It was a Saturday morning, and my dad and I had gone out hiking in the woods." Michael's grip tightened on her hand as he continued in a low, even voice. "Although it was a clear, sunny day, it had been raining heavily earlier in the week. The woods were still really muddy, and so was the trail. We were a good mile and a half from the starting point when a portion of the trail suddenly gave way beneath my dad." Michael tensed as he remembered, shook his head. "One minute he was there, the next he was just…gone."

"Oh, Michael," Kate breathed, imagining what that must have been like for a ten-year-old. "You must have been terrified."

Michael sighed, remembering as he looked at their tightly clasped hands. "Yeah, I was."

"What'd you do?" Kate asked, assuming from what his sisters had said about him feeling invincible ever since that it had been something heroic.

Michael shrugged, his expression impassive. "The only thing I could. I climbed down after him and helped make a crude splint for his broken leg."

Kate sensed it hadn't been anywhere near that easy. "Was your dad in a lot of pain?"

Michael nodded. "And he was also going into shock."

Which could, Kate knew, be deadly in itself.

Michael's eyes darkened as he continued. "My dad didn't want me to go for help—he was afraid if I left him I'd get lost in the woods, but I knew if I didn't get my dad out of there he probably wouldn't make it. So I put my jacket over my dad to help him stay warm and ran all the way back to the ranger station and brought help. The rangers got my dad to a hospital. And the doctors and nurses there saved his life.''

Kate regarded him with awe. ''Your parents must have been so proud of you,'' she said softly.

Michael grinned, brusquely admitting this was so. ''I even got some kind of citation for heroism from the park rangers.'' He paused, admitting after a moment, ''And that in turn did a lot for my self-esteem.''

''You say that as if your self-esteem needed work,'' Kate remarked lightly.

''I was small for my age when I was a kid and not particularly good at sports, and the other kids used to razz me something fierce about my lack of athletic prowess. When I saved my dad's life, I realized I could do just about anything I set my mind to—I just had to believe in myself. And so I did. And I grew taller and got better at sports and had a lot of success in most areas of my life, and was—in return—then razzed to death by all four of my sisters for what they call my take-charge, can-do attitude.''

Kate grinned. ''I can see that in you now.''

''In fact, they like to say the whole incident has given me a swelled head that has yet to recede.''

Kate laughed softly. ''You don't seem unduly confident to me.'' She paused, studying the guilty look on his face. ''You think you are, though, don't you?''

Michael shrugged his broad shoulders matter-of-factly. ''I think I've got a problem knowing when to give up. There's a part of me that refuses to concede defeat.''

''And yet,'' Kate said, turning to face him, ''you did acknowledge defeat of some sort when you ended your marriage to Val.''

Michael looked at the place where her knee lightly nudged his thigh. His expression softened as he traced the shape of her knee through her tights. ''Boy, they really gave you the lowdown on me, didn't they?''

Kate looked at his stroking fingers and tried not to think what his touch was doing to her senses. Aware her heart was pounding, she lifted her shoulders in an elegant shrug. ''They just said she really did a number on you.'' She lifted her chin and angled her head until she could see into his eyes. ''I had the feeling, from the looks they gave each other, that they felt Valerie hurt you pretty badly.''

Michael drew in a deep breath. ''It was a rude awakening,'' he admitted, his mouth thinning unhappily as the talk turned to his first marriage. ''But it wasn't all Valerie's fault. She told me when we were in our first year of med school that she'd be happy just being married. She didn't necessarily need or even want to have kids.'' Michael's eyes darkened unhappily. ''That went counter to the way I felt—I knew I wanted the kind of big, lively family I grew up in. But I figured we'd work it out.''

''Meaning you'd be able to talk her into it?''

Michael reached for the water bottle and took another long, thirsty drink. ''Right.''

Silence fell between them. Their gazes meshed. ''Were you happy?'' Kate asked.

Michael shrugged. ''As happy as two people can

be who spend so much time studying and going to school that they rarely see each other.''

"But eventually that changed," Kate guessed.

Michael's lips tightened. "Yeah, and when it did, when we had completed our residencies and gotten jobs, I wanted to talk about kids again. Val was less enthusiastic, but I figured that would pass because I knew Val—who's a pediatric surgeon—really loves kids." Regret glimmered in his eyes. "My biological clock was ticking like crazy. Hers had yet to really start. But Val promised me she would talk about it as soon as she settled into her practice and we'd saved some money and bought a house."

Michael shook his head in mute aggravation, remembering. "We did all that and she still wasn't ready. Finally, I got tired of being put off and said, 'If not now, when?' And that was when she admitted to me that she didn't want children, not any, not ever. She said she didn't think she had it in her to do it all, to have a full-time career in medicine and a marriage and kids. And she loved being a doctor too much to give it up."

"So it ended," Kate guessed.

Michael released a short, rueful breath. "No. I was still in invincible mode and I continued to try and talk her into it, to figure out a way we could make it work."

Ooh, Kate thought. "How'd she take that?"

"As you would expect," Michael retorted dryly, "with a great deal of irritation." He sighed, the defeat he'd felt then showing clearly in the handsome features of his face. "Finally, we both realized we were not going to be happy together and we split. That was two years ago."

Kate was sorry his marriage had ended but glad he was single now. She searched his face. "Do you regret the divorce?"

"No," Michael said softly, and on that, to Kate's relief, he was very firm. "In retrospect, I realize we had medicine in common, but we never should have married. We were meant to be friends, not husband and wife. The signs were there from the start. I just ignored them. Anyway, since then, I've made myself a promise. I no longer want to be the patron saint of lost causes." His hand tightened on hers. "I can no longer afford to let my natural optimism keep me from facing reality. I know that there are going to be times when, like it or not, I just have to be able to give up, to stop thinking 'time' will fix everything, because sometimes it just won't, and when that happens, I have to be able to move on if I'm ever going to have the happy family and fulfilling home life I want."

When Kate's marriage had ended, she had decided the same thing. There would be no more going through life with blinders on. No more refusing to see what was right before her eyes.

"It's hard, though, isn't it?" Kate said sympathetically, as she thought about the years she and Michael had both invested in unions that were fated to fail from the very beginning. "Making a decision to end a marriage and going through a divorce?"

Michael nodded, his mood as sober and reflective as hers. "Even when all the odds are stacked against me, I still really hate giving up."

Kate sighed, completely in sync with his feelings about that. She studied the way their hands were twined together and resting on his thigh. "I always thought I'd be married when I had a baby."

"Me, too. But—" He smiled and glanced at the clock. Noting it was now well after one, he helped her to her feet. "In the meantime, I'm glad you and my sisters got acquainted."

Kate steadied herself by curling a hand around his biceps. "We found we had a lot in common," she said as she felt his muscle flex beneath her fingers.

Michael grinned and looked like he wanted to kiss her again, even as they moved apart. "Oh, yeah, like what?"

Kate smiled. "We all care about you."

WE ALL CARE ABOUT YOU. Kate's words echoed in Michael's head long after he had retired to the guest bedroom for the night. Her words were so innocent, but truthful. For all her planning, Kate hadn't planned this. Any more than he had planned his reaction to seeing every slender, curvaceous inch of her in Lycra. He'd never seen a woman's body bounce back from pregnancy so quickly. He'd never wanted to make love to a woman so much. The more time he spent with her, the more he wanted to make her his. And the first roadblock to making that happen was getting her mother well—or at least to confide in Kate.

"So how'd the appointment go with Saul Zimmerman?" Michael asked Carolyn when they met in the hospital cafeteria the next afternoon.

"At this point Dr. Zimmerman's not ruling out anything." Carolyn's frustration was evident as she cupped her coffee mug between her hands. "He wants to do a series of tests on an outpatient basis. We're going to start with urinalysis, extensive blood work, a routine chest X ray and an EKG to help rule out heart-cardiac causes. If nothing definitive comes up in those, they'll do a radiographic bone survey and a CAT scan and possibly even a bone marrow exam. He said it could be weeks before we know what's causing my symptoms.''

"Waiting for a diagnosis is tough, I know, but you don't have to go through this alone.''

"I know.'' Carolyn sighed with relief. "And I feel a lot better, knowing you're watching over me.''

Though he was glad to help out, that wasn't what Michael had meant. "Kate's worried about you.''

Coffee sloshed over the cup's rim as Carolyn's hands plummeted to the table. "You didn't tell her!''

"No,'' Michael retorted, "but she knows something is wrong. She just can't figure out what, and it's got her pretty upset.''

Carolyn frowned. "She'd be more upset if she knew I could be dying, and I won't do that to her, Michael. I won't ruin her happiness. Not at the holidays. Not when she's just had a baby.''

Michael smothered a sigh of frustration. Although Carolyn could be in the early stages of a deadly illness, she could also be suffering from something far less severe. Only time would tell. In either case, he felt she needed her family around her. "How about confiding in Lindy, then?'' he suggested calmly.

Carolyn soaked up the spilled coffee with a paper napkin. "She has semester exams. She'd never be able to concentrate on her studies if she knew. I won't have her ruining her stellar academic record because of me.''

"Ted, then?'' Michael persisted.

Carolyn shook her head stubbornly. "Ted would

never be able to keep it from the girls if he knew.'' Carolyn's green eyes clouded with worry. ''Besides, I don't want to have to put him through this, either. And if I allowed myself to spend any time at all alone with him, he'd know I still love him, and then where would I be if my worst fears were realized?'' Carolyn demanded, tears shimmering in her eyes. ''He'd have to see me through the illness, and then so would the girls, and I've told you before, I will not subject anyone in my family to that!''

Silence fell between them. ''I've put you in a difficult position, haven't I?'' Carolyn said after a moment.

''I don't like keeping things from Kate,'' Michael said honestly.

''The two of you are getting close, aren't you?''

Not close enough, Michael thought, his frustration mounting by leaps and bounds. ''You don't disapprove?'' Michael asked cautiously, knowing more than anything he wanted Kate's entire family on their side.

''Far from it.'' Carolyn smiled.

Michael quaffed his coffee. ''I'm trying not to rush her.'' But, as always, he thought, frowning, he wanted everything to happen yesterday!

Carolyn nodded contemplatively. ''It's probably wise to take a slow, very well-thought-out approach. Kate's divorce from Kirk left her justifiably skittish— she doesn't want to make another mistake when it comes to picking a life partner. And you know what a planner Kate is. She doesn't want it to happen unless she's already penciled it in her calendar.''

Michael sat back in his chair. Slow, very well-thought-out approaches were definitely not his specialty. He preferred to go with what he felt like at the moment and let things happen as they were meant to happen, just as he had with his kisses. But Carolyn was right—that was definitely not how Kate did things. And right now, it was Kate who mattered most.

"So how should I proceed if I'm going to win your daughter's heart?" Michael asked. Heaven knew he didn't want to screw this up.

"Lay the groundwork. Continue to let her see what a good match you are." Carolyn smiled encouragingly. "Before you know it, you'll be penciled into a big chunk of her calendar."

"So how are things with Timmy's daddy?" Dulcie asked the day before Thanksgiving as she picked up the last of the baskets Kate had assembled in her living room.

"He's been great." Kate helped load them in the back of the Gourmet Gifts To Go van for delivery. "Since he moved in with me two weeks ago, he's rocked and held and bathed and diapered Timmy and helped me in every way he could. Laundry, grocery shopping, chores—he's done them all."

Dulcie grinned. "A real Super Dad, hmm?"

"You got it." And it was driving Kate crazy.

"Any romance in the bargain?" Dulcie asked slyly.

Kate wished! But in the last two weeks, there'd been nothing. Nada. Zip. Lots of looks as though he wanted to kiss her again. Lots of tension between them when those looks came up. But something mysterious was holding them back. "It's almost as if there's a wall between us sometimes," Kate said, glad to voice her frustration to someone. "We'll be talking about my mother or my father or Lindy or the upcoming holidays, and he'll get really quiet. Brooding, almost. Then he'll change the subject abruptly and move on to something else."

Dulcie loaded the last gift basket in the van and slammed the door closed. She leaned against the vehicle. "You think he's uncomfortable with the fact your parents are still separated?"

"Maybe," Kate said.

Dulcie paused. "How are your parents doing, anyway?"

Kate shrugged. "My father's depressed." *And still suspicious there might be someone else in my mother's life.* "And my mother's busy going way overboard on Christmas this year." In fact, she'd been shopping so much, Kate and Lindy had hardly seen her! "You ought to see the stacks of presents she's got over at her house."

Dulcie and Kate walked toward the driver door. "You think she feels guilty because she initiated the separation from your dad?"

"It's possible," Kate said, as she watched Dulcie climb behind the wheel. That made sense, since it was Carolyn who had broken up their family. Unfortunately, she had the nagging sensation there was more to it than that, a lot more.

"Look, it's bound to be tough for everyone in your family this year," Dulcie soothed, as she fit her key in the ignition. "It'll get better. In the meantime, just concentrate on getting through tomorrow."

Deciding Dulcie was right, Kate concentrated on forgetting about Michael's newfound reserve where she and romance were concerned, and on delivering the invitation her mother had extended.

"You're invited to my mother's home for Thanksgiving," Kate told Michael that evening, shortly after he got home from the hospital. "Dinner's at noon."

"I'd love to come…"

"But you can't," Kate guessed, obviously disappointed.

Michael frowned apologetically. "The holiday shifts are set months in advance. I'm pulling a double on Thanksgiving so I can have Christmas Eve and Christmas Day off this year. I have to be there at six tomorrow morning, and I probably won't get off till after midnight."

Kate hid her disappointment and gave him a sunny smile. "We'll miss you," she said breezily.

Not half as much as I'll miss you, Michael thought.

But with only half the test results in and the diagnosis still not made on Kate's mother, perhaps this was best.

He paused and looked deep into her eyes. "I wish things were different." *I wish I could tell you everything.*

Kate touched his arm. "It's okay, Michael. This is your job. I understand." A determined smile on her face, Kate shifted Timmy to her other arm. "Timmy and I'll see you Friday."

Michael nodded. Yes, they would.

They stayed up a while longer, talking, then all headed for bed. Too soon, his alarm went off at five. Groggily, Michael headed for the hall bath and the shower. Aware he was feeling sorry for himself for missing out on Timmy's very first Thanksgiving and the chance to be with Kate, he quickly ran the electric razor over his face and brushed his teeth, then turned on the shower, shucked his boxers and stepped in.

Not until he turned off the tap and started to step out did he realize what he had forgotten. The only linen he had was a wet washcloth, roughly the size of a fig leaf.

Michael stood there dripping, muttering a string of curses, then figured what the heck, Kate was still asleep. The house was dark. The linen closet—and a big supply of fresh towels—was only a few feet away. Easing the door open slightly, Michael scanned the hall. All was quiet, dark.

He switched off the bathroom light and waited a moment for his eyes to adjust, then stepped out, padded quietly past the nursery door and the master bedroom to the linen closet, eased the door open. Still dripping, he grabbed a towel, knocking over something cold and metal in the process. It rolled across the shelf and landed on his foot with a muted thud. The stack of towels came tumbling down on top of it. Swearing softly in surprise, Michael hunkered down in the dark and began to try to pick up everything at the same instant Kate stumbled out of the master bedroom, sleepily rubbing her eyes. Before he could do more than vault to his feet, she had stumbled into the length of him.

''What in the world!'' Kate exclaimed.

Michael swore again as she switched on the hall light.

Chapter Eight

It took two seconds for her eyes to adjust, another three to get the full view, and what a view it was. "Well, this is certainly one way to wake up," Kate drawled as she shoved the hair from her face and her eyes focused on the most masculine part of him. A part that seemed to be blossoming before her eyes. Stunned, she let her gaze rove his nakedness from head to toe, taking in a sea of smooth skin and hard tendon feathered with whorling brown hair. Heavens, he was beautiful, every inch of him.

Michael fumbled with a towel and wrapped it around his waist. "I was trying not to wake you."

Kate tried to ignore the tingling warmth in her chest that was spreading with alarming speed to her tummy and the backs of her knees. She tore her eyes from his golden skin and shot him a teasing glance. "Ah, well, then try not to stumble around in the dark and knock over stacks of towels and cans of spray starch." Her pulse still racing, her throat unbearably dry, Kate knelt and picked up the can. She held it up. "'Cause that will do it every time."

Unable to hide his arousal, no longer really inclined to, either, Michael folded his arms in front of him and studied her wryly. "You're enjoying this, aren't you?"

"Well, let's put it this way. To date, you've managed to see every part of me, unclothed, at one time or another." Kate patted him on the arm and returned his sexy smile with one of her own. "Now I've seen all of you."

"KATE, you haven't heard a word we've said all day!" Lindy complained over Thanksgiving dinner.

"You have been distracted," Carolyn agreed, as she pushed the food around on her plate.

"What have you been thinking about?" Lindy persisted.

Michael. Dripping wet. Naked. Aroused. Kate's heartbeat sped up as she dug into her peas. "Nothing."

"Well, nothing is making you blush," her mother noted.

That's because I've been fantasizing all day, Kate thought. *Imagining what it would be like to forget about the need for caution and planning and common sense and parental responsibilities, and just hold him and touch him and kiss him and be with him to my heart's content.*

"Too bad Michael couldn't be here," Lindy continued, as she helped herself to more sweet potatoes.

"I thought you didn't approve of me seeing so much of him," Kate said, remembering her sister's caution.

Lindy blushed. "I've changed my mind."

"Again?" Kate teased as she forked up some of her mother's delicious cranberry sauce.

"He's been really good to you and Timmy. Good for you," Lindy replied.

That he had, Kate thought wistfully. Whenever she was with him, she felt more alive, more excited. And never more excited than this morning when she'd run into him in the hall. Mercy, that man was built. And he was most definitely not—as the physical evidence had clearly borne out—as physically immune to her as she had begun to fear!

Carolyn studied Kate. "You miss Michael today, don't you?"

"Yes, I do." Kate smiled at her infant son, who was next to her in the bassinet. "But next year he should have Thanksgiving off." *And then we'll spend it together.*

"Speaking of missing people, I miss Dad," Lindy sighed.

"It doesn't seem like Thanksgiving without him," Kate agreed.

"Sometimes things change even when you don't want them to," Carolyn said cryptically, seeming suddenly tense and depressed, "but life still goes on, and so do we. Besides, the three of you are going over to his place later for coffee and dessert," Carolyn reminded her daughters gently.

"It's not the same, and you know it," Lindy said grimly, her resentment over the situation obvious.

"I agree." And though she might not have a choice about what was going on between her mother and father, or even any right to weigh in with an opinion, Kate thought, since it was their life not hers, there were things in this life that she did control. Like her future. And her relationship with Michael.

MICHAEL LOOKED UP from his place at the end of the hospital cafeteria line to see Kate walk in, Timmy in one arm, a wicker basket in the other. Her pale blond hair was windblown, and she was wearing a high-waisted, deep blue velvet dress that fell to midcalf. He headed straight for her and greeted them both Southern style, with a quick hug hello and a kiss to the cheek. Keeping his eyes locked on hers, he laced a possessive arm about her waist as they walked to a table for four by the windows. "What are you doing here?"

"Bringing you some of my mother's Thanksgiving dinner."

Michael helped Kate with her coat, then held Timmy while Kate set a place for Michael. A moment later, Timmy was in Kate's arms as Michael sat down to a turkey dinner with all the trimmings. "Did you have a nice time with your mom?" he asked, as he dug into the moist, succulent turkey.

"Actually," Kate replied unhappily, as she cuddled Timmy in her arms, "it was pretty depressing."

Michael could imagine how miserable this holiday was for Kate. "Because your dad wasn't there?" he guessed.

Kate nodded, her green eyes taking on a troubled sheen. "It feels lousy being torn between two parents on a holiday." She paused and raked her teeth across her lower lip. "I don't ever want us to do that to Timmy."

Michael wanted to take Kate in his arms and kiss her unhappiness away. He covered her hand with his. "We won't. I promise you that."

Kate relaxed at his reassuring tone. They smiled at

each other. "Have you seen your dad yet?" Michael asked.

"I'm joining Lindy at Dad's apartment this evening, to watch a football game with him and have dessert and coffee. He had dinner with some friends from work this afternoon. But right now, I wanted to be with you. And I wanted Timmy to be with you, too. So I called the ER and asked when your dinner break might be, and here we are."

A mixture of joy and contentment flowed through Michael. "This was the best surprise I've had all day."

Kate grinned as she fit a rattle into Timmy's tiny fist. "I'm glad you're as happy to see us as we are to be here."

Michael watched as Timmy cooed happily. "You weren't the only one feeling sorry for yourself," he confided as he finished his meal and dug into his pumpkin pie. "I started last night, when I realized I probably wouldn't see either you or Timmy at all today."

A mischievous sparkle came into Kate's eyes. She laughed softly and teased him with a wink. "Actually, as I recall, I saw quite a bit of you this morning."

It was Michael's turn to flush. If she only knew how much he hadn't wanted it to stop there. "You aren't going to let that go, are you?"

Kate wrinkled her nose at him. "Let's just say— as far as recently suffered indignities go, it put us on a level playing ground."

That it did, Michael thought, as they continued to look at each other. "So how was your dinner?" she asked, looking at his empty plate.

"Delicious." The only thing that would have made

it better was if he could have eaten at home with Kate and Timmy.

"I'll be sure to pass that along to Mom."

"Along with my heartfelt thanks to both of you," Michael said as the beeper on his belt went off, signaling he was needed in the emergency room. Michael stood reluctantly. "I've got to go." He leaned over and cuddled Timmy and kissed the top of his head, then wrapped his arms around Kate and Timmy both. "I'll see you at home later," he promised as he kissed her cheek. And he knew, even if Kate hadn't quite admitted it to herself yet, that their situation was beginning to change. Their relationship wasn't only about forging a connection with Timmy these days. It was about forging a bond with each other, too.

"I WANT TO HELP, Kate," Michael urged on Sunday afternoon.

Lindy, who'd come over to baby-sit Timmy, agreed. "You know there's no way you want to have to do all that work yourself, Kate, even if you are going stir-crazy after being at home for three weeks straight!"

But to Michael's frustration, Kate continued to worry and delay as she turned to him and propped her hands on her hips defiantly. "It's not right, asking you to spend your day off setting up a nursery for Timmy at my shop. I feel like I'm taking advantage of you."

Michael fervently wished she would take advantage of him. In more ways than one!

"Especially when you consider this is the first time to yourself you've had in days!"

No one had to remind him how hard he'd been

working over this holiday weekend or how little time he'd had to spend wooing Kate, Michael thought. He'd worked grueling eighteen-hour shifts three days straight. "Kate, I want to do this. I am going to do this," Michael told her firmly as he picked up his coat and handed Kate hers.

"All right. But just remember, I tried to get you to take it easy." Still looking anxious, Kate turned to Lindy. "What about you? Are you all set?"

Lindy regarded Kate with exaggerated patience. "Yes, Kate."

Kate continued down her list. "The bottles of milk are in the fridge."

"You already told me that—twice."

Kate ignored her sister's sarcasm. "And the number of the shop—"

Lindy rolled her eyes in utter exasperation. "Kate, I work there, too, and even if I didn't, I've had it memorized for a very long time."

Knowing strong action was called for, Michael took Kate's arm and pushed her willy-nilly toward the door. Kate called over her shoulder, "The diapers—"

"Are upstairs in the nursery and down here in the pantry. I know, I know." Lindy followed them and looked at Michael plaintively. "Will you get her out of here?"

With pleasure.

Once in the car, Kate buried her face in her hands, and moaned. "I'm making a fool of myself, aren't I?"

Michael thrust the car into reverse and backed out of the parking space before she could change her mind. "Let's just say you're a typical new mother," he said as he drove toward the shop.

Kate looked over her shoulder anxiously. "Maybe it's too soon for me to leave him."

"Kate, you are five minutes away," Michael repeated patiently. "You can call and or go back to your condo at any time."

Kate groaned in distress. "I know."

As Michael looked at her, his heart went out to her. She wasn't the first new parent to act this way. "It's natural to worry the first time you're away from your baby," he soothed, reaching over to give her arm a reassuring pat before putting his hand back on the wheel. "I did it, too." Michael watched the cars at the intersection, then preceded cautiously when it was his turn. "Remember all those calls?"

"You're still calling," Kate reminded as Michael turned into the parking lot behind Kate's shop.

"And still worrying myself silly for no reason," Michael affirmed as he parked. "Timmy is going to be fine. But," Michael continued as he searched her face and left the motor running, "if it will make you feel better we'll go back right now and get Lindy and Timmy and bring them over to the shop, and they can stay here while we work."

Kate shook her head. "No, it's too uncomfortable. And it's too cold outside." Kate cast a glance at the gloomy sky. "And besides, it might snow. And Timmy sleeps better there. And Lindy has to start studying for her exams."

Michael turned to her, aware she had never looked prettier than she did in the worn jeans and old UNC sweatshirt. "You going to be okay?"

Kate inhaled deeply and looked at him with wide eyes. "Uh-huh."

Michael grinned as he went around to help her with her door. "Try saying it with a little more conviction," he teased as he wrapped one hand around her waist and gave her a hand down.

Kate rested her hands on his shoulders. "I'm going to be fine."

"WELL?" Michael said dryly, when Kate hung up the phone.

Kate blushed. "Lindy said if I call one more time she is personally going to come over here and throttle me."

Barely suppressed amusement glimmered in Michael's dark brown eyes. "Too much, huh?"

Kate wasn't sure what the big deal was. Could she help it if she kept forgetting to mention things until after she'd already finished talking to Lindy? Especially when these were things Lindy needed to know about Timmy to make Timmy happy.

Then again... Kate shrugged. "I guess five calls in thirty minutes is overdoing it a bit," she admitted. Especially when she knew Lindy had the number of the shop and Michael's beeper number, and Michael's beeper was on his belt.

Michael held out his arm and gestured her to where he was working. "Why don't you come over here and give me a hand in making room for the crib here in the corner?"

Kate sighed and walked to Michael's side. "The problem is I can't concentrate," she complained.

"You don't have to concentrate to move stacks of catalogues and books."

Kate bent to pick up a stack, then swayed unexpectedly as the room twirled around her. She sat down swiftly on a stack of catalogues and put her head between her knees. "I don't believe this," Kate huffed. "Now I'm hyperventilating." And she never did that.

Michael knelt in front of her. "Slow down and stop taking so many breaths."

"Easy for you to say," Kate wheezed.

"Easy for you to do," Michael corrected. He took her hand and rose, drawing her to her feet and into his arms in one smooth motion. She made a protesting squeak of dismay. Michael framed her face with his hands. "Just relax with me a minute here, Kate," he urged softly as his lips came down on hers, and she was kissed into silence. Kate groaned as the seductive sensations overwhelmed her, and then his kiss turned warm, gentle, coaxing. She wreathed her arms about his neck and melted against him, shaken by how thoroughly she was under his spell. When he held her like this, when he kissed her like this, like she was his woman, she wanted only for it to go on and on. Being in his arms was like being home. Like being safe. It was too soon, yet it felt so right. So very, very right...

Michael knew he had taken unfair advantage. He didn't care. He wanted Kate to be his. And his alone. And putting the moves on her was the only way. Desperate for more, unable to get enough of her, he kissed her with an intensity that left no doubt about what he was feeling. He kissed her until the rest of the world fell away, until she was clinging to him, molding her slender body to his, until there was no doubt about the depth of his arousal and hers. And then, and only then, did he lift his lips away.

"Better now?" Michael asked huskily.

So much better, Kate thought, and so much worse because now she wanted to take it a million steps further and make love to him, heart and soul.

"THAT GLOW in your cheeks does not come from moving stuff at the shop," Lindy claimed upon their return.

"You're right," Michael drawled as Kate rushed to check on their son and found him sleeping peacefully. He grinned at Lindy as he joined Kate at the bassinet. "It comes from kissing. Lots of kissing."

Kate whirled and playfully thumped his chest. "Michael!"

Lindy grinned and looked all the more interested as she sidled forward. "I thought gentlemen weren't supposed to kiss and tell."

"They don't." Michael hugged Kate from behind and wrapped both his arms about her waist. "Unless they're staking a claim."

Lindy's eyes widened as Michael trailed a string of shivery kisses down Kate's neck. "Are you?" she whispered.

Michael nodded as Kate settled her body into the curve of his. "Whether that claim has been accepted or not is yet to be seen." But it felt like she was at least considering it.

"I think I'll leave you two alone to discuss this. Later!" Lindy slipped out the door with a wave.

Kate turned to Michael. "I can't believe you said that!" she chided softly, as a blush climbed her neck into her face.

Michael slid his hands behind her until they overlapped, then drew her against him. "Part of me can't, either." He chuckled affectionately as he stroked a hand through her hair. "I had it all planned out. I was going to go slow, take months to court you, do everything strictly by the rules according to Kate. But whenever I'm alone with you, all my good intentions go out the window." His voice dropped a notch. "Be honest, Kate. You've been thinking about the kisses we've shared, too."

"Well," Kate said, a contemplative grin tugging at the corners of her lips, "they were good."

"Just good?" he teased, knowing the feel of her lips beneath his was sweet, soft and all too intoxicating.

Kate's eyes danced. "Incredibly good, and you know it," she said, surprising him with her honesty. "But that doesn't mean we should complicate matters further by rushing into a love affair."

Michael knew they were fooling themselves if they thought they could keep their relationship platonic much longer. It was time Kate dealt with that fact, too. And not just while in the throes of passionate kisses. "I don't want an affair, either, Kate," he told her solemnly, as he slid his hand beneath the curving ends of her hair and caressed her nape with his thumb. "I want to get married again. I want us to take this situation we've been handed and be a family."

The emotional part of Kate wanted that, too. But the pragmatic part of her reminded her that they'd only known each other a matter of weeks. She had known Kirk for a year before they'd gotten married, and the marriage had still failed. She drew a breath, aware the plans she'd made on Thanksgiving Day to win his heart had not included a marriage proposal before Christmas. Probably not before next summer, at the very earliest. Panic assailed her. She broke his hold and stepped away from him. "Michael, it's too soon."

Michael followed her to the window. Outside, the condo association was putting up Christmas wreaths, decorated with red velvet ribbons, on every door. He stood behind her and cupped her shoulders with his palms, the warmth of his touch as soothing as his words.

"We have a child, Kate, who needs us both now."

Kate turned to face him. Her heart was pounding. "We also have a very complicated situation."

"We get along—our living together with nary a complaint has proven that. We also desire each other—our long, delicious kisses have shown us that."

If he only knew how much the reckless part of her wanted to give in to him here and now and just elope! But she couldn't do that. For Timmy's sake, for all their sakes, she had to approach this in a reasonable, thoughtful manner.

"Desire isn't love. Sharing a baby the way we do isn't love, either. And marriage, relationships, need love, and lots of it, to survive." Kate twisted her hands in front of her and began to pace. "I don't want to take advantage of the situation or you and I'm very much afraid I am. I don't want to rely on you for all the wrong reasons." Because that, she knew, would bring disaster.

"I admit I was initially confused by all this, too. But there's one thing I'm very certain about, Kate, and that's how I feel about you. You and Timmy are the last thing I think about when I go to sleep and the first thing on my mind when I wake up. I miss you both when I'm not with you. And I can't imagine a

future without you. I don't want to live the kind of
life-style that has our son caught between us, going
to your place half the time, mine the other. Nor do I
want to be a weekend-only kind of dad who only sees
my son once or twice every week.''

''I don't want that, either, for me or for you,'' Kate
confessed.

''Good.''

Kate studied him. ''So what are we going to do
about it?''

''The only thing we can do,'' Michael whispered,
taking her into his arms once again. ''Rise to the challenge in front of us and let our feelings be our guide.''
As his lips lowered to hers, all the feelings Kate had
been suppressing flooded her heart. Soon, she was
kissing him back, needing him and wanting him as
desperately as he wanted her.

Michael smoothed a hand through her hair. He
kissed her again, teasing her tongue with the tip of
his until her breath was as short and shallow as his,
until she moaned low in her throat and arched against
him pliantly. ''Oh, Kate, I want to make love to you
so badly.''

His body was hard and demanding against hers.
She burned and throbbed everywhere they touched.
Still reveling in the pleasure of the kiss and the utter
recklessness their passion engendered, Kate leaned
her forehead against his. ''I want that, too,'' she murmured honestly, as he dragged her nearer, so close
their bodies were almost one. ''But we can't.'' For
so many reasons. ''It's too soon after the birth—''

Michael hooked his thumbs beneath her chin and
tilted her face to his. ''We can still cuddle and kiss
to our heart's content,'' he suggested on a thready

whisper. "And maybe—" he lowered his mouth to hers, felt her tense and gasp softly in anticipation of his kiss "—even sleep together in one bed."

Kate grinned as his lips claimed hers lightly, evocatively. She jerked in a halting breath and shook her head at him. "You're relentless."

Michael grinned. "When it comes to claiming you as mine, you better believe it." He lifted her in his arms and carried her to the sofa. He set her down and came down on top of her. "We're going to kiss, Kate, that's all," he promised. And as they cuddled and kissed, she realized she felt better than she had in a long time.

"You look upset," Michael told Kate the following evening when she came in the front door. Since he'd had the day off, he'd stayed home to take care of Timmy while Kate went to the shop. She charged in at six-thirty, looking tense and stressed, and he wondered if it had been a good idea for her to go back to work so soon after Timmy's birth, never mind put in what had turned out to be a very full day.

Kate flung her briefcase, coat and purse on the sofa. "I *am* very upset."

"What happened?"

Kate slipped off her shoes. She threw herself on the sofa and began opening the brightly colored holiday envelopes that had come in the mail. "One of my mother's friends from bridge club came by the shop today. She told me how much she had missed my mother at bridge the past month, but they understood she'd been helping me out with the baby, both at home and the store."

"I wasn't aware she had helped out with either," Michael said.

"Which is exactly the point!" Kate tossed the cards onto the coffee table and vaulted to her feet. She began to pace. "Michael, she lied to them. And she lied to me. She told me just two weeks ago she was late for her bridge club gathering. When I questioned her about the time because it wasn't even the right day of the week, she told me there was something extra going on that week. I assumed she meant a tournament or something. Well, guess what? There was no tournament or anything else on any day but a Saturday this entire fall!"

Michael knew something like this was bound to happen sooner or later, given the enormous number of lies Carolyn had told to cover the time she'd been spending at the hospital. And her tests weren't over yet.

"Maybe you should talk to her, tell her how upset you feel," he suggested, wrestling with his guilt at having been unwittingly put in the middle of this. He didn't want secrets between himself and Kate.

Kate shook her head. "No. I'm not giving her the third degree. I hate it when people do that to me, and I'm not doing it to her. Besides, I know there's a perfectly good reason for all this. I know in my heart my mother can't be having an affair."

Good for you, Michael thought.

Kate pivoted to Michael and drew a breath. When she spoke again, her voice was noticeably lower and calmer. "I just have to wait until my mother tells me what's going on."

Michael hoped that was soon.

"Meanwhile, you look exhausted," Michael said,

stepping behind her to rub the tenseness from her shoulders.

Kate closed her eyes and gave herself over to his soothing touch. "That's what happens when we're trying to fill the huge semester-exam care basket orders for the university. But we'll be finished in another day or so, and then it will be on to the Christmas orders."

Michael turned her to face him and gently touched her cheek. "No rest for the weary?"

"Not this month." Kate met his eyes and confided softly, "But I'm in the process of hiring more people. It'll cut down on my profits. But it'll be worth it in the end. Because I'll have more time to spend with Timmy and you."

"I like the sound of that," Michael said, as he kissed her and drew her close. "In the meantime, I prescribe some R and R."

Kate cuddled against him and wreathed her arms about his neck. "Oh, you do, do you?"

Michael nodded. He took her hand and led her up the stairs. Scented candles were lit in the bedroom and master bath. New silk pajamas and a matching robe had been laid out on the bed.

Kate turned to him, stunned. "I can't believe you did all this for me."

"It's just the beginning, Kate," Michael promised, knowing there was nothing he wouldn't do to win her heart—and hand. "Just the beginning."

TIMMY WOKE just as Kate went in to draw her bath. Michael changed him. Kate nursed him. They took turns cuddling and playing with him, then Michael rocked him to sleep while Kate retired to her bath.

By the time Kate walked downstairs, the fire was lit, Christmas carols were playing on the stereo and dinner was made.

Kate offered to help serve, but Michael made her sit down. She marveled as he brought chicken parmigiana, fettucini, Caesar salad and bread to the table. "No one has ever done anything like this for me before."

Michael poured sparkling water into her glass. "Not even your husband?"

Kate sat back in her chair and sipped her water. "Our marriage was all about me meeting his needs."

Michael sat opposite her. He leaned toward her earnestly, his entire attention focused on her. "Did you know it was going to be that way when you married him?"

Kate shrugged. "I thought it'd be a fifty-fifty sort of partnership, but…" Kate frowned, recalling. "Kirk quickly disabused me of that notion with his long hours at the office and incessant demands."

"What kind of demands?" Michael pinned her down in the same low, confident voice.

Kate spread her napkin across her lap. "When we got married, Kirk was a junior hotel executive working his first job out of business school. His assignment was to take hotels with low performance ratings and profit margins and turn them around. It was part of his training as an exec, and it was only supposed to be for a year or so."

He reached for her plate and ladled salad onto it. "Were you able to work?"

Kate accepted her plate with thanks. "I wanted to, but with us moving every two to three months it was impossible. Anyway, after that first year Kirk did get promoted to the next level, but it was just more of the same, only instead of supervising operations at one hotel at a time, he usually had three or four under his control. Plus, these were five-star hotels in major cities all over the country, and there was a lot of entertaining to be done.'' Kate's tone darkened along with her mood. ''I was constantly being asked to throw dinner parties and entertain other executives and their wives.''

''And you didn't like it,'' Michael guessed as he broke open a soft, fragrant roll.

Kate shrugged, knowing it wasn't the socializing that had gotten to her, it was the fact she'd been so habitually and thoroughly taken for granted. ''I wanted something of my own. I had an undergraduate degree in business, and I wanted to use it. I thought maybe if I had my own business, or at least worked for the same hotel corporation he did and could transfer jobs whenever he did, I'd be happier.''

''You didn't want a family at that point?''

Kate drew a breath, recalling how miserable she had been. ''Kirk wasn't ready to have children. With the incredibly long hours he was working and my misery with our gypsy existence, we were not all that happy, and it seemed a wise idea to put it off. Anyway,'' Kate continued, cutting into her chicken, ''I put in an application at the company where he worked and was turned down. The same thing happened with a rival corporation, and every other job I applied for. I thought it was because we had moved so many times in the three years we had been married. Meantime, Kirk had managed to get a permanent position in Charlotte, with an investment banking firm that specialized in acquiring hotels, so we moved back to North Carolina and bought a house.''

Michael observed her candidly. ''You must have been happier then.''

''Yes, but I still wanted to work and I had realized by then I also wanted my own business, so I pulled together a business plan and began looking for a place to open up shop. Mysteriously, something went wrong everywhere I looked. I lost a small-business bank loan that, up until the very point I was denied credit, looked like a sure thing. The location I wanted was leased out from under me, and so on down the line.''

Michael's eyes darkened angrily. ''Kirk?''

Kate nodded as the bitterness rose in her throat. ''He didn't want me to work. He figured if he sabotaged my efforts long enough and well enough I'd decide it was too much trouble and give up and concentrate on him and his needs. Instead, I found out what he'd done, realized he couldn't possibly have loved me if he could do something like that, and asked for a divorce.''

Michael gave her a look that said he backed her up. ''Was he remorseful?''

Kate sighed and looked directly into Michael's velvety brown eyes. ''It would have been great for my pride if he had been, but no, not really. He said he had married me because he thought I would make a good executive's wife and because my family had great social connections. He felt both would help him in his career, and would have, if I had only been more cooperative.''

Michael summed up Kirk's character with a single descriptive phrase, then asked, ''Where is he now?''

Kate grinned. "Still in Charlotte, happily remarried, to a socialite who can *really* help his career."

"You must've been devastated by his betrayal," Michael said gently.

Kate sighed and lifted her shoulders in an indifferent shrug. "Actually, I wasn't all that unhappy," she admitted candidly. Finished, she pushed her plate away from her. "More like relieved. Which in turn made me realize that I hadn't loved him, after all. I had married him to try to find myself—my life's direction. And I did. I'm just sorry we had to put each other through such misery for that to happen. But, painful as it was, some good came out of it. I know now I have to have my own work, that my needs and ambitions have to count as much as my husband's if I ever do get married again."

"Good for you." Michael praised her warmly. "That's the way it should be."

Kate studied him. He was wearing a soft crew neck sweater and khaki slacks. His skin was golden, his jaw freshly shaven and scented with brisk, wintry aftershave. His dark lashes looked silkier and longer than ever, his face more ruggedly handsome in the soft, warm glow of candlelight.

"You mean that, don't you?"

He nodded and reached across the table to cover her hand with his. "I'd never stop you from pursuing your own happiness or assume I knew more about what would make you happy than you do."

"ONE MORE THING," Kate said, as Michael got ready for bed later that evening. "My mother is having her annual Christmas open house on Saturday. She said it might be her last one."

Michael tensed, aware he knew what Kate and the rest of the Montgomery family didn't, that Carolyn was scheduled for one last round of tests that would bring either very bad or very good news. Thus far, cardiac and lung problems had been ruled out, but that still left some very serious illnesses as a possibility, including the one that had claimed Carolyn's mother. "Did she say why?" he asked cautiously, as he went into the bathroom to brush his teeth.

Clearly used to her mother's vagueness and unpredictability of late, Kate shrugged. "Just that she might not feel like entertaining next year—I'm assuming she meant that if the divorce goes through she won't want to continue a yearly tradition that was, in the past, very much a big deal not just for our family and friends, but all the colleagues and clients at my father's law firm. Anyway, in an effort to have our 'family' together at least once during the Christmas holidays, she's invited my father to be there, too, to help her host it." Kate picked up her toothbrush, too, and layered on mint toothpaste. "I'm hopeful what that invitation really means is that she is reconsidering her request for a divorce, and this is her way of inching back toward my dad, without having to sacrifice her pride, after all that silly talk about needing her 'space' to recapture her 'individuality.'"

No, what it really meant, Michael corrected silently, was that Carolyn was throwing herself one last hurrah in case the news was bad and she decided—against his and every other doctor's advice—to disappear into parts unknown to live her last days on earth completely alone. She had probably asked Ted to cohost in case she became indisposed with either chest pain or light-headedness during the evening's festivities.

"Plus," Kate continued happily, oblivious to his thoughts as they headed for the bedroom, "Dad told me today his gut sense is that my mother still loves him, regardless of who she may have been seeing during their separation. He's thinking about starting from scratch and courting Mom all over again." She drew back the covers and climbed into bed. "Isn't this good news?"

It was and it wasn't, Michael thought, as he climbed in beside her. If Carolyn's report from Saul Zimmerman was good, Ted's actions would no doubt speed a reconciliation. If the report was as bad as Carolyn continually feared, however, Ted's desire for a reconciliation and Carolyn's subsequent spurning of him would only lead to more heartbreak on all their parts.

Kate turned to face him and studied his sober expression with serious light green eyes. "You don't think my parents are going to get back together, do you?"

Not if the news was bad, he didn't. Carolyn was one stubborn woman. But he couldn't tell Kate that without reneging on Carolyn's request for complete confidentiality. All he could do was hold Kate close and tell her what was in his heart. Michael guided Kate into his arms and smoothed the hair from her face. "I really hope, for all your sakes, the news is good."

Kate put her head on his chest and relaxed against him. "I do, too." She brushed her lips across the back of his hand, then continued to nestle against him. "Mom wanted the three of us—you, me and

Timmy—all to be there. So—'' She lifted her chin and looked at him with sparkling eyes. "Will you attend with me?"

Michael tightened his arm around her, knowing he had never wanted to protect a woman more. "You have to know," he told her huskily, as they cuddled together before drifting off to sleep, "it would be my pleasure."

MICHAEL LET OUT a low wolf whistle the moment Kate walked into the nursery Saturday evening. "Now that," he enthused as his eyes moved over her, "is one very sexy dress."

"Like it?" Kate twirled in her short and Christmassy red velvet dress.

Michael gave her a sexy once-over that quickly had her mouth dry and her heart pounding. "Love it."

Kate paused next to the crib, where a velvet-suited Timmy was cooing and kicking beneath his Winnie the Pooh mobile, and straightened Michael's tie. "You look great, too," she said, admiring his dark blue suit, pale blue dress shirt and reindeer tie. "As does Timmy." In fact, they made one picture-perfect family.

Michael hauled her into his arms and stood with her locked in his embrace. "Ready to go out and celebrate the season?" he asked softly.

Her heart bursting, she was so happy, Kate nodded.

The party was in full swing by the time they arrived. Kate threaded her way through the throngs of people—many of whom had attended the Montgomery Christmas bash year after year—and hugged Lindy. "Where are Mom and Dad?" She hadn't seen them when she walked in.

"Over there." Lindy nodded at a crowd of people by the living room fireplace. "Can you believe it?"

Kate spotted her parents and studied the flushed, happy looks on their faces as they stood side by side. Aware it was almost too much to hope for after everything that had happened, Kate caught her breath. "You don't think—"

"That they're still in love with each other?" Lindy exclaimed. "Of course I do!" She clapped a hand across her heart. "Isn't it obvious?"

"I have to admit it looks that way even to me," Michael said, as he cradled a cooing Timmy in one arm and grabbed a glass of warm cider from a passing tray.

"If only there were some way to reunite them," Lindy said.

Kate grinned as a plan began to form. She shot Lindy a mischievous look. "Maybe there is."

Chapter Nine

"I thought I was going to baby-sit Timmy today," Ted Montgomery said as he entered Kate's condo the following morning.

An equally stunned Carolyn laid a hand over her chest. "I distinctly remember Kate asking me."

"Actually," Kate said, pretending there'd been a mix-up, "Michael asked you, Dad. And I asked Mom because Lindy told me last night she couldn't do it. And we do need a sitter for Timmy because Michael and I are going out to buy Timmy some Christmas presents. So," Kate summed up breezily as she shrugged into her coat with Michael's assistance, "as long as you're both here..."

"You're not fooling us for one minute, Kate Montgomery," Carolyn admonished sternly.

Her father agreed. "We know a matchmaking ploy when we see one."

Kate threw up her hands. "I confess." She shook her head in comic dismay. "You're on to me. I had a baby, found his father, got woefully behind on my shopping and indeed all yuletide preparations—as you can see the three of us don't even have a tree up yet!—and invented the Christmas holiday, all to bring my parents together.''

Ignoring the exaggerated exasperation on the faces of both her parents, Kate bent to kiss her son goodbye, then watched as Michael handed him over to his grandparents.

''Bottles are in the fridge, instructions and phone numbers are on the kitchen table, along with Michael's pager number. Beep us if you need us. If you don't, even better. Meantime—'' Kate paused in her breathless delivery long enough to kiss her mother's cheek, then her dad's ''—just enjoy being grandparents even half as much as we love being parents, and you'll all do fine. Michael—'' grinning, Kate laced her arm through his ''—we are outta here!''

''SO WHAT DO YOU GET for a baby who is just a few weeks old?'' Michael asked minutes later as they roamed the packed aisles of the nearest toy superstore.

Kate sidestepped a towering display of Barbie dolls, while Michael pushed the basket behind her. ''Lots of things,'' Kate—who had been reading up— said as he drew beside her once again and they turned into the infant aisle. ''Books, blocks, stuffed animals, bath toys, things to chew on. Anything Timmy might want to play with throughout his first year.''

Michael laced an arm about her waist. Ducking his head, he whispered into her ear, the soft warmth of his breath brushing her neck and sending tingles of awareness down her back. ''Think it's too early to get him a catcher's mitt?''

Kate tilted her head so she could look into his eyes. ''Probably.''

Arm in arm, they continued to roam the aisles, contentedly selecting gifts. Without any planning at all, they'd become a couple, Kate realized. And more important still, she and Michael were more family to each other than she and Kirk had ever been. She put her hand in his. "Michael?"

"Hmm?" He gave her that gentle smile, the one that made her heart swell with tenderness.

Kate rushed on before she could stop herself, her words low and urgent. "Let's make ourselves a promise. No matter what happens, let's promise we'll shop for Timmy together every year and give him his presents jointly, so he doesn't feel torn between the two of us."

"Agreed."

They hit two more stores, then headed home. As they entered, her parents were sitting side by side on the sofa. Carolyn was snuggled contentedly in the curve of Ted's arm, which was draped along the back of the sofa. Timmy was cuddled in Carolyn's arms. Both her parents were so intent on watching their first grandchild sleep they didn't hear Kate and Michael come in. They jumped when they saw them. But Timmy, bless his little heart, slept on.

"You're supposed to put Timmy down when he drifts off to sleep, Mom," Kate said. "Otherwise, he won't want to sleep in his crib."

"I know." Carolyn sighed as she awkwardly disengaged from Ted's sheltering embrace.

"We couldn't get enough of him," Ted added softly, sending his estranged wife an affectionate glance rife with feeling. "It's such a miracle, having him in our lives."

Kate reached over to squeeze Michael's hand.

Their ploy to bring her parents back together was working! "We feel that way, too."

She helped her mother put Timmy down while Michael and her father checked the score on the Carolina Panthers game.

"You and Dad looked awfully chummy just now," Kate said happily.

Abruptly, Carolyn's eyes filled with sadness that was almost unbearable in its intensity. "Oh, Kate—"

Kate felt disappointment coming on.

"Nothing of importance has changed," Carolyn stated sadly.

"Then it should!" Kate insisted stubbornly. "Don't tell me you don't love him, Mom. I saw the way you looked at him at the open house last night, the way you were sitting together on the sofa just now—" Abruptly, her voice caught and tears filled her eyes. She couldn't go on.

Twin spots of color filled Carolyn's pale cheeks. "I admit I still have feelings for him—"

"Then stop this nonsense and go back to him!" Kate whispered plaintively.

Carolyn took Kate—and their conversation—into the hall away from Timmy. "Kate, I can't!"

"Why not?" Kate squared off with her mother at the head of the stairs.

Carolyn turned away, face paling. "You wouldn't understand."

"Then that makes two of us," Ted said grimly from the landing. He looked at Carolyn. "I thought we were making progress the past few days, beginning to get in sync with each other once again."

"We have been," Carolyn replied evenly.

"And yet you still won't give me an explanation as to why you need to leave me!"

Carolyn flushed as she put a hand to her breastbone and held it there. "I told you it was for the best! Why can't you accept that?" she cried emotionally, as Timmy let out a gosh-awful wail.

"Because it doesn't make any sense!" Ted exploded.

"To me, either!" Kate interjected emotionally, as Michael swept unobtrusively past them and went to tend to Timmy. "I'm sorry, Mom," Kate continued as the tears fell. "I tried to stay out of this. But when I think about how long the two of you were married, I know it has to count for something. And don't tell me the two of you don't love each other because Lindy and I lived with you all those years and we know you do!"

"Honey," Carolyn said in a low, quavering voice, "the holidays are a very emotional time. Everyone feels sentimental. Your father and I are no exception."

"Tell me you'll at least keep an open mind about all this," Kate pleaded.

But her mother only shook her head and turned away. Fist still pressed against the center of her chest, she marched down the stairs.

Michael handed Timmy to Kate. Downstairs a door opened and shut rapidly. Kate looked in the direction her mother had headed, then at her dad. She'd never felt more torn or less in the Christmas spirit than she did at that moment.

"I'll go make sure she's all right," Michael said.

Kate and her father were still regarding each other in silence as the door shut behind him.

MICHAEL CAUGHT UP with Carolyn at her car. She still looked very shaky. "You're in no condition to be behind the wheel," he told her sternly. "I'm driving you home."

He helped her into the passenger side, then got behind the wheel. "Are you okay or do you want to go to the emergency room?"

"I'm fine."

"The pain in the center of your ribs is back?"

Carolyn nodded. "As well as the light-headedness. And I haven't had either symptom for at least two days. Both came back with a vengeance when Kate and I started arguing."

Which could mean, Michael thought, that her illness was at least in part stress-related. "Have you finished all your tests yet?"

Carolyn shook her head. "I still have two left—a CAT scan and a bone marrow test. The CAT scan is going to be next Friday, the bone marrow the Monday after that. When they are finished and all the results are in, Dr. Zimmerman is going to meet with me to give me the results." She pressed a hand to her lips and burst into tears.

"Need someone to be with you?" Michael guessed.

Carolyn nodded vigorously and continued to cry great gulping sobs as Michael turned the car into a parking lot of a convenience store and put it in park.

It should have been family helping her through this, Michael thought. But given the way things were going with Kate, maybe he already was family in a sense. Michael reached over and held Carolyn's hand. "Then I'll go with you," he said gently, as the tears continued to stream down her face. "But you—" he hugged her briefly, reassuringly, then handed her a tissue "—also need to do something for me."

Carolyn smiled through her tears as she wiped her eyes. As the moments drew out, Michael could tell by her color and demeanor that her chest pain and light-headedness had subsided.

"What could I possibly do for you?" Carolyn sniffed.

"Easy," Michael grinned. "Go shopping."

KATE WAS STANDING in the window of her condominium when the taxi pulled up and Michael got out. "Your dad get off okay?" Michael asked, once he came inside.

"Yes. My mother?"

"She's okay now. I drove her home. It seemed the gentlemanly thing to do."

"Thanks."

Silence fell between them, punctuated only by their sighs. "Well." Kate looked at the bags full of toys they'd bought for Timmy. She put them on the kitchen table, along with wrapping paper, ribbons, scissors and tape. "Lindy and I really asked for that one, didn't we?"

Michael cut a length of paper decorated with candy canes. "Given the situation, it's only a miracle it didn't happen sooner."

Kate wrapped a box of oblong plastic pull-apart links. "I should have known better than to do something like that on the spur of the moment." She tore off a piece of tape with a vengeance. "How could I have been so foolish?"

Michael took her by the shoulders and forced her to face him. "Kate, come on, stop beating yourself up over that. It happened. It's over. Your parents are fine and they're going to go on.''

"But they're not married anymore, Michael, not like they were, and I can't begin to tell you how upsetting this is for me!" Kate burst into tears.

Michael sank into a kitchen chair, tugged her onto his lap and gathered her close. "I think I have an idea how difficult this must be for you." He stroked a hand through her hair.

"How?" Kate drew back slightly, dashed away her tears and sent him a baleful look. "Your parents aren't divorced!"

Michael looked deep into her eyes. "I know how much I've always counted on them to be there for me. The incredibly connected, incredibly loving family unit they've forged has grounded me all my life. And I know it's done the same for my sisters."

Kate sighed as she splayed her hands across his chest. "That's the way it used to be for them—and us," Kate confided sadly.

"And maybe it will be again someday," Michael prophesied quietly.

"I guess you have a point." Kate wiped her eyes. "If ever there's a season for miracles, this is it."

Without warning, Michael seemed a million miles away. Finally, he swallowed and said, "I hope it works out for you all."

Kate nodded wistfully. "So do I, because if there's one thing this Christmas has shown me, it's that families should be together."

Michael held her close and kissed the top of her head, her cheek. "And speaking of families," he said softly, as he looked deep into her eyes, "isn't it about time we called mine and asked them to come and visit Timmy, too?"

"THANKS FOR COMING to baby-sit for us," Kate told Michael's parents when they came to visit the following Saturday evening.

"Are you kidding? It was our treat!" Ginny Sloane said, bringing in several containers of home-baked holiday goodies.

"We've been wanting to spend some time with our new grandchild," Hugh Sloane said. "So we're only too happy to help out."

Glad Michael's parents were so enthusiastic about the unexpected addition to the Sloane family, Kate briefly showed them around the first floor of the condo, letting them know where everything was, then led the way upstairs, giving a guided tour as she went, while Michael and Timmy brought up the rear. "Here's the master bedroom, the nursery and the guest room where Michael has been staying."

Hugh and Ginny's jaws dropped simultaneously. They weren't the only ones who were stunned.

Kate looked at Michael and lifted a brow. "You didn't tell them you had moved in with me temporarily?"

"Didn't see any reason to get into it." Michael handed Timmy over to his mother and then clamped a hand on Kate's shoulder. "We'll be back in a few hours, folks."

"Take your time," Ginny said.

"We'll be just fine," Hugh added.

"Not good, Michael," Kate remarked as they braved the cold and misty December weather and got into his Jeep.

"What?"

Kate frowned as he fastened his safety belt and started the Jeep. "You know what!" she chided, making no effort to hide her disapproval of the way he had handled the situation. "Not telling your folks you were staying with me!" She turned to study him and breathed in the tantalizing fragrance of his aftershave. "Why didn't you, by the way?"

Michael shrugged his broad shoulders and concentrated on adjusting the Jeep's heater, then let the vehicle warm up. "For the same reason you didn't initially, mention it to your parents, Kate. I knew they'd disapprove."

Kate met his gaze equably. "Under the circumstances it might make them feel better."

He shook his head, his reluctance to disappoint his family evident. "They don't believe in living together. As far as my parents are concerned, marriage is the only way to go."

Under normal circumstances, Kate agreed with Michael's parents. Unfortunately, these were not normal circumstances. Still feeling irritated—and not sure why—Kate folded her arms. "You should have told me. I'm sorry it came out the way it did." She didn't want Michael's parents thinking ill of her. She paused and bit her lip. Despite the Sloanes' quick recovery, she had the feeling the subject was far from closed. "Do you think your parents are going to speak to you about it?"

"My dad probably will, but don't worry, I'll handle it." He reached over and squeezed her hand. "Meantime, we've got to get a tree up for Timmy. So what kind do you want, real or artificial?" Michael asked as he drove out of the condo parking lot.

Maybe Michael was right. Maybe it was best they forget about the problems of their families and concentrate on making this the best first Christmas Timmy could ever want. Deliberately putting her worries aside, Kate tilted her head at Michael playfully. "What kind do you think?"

Michael paused at a stop sign and sized her up facetiously. "Real—I'm betting a fir, trucked down fresh from the western Carolina mountains."

Kate grinned as she pushed the scan button on the car stereo until she found a station playing Christmas carols. "You guess right," she said dryly, as the cheerful lyrics of "Deck the Halls" filled the interior of the Jeep.

Michael hummed a bit of the melody, and Kate joined in. "Any place in particular you usually buy one?" Michael asked.

"Actually, there is." Kate directed him to the lot where the seasonal stand she favored operated. Minutes later, they had parked and were roaming the lot. It was still misty, and they could see the moisture in the glow of the bright lights overhead. The hauntingly beautiful strains of "Oh, Come All Ye Faithful" flowed from the speakers overhead, and their breath was frosty in the cold, crisp December air. Tape measure in hand, Kate and Michael prowled the rows and rows of beautiful fragrant trees, along with many other couples in search of the perfect tree.

Kate went from one to another to another. They all looked stunningly beautiful to her. She stood, hands braced lightly on her hips, as she studied an eight-foot tree. "I don't know. I can't make up my mind."

Michael moved up and down the rows, then selected the last one in the fourth row. "This is it," he said, "the perfect tree."

Kate tucked her scarf around her neck to ward off the chill and went to stand beside him. "How can you tell?"

Like you even have to ask? his look said. "It's obvious," he said.

Kate shook her head. "Not to me. To me, they all look pretty much the same, although some are a little taller, which is why I have to measure. 'Cause I want one that is exactly eight feet tall and no more than six feet in diameter at the bottom." She studied the ruggedly handsome lines of his face. "How big a tree do you think we should get?"

Michael pointed to the tree in front of them. "I like this one."

He'd made his decision awfully fast. Too fast, Kate thought. "Well, I want to look around a little more," she said.

For the next thirty minutes, they measured and checked the freshness of every tree in the lot, only to return to the one Michael had initially picked out. When they finally got around to sizing it, it measured exactly what Kate had figured they needed and was as fragrant and soft as only a fresh-cut tree could be. Kate shook her head in awe. "I don't know how you did it, but you're right, this is the perfect tree."

Michael grinned and signaled to the tree-lot employee to cart this one off and ring it up for them. "Sometimes you just have to go with your gut and wing it."

Kate walked with Michael to the cash register while two lot employees secured their fir to the luggage rack on top of his Jeep with ropes. "I know that works for you, but I'm uncomfortable just letting life unfold. I like to plan things out to the tiniest detail. I like order in my life.''

''You know what they say,'' Michael teased, after he had paid and they headed to his Jeep where their tree awaited carting home. ''Too much order makes Jill a dull girl.''

Her heart thudding in her chest, Kate leaned against the passenger door of the Jeep. Michael probably didn't realize it, but his playful gibe was uncomfortably close to something Kirk had used to say to her, when he'd razzed her about her seeming inability to cope with the gypsy existence required by his career. Telling herself firmly that this was not the same thing—not by a long shot—Kate stuck her hands in the pockets of her coat and tilted her head to his. ''So you're saying what?'' she asked, unable to hide her insecurity. ''That I should loosen up a bit?''

Michael shook his head as he reached up to catch her face in his hands. ''I'm saying you should let loose a little and go with your feelings, Kate, like I intend to go with mine.''

Kate had only to look into his eyes to know he wanted to make love to her then and there. Trembling, she rested her hands on his chest. ''I think we better get home.''

He gazed at her ardently. ''Me, too.''

The drive home was fraught with a new kind of tension. He hadn't even kissed her—had barely touched her—and yet Kate knew she and Michael were going to make love soon. In fact, she admitted to herself frankly, they probably would already have done so if she hadn't just had a baby.

And Michael knew it too.

When they arrived home, Kate started to help Michael with the tree before he stepped in to stop her. "It's too heavy for you, Kate. You go check on my mom and Timmy, and I'll go in and get the tree stand and get my dad to help me with this."

Seconds later, Michael's dad had his coat on and both men were outside, cutting through the rope that held the tree to the luggage rack. As Michael had expected, his dad wasted no time in speaking what was on his mind. "That was quite a shock you handed to your mother and me, son," Hugh said.

"Sorry." Michael sawed through one of the ropes at the rear. "I meant to tell you."

Hugh cut through the rope on the other side. "Where do you expect all this to lead?"

Michael went around to the ropes securing the tree at the front of the luggage rack. He wished he could tie all this up in a neat little package with a tidy bow, but it was too soon for that. "I don't know," he said honestly. He knew he was falling in love with Kate. He knew he wanted to make love to her. But how did she feel?

Hugh helped Michael pull the tree to the ground. "I think there's an agenda, even if you haven't admitted it to yourself. You want to be part of your son's life. You see romancing his mother as a way to achieve that."

Guilt assailed Michael as he thought about the way Kate melted against him when they kissed and the way they were already sharing not just a son but a bed, even if they had yet to do more than kiss and cuddle. There was nothing wrong with the relationship they were forging. "It's more complicated than that, Dad," Michael told his father gruffly.

"I know it is, son." Hugh knelt and helped Michael fit the tree into the stand and tighten the screws. "I'm just saying don't romance Kate on a whim or simply because it feels good at the moment."

"Meaning what?" Michael glared at his father. "My actions should be more calculated?"

Hugh closed the distance between them. He clapped a fatherly hand on Michael's shoulder. The concern he felt for both Michael and Kate was evident. "What I'm saying," Hugh continued gently, "is that it takes a lot more than the shared love of a child to sustain a marriage, Michael. It takes a hell of a lot more."

Michael swallowed as he realized all that was at stake. "I know that, Dad," he replied just as softly and just as honestly. "And I know you're right. I have been acting on impulse." *Following my heart.* For the next few seconds, both of them were extraordinarily quiet. "But I can't back away from Kate and Timmy."

Hugh studied his son, his disappointment obvious. "Are you telling me you know her well enough and love her enough to make the kind of lasting, lifelong commitment that a marriage is built on? Because from where I'm standing, it looks like you've known her a few weeks, and during that short time, your feelings have been complicated by the fact she has just borne your first and only child, a child you've wanted for a very long time."

"I can't explain it, Dad. Other than to say I know what I feel for her is real and lasting." In fact, he could no longer imagine his life without her. "But you're right. I should take more substantial action if I want to make her mine permanently."

Hugh paused. "You always have made up your mind pretty quickly about things," he said slowly, after a moment. "Just make sure you give her the time she needs to think things through, too."

"I'VE NEVER KNOWN YOU to be spontaneous," Lindy said Sunday at noon, when Kate called and asked her to baby-sit.

Kate thought about the talk Michael had had with his dad the previous evening, when they were bringing in the Christmas tree. She didn't know what had been said outside. Michael hadn't volunteered. And it would have been rude to pry. She'd just known whatever it was had given Michael pause and that he'd been unusually quiet while they decorated the Christmas tree with his parents and affectionate but unusually preoccupied after they'd left. From the way he'd been looking at her earlier in the evening, Kate had expected a really hot necking session when he joined her in her bed. Instead, they'd cuddled but barely kissed.

Kate didn't know why he'd put on the brakes, she just knew she wanted things where they had been, open and easy, and felt maybe giving him some of the much needed R and R he'd already given her might be the way to achieve it.

Kate shifted Timmy to her other side to finish nursing. "Michael's done so much for me and Timmy, Lindy. I realized the other day I hadn't really gone the extra mile for him, so I want to do the kind of thing he likes and take him out to lunch on a whim." Since he had the day off, now was the perfect time.

When Lindy arrived ten minutes later, Michael answered the door. Hands on her hips, Lindy looked him up and down facetiously. "You're not ready to go!" she teased.

Michael blinked and asked laconically, "Go where?"

Glad to see she really had surprised him, Kate came up behind him and laced a hand around his waist. "Out with me."

"Where are we going?"

Kate grinned and gave him a sassy glance she hoped would get his engine revving. "You'll find out soon enough." She linked her fingers through his and tugged him out the door. "See you later, Lindy." She waved cheerfully.

"Have fun, you two."

MICHAEL MIGHT NOT have had a clue what Kate was up to, but she couldn't have picked a better day for it, he thought, as he followed Kate's trim, blue-jean-clad figure to her sedan. The day was unseasonably warm. With the temperature hovering around the fifty-degree mark, the sky overhead sunny and clear despite a prediction for a slight chance of rain that so far had not materialized, it was shaping up to be a perfect day to be out and about.

Michael relaxed in the passenger seat, his gaze discreetly following the deft movements of Kate's sensationally curved leg from accelerator to brake to accelerator again. "So where are we going?" Michael asked, unable to help but notice the enticing curves of her breasts beneath the form-fitting white T-shirt and heavy blue denim work shirt she had on.

"That depends." Kate shot him a sexy smile before returning her attention to the road. "What kind of food have you been craving lately?"

Michael thought about it. "I haven't had Carolina barbecue in a long time."

Kate grinned and turned in the direction of nearby Durham. "I know just the place."

Michael studied her profile. "Determined to be mysterious, aren't you?"

"Uh-huh."

Ten minutes later, Kate pulled into the parking lot at Bullock's in Durham. She frowned at the lack of cars while Michael silently berated himself for not having figured out this was where Kate was headed. It was, after all, *the* place to go for barbecue in the Triangle area.

"That's strange," Kate's eyebrows knitted together in a frown. "Usually there's a line out the door at lunchtime."

Realizing he was the unfortunate person who was going to have to burst her balloon, Michael put a staying hand on her forearm before she could turn off the car motor. "Uh, Kate," he said reluctantly, "Bullock's is never open on Sundays."

Momentarily, Kate looked taken aback, but she quickly pulled herself together. "We'll just go somewhere else," she said, smiling cheerfully.

Aware they didn't have all that long before Kate would have to be back to relieve Lindy, Michael suggested, "How about one of the fried chicken places we just passed?"

Kate turned her car onto the road. "Chicken it is, then. In fact, it's warm enough to eat outdoors if you'd like."

"Sounds good." Michael settled back for the ride.

They pulled into the drive-through lane. Kate placed her order at the speakerphone for the holiday special—a bucket of chicken with all the trimmings—only to be told they were out of fried chicken.

"We've got a problem with our fryers this morning. All we have are the trimmings. You know—baked beans, cole slaw, mashed potatoes and gravy, biscuits, corn bread. Stuff like that."

Kate thanked them and drove on. "There's another chicken place up the street. We'll just try there."

"Sure," Michael said. He was glad Kate was taking this in stride.

Fortunately, that restaurant's chicken fryers were all in perfect working order. In no time flat, Kate had purchased a nearly identical holiday meal in a yuletide bucket, and she turned her car toward a nearby park. Only to find there was an end-of-season soccer tournament going on and there were no parking places or empty picnic tables.

"We could go somewhere else," Michael said. "Or we could eat in the car."

Kate shook her head. "There's another park close to here. We'll just go there." Unfortunately, when they reached the second park, the place was packed with people enjoying the unseasonably warm weather. By the time they located a vacant picnic table, the sky had gone from a crystal blue to a deep gray. They got out of the car and lugged their meal to the picnic table. "I don't believe this," Kate moaned in obvious distress as she sorted through the contents of the bag. "They didn't give us any silverware or napkins!"

Not good, Michael thought, since there was no way they could eat mashed potatoes and gravy and cole-slaw without silverware. "We'll just have chicken and biscuits. We can wipe our hands on the bag and eat the rest of the dinner at home."

Kate smiled. "You're right, of course." They set out their meal. And that was when the first fat, wet raindrop hit their table.

"SO HOW was your day out?" Lindy asked as Michael and Kate came in the door forty minutes later, both of them drenched to the skin. Lindy looked at Kate's stormy expression. "Or shouldn't I ask?"

"It was fun," Michael said.

Kate merely rolled her eyes at his pronouncement and shucked her wet shoes on the rug by the front door. "Has Timmy eaten yet?" she asked Lindy.

"No. He should be waking any minute, though."

As if on cue, Timmy let out a loud wail. Kate pushed her fingers through her damp hair and exited quietly. "I'm going up to nurse Timmy."

"Is she okay?" Lindy asked Michael.

Michael looked at the way Kate's slender shoulders sagged in defeat, and his heart went out to her. "She will be," Michael promised Lindy quietly. He would see to it.

Michael thanked Lindy again for baby-sitting for them and saw her out, then headed upstairs. He changed into dry clothes while Kate finished nursing their son, then went in to relieve her while she changed and used the blow dryer on her hair. By the time Kate emerged from the bathroom in her robe, Timmy was in his crib, fast asleep, and Michael had a tray of tea and shortbread cookies waiting for her in the master bedroom.

Kate tucked one slim leg beneath her and plopped down on the edge of the bed. Hot, agitated color poured into her cheeks. "How can you be so cheerful?"

"Easy." Michael sat opposite her. "We had a great afternoon."

Abruptly, tears pooled in Kate's eyes, turning them a deep, luminescent green, as she tugged a brush through the silky ends of her hair with short, choppy strokes. "I don't see how you can say that," she stormed, "when everything that could go wrong did go wrong." Finished brushing her hair, she flung the brush aside. "I was trying to be spontaneous, and the entire day turned into an example of Murphy's law— whatever could go wrong did."

Michael had an idea what it had cost Kate to embark on anything without a detailed road map to success. He also knew how she hated to fail at anything. "You want spontaneous?" he teased.

"Yes!" Kate fumed, as she vaulted to her feet and began to pace barefoot across the room. "For once in my life, I want to know what it's like to feel like doing something and just do it!"

Michael stood and faced her. He braced his hands on his hips and lazily looked her up and down. "Okay," he drawled, "I'll give you spontaneous."

KATE LOOKED directly into his velvety brown eyes, unable to help but note the lusty promise in his low, husky voice and take-no-prisoners stance. "What?"

Michael spread his hands on either side of him and continued to survey her. "What do you feel like doing this very instant?" he asked in a soft, self-confident voice.

He was offering her the world. All she had to do was be brave enough to take it. Kate licked her lips as she stalled for time. "What do you mean?"

"You and I are alone, here in your bedroom. The

rain's pounding on the roof. Our baby's asleep, and we've just spent the afternoon together. Christmas is a week and a half away. What do you feel like doing?''

Afraid of the passion shimmering through her, Kate started to turn away. "I don't know what you mean," she whispered.

Michael closed the distance between them in two long strides. "Yes, you do, Kate." He caught her before she could flee and held her close. Close enough to inhale the intoxicatingly male scent of his skin and cologne. Close enough to face what they'd both been feeling almost from the moment they met.

"What do you feel like doing?" he repeated huskily, sifting his fingers through her hair, tilting her face to his and staring into her eyes. "Not tomorrow or the next day or the next month, but this instant, Kate."

This instant? Making love to you.

Kate didn't know where the thought had come from. She only knew it was true. As true as her love for the baby they shared and the love she felt for Michael.

Aware her heart was pounding in her throat, her insides were tingling and her knees were weak, Kate started to speak.

He laid a finger across her lips. "No. Don't tell me, Kate," he whispered raggedly. "Show me."

Kate took a deep breath as every romantic, sexy fantasy she'd ever had about him—and there'd been plenty—came to mind. Their eyes locked as she listened to the rain pounding on the roof on this lazy Sunday afternoon. This was it, Kate thought, the moment of truth, the moment—the man—she'd been waiting for all her life. "Just like that?" she whispered hoarsely.

Michael nodded as a pulse worked overtime in his throat. "Just like that."

You wanted to take some risks, just go for the gusto. Here's your chance. "All right." Deciding to take the challenge he put in front of her, Kate said, "I want to open my robe, like this."

And she did. Michael sucked in his breath as his dark eyes dropped to the revealing tightness of her breasts, caressed the rounded slope of her tummy and grew to know the shadowy vee of her hips. Her heart pounded as he took his time, letting his gaze stroke and caress and incite every inch of her to a fever pitch. Able to see the desire in his eyes, the tenderness, the love, Kate stood in front of him proudly and drew in a trembling breath. "Okay so far?" she asked.

"Oh, Kate, this is more than okay. You're so beautiful."

As was he. "Then you won't mind if I do this." Kate put his palms inside her robe, on her waist, then moved them slowly and purposefully upward, until satisfaction flowed through her in effervescent waves and her nipples pressed urgently against his palms. Her knees were trembling, her insides pulsating, as he continued to caress her breasts. "Still okay?"

Michael's touch radiated the same heat and gentleness as his gaze. "Very much so," he said softly, then bent and kissed her lips. "How about you?"

"So far so good," Kate murmured against his lips as she tugged his sweatshirt up and off. She ran her hands over his chest as her breath soughed out in a rush. Then she moved closer, until skin met skin and her thighs rubbed with delicious friction against his.

Threading her hands through his hair, she kissed him, not the tentative, learning kisses of their initial courtship, but deep, sexy, urgent kisses.

Michael's hands moved down her hips, fitting her against him with an intimacy that was at once erotic and unmistakable. Kate closed her eyes and arched against him, feeling the rigid proof of his arousal through his jeans.

"As long as we're being spontaneous," Michael said as he trailed kisses down her breasts to her ribs, to her waist, "is it okay if I improvise, too?"

Kate laughed. "Heck, yes." Desperate to touch everything she'd already—albeit accidentally—seen, Kate tugged at the zipper on his jeans and shoved them—along with his boxers, off his hips. "I'd be disappointed if you didn't."

Michael stepped out of his jeans. He was gloriously naked, gloriously beautiful and aroused. "This is what I feel like doing." He ran his hands from breast to hip and back again before settling in the apex of her thighs.

Kate sighed as he touched her there. He was making her want, making her need. She moaned as a hunger unlike any she had ever known built within her. "Oh, Michael," she whispered tremulously, "I like that, too."

Michael kissed her languidly until her skin was so hot it sizzled to the touch. "Then maybe," he said softly, "you'll also like this." He divested her of her robe, swept her up in his arms and carried her to the bed. Planting an arm on either side of her, he followed her down. Awash in sensation, Kate closed her eyes.

She wanted him so much, and yet… "I haven't gotten the green light from my doctor."

Michael knew. It didn't matter. He threaded his hands through her hair. "Trust me to stay within the limits and still make you feel as good as I know how."

He kissed her again, his hands claiming her first, then his lips and tongue. Kate surged against him, amazed he could know just how and when and where to touch, amazed she could want him so much. Seconds later, she fell apart in his hands. He took her higher still, until she heard the soft, whimpering sounds in her throat, until her body was taking up the same timeless rhythm as his. So, this is what it will be like when we finally do make love, Kate thought, as she found him in exactly the same way, and then all was lost in a blinding explosion of heat.

They came back to earth slowly. Both of them trembled. Both were damp with sweat, sated with love, dewy with passion. No one, Kate thought, had ever loved her so fiercely and possessively. No one had ever made her want, made her need in quite that way. But he had, she thought as dizziness continued to sweep through her in tantalizing waves, and he always would.

"Michael?" Kate curled against him contentedly and rested her head against his chest.

"Hmm?" Michael responded softly as he wrapped his arms around her.

Kate lifted her head to look into his eyes. They might not have said the words yet, but she knew she was in love with him. "Our afternoon may not have started out perfectly, but it certainly ended that way."

He grinned and pulled her close. "For me, too."

Chapter Ten

Lindy and Kate put the Closed sign on the front door of the shop at six but left the door unlocked for Michael, who was scheduled to pick up Kate and Timmy when he got off around seven. Kate didn't like to stay late these days, but tonight was an exception. They were still working on a half dozen yuletide baskets that needed to be ready for morning delivery while Timmy sat in an infant seat perched between them on the worktable, watching contentedly.

"You've changed since the holiday season started, and Michael Sloane came into your life," Lindy said.

Kate felt different, but she was curious to see how her sister perceived her. "How so?" she asked as she smiled at her son and then added carefully scripted amounts of fruit and chocolate to the basket in front of her.

Lindy tied an elegant gold bow to the handle of hers. "You're looser, more relaxed."

Thanks to Michael, the feeling of constantly having to prove herself and make up for lost time had faded significantly. Kate smiled as she bent to kiss a cooing Timmy's cheek. "Well, I'm a mother now and I can't afford to worry about every little thing."

"It's more than that. It's that special glow in your face—the one that magically increases whenever you mention Michael's name."

Kate felt her cheeks pinken self-consciously as she smoothed plastic wrap over the finished basket in front of her. "Is it that obvious?"

Lindy nodded. "You're in love with him, aren't you?"

Kate tensed. Michael was serious about sharing parenting of Timmy and making slow, delicious love to her, which would soon be even better, given the fact she'd had her postpartum checkup earlier in the day. But love was something that hadn't come up, even if he had made her happier than she'd ever been in her life. "Love wasn't in the plan, remember?"

Lindy shrugged, put her finished basket on the delivery shelf and went to get another basket. "Then maybe it's time you changed your plan."

Kate watched Timmy maneuver his rattle rather clumsily toward his mouth. She shook her head. She didn't want to rock the boat, and she was afraid, given the difficult, emotional circumstances that had brought them together in the first place, that would be all too easy to do. "We have enough pressure on us already."

"From the families?"

Kate picked up another order, studied it, then selected the appropriate basket from the shelves and brought it to the worktable. "His parents think we ought to get married if we're going to be living under the same roof."

"What do you and Michael want to do?"

I know what I want to do—marry him. But as far as Michael went, she hadn't a clue what he wanted to do. Up to this point he'd been as careful with his feelings as she had been with hers, and for good reason. They were in a very delicate situation here. Aware Lindy was waiting for an answer, Kate shrugged and said, "We haven't discussed it."

"Don't you think you should?"

Kate made a face that conveyed her reluctance. "It was enough to try and come up with a plan that would take us through Timmy's first six weeks and the Christmas holiday. I don't want to push it."

"Once burned, twice shy?"

Kate sighed. "He's already weathered one divorce. He doesn't want another one, and frankly, neither do I." It was enough to have rushed into an ill-fated marriage and failed once, Kate thought resolutely, without doing the same thing all over again. Besides, what they had right now was fine. It was more than what she had anticipated when she set out to have a baby on her own.

"Michael's not Kirk," Lindy said gently.

"No, he's not," Kate agreed. In some ways they were the direct opposite. Kirk had planned out his entire life from the time he was a kid, whereas, outside of his medical career, Michael rarely planned more than a few days in advance. Both ways of living had left her feeling off balance.

"So how serious are you about him?"

Realizing they were headed into dangerous territory again, Kate chose her words carefully. "I want him for a friend. And of course he's Timmy's father."

"Uh-huh." Lindy gave her a knowing look that spoke volumes about all Kate wasn't saying. "Is he husband material?"

"Of course," Kate admitted easily. "For someone,

not necessarily me.'' Although, Kate admitted silently, given her druthers, she knew what she'd wish.

Lindy's eyes sparkled mischievously as she finished the basket she was working on and put it on the shelf, too. ''What about in the romance department?''

At the mention of that, it was all Kate could do to suppress a wistful sigh. Since that rainy Sunday afternoon when he'd first shown her just how wonderful the love between a man and a woman could be, they'd taken kissing, caressing and cuddling to the absolute limit. And yet, because she'd so recently had Timmy, they still had one threshold they had yet to cross.

Trying not to show just how much she was anticipating making love with Michael all the way, Kate turned from her sister's probing. ''What *about* the romance department?''

''Does he kiss as well as he looks like he does?'' Lindy teased.

Kate successfully fought an incriminating blush. ''Come on!'' she chided, as she finished another basket and began working on her last. ''You've seen him. You know what a sexy guy he is.''

Lindy rolled her eyes and stepped up her pace. ''Being naturally sexy, which I'll be the first to admit Michael is, and behaving in a romantic fashion are two entirely different things, Kate.''

Don't I know that.

''So rate him on a scale of one to ten as a potential lover. Assuming, of course, you don't already know the answer to that, too!''

She did and she didn't, Kate thought, wishing the two of them had already had the opportunity to make love all the way. She wanted to know what it felt like to have Michael deep inside her, to have him claiming her as his, not just for today or tomorrow, but all time. Aware her baby sister was waiting for her to rate Michael's potential as a mate, Kate dropped her eyes and chided, "Lindy!"

"C'mon, Kate. Just do it!"

"Okay. Fine. He's a nine and a half," Kate fibbed.

Lindy regarded her speculatively. "Just nine and a half?"

Knowing full well that on a scale of one to ten, Michael would rate about a thousand, Kate shrugged indifferently and tossed her head. "Ten would be the perfect man, and they don't make tens."

"I don't know about that!" Michael's deep, sexy voice suddenly sounded in front of them.

"Michael!" Kate flushed with embarrassment as she looked up to find him lounging in the workroom doorway. She had no idea how long he'd been standing there, but with the faint shadow of an evening beard lining the handsome features of his face, his tie loosened and the first button of his shirt undone, he certainly looked comfortable. Kate swallowed. "We were just talking about you."

He regarded her wryly. "So I heard." He paused in front of the infant seat and tucked his index finger in Timmy's fist. "You and Timmy ready to go home?" he asked, lifting Timmy's fist to his lips for a gentle, affectionate kiss.

"Just about." Kate put the bow on the last basket.

Still holding Timmy, Michael tucked an arm about Kate's waist and kissed the top of her head before turning to Lindy. "Need a ride?"

"No. I've got my car out back."

"I know, but it doesn't have four-wheel drive, and it's a little slick out there."

"I didn't hear it start to rain," Kate said. Usually she could hear the rain on the roof of the shop.

Michael hoisted Timmy into his arms while Kate got his powder blue cap and snowsuit. "It's not raining. It's snowing!"

Kate and Lindy both did a double take. In that part of Carolina, it snowed more frequently after Christmas than before. "I thought it was supposed to rain!" Kate said as she fit Timmy's arm into his snowsuit.

Michael nodded as he continued to hold Timmy and assist Kate in getting their son ready to go out into the cold winter weather. "That's what the forecast said until the temperature dropped below freezing."

Quickly, they closed up shop. Outside, picturesque Franklin Street was quickly turning into a winter wonderland. They drove through the college town, admiring the pristine white layer of snow adorning the stately redbrick buildings and rolling hills, abundant shade trees and redbrick sidewalks. Michael dropped Lindy at her off-campus apartment, then drove Kate and Timmy to her condo. With the university on break and the majority of students home for the holiday, the town was a lot quieter.

They knocked as much snow off their shoes as they could before heading inside. Kate took off her shoes while Michael held Timmy, then did the same for him. "Want me to bathe Timmy or whip something up for dinner?" Michael asked, as together they got Timmy out of his snowsuit and cap.

This is what it would be like, Kate thought, *if Mi-*

chael continued to live here even after the Christmas holidays. But that hadn't come up.

Telling herself to let the future take care of itself, Kate promised herself she would revel in what they had, forgo her inherent need for plans and concentrate solely on the present from now through Christmas.

Kate smiled. "Why don't we both cook dinner and bathe him together tonight? Then I can nurse him and put him down for the night." Kate knew they didn't have a lot of time left before the holiday—less than a week—but she wanted it all to count. So that when she did ask the question she was planning to ask him, Michael wouldn't be either surprised or likely to oppose her.

DINNER WAS a relaxed affair, and so was Timmy's bath. Half an hour later, the condo was quiet except for the sounds of the Christmas carols playing softly on the stereo.

The mood for love was set.

"Timmy asleep?" Michael asked, as she joined him in the living room.

Kate nodded and sank down on the sofa beside him. She was still wearing what she'd worn to work—one of her prettiest dresses, a silky tea-length navy Laura Ashley with a close-fitting bodice and lacy round collar and a row of close-set pearl buttons down the front. Navy stockings and matching suede shoes had completed her outfit. "He's out like a light. He was up most of the afternoon, so he should sleep like a lion tonight."

Michael laced an arm about her shoulders and drew her into the comforting curve of his arm. His only concession to being home for the evening had been to take off his tie and roll up his sleeves. He looked incredibly handsome in his khaki slacks and dark green, ecru and khaki plaid dress shirt. "It's hard to believe he's already sleeping through the night, isn't it?"

Kate turned her head into the solid warmth of Michael's shoulder as she surveyed the glittering Christmas tree they had picked out and decorated together. She inhaled the brisk masculine scent of his cologne and skin that was uniquely him. "I know what you mean. He's changing so fast," she murmured. And their six weeks together was going by much too quickly.

"We say that now," Michael replied in a hushed, deeply sentimental voice. "Wait another seventeen years."

A poignant silence fell between them. Kate sighed as she toyed with one of the buttons on his shirt. "It's funny, he's been here less than six weeks, yet I can hardly remember what it was like before I had him."

Michael's gaze gentled compassionately. "I know what you mean. He's come to be such a big part of my life—of both our lives now."

"Which is the way it's supposed to be," Kate said softly.

Michael grinned. "I think so, too. And speaking of the way things are supposed to be," he teased, waggling his eyebrows and shifting her onto his lap, "let's go back to that conversation you and Lindy had in the shop this evening, and you can tell me how I can improve on that nine and a half rating on the red-hot lover scale and make it a ten."

Kate flushed at the immediate—and ever present—resurgence of his desire for her. A roller coaster of thrilling tension and unbearable anticipation swept through her. She lifted her chin and tried not to feel so much like a newlywed anticipating her first night with her new husband. "You're serious, aren't you? You really want me to get into that."

His eyes glittered with an ardent light. Lower still, she felt the burgeoning of his desire. "I don't want you yearning for anything, Kate," Michael told her, as his body grew ever warmer next to hers. "So let's start with the way I hold you in my arms. What do you think about this?" He tried but could not quite quell a grin as he settled her more firmly on his lap and anchored both arms about her waist. "Is this okay?" he drawled with comically exaggerated seriousness.

Kate's heart pounded and she felt the oh-so-familiar fluidness between her thighs, the feeling she had every time Michael kissed her. "It's great."

Michael surveyed her from head to toe. "And this?" The roguish amusement in his eyes deepened as he tunneled his hands through her hair. He cupped the back of her neck and tilted her head to his. "What do you think of this?" he said as his lips descended ever so slowly to hers.

His kiss was both harder and sweeter than what she expected. It left her feeling ravished and wanted and utterly sure he was the man she had been waiting for all her life. "Definitely a ten," Kate decreed breathlessly, when at last he broke it off and lifted his head.

"Aw, shucks," he drawled humorously, as his tongue traced down her throat and he began opening the buttons on the front of her dress with exasperating slowness. "And I was shooting for a hundred."

"Then let's try again." Needing to prove he wasn't

the only one capable of throwing their senses into an uproar, Kate fit her lips to his and kissed him as thoroughly and completely as she knew how. She knew this wasn't what he had planned—her taking the lead in this little experiment of his—but right now she couldn't help herself, she thought as she moved against him pliantly, arcing forward and fitting her breasts against his chest. She wanted to taste the flavor that was uniquely him. She lifted her arms to wreathe them around his neck and kissed him deeply, over and over, until all the layers of restraint fell away. Finally, she lifted her lips from his and rested her forehead against his while they both caught their breath.

"Damn, Kate." Michael sighed his contentment.

Kate knew she'd done well. So far all they'd done was kiss, and he was hard as a rock.

Leaning back, she began to unbutton his shirt. "I know," she teased. "I'm shameless, aren't I?"

Michael nodded. "But then," he kissed her again as his hands resumed unbuttoning the front of her dress, "so am I."

He worked his way to her waist, then parted the edges of her dress. He slipped his hand inside the fabric and smoothed from the silk of her shoulders to the uppermost curves of her breasts. Ever so delicately he traced the white flesh spilling out of the lacy cups. She trembled in response, her flesh swelling to fill his palm. "I want to send you right off the scale and beyond," he confessed as he continued to caress her. "But first I need to know how that doctor visit of yours went this morning."

Kate drew a breath and kept her eyes on his. With

her whole body throbbing and yearning for him, now was not the time to be shy. "I got the all clear."

His eyes darkened dangerously. "So we can…"

Kate nodded, knowing she would go mad if he didn't take her to bed this instant. "Make love all the way, yes, absolutely."

Michael unfastened the front closure of her bra and bared her creamy breasts and rosy nipples to view. His fingers traced from base to tip, then he bent and laved the nipples with his tongue, until they were tight and achy and her hips rose instinctively to meet him. "When?" he whispered.

Dizziness swept through Kate in waves. "Now's good for me."

Michael looked at her and smiled. The hot, melting feeling in Kate's stomach grew. His lips covered her in a desperation and a hunger she not only felt but also understood. "For me, too," he whispered.

Michael turned off the light so the only illumination in the room was the beautifully lit Christmas tree. "Wait here." He went up the stairs and returned with a blanket and several pillows. He put them on the floor next to the tree, then took Kate's hand and led her to the makeshift bed. With Christmas carols still playing softly on the stereo, he began to undress her, removing dress, bra and panty hose until she stood before him dressed only in her navy blue bikini panties. He bent and kissed her breasts, laving the raised nipples with his tongue until a hunger and a need built within her unlike any she had ever known.

Kate gasped.

"More?"

She nodded as his mouth met hers, his kisses as hot and searching and rapacious as his touch. His fingers slid inside the elastic of her bikini panties. He touched and rubbed and stroked. It had never been like this for her. No one had ever loved her so fiercely and possessively.

"That's it," he murmured as she opened his shirt and caressed his chest. "Touch me, too." She slid her hands across the rock hard muscles of his stomach. Lower still, to the cold metal of his belt buckle. Still kissing him, she unbuckled his belt, sucked in a shallow breath and slid down the zipper. Like hers, his skin was so hot to the touch it burned. She pushed away the fabric, lowering his trousers, then his boxers, not stopping until the hard ridge in his pants sprang free. Marveling at his smooth, velvety hardness, the depth of his need, she caressed him from base to tip. Desperate to feel all of him against all of her, she surged against him. She wanted to feel everything, every tremble, every gasp. As did he.

"I've got to have you," he whispered against her mouth.

"Now," she agreed.

He whisked aside her panties, kicked off his trousers and dispensed with his shirt. His arms still around her, he guided her to the blanket, his body trembling with the effort it took to contain his need. He stretched out beside her. Kate found herself on her back, knees raised, cupping the outside of his hips. His hands found her first, then his lips, then his tongue. Too soon, he was pushing her past the edge. She shuddered as he slid his way up her body. He kissed her again, not stopping till she moaned, then, eyes glazed with passion, cupped her hips and ever so slowly and carefully settled against her, the tip of his manhood pressing against her delicate folds. She moved to receive him, and he pushed all the way inside, penetrating her with his hot, hard length. He groaned and began to move inside her, slowly at first, deliberately, until she spread her thighs and arched her back and brought her whole body to meet him.

Kate moaned and writhed beneath Michael. So this is what it felt like to be loved, really loved, she thought, as her whole body urged him on to release. Awash in sensation, she closed her eyes, accepted his kiss. Their bodies took up the same timeless mating rhythm as their mouths until Kate was once again quaking with sensations she could hardly bear.

Michael pressed into her as deeply as he could go, then withdrew. And then he filled her again. Withdrew. Taking her again and again. Until both of them were so lost in the pleasure and each other that satisfaction exploded inside her like fireworks on the Fourth of July. Then he thrust forward, surging into her, his release coming quickly, explosively on the heels of hers.

Unable to let each other go, they cuddled close and eventually made love again with the same thorough, soul-satisfying blend of passion and tenderness. Afterward, they drifted off to sleep, still wrapped in each other's arms.

When they woke, Michael carried Kate up the stairs to the master bedroom. He followed her down to the mattress and stretched out over her.

"I wish we'd made Timmy the old-fashioned way," he whispered as he looked into her face and stroked her hair with gentle fingers.

"Me, too," Kate whispered as she wrapped her arms around him and surged up to meet him. She realized she felt more connected to Michael than she had ever felt to anyone before.

"But since we didn't, we're going to have to make do," Michael whispered as he bent to kiss her again with shattering intensity. And make do they did. Binding minds and hearts, souls and lives, in a way that could not—would never—be undone.

WHEN MICHAEL AND KATE woke the next morning, she had only to look at the expression on Michael's face to realize he felt as blissfully at peace, as glowingly content as she did. She realized she had never felt more loved in her life, even if Michael hadn't said the words she wanted to hear.

She knew "I love you" would come in time. And so would Christmas. With only five shopping days left, she had very little time to decide exactly how to show Michael how much she cared about him and wanted him to stay in her life.

"Can you baby-sit for me this morning?" Kate asked as soon as she and Michael had finished the breakfast dishes.

Michael closed the distance between them in a single stride and anchored a hand around her waist. "Not running away from me, are you?" he teased, tugging her close.

"On the contrary," Kate said as she splayed her hands across the warmth and solidity of his chest and breathed in the sexy masculine scent that was uniquely him. She was running *to* him. Trying to figure a way to keep him in her life.

"Because I wouldn't want that," Michael continued softly as he traced the curve of her lips with his fingertips. "Not today. Not ever."

"I just need to do some Christmas shopping." Kate smiled. "I want to get something special—" *for you,* she added silently "—and I haven't had much of a chance. And since you've got the day off, too, maybe we could spend the rest of it together, doing something special." Something that would add to the love they'd expressed for each other last night.

Michael frowned. "I'd like to—"

"But you can't," Kate guessed, unable to contain her disappointment. Was it her imagination or was he pulling away from her again?

"I can sit for Timmy this morning, but this afternoon I have some shopping of my own to do," Michael said, giving Kate the impression he was choosing his words with care. "And after that I promised a friend a favor," he stated more easily. "Between the two, it's liable to take all afternoon, at the very least."

Kate waited, but Michael didn't elaborate.

With effort, Kate pushed her uneasiness away. Just because Michael didn't want to tell her every little detail of what he was doing did not mean he was hiding anything from her the way Kirk had hid things from her. It didn't mean he had a secret agenda she knew nothing about.

"So, what time do you need me to be back?" Kate asked, refusing to let herself worry over problems that did not exist.

"Noon."

"No problem." Kate could easily accommodate his schedule. "When should Timmy and I expect you back?" she asked with a smile.

Michael paused. A distant look came into his eyes. "I'm not sure how long all this is going to take," he replied cautiously after a moment. Still holding her close, he kissed her brow and held her tight. "But I'll come home as soon as I can, I promise."

MICHAEL WAS still wrestling with his guilt over having deliberately misled Kate when he met up with her mother hours later. Thankfully, he told himself, the days of keeping Carolyn's confidence would soon be over. And then there'd be nothing between he and Kate.

"Saul Zimmerman said he'd call you?"

Carolyn nodded. "As soon as the last of the test results are in, which should be sometime this afternoon. And then I'm to go right over to his office and discuss the treatment in depth." She seemed nervous, jittery as she slid a slim cell phone into her purse before heading out of her house. "I can't believe I'm finally going to find out what's wrong with me."

"The last six weeks have been an ordeal, I know," Michael sympathized bluntly as he assisted Carolyn into his Jeep.

Carolyn shot him a grateful look. "I'm not sure I could have weathered it alone."

"No one should have to go through something like this alone." Michael held her door and waited for her to get situated. Which was why Carolyn should have told her family. And why, when she wouldn't, he'd had to step in in their absence.

As he drove the short distance to the shopping mall, Michael and Carolyn talked about the last round of medical tests she'd had. By the time Michael had explained what kind of results Carolyn could expect from each, they'd arrived. Unfortunately, that close to Christmas, even on a weekday, it was difficult to find a parking place. Michael had to drive around twice before they spotted one. Inside the mall, it was just as busy. "Next year we'll be bringing Timmy to see Santa," Michael said, as they walked briskly past the children and parents in line at Santa's workshop.

"We as in you and Kate?"

Michael nodded as joy over what he'd found with Kate filled his heart. If all went as he hoped, this time next year they would really be a family, and he'd have a wife and a son to come home to every night.

"So what's going on here, Michael?" Carolyn asked as they entered the jewelry store. "You strike me as a man who is perfectly capable of picking out a gift for a woman without any help whatsoever."

Michael stopped in front of a display of necklaces. Carolyn was right. He'd never had trouble picking out a gift for a woman before, but this last week he had been to the mall three different times to look at jewelry and been unable to even come close to making a decision. "I wanted to get Kate something really nice for Christmas."

"Good idea." Carolyn smiled her approval.

"The only problem is I haven't known Kate long enough to know her taste in jewelry." Michael studied the array of necklaces and still had no clue what to get.

Fortunately, Carolyn wasn't shy about putting in her two cents. "She already has an excellent set of pearls, but she doesn't have any emeralds, and they'd probably be beautiful with her green eyes."

Michael knew Kate would be beautiful in anything, but he liked the idea of her in great jewelry, too. Yet, when the clerk behind the counter lifted the emerald display out of the case and put it in front of him, Michael was unmoved.

"You don't like any of these, either?" Carolyn asked.

Michael shrugged. "I can't really tell how they would look on."

The clerk smiled. "Perhaps your companion would be so kind—"

Carolyn shrugged. "Certainly."

Michael watched as the clerk put a necklace around Carolyn's throat.

"The matching earrings are lovely, too."

At the clerk's urging, Carolyn put those on. "What do you think?"

Carolyn seemed to like them a lot. Michael still couldn't imagine them around Kate's neck. "It's a beautiful set."

Carolyn caught the hesitation in his voice. "But?"

"I'm not sure it's really Kate." He wanted this to be a Christmas Kate never forgot. Belatedly, he realized a necklace and earrings set weren't going to do it, and he told Carolyn so.

"Maybe perfume, then?" Carolyn suggested helpfully.

Michael shook his head, knowing that wouldn't send the message he wanted to send, either. "She has a huge bottle of her favorite on her dresser."

Without warning, the cell phone in Carolyn's purse began to ring. Looking abruptly apprehensive, Carolyn withdrew the slim phone from her purse, unfolded it and put it to her ear.

She listened intently, tears that could have been happy or sad streaming down her face, then thanked the person on the other end for letting her know and said she'd be in to see him right away.

Michael waited for her to cut the connection. "That was Saul Zimmerman?" he asked tensely.

"Yes." In a choked voice, Carolyn told Michael, "The news was so good he couldn't wait to tell me. Michael, I have a form of arthritis in my ribs, not cancer."

Christmas had just come early, Michael thought in relief. "Costochondritis." Michael murmured the medical term for her illness.

Carolyn nodded, confirming that was indeed it. "Dr. Zimmerman says it can be controlled by medication. My weight loss and the light-headedness were due to anxiety." Sobbing openly, Carolyn threw her arms about his neck and hugged him fiercely. "Oh, Michael, can you believe it? I'm actually going to be okay!"

"YOU HAVE TO tell Kate, Lindy and Ted," Michael said firmly after they had cut short their shopping excursion and headed to his Jeep so he could drive her to Saul's office to pick up her prescriptions and talk to Saul about her treatment.

For a moment, Carolyn said nothing. "The girls may forgive me, but Ted's not going to want to hear it after all I put him through the last few months. In fact," she continued, as she stopped in front of the Jeep's passenger door, "after the way I've hurt him, he may not want me back after all."

Michael opened her door for her. "He may surprise you. And being honest with your family could be the best early Christmas present you could ever give them."

Carolyn blew out a gusty sigh. "All right, you've convinced me to tell them everything," she conceded as he slipped behind the wheel, "but only after I've had a chance to start the medicine and know for sure it's working. How long does it usually take?"

Not long, Michael thought, relieved this ordeal of not knowing if Carolyn was going to live or die was coming to an end. "Generally, the medication takes effect anywhere from a few hours to a few days. It depends on the severity of the symptoms and the person."

In the meantime, Michael thought, he had his own future to insure. So, after he dropped Carolyn off at home, he called Kate, told her he was going to be even later than he had first thought, but he definitely would be home by nine.

He had to face it, he thought, his mind revving with excitement, as he headed to the mall. There was only one Christmas present he wanted to get for Kate, only one thing that would properly convey the way he felt about her. And it was something he had no qualms about picking out alone.

Chapter Eleven

"Christmas is still five days away," Kate reminded Michael hours later as the two of them sat in front of the Christmas tree.

Michael's eyes sparkled. "I know, but I want to give you your present early."

Kate grinned at Michael, knowing she'd never been this crazy in love with anyone in her life. "I want to give you yours, too." In fact, she was brimming with holiday spirit. Maybe because Christmas—in the form of Michael and Timmy—had come early this year.

She handed Michael a small box. "Any guesses?"

Michael eyed it with mock solemnness. "A new billfold?"

"Nope."

"A cassette."

"Wrong again." Kate's eyes glowed with teasing lights. "You've got one guess left."

"A photo of you and Timmy that I can put in my billfold."

Almost, Kate thought, except what she was giving him was better than any photograph. "Open it."

Michael unwrapped it. Inside was a gold key ring. On it was a house key with his name engraved on it.

He looked at Kate, not sure he understood. Kate took his hands in hers. "I don't want you to leave after Christmas, Michael. I want you to continue to live here with Timmy and me." *For now and forever,* she thought.

Michael grinned as though he'd just won the lottery and had a secret besides. Kate paused. "Why are you smiling?"

Michael handed her a large box wrapped with silver and gold paper and matching ribbon and bow. "Open your gift from me and you'll see."

With trembling fingers, Kate unwrapped the big box. Another smaller box was inside that, and so on, and so on, until she came to a small square velvet ring box. Was it what she thought—what she hadn't even dared hope for? Kate wondered.

Her hands were trembling.

"Go on," Michael said softly, watching her with serious velvety brown eyes. "Open it."

Eyes brimming, hands still shaking, Kate flipped open the lid. When she saw what was inside, her breath escaped in a rush. She laid a hand across her heart. "Oh, Michael," she whispered emotionally, as she stared at the marquis-cut diamond ring in a platinum gold setting. "It's beautiful," she breathed.

"Marry me, Kate," Michael said in a low, rusty-sounding voice. As she looked into his eyes, she saw he was as happy as she was. "Marry me and make it official. Make the three of us a family once and for all."

KATE AND MICHAEL bundled Timmy up and applied for a license and got their blood tests first thing the next morning. "Now all we have to do is set a date," Michael said as the trio returned home.

"Any particular time you have in mind?" Kate asked, as she brought Timmy inside and helped him out of his snowsuit.

Michael nodded. "Christmas Eve."

"Then Christmas Eve, it is," Kate said.

Anxious to share their good news, they telephoned Michael's parents and talked to them together via speakerphone.

"That's great news!" Hugh said.

"Absolutely fabulous," Ginny agreed. "When's the date?"

Michael told them as he linked hands with Kate. "Naturally, we want you all to be there," he finished.

"We wouldn't miss it for the world!" his parents said, and promised to spread the word to Michael's four sisters and their families, too.

"One side of the family down, one to go," Michael said when he hung up the phone.

The happiness in Kate's eyes faded a tiny bit before she recovered with a sunny smile. "I want to tell my parents together, too, and the only way to do that, since they're still separated, is to get them here in person." She picked up the phone. "I'll call them and ask them to come over right away."

"So what's all this about?" Ted asked Michael and Kate the moment he and her mother walked in.

Michael took their coats while Kate ushered them to the sofa, waited until they sat down, then delivered the news. "Michael asked me to marry him, and I said yes," she announced proudly. "We're getting married on Christmas Eve."

Her father's expression went from curious to disapproving in nothing flat. Then he bellowed, "Over my dead body!"

KATE BLINKED. "I know you don't like impetuous decisions, but given how strongly I feel about Michael and vice versa, I thought you'd be happy for me!"

"I'll second that," Carolyn said, sending a resentment-filled glance Ted's way.

Ted glared at Carolyn before turning to Kate. "Honey, I was hoping not to have to tell you this until I was absolutely sure what had been going on and why, but you've left me no choice. I really think you should know." Ted went out to his car, then returned with a thick manila envelope stamped Confidential in his hand. Wordlessly, he handed it to Kate.

She stared at it as if it were a bomb about to go off. "What is this?"

Ted grimaced and glared at Michael, then Carolyn. "Proof of the duplicity that's been going on."

As Kate stared at them, stunned, Michael shot Carolyn a helpless look. "Tell her," he directed flatly, "before she finds out another way."

"Tell me what?" Kate demanded as she continued to wonder what in heaven's name was going on. She looked from Michael to her mother and back again. And then, with a sinking feeling of been-there, done-that, it began to hit her. "You two know what's in this envelope, don't you?" she guessed, beginning to feel a little sick.

"I have an idea," Michael admitted reluctantly.

"You should," Ted shot back cantankerously, continuing to send accusing looks Michael's way. "Since you've been having an affair with my wife!"

"WHERE IN THE WORLD did you ever get an idea like that?" Kate demanded of her father, aghast.

"They've been secretly meeting for weeks now." Ted removed the manila envelope from Kate's limp fingers and withdrew a stack of neatly typed papers and photos. "Here's a list of dates and times. Initially, I thought the detective I hired had to be wrong. I figured the meetings were about you and Timmy. But then I saw these photos, and I knew we'd both been had."

Reluctantly, Kate looked at the photos her father handed her. She saw Michael wrapping his arm about her mother's shoulders, helping her into his Jeep. The two of them conversing with unmistakable intimacy and emotion. Kate's lower lip trembled. A horrible feeling of déjà vu swept over her as Ted produced more photos of Michael and Carolyn in a popular local jewelry store. It didn't take a rocket scientist to see that her mother was trying on expensive jewelry for Michael's benefit. More incriminating still, Carolyn looked happier, more elated, than she had in weeks. Kate felt sick inside at the depth of the betrayal.

She looked at Michael, whose guilt and misery were written all over his face, and then at her mother, who looked equally upset. Tears blurred Kate's eyes as she advanced on her mother and demanded hotly, "Tell me you were just helping Michael select my engagement ring!"

Carolyn sighed.

Michael gave Carolyn a look filled with intimate knowledge and some sort of telegraphed command that neither Kate nor Ted could begin to decipher.

Carolyn sighed. "I'm afraid I can't take credit for

that. We didn't even look at rings when I was in the store with him,'' Carolyn told Kate honestly. ''But jewelry was something he was considering for you as a Christmas gift. That's why I was trying the necklace and earrings on for him.''

''And that must also be why you're hugging him like you just won the lottery,'' Ted said jealously to his wife.

''You can't seriously think Michael and I are involved!'' Carolyn said to Ted, irate.

''Then you tell me what to make of all this!'' Ted hollered.

An angry silence reigned. Kate continued to study the photos. The hugging and even the secret yuletide shopping expedition she could dismiss as something that just looked bad on the surface.

But the list of dates, times and places where Michael and her mother had met repeatedly and secretly was something else again.

She couldn't believe how effectively she'd been cut out of the loop! For what purpose, Kate thought furiously, she could not begin to imagine.

''Now, Kate,'' Carolyn said hastily, reading Kate's mind. She grabbed Kate's arm before she could flee. ''Before you and your father jump to any more conclusions, let me explain.''

''So you see,'' Carolyn concluded happily when she'd told one and all the whole sad story, ''everything's going to be fine! I'm not dying after all! And furthermore, I'm going to be feeling much better now that I know what's wrong with me and have started on medication to control my symptoms. It's only been eighteen hours, and already I'm feeling a lot of relief."

Michael watched as Ted shot his wife an accusing look. "You should have told me you were ill," he said gruffly.

Carolyn looked deeply into Ted's eyes, the heartache and regret on her face unmistakable. "You're right. I should have. Believe me, if I'd have known then what I know now, I would have. At any rate—" Carolyn dashed away a tear or two before she sent Michael a grateful look "—I'm sorry I kept you all in the dark."

"I'm just glad you're okay." Kate hugged her mom as she choked back tears.

"Me, too," Ted said, though—unlike Kate—he made no attempt to hug his estranged wife.

Carolyn looked at Ted and shook her head at the photos spread out on Kate's coffee table. "I can't believe you hired a detective!"

Neither could Michael.

Ted shrugged. "The firm has one on retainer anyway. If I was losing you, I wanted to know why."

Carolyn looked at Kate and Michael, then at Ted. She closed the distance between her and her husband, and after a moment's hesitation took his hand in hers. "Maybe you and I should go somewhere and talk now that the situation is under control," she suggested.

Ted looked at their joined hands. After a moment, he nodded and said tersely, "Maybe we should."

But whether or not there was going to be a reconciliation in the works was yet to be seen, Michael thought, as the two elder Montgomerys said their goodbyes and left.

"So what do you think?" Michael asked Kate the moment they were alone. He echoed Carolyn's conciliatory words. "Is the situation under control?"

Kate frowned. "You tell me."

MICHAEL STUDIED the expression on her face. "You're angry," he observed quietly.

"You bet I'm angry!" Kate shot back, thinking about all the times she had been worried sick about her mother and father and had poured her heart out to Michael. She thought about all the times he had gone behind her back. And she had trusted him so much, she had loved him so well and so blindly, that she hadn't had a clue anything was amiss! Kate continued to pace. "I can't believe my mother was sick for weeks and didn't tell me!"

Michael drew a deep breath. "She was trying to protect you."

Kate whirled to face him. Resentment stiffened her from head to toe, forced her shoulders back. "And what about you, Michael, what's your excuse?"

Michael grimaced and drove a hand through his hair. He'd been afraid Kate would react like this when she finally found out. "I wanted to tell you—you don't know how much—but I knew if I did your mother might just get scared and run off somewhere without getting the medical treatment she obviously needed. I couldn't take that chance."

"So instead you lied to me for weeks." Kate bristled. She gave him a deeply disappointed look. "You hid behind the drapes when my father showed up unexpectedly, which caused no end of grief and humiliation for him, and you went behind my back and saw my mother and blithely made a fool out of me."

"Your mother pushed me behind the drapes to spare your father's feelings." Michael scowled as his patience was tested to the absolute limit. "I didn't come out and confront your father because I didn't want to make their already strained relationship worse! And as far as what went on between you and me as I very reluctantly kept your mother's confidence, there was nothing blithe about anything I said or did."

But none of that mattered, Michael swiftly realized as he studied Kate's face, because she thought he had betrayed her, pure and simple.

Kate folded her arms. "Tell me something, Michael. Why did you sign that agreement my father drew up that pledged you would never sue me for custody of Timmy?"

"Because," Michael explained as he attempted to comfort her by putting a possessive arm about her shoulders, "you needed to trust me, and I knew you couldn't do it unless I gave you reason to do so."

Kate extricated herself from his arms, crossed to the other side of the room and stood with her back to their beautifully decorated Christmas tree. "Or were you buying time to romance me?" Kate asked icily.

It hadn't been like that, but Michael knew he'd be wasting his breath if he tried to defend himself on that score.

Kate propped her hands on her hips and turned to face him like a warrior prepared for battle. "Tell me, assuming our romance ends today, what are your intentions toward Timmy?"

Michael's outward demeanor remained calm, but his voice was a dangerous purr as he reminded her,

"He's my son. I love him. Just the same way I love you."

"I see." Kate leveled an accusing finger at his chest and advanced a step. "And if I were to try to take him away from you at this point, then what, Michael?"

Michael sighed and retorted wearily, "You'd never be that cruel, Kate."

"Suppose I was." Kate angled her chin a notch higher and kept her eyes on his. "Would you stick to the agreement my father had you sign?"

His voice quiet in deference to the sleeping baby upstairs, Michael replied, "If you were that cruel now, which again I do not believe, I'd do whatever I have to do to stay in his life."

"I see," Kate said icily. "Including getting me to marry you?"

A muscle worked in Michael's jaw. "You know that's not true."

"Do I?" Kate shot him a look that all but accused him of being a traitor. "Our agreement that you live in was only for the first six weeks of Timmy's life. *If* you hadn't made love to me, *if* you hadn't proposed marriage, *if* I hadn't accepted, you'd be moving out a few days from now. Which no doubt explains the rush to get married on Christmas Eve."

Silence fell between them before Michael said, "My actions aren't the problem here, Kate."

"They aren't?" she echoed hollowly, as she began to pace agitatedly back and forth.

"No, they aren't." Michael fell into step behind her. "You're just looking for an excuse."

"To do what?" Kate demanded, whirling to face him.

Michael grabbed her and hauled her into his arms. "To wedge some distance between us."

Kate scowled at him. She wrested herself from his grip and pushed her hands through the silky ends of her pale blond hair. "Maybe that isn't such a bad idea."

Michael stared at her. "What are you talking about?" he demanded.

Kate drew a tremulous breath as all her doubts were telegraphed plainly on her face. "We rushed into this."

Michael knew that. He also knew that all the time in the world would not have changed anything. He still would have fallen head over heels in love with Kate. And she still would have fallen head over heels in love with him.

But figuring Kate was not about to concede that point in her current frame of mind, Michael let it go and said wearily, "Look, why don't we forget having a wedding with both our families present, forget making a big deal about this, and just elope?" Maybe if they went with their feelings, concentrated on the bond they'd forged with each other and with Timmy, they could work everything else out later.

Kate looked at the diamond engagement ring on her left hand. "Eloping isn't a solution, Michael," Kate said sadly.

"Meaning what?" Michael demanded, refusing to consider letting all the love they'd found be thrown away. "You want to go ahead with our plans to marry here in the condo Christmas Eve?"

"No." Kate spelled it out plainly. "I mean I don't want to get married at all right now."

"Why not?" Michael demanded.

"Because this is all happening way too fast."

Michael stared at her, wondering what the last weeks had been about. Had he been fooling himself? Seeing things in Kate—and in their relationship—that didn't exist? Or had it all been real—the love, the tenderness, the laughter, the passion—and was it Kate who was refusing to see the truth? He walked closer and took her by the shoulders. "What are you saying?" he whispered hoarsely, unable to contain his hurt, "that you don't trust me?"

"No. That's just it." Tears filled her eyes as she looked at him. "I do trust you and know that you would never intentionally do anything to hurt me or Timmy." She swallowed hard and pushed on in a low, trembling voice. "But I also know that we would never have met if it hadn't been for Timmy. We would never have lived under the same roof. I also know we wouldn't feel this close."

And that was a problem? That they'd grown close? None of this made sense! But then, maybe it didn't have to, he thought, his every protective instinct going into overdrive. He gently touched her face, said dryly, "I didn't ask Timmy to marry me, Kate, I asked you."

Kate was silent, refusing to acknowledge his attempt to gently goad her into a better mood as she backed away from him. Impatiently, she rubbed the back of her neck, then crossed her arms at her waist. "I know that, and I know there's been a lot of romance between us." Kate drew in a breath. "What I *don't* know is if we would have felt that giddy and romantic if we hadn't shared a baby." She turned her troubled glance to him. "What I don't know is if that kind of euphoria will last as the baby grows older.

All I know for sure is that everything is happening way too fast for all of us and that we need more time. Time apart as well as together. Before we make any major life-changing decisions."

"Meaning you want me to move out?" Michael guessed grimly as all his hopes and dreams for the future came crashing to the floor.

"I think it's best," Kate said sadly, even as her eyes filled with a mixture of bittersweet resignation and longing, "yes."

MICHAEL HAD BEEN this route before. With Valerie, when she kept saying she wanted to have children, too, she just wasn't sure when. He wasn't going through it again with Kate on the issue of marriage. He wasn't going to give everything he had to give and have his hopes raised only to have his heart smashed into a million pieces.

"Time won't help, Kate," he said, aware he'd never felt more bitterly disillusioned or hurt than he did at that moment. "I already know how I feel." He raked her with a glance. "Obviously, you do, too."

Kate looked at him as if he were a stranger she had no idea how to deal with. "Michael—"

"Look, Kate. I love you and want to marry you. You don't want to marry me." *What else is there to say?* he wondered bitterly. *I don't love you and never did? Everything we felt for each other—or thought we felt—was a lie?*

She looked as though she wanted to punch something. He knew just how she felt. Finally, she gritted her teeth and spelled it out for him. "I want time, Michael."

"To do what?" he demanded impatiently.

Color flowed into her cheeks, and her chin took on a stubborn tilt. "Time to plan things better. I want to back up and start over and have a long, slow courtship and maybe an even longer engagement—one where there are no secrets and I don't feel so clueless. I want us both to think about this and know it's the right thing for the long haul."

On the surface, her request sounded reasonable. Underneath, it was the end to all his dreams. Michael sighed, the weariness in him, the disillusionment, the disappointment going soul deep. "If I thought that was all it was, I'd give it to you, Kate, no problem. But my gut tells me you're scared and are looking for a way out—a way to end things more gracefully." And that, he didn't want to give her. If it was over, he wanted it over clean and quick. No drawn-out endings. No dead-end love affairs or marriages destined to end in divorce. No dashing his heart—and hopes—to pieces.

Her emotions in turmoil, Kate bit her lip and tried again. "Look, I know you think I'm being unreasonable here—"

"And then some."

"But I can't help it, Michael! I'm uncomfortable when things happen too quickly and spontaneously." Kate waved her arms, then began to pace like a lecturing professor in front of a class. "The bottom line is, my life is always fine when I take my time and plan things out and then follow the plan I've devised for myself to the letter." She turned to him, green eyes blazing, determined, it seemed, to put him in his place. "It's when I do things on impulse—like marry Kirk shortly after I decided not to go to law school— or inviting you to move in with Timmy and me on the spur of the moment because I wanted to give you a chance to bond with him—that things go all wrong.''

Michael decided to deal with this situation calmly even if she wouldn't. ''You can plan things and organize your life all you want, Kate, but you can't organize your feelings away. Feelings—like love—just happen. And you either trust in that or you don't. But if you don't trust what you feel in here—'' Michael indicated his heart as he loomed over her ''—there's not a chance the rest of it will ever work.'' It didn't matter how much time they took or how well they planned.

''Then it's over?'' Kate said.

Michael nodded. He stepped closer, his commanding look intensifying with every second that passed. ''If you delay the wedding, it has to be.''

Obviously not about to be pressured into anything, Kate removed her ring.

''I'll still want to see Timmy,'' Michael warned grimly.

Tears streamed down Kate's face. ''I want you to do that, too.'' A sob caught in her throat. She turned and ran from the room.

Chapter Twelve

"I know it's none of my business," Lindy told Michael several days later in the emergency room staff lounge. "But I just can't sit around and do nothing when Christmas is tomorrow and my sister's more miserable than she has ever been in her entire life!"

Michael steeled himself against any more heartache where one very fetching blonde was concerned. "What do you mean?" he asked grimly as he grabbed the Santa suit out of his locker. He didn't know why he'd let the nurses in pediatrics talk him into handing out toys. He didn't have any Christmas spirit, either. But the busier he stayed these days, the better.

Lindy lounged against a tabletop and watched Michael attach the pillow stomach to his midriff. "Kate's lost every ounce of Christmas spirit since you two split up. Oh, she talks to Timmy and plays with him and is a good mother and all that, just as you would expect, but the happiness that was in her face every time I looked at her—the joy she'd been taking in life lately—it's all gone."

Like that was his fault? Michael fumed, exasperated. "It was her decision to call off the wedding and ask me to move out." He hadn't wanted to go. If it were up to him, he'd still be there. Hell, if it were up to him, they'd be getting married today!

"I know that."

"So why are you here talking to me?" Michael kicked off his shoes and hitched a pair of red velvet pants on over his scrubs.

Lindy put the candy canes Gourmet Gifts To Go had donated to the children's ward into the burlap sack of goodies Michael would fling over his shoulder. "Because you're the only one who can fix things!"

Michael added spirit gum to the back of Santa's snowy white beard and smoothed it into place. "That kind of thinking, Lindy, along with my habit of taking way too much for granted, is what got me into trouble in the first place." With short, irritated motions, Michael hooked a pair of gold-rimmed spectacles over his ears and nose.

"I thought if I loved Kate—and Timmy—well enough she'd love me back." Michael shook his head as he shoved his arms through the sleeves of the fur-trimmed jacket. "Just like I figured if I wanted children badly enough and was able to communicate that enthusiasm to my first wife, Valerie would lose her lukewarm attitude toward parenthood and want children, too. Well, guess what?" Michael plumped his fake stomach into place and cinched on a thick black leather belt. "It didn't happen with Valerie." Michael shoved his feet into a pair of black boots. "And it didn't happen with Kate, either. The simple act of my wanting something doesn't make the person I'm with want that same something, too." Michael tugged on the white wig and added the Santa hat, all the disillusionment and disappointment he felt rushing to the fore. "And I'm tired of being the patron saint of lost causes."

Lindy emptied the last of the things from Gourmet Gifts To Go into the Santa sack and stood, arms akimbo. "So instead you're going to just blow off this chance to be with Kate and Timmy?"

Christmas was the season of miracles, but Michael didn't see any happening in his future. "As much as I love Timmy and Kate—" he regarded Lindy grimly "—I don't see I have any other choice."

"I KNOW what you're thinking," Kate told Timmy as she drove toward her mother's house that afternoon. "First, you're thinking you wish the weather lady was right for a change and that it really is going to snow tonight. And two, you're wondering why I'm going over to see my mother two hours earlier than we arranged."

Timmy cooed in the infant seat and kicked his feet in response.

Kate smiled at her son. "Well, my answer to the first is I wish it would snow, too. Even though snow would make it a much more romantic Christmas Eve, and at this point in my life, more romance is the last thing in the world I need. And two—" Kate forced back a sigh "—as for us arriving here way ahead of schedule, what can I say? Since Michael left, the condo has seemed really empty." And so lonely, Kate thought, as tears welled in her eyes. She swallowed hard around the lump in her throat, and her voice dropped to a tremulous whisper more suitable to a funeral than the day before Christmas Eve. "I can't believe how much I miss him, Timmy," she whispered, choking back a sob. "And I'm wondering if those feelings I have for him are ever going to go away.''

Timmy waved his arms in front of him like an agitated referee.

Kate tightened her hands on the steering wheel in front of her, barely able to believe she felt so distressed and disillusioned during what should have been the happiest time of the year for them all. Even staying up half the night baking Christmas cookies for all her friends and family hadn't lifted her mood any. Nor had the impromptu visit she and Timmy had made—sans Michael—to see the mall Santa.

She sighed again louder. She knew what her son was likely thinking she ought to do—the same thing everyone was thinking. "You want me to give him a call and tell him I take it all back, don't you?" Timmy kicked in his car seat and waved his arms harder.

Kate took a deep breath and pushed back the tears she felt gathering behind her eyes. "Well, sport, I would if I thought there was any chance at all we could make this family thing work. Not just for a few weeks, but for the long haul. But there really isn't.'' Because Michael had not only betrayed her, he seemed to think what he'd done was no big deal. And it was. Kate needed a man she could trust not to go behind her back for any reason—a man who appreciated the value of planning—a man who would give her the time she needed, and then some, to know she was doing the right thing. And sadly, that just wasn't Michael.

Her mood sobering, Kate parked in front of her mother's house and cut the motor.

When she reached the front door, she used her key,

as was custom, and let herself and Timmy in. The house was unusually silent.

"Mom?" Kate called as she made her way to the sitting room her mother favored. "Mom, are you here?"

There was no answer. There were, however, stacks of cookbooks, flyers from several bakeries, guest lists and several cases of champagne. It looked, Kate thought, as though her mother was planning a party. Which was odd, Kate ruminated, since her mother had already had her annual Christmas open house. Kate looked at Timmy, who seemed not to know what to make of it, either. "Maybe she's upstairs. Let's go see."

Kate climbed the stairs, Timmy in her arms. When she reached the top, she called again. "Mom? Are you home?"

From the far end of the hall, something hit the floor with a definite thud. "Just a minute, Kate!" her mother called, somewhat frantically. "I'll be right there." Before Kate could turn the corner, the master bedroom door slammed.

Kate looked at Timmy as she ducked into her old room and sat on the bed to wait. "If I didn't know better, I'd think my mother really is having an assignation," she told her son drolly. But she knew better. Didn't she?

Seconds later, her mother came into the hall. Hastily belting a robe, she blocked the way to the master bedroom suite. "Kate! You're early!"

Kate studied her mother's flushed, disheveled appearance. "Why aren't you dressed?" she asked curiously, recalling all too well the last time something like this had happened. "It's the middle of the afternoon."

Her mother clapped a hand over her heart. "Oh, dear. Your father and I really didn't want you to find out this way."

"Find out what?" Kate demanded.

Her father stepped out into the hall. He was wearing a robe and grinning from ear to ear. "Your mother and I have decided to reconcile," he announced happily. "We're calling off the divorce."

"Thank heavens!" Kate said, relieved they'd finally come to their senses. Although she couldn't believe she'd caught her own parents en flagrante!

Carolyn and Ted linked hands. Shyly, her mother continued to explain, "Your father came over for dinner last night, and we were up all night talking about everything that's happened over the last six months. And we realized we could have fixed things sooner if we had only talked openly and honestly about our fears as well as our feelings. And helped each other through the rough and uncertain times in our lives, instead of stubbornly trying to go it alone," Carolyn finished.

Ted wrapped a comforting arm around Kate's shoulder. "We think you and Michael are in the same predicament."

"And how is that?" Kate asked dryly as her mother took a cooing Timmy into her arms.

"You got together because the two of you had a baby and you wanted to do the right thing by Timmy. Neither of you expected to find love with each other, but it blossomed right along with your friendship."

That was true, Kate thought. She had loved Michael. Would always love him.

"And you'd still be together if I hadn't pressured Michael to keep my illness secret," Carolyn said, sighing with regret. "And your father hadn't been so suspicious and forced Michael to sign that agreement from the get-go and hired a private detective and spilled the beans to you before Michael and I had a chance to confide in you."

It had been a fairly eventful six weeks, Kate thought with a sigh.

"Which is why your father and I asked you to meet us here later this afternoon," Carolyn finished seriously. "We wanted to tell you what we'd done to try and make it up to you and Michael."

Ted nodded. "And we hope, for Timmy's sake, as well as your own, you'll give it a try."

KATE'S HEART POUNDED as she parked her car in front of Michael's apartment building. Odd that in the six weeks they had lived together, she had never once been here or really felt any curiosity about his life before her. It was almost as if their lives had started the moment they'd found out the two of them were biologically and forever linked as parents to their son, Timmy. It was almost as if she hadn't wanted to acknowledge that he might be able to go on with his life as surely as if they'd never met and been linked together through Timmy.

But now that Michael had reluctantly returned to his previous life and home, she had to wonder if things were really as simple as she—and her parents—wanted to believe. Would Michael forget everything she'd said and done and give her another chance?

There was only one way to find out.

Kate got out of her car and walked through the first flakes of swirling snow to the door. Christmas was the season of miracles. And they were going to have a white Christmas in Chapel Hill for the first time in she didn't know how many years. Maybe, she thought hopefully, there was a miracle here, too.

Before she could even knock, the door opened. Michael, clad in a long wool coat, suit and tie, started through the portal, a stack of gaily wrapped Christmas presents in hand. He stopped short when he saw her. His expression became wary, tense. "Kate." There was no masking his surprise.

"Hello, Michael," Kate said softly.

Michael shifted the packages in his hand as the moment drew out awkwardly between them. He looked her over from head to toe, wordlessly taking in her sexy black evening boots and the long green velvet Christmas dress peeking out from behind the unbuttoned edges of her black wool coat before returning his gaze to the wind-tossed layers of her light blond hair. "Merry Christmas."

Kate licked her suddenly dry lips and felt the self-conscious flush in her cheeks deepen. "Merry Christmas to you, too," she said hoarsely.

"I was just about to leave to bring some presents over to you. They're for Timmy."

Was it too late for a second chance? Kate wondered as she looked at the snow falling overhead. She hoped not. "Timmy's with my mom and dad, at their house. Maybe we can go over there later, after we talk." That was, if everything worked out the way she hoped.

"Sure." Michael stepped back to let her pass.

"Come on in." He shut the door behind them and put down the packages.

Kate immediately noted the absence of a Christmas tree and yuletide decorations among the soft tan leather sofa and chairs, distressed pine furniture and Southwestern rug. "This is nice," Kate said as she looked at the abundance of books and CDs. A real single guy's domain, complete with large-screen TV and stereo. When it came to material possessions, Michael did not seem to be wanting for anything.

"Thanks." Michael tossed off his coat, then helped her with hers. He strode toward her with a determined lazy grace that quickened her pulse. "Listen, before you say anything else, I wanted to apologize for the way I laid down the gauntlet the other day."

Kate stared at him, not sure whether to launch herself into his arms and hope for the best or burst into tears. Only knowing she wanted to do both so badly. "You don't have to do that," she said hoarsely.

"Yes, I do." He braced his hands on his waist, and his brown eyes, so shrewdly direct, lasered in on hers. "I pushed you unconscionably, Kate, and I never meant to do that." He took her hands in both of his. His voice turned low and gravelly. "I promise from now on I'll take things as slowly as you need me to take them, if you'll just give me another chance."

"Oh, Michael," Kate whispered joyfully as tears of happiness slid down her face. "Of course I'll give you another chance. But before we talk about that, I have to tell you something." She swallowed and tipped her head to his. "My parents have done something."

Michael's eyes glinted with a combination of humor and wariness. "Again?" he drawled.

"But I think you're going to like this."

"Let's hope so," Michael quipped as he wrapped his arms around her waist and guided her against him so they were touching length to length. Threading a hand through her hair, he tenderly pushed the silky strands from her face and waited for her to go on.

"They've arranged for a minister and a small gathering of family and friends to be at my mother's home at seven-thirty this evening," Kate told him with a quiet confidence born of love. She leaned against the warm cradle of his arms to look into his face. "The idea being that a wedding would take place," she said softly. "And your family has been invited, too."

Michael's eyes narrowed at her thoughtfully. "Who's getting married?" he asked, his expression giving nothing of his feelings away.

Kate's heart took on a slow, heavy beat as she laid her hands across his chest. "That all depends." *Please...let this work out.*

Michael tightened his grip on her waist. "On what?" he asked, the passion he'd always felt for her gleaming in his eyes.

Kate paused, knowing she was about to take the biggest risk of her life, knowing that she had no plan past this very moment. But knowing if Michael loved her as much as she thought he did, everything would be absolutely okay. Marshaling every ounce of courage she had, she replied tremulously, "On you and me and whether or not you still want to marry me absolutely as soon as possible."

"What about your doubts?" Michael demanded, guiding her closer yet. "Your feeling that we were rushing into this way too fast?"

Finally, Kate noted with a mixture of aggravation

and relief, he seemed to think those were valid concerns. She swallowed around the lump of emotion in her throat. "I don't want to go slow anymore, Michael, just for the sake of going slow. There's no need." Kate ran a hand through his dark hair and looked deep into his eyes. "I know what's in my heart. I've known for weeks now. I love you with all my heart and soul and always will."

Michael hugged her fiercely. He tilted her head to his and kissed her with a thoroughness that was just the beginning. "Oh, Kate," he confessed emotionally, "I love you, too."

Kate released a shaky breath as they drew apart. She needed to tell him everything she had learned about herself. "I admit I was scared, my feelings for you were so strong. I realize now there's a certain amount of discomfort and risk at the beginning of any relationship. But those risks are worth it." Kate stood on tiptoe, wreathed her arms about his neck, and delivered another euphoric kiss "I want to follow my heart, Michael. And my heart is telling me to marry you—now, tonight, just as we originally planned." And she couldn't think of a better time to do that than on Christmas Eve.

"I want that, too." Michael grinned as he pulled an oh-so-familiar ring box from his suit jacket pocket. He opened it, removed the ring and slipped it onto her left hand. "In fact, I was headed over to your place now to try to convince you of the exact same thing."

Kate looked at the engagement ring on her hand and knew it would soon be joined by a wedding band she would wear the rest of her life. "This has certainly been a Christmas season to remember." She sighed contentedly.

Michael kissed the back of her hand. "I'll second that."

Kate grabbed his hand and led him toward their coats. They stepped into the snow. "If we hurry, we have just enough time to make it to the wedding on time."

KATE GLIDED toward Michael in her tea-length green velvet dress. She had never looked more radiant. Michael had never felt happier or more content. With their family surrounding them, they joined hands in front of the Christmas tree and said their vows.

"I take thee, Michael, for my lawfully wedded husband...."

"I take thee, Kate, for my lawfully wedded wife...."

"For richer, for poorer..."

"In sickness and in health..."

Their vows completed, the minister beamed at them and pronounced them man and wife. "Michael, you may kiss your bride."

Michael took Kate into his arms. She looked into his eyes. He looked into hers. The love they felt for each other binding them together, he bent his head and delivered a long, stirring kiss.

Hours—and much celebrating—later, they ended up at Kate's condo, Timmy sleeping soundly in the next room. They came together in the center of the bed. "You've made all my dreams come true," Michael said, as he took Kate into his arms once again.

Kate sighed contentedly as she nestled against him. "Mine, too."

"Merry Christmas, darling."

"Merry Christmas to you."

THE UNLIKELY SANTA
Leigh Michaels

CHAPTER ONE

BRANDI Ogilvie was not having a good day.

A shipment of Christmas supplies—twinkle lights, wrapping paper, and tree ornaments—which had been promised for delivery that morning had gotten lost somewhere between the warehouse and the store, and Brandi spent the better part of two hours on the telephone trying without success to track it down.

A sudden, virulent flu had taken out a half-dozen workers in the course of the morning and was threatening to decimate her staff before the week was out—hardly a cheerful thought for the first Monday in December. It was the crucial second week of the Christmas shopping season, and the Tyler-Royale store in Oak Park, Illinois, was a major department store, not a self-service discount outlet. As its manager, Brandi needed every person she could get on the sales floors.

And as if all that wasn't enough for one day, her secretary paged Brandi away from her lunch break before she'd eaten the first half of her hot pastrami sandwich. She sighed and picked up the other half to take back to her office, and as she was leaving the tearoom, two youngsters who were playing tag around the tables crashed into her. Mustard squirted from the sandwich over her new cream-colored silk blouse.

"Urchins," she said under her breath. "What are they doing in here anyway? And where are their parents?"

Brandi didn't expect an answer, and she was startled when a voice at her elbow murmured, "Right over there, drinking coffee and peacefully oblivious to their children's antics." Casey Amos, the department head of ladies' active wear, reached past Brandi to pick up a linen napkin from the nearest table.

Brandi took it and dabbed at the stain on the front of her blouse. "I'd like to ban kids from the tearoom altogether. That's why we put in the cafeteria downstairs, you know."

"You'd feel better if you sat down and ate something reasonable," Casey diagnosed.

"It's got nothing to do with where and what I eat. It's the season. Just between you and me, I hate Christmas, Casey."

"Now is that a proper attitude for the manager of a Tyler-Royale store? Don't you remember what Ross Clayton said at the sales conference just last week?" Casey struck a pose in imitation of the chain's chief executive officer and deepened her voice. "Always remember Christmas is the engine that drives retail sales. We'll do a third of our year's business between now and New Year's Day. And every single one of our customers is apt to walk through our doors in the next six weeks. Catch that customer and keep him or her happy!"

Brandi feigned a frown. "Does that mean you think our beloved leader would object if I spanked the brats?"

"Darling, I doubt you could catch them," Casey said frankly. "If you were eating properly and taking your vitamins, I'd put money on you, but…"

Brandi laughed. "All right, I'll order a salad next

time. I suppose this serves me right for being in such a hurry—I shouldn't carry food around.''

She could hardly go back to work drenched in mustard; her secretary would just have to be patient for another few minutes. Brandi stopped in Salon Elegance, the department that handled upscale women's clothing, and bought a duplicate of her blouse.

The clerk charged the sale to Brandi's Tyler-Royale credit card and offered to send the original blouse out for cleaning. ''It may be too late already, Ms. Ogilvie,'' she said. ''Mustard's a tough one. But we'll do our best.''

Brandi pinned the white carnation that marked her as a manager to her shoulder, gathered up her receipt and wallet and made a mental note to compliment the woman's supervisor about her helpful attitude. Then she headed for the escalator and her office. She was feeling much better, now that she was properly dressed again.

Christmas was just a state of mind anyway—in less than four weeks the holiday season would be over. She'd survive the pressure this time just as she had for the past half-dozen years. It was simply part of the job. And someday, when she moved farther up in the corporate structure, she wouldn't have to deal with this sort of pressure around the holidays.

In Tyler-Royale's anchor store in downtown Chicago, the executive offices took up two whole floors, but in the rest of the chain—even the big suburban stores like this one—space was precious and managers made do with much smaller quarters. Brandi's office lay at the end of a narrow corridor on the top floor, cramped between the employees' lounge and a storeroom, and her secretary's desk occupied a tiny alcove just outside her door.

The secretary looked up with obvious relief at seeing her boss. No doubt, Brandi thought, that was because today the alcove seemed even smaller than usual—the single visitor's chair beside Dora's desk was occupied.

"Sorry I took so long, Dora," Brandi said briskly. "I had a little accident and had to change my blouse. Have I forgotten an appointment?" But she didn't remember scheduling a supplier or a sales rep today, and Dora usually let people like that sit in her office rather than subject them to the cramped alcove. So who was waiting for her?

The man rose with an easy, athletic grace Brandi couldn't help but admire. She was tall herself, but her nose was on a level with the knot in his tie—a black tie, over a white shirt, under a V-necked sweater in a bold black-and-white pattern. His eyes were almost black, as well, or was that just the effect of the dramatic clothing? And his hair was black; it looked silky and fine and soft.

Dora said, under her breath, "He's waiting for you, Ms. Ogilvie. He says he's your new Santa."

Brandi blinked and looked up at the man again. Mid-thirties, she estimated. There was not a strand of silver in his hair; his shoulders were broad and his stomach perfectly flat, and his face—though far from unpleasant to look at—was too well chiseled to be called merry. His was hardly the sort of physique she normally sought for the job; this man looked more like a model—the rugged, outdoor kind—than a stand-in for jolly old Saint Nicholas.

Furthermore, Brandi thought, he ought to have realized that much himself—unless he was suffering from some kind of delusion. Maybe he really thought he *was* Santa Claus?

"Did you call security, Dora?" she asked softly.

Despite her low tone, the man heard her. "No need for that, Miss Ogilvie."

His voice was low and warm and rich and reassuring; that much was exactly right for the part. But the rest of him...

Dora shook her head. "He didn't seem threatening, exactly, just determined."

Brandi didn't have any doubts about the determination. She turned to face the man. "It's *Ms.* Ogilvie, please. And if you're looking for a job..."

His eyes dropped to her left hand, where a diamond cluster sparkled on her ring finger, then met hers again, without hesitation. "It's not a matter of looking, exactly, Ms. Ogilvie, I *am* your new Santa."

Brandi said dryly, "You'll pardon me for not recognizing you. Perhaps it's because you're out of uniform?"

His smile started in his eyes, she noted. It was quite a nice smile, slow and easy; it lit up his whole face and showed off perfect teeth and an unexpected dimple in his left cheek.

Dora cleared her throat. "Also, Ms. Ogilvie, there's a call for you from Mr. Clayton." She said the name with the same reverence most of Tyler-Royale's employees used when referring to the chief executive officer.

Brandi frowned a little. "And you've kept him waiting? Why didn't you tell me that right away?"

"He said not to disturb you, that he'd wait till it was convenient."

Brandi's frown deepened. That didn't bode well; Ross Clayton was a good and thoughtful employer, but it wasn't like him to be so very considerate of his manager's schedules. "I'll take it right now," Brandi murmured and turned back to her unlikely Santa. "Hiring isn't my department anyway. Perhaps you'd best speak to the personnel director—third door down the hall, on your right." Without pausing to see whether he obeyed, she closed her office door behind her and picked up the phone. "Ross, I'm sorry to keep you waiting."

"It's no problem. This is in the nature of a favor, so I didn't want to disturb your lunch."

"Don't let it worry you. You'd have been the least of the disturbances. What can I do for you?"

"I'm sending a man out to see you this afternoon."

Brandi closed her eyes. "Very tall?" she said warily. "With black hair and a grin so charming it almost makes you overlook the fact he's a maniac?"

"That sounds like Zack. He's showed up already, has he?"

Brandi rubbed the bridge of her nose. "Oh, he's here."

"He's generally on the ball. Good, you can put him to work right away. I know you can always use an extra Santa."

"With all due respect, Ross, I don't need another Santa. I have three perfectly good Santas hired already. Their work schedule is set up through Christmas Eve, and..."

"I hear the flu's getting really bad. What if you lose one?"

"That's why I've hired three. Ross, they're all honest-to-goodness grandpas, with real white beards and real white hair. They're even just about the same height so they can swap costumes. Tell me, where am I supposed to get a Santa suit for your Goliath? Besides, those kids are a tough audience. I can't just stick a couple of cotton balls on your friend's face and make him look believable!''

"I know you're a stickler, Brandi. But as a favor to me…''

Brandi wanted to groan. "Let me guess," she said crisply. "He's an old friend of yours who's fallen on hard times, and you're finding him a job?''

"He's got some problems just now," Ross agreed.

"That figures.''

"It's only a seasonal job, Brandi. Just through Christmas.''

"I don't need a Santa," Brandi muttered. "I need an assistant manager and another six clerks who can float to any department.''

"What?''

"Never mind. Is this a direct order, Ross?''

"Brandi, you know I like to give my managers maximum authority. I try never to issue direct orders in matters that affect a single store.''

"That means it is. All right, Ross—your Santa has a job.'' She put down the telephone and dropped her head into her hands for a few seconds. Then she punched the intercom. "Dora, is Santa still out there?''

"Yes.'' The secretary's voice was little more than a whisper. "He won't leave.''

"I'm not surprised. Send him in.''

Brandi sat at her desk and watched him as he crossed the narrow room and took the chair opposite her. He moved like an athlete, perfectly at ease with his body and in command of every muscle. She wondered if he was a dancer, too—there was something about the way he moved....

As if it mattered, Brandi reminded herself. She eyed his cable-stitched sweater and houndstooth-check trousers. He wore his clothes with an ease that said they weren't brand-new, as she'd half expected them to be. So Ross hadn't fitted his friend up at the downtown store before sending him out to Oak Park. And his clothes were expensive; Brandi had no trouble recognizing the quality of the whole outfit. Whatever hard times this man had fallen on were obviously recent ones.

She picked up a pen and doodled a square on the edge of her desk blotter. "Ross said your name's Zack?"

"That's right. And I'll happily let you call me that if you tell me your first name in return."

Brandi looked at him levelly, eyes narrowed. "Don't be impudent. I may have had to give you a job, but I don't have to make it easy for you."

He bowed his head. Brandi couldn't help but feel the submissive gesture was tinged with a good deal of irony. "Zack Forrest, at your service."

"That's better. Mr. Forrest, I'm sure you understand that Ross doesn't assign entry-level jobs in his stores. That's up to the managers. And right now I don't need a Santa. What I could use is floor help—clerks who float throughout a department and assist the customer to find what he or she wants. If you're interested, I can put you down in men's active wear this afternoon for training, and—"

He was shaking his head. "Ross sent me here to be a Santa."

"I just told you…" Brandi paused. "Look, I'm sure Ross meant well. But he doesn't know what's going on out here."

Oh, that was great, she told herself. The last thing she needed was for Ross Clayton's friend to go back and tell him that the manager of his Oak Park store said he had no idea what was going on!

"I want to be a Santa," Zack Forrest said. "In fact, I insist on it." If his voice hadn't been so deep, Brandi would have sworn he sounded like a stubborn three-year-old.

"Or what?" Brandi said in disbelief. "You'll report me to Ross? I don't know what kind of hold you have on him, but—"

"I wouldn't call it a *hold*, exactly," he said thoughtfully.

Brandi gave it up. "Why did he send you to me anyway?"

Zack shrugged. "He said this store has the busiest Santa's Workshop of any Tyler-Royale location."

"That's partly because I'm so careful who I hire to man that department." Brandi paused and thought, I can't believe I'm explaining my hiring practices to him!

He treated her to another slow, unrestrained smile. "I thought you said hiring wasn't your responsibility, Ms. Ogilvie."

"You know, with that kind of attitude it's no wonder you're out of a job." Brandi stood up. "You can report to the personnel manager and fill out the paperwork. Be sure to leave a phone number. Since it will take some time to find a Santa suit your size—"

Zack Forrest had risen, too, and Brandi let her gaze run from his face to his well-polished black wing tips and back, hoping the curt appraisal would take him down a notch. But he didn't even blink, just stood quietly and watched her face while she looked him over.

Brandi went on, "We'll be in touch when we can put you to work. Don't expect a call for a few days, though, because I'm sure finding a suit to fit you will be—"

"No problem at all," Zack interrupted. "I happen to have one in my car right now. I can go to work this afternoon." There was a glint in his eyes. "If you like, that is."

Brandi was taken aback. "Fill out the paperwork first and we'll see," she said finally. "I'll call the personnel director and tell him you're on the way."

The corner of his mouth quirked as if with satisfaction, but he didn't say a word till he was at the door of her office. Then he paused and turned. "You owe me one, though," he said gently.

Brandi had already picked up the telephone. She looked up from it, her mouth ajar. "One what? Listen, buddy, if you think you're the one who's doing *me* a favor here—"

"Oh, no. I appreciate everything you've done for me." There was a faint note of irony underlying that rich, warm voice. "I just mean I've earned equal time to look you over as thoroughly as you've studied me, Ms. Ogilvie."

"I beg your pardon?"

"And I reserve the right to do so…someday." He sketched a salute and pulled the door closed behind him.

Brandi sank back into her chair. At this rate, it was going to be a very long time till Christmas.

* * *

Brandi couldn't settle to anything constructive that afternoon, because the face of her unlikely Santa kept popping up between her and whatever she was trying to do. Finally, she pushed all her paperwork into a desk drawer and went out to do her daily tour of the store.

Early in her training, Brandi had learned to pop into every department frequently but unexpectedly, just to be certain her staff was performing up to specifications. It had turned out to be a good habit; in her two years as manager of the Oak Park store, Brandi had avoided a lot of big trouble by catching problems while they were still small enough to handle. It was one of the reasons that her store consistently ranked near the top of the Tyler-Royale chain when it came to profitability.

Though if the CEO kept sending her employees she didn't need or want, her record was likely to be chipped away. What had gotten into Ross Clayton anyway? Zack Forrest had denied having any hold over him, but Brandi didn't believe it for a minute. It just puzzled her to think what it could be.

Mondays were always the least hectic day of the week in the retail trade, but already this was shaping up to be the busiest Christmas season Brandi had ever experienced, and despite the day the store was comfortably full of shoppers. Some were admiring the long double row of decorated trees that lined the atrium entrance, inviting the public to come in for a closer look. Others were already heavily loaded with bags and boxes in Tyler-Royale's trademark blue and silver. In the toy department, several women browsed, and nearby a line of children waited to reach the big chair that sat just in front of the elaborate facade of Santa's Workshop.

Wait a minute, Brandi thought. There wasn't supposed to be a Santa on duty this afternoon—not till evening, when children were out of school and families came to shop.

She paused at the railing that surrounded Santa's Workshop and helped to keep the line orderly in particularly busy times. This wasn't one of those times; at most, a dozen children were waiting to talk to the man in the red suit who sat comfortably in the throne-size chair with a child on each knee.

Brandi went to the nearest checkout station and called the personnel director. "Did you assign our new Santa to work this afternoon?" she asked bluntly.

The man sounded stupefied. "Of course not. I gave him the employee handbook and said we'd call him when we got the schedule straightened out, just like you told me to do."

"That's what I thought," Brandi muttered. She put the phone down. By the time she got back to Santa's Workshop, the two boys had gotten off Zack's lap and a little girl had climbed up.

Brandi leaned against the rail and watched for a moment. She had to admit that Zack Forrest made a better Santa than she'd expected. Despite some padding around the middle, he was still a bit on the lean side, and Brandi could tell from across the room that his beard was fake. But he'd brushed something into his eyebrows to turn them gray, and his suit was perfect—the heavy red velvet was trimmed in what looked like real white fur. And he hadn't settled for cheap black patent accessories, either—this Santa's belt and boots were top-grain black leather, polished to a gleam. So was the cover of the notebook that lay open on his right knee.

A notebook? Brandi thought in disbelief. Why on earth was he taking notes? And why was he even *here*, without orders? The sooner she dealt with this mutinous employee the better.

Brandi slipped through the gate and went to the head of the line. "I need to talk to you," she murmured.

Zack ignored her. All his attention was focused on the child in his lap. The little girl was about four, and she was chattering merrily in what could have been a foreign language as far as Brandi was concerned; she could make out little resemblance to standard English. But though Zack's brow was furrowed a little as if he, too, found it difficult to understand the child, he was writing down a word now and then as she talked.

"Did you hear me?" Brandi muttered.

Zack's gaze lifted to study the line. "Certainly. I'll see you after I've finished with the kids."

Brandi had to bite her tongue to keep from firing him on the spot—but how would that look to the dozen children, and their parents, who were waiting in line?

She waited impatiently, trying not to tap her toes, as he eased the little girl off his lap, then beckoned the next child up and began to chat. At this rate, she thought, he'd be all afternoon getting through the remaining dozen kids. Which was no doubt exactly what he had in mind—stalling till Brandi got tired of waiting.

She shut the gate so the line wouldn't get any longer and put out the sign, kept handy for all the employees' breaks, which announced that Santa had gone to feed his reindeer but would return soon. Then she went back to stand beside the big chair. There was an infant on Zack's lap now, and his mother was backing off to get a photograph.

But finally the line was gone. Brandi waited till the last child was well out of earshot, and then turned on Zack. "What are you doing here?" she demanded.

"I don't see how it could be any more obvious."

"You were told you'd be called when we had an assignment for you!"

"And just when was that likely to be, Ms. Ogilvie? I don't think it would take much effort for you to find an excuse not to call me at all, so when I saw there was no Santa scheduled to work this afternoon, I volunteered."

"Don't you understand the store has a liability, Mr. Forrest? You can't just walk into this job without training."

"What's to learn? Your personnel director gave me a list of all the rules, and they're easy enough to memorize. Let's see—don't promise any toy unless the parent gives you a signal, just say *We'll see* instead. Never comment on a request for a little brother or sister. Just pretend you didn't hear it. Don't wear strong cologne or after-shave. Don't give candy without the parents' permission. Make a tour of Toyland every day before going on duty, in order to be familiar with the merchandise. Help the child to climb up, but don't lift—we're less likely to have scared little ones that way…" He paused. "And fewer injured Santas, too, no doubt, if they're not straining their backs lifting tots."

"That suggestion may have come from the corporate legal department,'' Brandi said stiffly. ''But I don't see what that has to do with—''

''It certainly sounds like it.''

She raised her voice. ''The point is—''

''The point is that I have the rest of the hundred rules down pat, too—so why shouldn't I be working? Why should the kids be cheated of their opportunity to talk to Santa, just because it happens to be Monday afternoon?''

Brandi folded her arms and put her chin up. ''There seems to be a basic disagreement about who's in charge here, Mr.—''

''Careful,'' Zack warned, and waved as a child stopped hopefully by the closed gate.

''*Claus*,'' Brandi said through clenched teeth. ''Perhaps we should have this discussion somewhere other than Toyland.''

Zack snapped his fingers. ''I think you've finally hit on a good point, Ms. Ogilvie.''

It was midafternoon, and the cafeteria should be practically empty. ''How about talking it out over coffee?'' Brandi suggested.

The child at the gate looked disappointed when Zack stood up. ''When will you be back, Santa?'' she called. ''How long does it take to feed your reindeer?''

''Just a few minutes,'' Zack said. ''I'll be back soon.''

''If I were you, I wouldn't make any promises,'' Brandi muttered.

The lunch rush was long over, and only a few patrons were in the cafeteria, having a soft drink and resting their feet while they checked over their lists and purchases.

Zack poured two cups of coffee and carried them to an out-of-the-way table while Brandi gathered up cream, sugar, and napkins and told the counter attendant to put the charge on her bill.

"I suppose Santa never carries money," she said as she set her awkward load down on the table.

"Of course I do. But you asked for this date, and judging by how sensitive you were when I got your title wrong, you're probably the sort to take offense if I insist on paying. I'd be happy to hold your chair, though, unless that would irritate you, too."

"Oh, sit down," she ordered.

But he held the chair for her anyway, before taking the seat across from her.

Brandi stirred sugar into her coffee and looked him over thoughtfully. "I feel as if I've walked into *Miracle on 34th Street*," she muttered.

Zack grinned.

The effect of his brilliant smile against the pure white beard and tanned face was stunning. He looked good in red, Brandi thought absently. The suit was a deep, rich ruby, and the color reflected nicely across his high cheekbones.

"If that's a polite way of asking if I think I'm the real Santa Claus, Brandi—no, I don't."

"Well, that's some relief. Wait a minute. How'd you know my name?"

Zack leaned forward confidingly. "Would you believe I used my X-ray vision to see through the file cabinets in the personnel director's office?"

"No."

"That's good. We've established two things. I don't think I'm either Superman or Santa Claus, and you admit I'm not deluded about it. Now we're getting somewhere.''

"We're getting nowhere. I could fire you for this stunt, you know. You can't just go around putting yourself to work because you see a job you think needs doing.''

"I don't expect to be paid for this afternoon. It's sort of like giving out free samples—I volunteered in order to show you how well I can do the job. And you must admit I'm good at it.''

Brandi didn't want to admit anything of the sort, but she could hardly deny it, either. "That's beside the point, don't you think?''

"Hardly.'' Zack leaned back in his chair. "Tell the truth. Would you have called me?''

"Not directly. It's not my job. But I'd have made sure the personnel manager kept you in mind.''

"What a comfort.'' His voice oozed sarcasm. "I might have got to work by Christmas Eve!''

"You have to remember you're low man when it comes to seniority. Knowing Ross doesn't make a difference where that's concerned, and it's only fair that the three Santas I hired before you will be considered first.''

"There. You see? That's why I felt it necessary to make my own hours.''

"Look, Mr. Forrest, I can't have employees setting their own schedules without considering what's best for the store.''

"I *am* considering what's best for the store. You've now got a dozen kids who are happier with Tyler-Royale than they'd have been if I wasn't on duty this afternoon. And you'd have a dozen more if you'd left me at work instead of dragging me down here to drink coffee. So if you'll excuse me, I'll get back to my job." He pushed his chair back and stood up.

"Just because you know the CEO doesn't mean you can make the rules," Brandi warned.

He looked at her, gray eyebrows lifted in what looked like long-suffering patience.

Brandi reconsidered. He'd been flagrantly in the wrong to put himself to work like that. Still, she had to admit she couldn't exactly fire him over it; she'd have a little trouble explaining to Ross Clayton what was so terrible about his friend volunteering an afternoon to play Santa in order to prove himself.

And Zack Forrest looked as if he knew very well what she was thinking. He was standing beside the table with an air of disdain, clearly waiting for her to admit defeat.

Brandi capitulated. "You will not set your own hours anymore."

Zack set a booted foot on his chair and leaned over her. "How about if I promise to tell you before I go on duty?"

"That's not the same thing at all."

He smiled a little. "Well, I'm sure you'll work it all out. In the meantime, you know where to find me." He didn't pause till he reached the cafeteria door, and then only to politely hold it for a couple of elderly ladies.

There was no point in counting to ten in an effort to control her temper. Instead, Brandi counted the days till Christmas.

CHAPTER TWO

By the time Brandi left the store that night, it was almost closing time and the late-evening rush was beginning to die down. In the parking area of the enormous shopping mall, the cars were beginning to thin out. The air was cold and crisp; she knew she'd have been able to see the stars if it wasn't for the powerful banks of lights that held the winter darkness at bay. There would be no snow tonight.

A few miles away, in the big apartment complex where she lived, the windows of almost every unit glowed. In many of them, Christmas trees sparkled with light as tiny red and green and gold and white bulbs twinkled on and off. Almost every door displayed a wreath or a Santa or a Nativity scene.

And she could hear Christmas carols as she walked through the courtyard to her building. The sound of it made Brandi's head hurt. The music wasn't obnoxiously loud, but it was so darned distinctive, and so very inescapable. Christmas, she thought, had gotten out of hand.

Her own apartment, in contrast, was dim and quiet. She closed the door with a sigh of relief, turned on a couple of lamps, and put a classical CD on to play. Then she poured herself a glass of sherry and sat down on the couch to enjoy a little peace.

The room was something like a cocoon, cozy and comforting. The overstuffed furniture was covered in subdued colors and subtle patterns, nicely framed prints decorated the neutral-colored walls, and soft deep carpeting cushioned the floors. A room to be at ease in, it looked just as it did the other eleven months of the year—and that was one of the things Brandi liked best about it.

Here, there was no tree, no tinsel, no mistletoe. She didn't have to deal with the sights and smells of the holiday. She didn't have to listen to perpetual Christmas carols. In fact, when she was safely snuggled into her own living room, she could pretend it wasn't Christmas at all.

And considering the day she'd had, that was a blessing.

She let her head rest against the soft back of the couch and closed her eyes. How on earth was she going to handle her new Santa?

In the two years she'd managed the Oak Park store, she'd never had an employee like him, that was sure. She'd never even *heard* of an employee who set his own hours in defiance of the store's schedule, who contradicted the boss, who acted as if he knew her job better than she did.

But then, she'd never hired a friend of the boss before, either. She'd like to call up Ross Clayton and ask what kind of blackmail material Zack had on him; it must be something extraordinary to account for the kind of special treatment the man seemed to expect. For the life of her, she couldn't think of anything that infamous.

She finished her sherry and wandered into the kitchen to dig through the freezer for something that would be easy to cook. There wasn't much variety left; she'd have to fit in time to stop at the supermarket in the next few days. Certainly she'd have to go before the weekend, when things would really get hectic again.

The phone rang. She made a face and thought about ignoring it, then sighed and picked it up anyway. There might be a security problem at the store.

Casey Amos said, "I saw you with Santa in the cafeteria this afternoon. What's going on, Brandi?"

"We were having a chat. Why?"

"You should hear what the grapevine's saying."

"Casey, I stopped being interested in store gossip a long time ago."

"All right, then, I won't tell you," Casey said cheerfully. "It's a good story, though. And I could see the sparks you were striking off each other."

"The only sparks you saw were pure irritation."

"Ah. Then it is true Ross made you hire him?"

Brandi kept her voice level. "I wonder who started that rumor."

"You just did—telling me you were irritated. If hiring him had been your idea, and he annoyed you so much, he'd have been out the door in two minutes flat."

Brandi wanted to bite her tongue off. Just yesterday she'd have had the sense to think it over before she spoke, and she'd have refused Casey's bait. Zack Forrest had struck once more. At this rate, by Christmas she wouldn't have a shred of judgment left.

"Instead," Casey went on, "he finished his shift and went home. In fact, since I was clocking out at the same time, he walked me to my car."

"Congratulations."

"He seems perfectly nice—but I didn't feel the same kind of sparks you were giving off this afternoon, so don't worry."

"Why do I put up with you, Casey?"

"Because I'm the best department head you've got, and when I get a store of my own next year you're going to cry over losing me."

"True. Still—"

"And because I'm so discreet. I won't pass along a word of what you've confided in me tonight."

"I wasn't aware I'd bared my soul," Brandi said acidly. "If that's why you called, I appreciate the thought, but—"

Casey's voice took on a more serious note. "No, actually I'm checking on the menu for the Christmas party. It's only two weeks off, you know, so I have to get an order to the caterer right away."

"Casey, you know I don't care what you serve at the Christmas party."

"We can do it for the same money as last year if we leave out the shrimp."

"Didn't you say the staff loved the shrimp last year?"

"Yes. Still, everything else has gone so high, and you did say we had to stick to the budget...."

"Have the shrimp. I'll make up the shortfall personally. Just don't tell anybody, all right?"

"And ruin your reputation as the biggest Scrooge in the chain? I wouldn't dream of it. Are you going to put your name in the gift-exchange drawing this year?"

"Of course not. Why do you think I insisted you make participation voluntary?"

"Still, you seem to be softening a little. Maybe it's Santa's influence. You seem inspired, somehow."

Brandi gritted her teeth. "The only thing my new Santa has inspired in me is fury."

"I wasn't referring to any person in particular," Casey murmured. "I was talking about the spirit of Christmas. But *you* assumed I meant your new Santa. How interesting that you thought of him right off!"

There were times when the cramped size of Brandi's office had its advantages; she'd found that meetings and conferences tended to move along very promptly when the participants found themselves sitting on bookcases and file cabinets.

Her usual Tuesday morning meeting with all the store's department heads was winding down, just a few minutes before the business day began, when Dora came into her office with a slip of paper and slid it across the desk without a word.

Brandi unfolded the note, still half-listening to the report from the head of the electronics department. "Mrs. Townsend of the Kansas City store wants you to call her," Dora had written in her cramped, neat hand.

That's odd, Brandi thought. If the matter had been crucial, Dora would have summoned her from the meeting. Since it wasn't, why hadn't the secretary just held the message till after the meeting broke up?

Then Brandi realized she'd overlooked the second part of the note. "And your Santa popped in just now to tell you he's going to work this morning," Dora had written.

Brandi sighed. Did everybody in the store now think of Zack Forrest as her very own private Santa?

She dismissed the department heads and followed them out to the alcove. "Dora, did Mrs. Townsend tell you what she wanted?"

"No. She just said to call her when it's convenient,

that she'd be in the store all day.'' Dora warily eyed the slip of paper in Brandi's hand. ''I didn't know what to do about your Santa.''

''Neither does anyone else,'' Brandi admitted.

''I'm not even sure what he was talking about. I asked him why he didn't just punch the time clock like the rest of the employees instead of reporting to you, and he said you were expecting him. So I thought I should tell you right away.''

I wish you hadn't, Brandi thought. If she didn't know Zack was down there in the big chair in front of Santa's Workshop, stirring up trouble, she could simply go about her business. Now that she knew, she'd have to do something about it—she couldn't simply pretend to be oblivious. No manager could let a brand-new employee go around creating his own schedule and making a fool of her. If that word got out, Brandi Ogilvie would be a laughingstock throughout the whole chain.

But she'd spent the night thinking about it, and she still couldn't quite imagine how she was going to stop Zack Forrest from doing precisely what he pleased.

She could refuse to pay him, of course, but she didn't think that would stand up long once he had another chat with Ross Clayton. After all, he was doing the work for which he'd been hired—and she didn't think the fact that he wasn't precisely up to Brandi's specifications would carry any more weight with Ross than it had yesterday when she'd tried to get out of hiring him in the first place.

Well, if she couldn't get rid of him, she'd better give him some regular hours. At least then she'd look as if she was still in control. ''Dora, will you find out when the next real Santa's due to come in?''

"Certainly." Dora looked a bit puzzled.

"Better yet, go over to the employees' lounge and make a copy of the schedule for the next week, and bring it into my office. Oh, and Dora—try not to let anybody see what you're doing."

Dora looked even more confused. Brandi just smiled and went back to her office.

She dismissed Zack from her mind for the moment and settled back at her desk to call Whitney Townsend in Kansas City. She always enjoyed talking to Whitney; the woman might have anything in mind, from a personnel swap to a practical joke on the CEO. And since she was not only a senior manager but a vice president of the Tyler-Royale chain, she could get by with either—or almost anything in between.

Brandi's call was passed to Whitney's office with machine-gun efficiency. "How are you?" Whitney demanded as soon as she picked up the phone. "I haven't heard from you in weeks."

"You know how things get this time of year."

"Exactly. That's why I expected a call before the Christmas season kicked into high gear. Don't you know you're supposed to phone your mentor once a month at least?" The smile in her voice took any sting out of the words.

"I've tried," Brandi said crisply. "But I didn't bother to leave a message last time I called, because you were in San Antonio sorting out the problems in the store there."

"Oh, that. Ross seems to be short a troubleshooter at the moment, so I got roped in to handle things."

"I assumed that's what happened. At any rate, I thought you probably had enough to deal with. The time before that you were vacationing in Hawaii when

I called. Your secretary offered me the number, but I know better than to disturb you on a second honeymoon.''

Whitney laughed. ''Good thinking. No problems, then?''

Brandi thought about Zack Forrest, and sighed. She couldn't even begin to put that particular difficulty into words. ''Nothing more than usual.''

''Well, that's good. Nevertheless, I want to check for myself, so I'm coming up to see you at the end of the week. Hold Saturday evening open for me, all right?''

Brandi flipped the page in her desk calendar to write the appointment down. ''You don't mean the night of the corporate Christmas party,'' she said slowly.

''That's exactly what I mean. And don't you dare miss it.''

''Whitney, you know I hate those things.''

''Yes, and I also know that every year you come up with another spectacular reason for not coming. In fact, Ross suggested I not call you, because he wanted to see what you'd use to get out of it this time. You're running so late at sending your regrets that he figures it'll have to be a doozy of an excuse.''

''But of course you didn't obey his wishes.''

''Well, it wasn't quite a direct order,'' Whitney said reasonably. ''So I just ignored him.''

Brandi wished she'd dared to ignore Ross on the question of Zack Forrest. Someday, she thought dreamily, she'd be a corporate vice president and she could. Not that it made any difference right now. ''Can't we just have lunch instead, Whitney? We won't really be able to talk at the party, you know.''

Dora opened the door and quietly laid the Santa schedule on Brandi's desk.

Whitney said firmly, "I'm flying up on Saturday afternoon and back on Sunday, so it's the party or nothing. I have a store to manage myself, you know."

Brandi capitulated. "Then I'll be at the party to see you. But I hope you don't insist on my having a good time otherwise."

Whitney only laughed, and Brandi put down the phone and picked up the Santa schedule. Dora hadn't stopped with the week's calendar; she'd brought the whole month's, all the way through Christmas Eve.

Brandi had worked like fury on that schedule. It was the perfectly arranged product of two seasons' worth of observation of the store's mix of customers. Any time there was likely to be a large number of children in the store—late afternoons, evenings and weekends, mostly—there would be a Santa on duty. And the hours were perfectly divided between the three elderly, white-haired, bearded men Brandi had hired to play the part.

Now, in order to leave room for Zack Forrest, she was going to have to throw it all out and start over.

She wanted to growl. No, what she really wanted to do was go down to Toyland and give one irrepressible Santa a black eye. But that was guaranteed to make things worse.

She got out a fresh schedule sheet and began to draw boxes.

Keeping things as fair as possible, while trying not to cheat any of the men she'd hired first, would be a challenge. In fact, just the idea of calling her handpicked Santas in and explaining the changes gave her heartburn. They weren't going to be happy at having their calendars rearranged for no reason, and she didn't blame them. But she could hardly come straight out and tell them they'd been displaced by an upstart who happened to know the boss.

Unless... Maybe there was another way.

She turned the original schedule this way and that, then smiled, reached for a red marker, and drew a series of neat lines. Then she tucked the page in the pocket of her suit jacket and left her office. "Dora, I'll be in Toyland talking to Santa."

"Good luck," Dora muttered. "I don't envy you the job."

The line outside Santa's Workshop was moving along faster this morning then it had yesterday; most of the children were very small, and the parents seemed more interested in photographs than in conversations. Brandi closed the gate, put the "Santa's Feeding His Reindeer" sign in place, and strolled to the head of the line to stand near the big chair.

Zack had seen her coming the moment she'd gotten off the escalator, Brandi was sure of that, though he didn't look up. In fact, an observer would swear Santa hadn't taken his attention from the child on his lap. But Brandi knew he was aware of her presence, because she could feel a sudden pulse of energy coming from him—as if he'd been waiting impatiently for her and was relieved that she'd finally appeared.

She stood beside the big chair, just inside his periph-eral vision, and folded her arms, trying to look as if she could comfortably stay there forever. She knew better than to suggest Zack leave even a single child waiting, but perhaps if she just stood there silently, he'd get nervous and hurry things along.

A couple of minutes later he looked up at her with

a quick smile and a quizzical quirk to his fake-gray eyebrows. "Are you certain the reindeer need feeding *again*, Ms. Ogilvie?"

Brandi kept her voice level with an effort. "I'm afraid they do, Santa."

"And you came all the way down to help me. How thoughtful of you!"

The year-old child on Zack's lap gurgled, and her mother picked her up. "Nice touch. I hope you both enjoy yourselves on your break." She winked at Brandi. "Bet I can guess what you'd like for Christmas from this particular Santa."

Brandi felt color rising in her face as she remembered what Casey had said about the sparks she'd seen passing between Brandi and Zack yesterday. The conclusion Casey had jumped to was an idiotic one, of course—and this young mother was being just as silly to think that the electricity she saw must have a romantic element to it.

But Brandi had to bite her lip hard to subdue the blush. She didn't look at Zack, but she could sense he was smiling, obviously enjoying her discomfort.

The next child had been listening to the exchange. He marched up to Zack, folded his arms, and announced, "Santa's just for kids. My mom says so. Big people aren't supposed to ask you to bring them things."

Zack's eyebrows soared. "Why on earth shouldn't they? Big people have dreams, too." He looked up at Brandi appraisingly. "What *would* you like for Christmas, Ms. Ogilvie?"

"For New Year's Day to come three weeks early," Brandi said.

Zack choked, and it was almost half a minute before he recovered enough to take the child on his knee and get back to business. With her equilibrium restored, Brandi settled back to wait for him to deal with the rest of the line. At least, she thought, he wasn't likely to ask her any more leading questions in public!

He was better than she'd expected at the job, she had to admit. He'd done his homework, or else he was a phenomenal actor, for not a toy was mentioned that Zack didn't seem to recognize. And he didn't simply acknowledge the requests, either; he engaged each child in conversation about his wishes, and asked how he'd decided on that special item.

Brandi shifted impatiently from one foot to the other. "That's charming, Santa, but—"

Zack's eyes widened. "You mean you actually think I'm doing something right for a change?"

"Yes and no. I don't see the point of asking them why they've chosen a particular toy."

"I'm trying to make certain they really want it, and haven't simply been swayed by television ads or what their friends say."

A mother waiting in line nodded in approval. "Last year my son got everything on his list and didn't play with any of it. I was pretty annoyed, I'll tell you, when all those expensive toys turned out to be just a fad. I appreciate your taking time to make sure, Santa Claus."

Zack shot Brandi a look that said, *See? Maybe I do know what I'm doing.*

She said, under her breath, "I still think it's more likely you're trying to delay till I get tired of standing here."

"You?" he murmured. "I'm beginning to think

you're inexhaustible, Ms. Ogilvie.'' But eventually the kids were all satisfied, and Brandi and Zack were alone outside Santa's Workshop. Zack stood up, stretched, and tucked his leather-covered notebook into a capacious pocket. "I must say it's nice to have a break. That chair isn't as comfortable as it looks. Coffee? It's my turn to buy, I believe.''

The same counter attendant was working in the cafeteria. "Two days in a row?'' she murmured. "This is getting to be a habit, Ms. Ogilvie.''

Oh, that's just great, Brandi thought. If Casey was right, the store's grapevine was already working overtime. By the end of the day, her two cups of coffee with Santa would probably have grown into a full-fledged affair. And if the tale escaped the Oak Park store and made the rounds of the chain, gossip would probably have her moving to the North Pole to live with him.

Zack stirred sugar into his coffee and looked thoughtfully across the table at her. "So what do you really want for Christmas, Brandi?''

She decided to ignore the name; complaining, she suspected, would only encourage him. "You're off duty now. Remember?''

He didn't seem to hear. "Emeralds? They'd look good against that auburn hair and fair skin of yours.''

"I hardly think Santa's likely to bring me emeralds.''

"Well, that's true—at least this Santa. We hardly know each other, so it wouldn't be at all proper for me to give you jewelry.'' His gaze dropped to the cluster of diamonds on her left hand. "To say nothing of the fact that Mr. Ogilvie would probably object. Tell me, *is* there a Mr. Ogilvie?''

This, Brandi thought, is getting out of hand. "I can't think why you'd need to know."

"Can't you? Well, never mind for now. Surely there's something you'd like for Christmas. Something simple, maybe, like peace on earth..." Zack snapped his fingers. "I know! How about a white Christmas?"

"That would be too late to do us any good," Brandi said crisply. "On the other hand, a nice half-inch snowfall sometime this week would put every shopper in the holiday spirit and raise the season's sales by at least ten percent."

Zack shook his head sadly.

"Only half an inch, though." Brandi sipped her coffee. "Much more than that jams up traffic and people stay home."

"You have a very unromantic view of the holiday."

"So would you, I expect, if you'd been working Christmas retail for a decade."

Zack looked startled. "Ten years? You're not old enough."

"Yes, I am. I started working part-time for Tyler-Royale when I was in high school, right in the middle of the Christmas season. But I didn't come down here to talk about me. I've got your work assignments for the rest of the month."

Zack pulled out his notebook and flipped it open.

"That reminds me," Brandi said. "Don't you think you ought to ditch the notebook?"

"Why?" He didn't sound argumentative, just curious.

"Surely I shouldn't have to explain to you that

Santa remembers everything a child says and does. It's part of the mystique.''

Zack frowned. ''You mean you haven't ever heard of the old guy making a list and checking it twice? I take back what I said earlier, Brandi. You're not unromantic about Christmas, you're downright oblivious.''

Something about his tone annoyed Brandi; he didn't need to treat her like Scrooge, for heaven's sake. ''I must say I don't see what good it does to write down what a child wants. It's not like you're seriously going to hunt up these kids on Christmas Eve and deliver toys.'' She wrinkled her brow. ''Are you?''

''Of course not.''

''Right. How could you, when you haven't the foggiest idea who the child is or where he lives? That proves my point, you know. Writing all this stuff down takes up time and paper for nothing.'' She reached for his notebook, and knocked loose the white carnation pinned to the lapel of her forest green suit.

Zack slid the notebook out from under her hand and tucked it back in his pocket. ''On the contrary,'' he said soberly. ''Taking notes make the kids feel that I'm listening to them very seriously. They're reassured to know their requests are written down safely in Santa's book. So, while I thank you for your concern, I believe I'll keep on just as I've been doing.''

Brandi glared at him for an instant, then turned her attention to her carnation. It was useless to argue with him, she thought. She was obviously not going to convince him she was right, and the issue simply wasn't important enough to issue a direct order. That was why she'd asked a question in the first place, instead of just telling him to leave his notebook at home; Brandi had learned long ago to choose her battlefields more carefully than that.

Zack reached across the table. For an instant, his fingers almost encircled her wrist as he pulled her hand away from the carnation. Then he straightened the flower himself, setting the pin firmly into the wool of her lapel.

Brandi thought she could feel the warmth of his fingertips against her collarbone. The sensation was strictly imaginary, of course, she reminded herself, since not only the suit but a silky blouse lay between his hand and her bare skin. Still, the contact seemed to burn all the way to her bones.

"You said something about my work hours?" Zack reminded her.

Brandi pulled the Santa schedule out of her pocket and slid it across the table. "The blocks I've marked in red are yours."

Would he argue? she wondered. Or threaten? Would he get angry, or try to negotiate?

Zack studied the page, and then his gaze lifted to meet hers. At this distance, his eyes looked even darker than usual against the spun white floss of his beard. "You've marked all the times you hadn't already scheduled a Santa."

"Yes," Brandi admitted. "Since you seem to have adopted a good number of those hours anyway, I thought you might as well have every last one of them."

"It's generous of you, but—"

Brandi smiled. "Isn't it?" she said easily. "I *have* given you more time than any of the other Santas will work, so I hope you won't make an issue of it. They might feel left out.''

''Considering the way these hours are spread around, I doubt they'll be jealous.'' Zack glanced at the paper again. ''Two hours in the morning, one at closing time, a half hour through the supper break… this ought to keep me busy.''

''If you don't like the schedule, Zack…''

''Oh, I absolutely adore it. I can get all my Christmas shopping done while I'm between shifts.''

Brandi started to feel just a bit uneasy. The schedule she'd given him was nasty—the man wouldn't have an entire half day to call his own for the next month, but his work was so split up that all of his hours didn't add up to a full-time paycheck, either. Shouldn't he have at least tried to change her mind, to talk her into giving him some more reasonable hours? She studied him covertly. She couldn't detect a hint of strain in Zack's smile, and that worried her.

''Of course, I may have to pitch a tent in the parking lot to be sure I'm not late for any of my numerous curtain times,'' he said, ''but as long as you don't mind that little nuisance—''

Brandi relaxed a little. There was an edge to his voice, so slight that if she hadn't been listening intently, she'd have missed it. So he wasn't as sanguine as he'd pretended. Now he'd no doubt start to negotiate.

Well, that was all right with Brandi; she was perfectly willing to compromise. At least this time she'd be dealing from a position of strength, unlike the matter of his notebook. Brandi thought it made a nice change, everything considered.

''That's why I gave you your schedule for the

whole month," she said agreeably. "So you could plan ahead."

"I'll do that. Now, since I'm supposed to be working at the moment, I'd better get back to it or you'll probably fire me for not showing up for my assigned times."

He folded the schedule, tucked it into an inner pocket, and left the cafeteria without a backward glance.

Guilt washed over Brandi like a wave across the deck of a sailboat. The schedule she'd given him was worse than nasty, she admitted; it was unconscionable. She'd never before assigned an employee to that kind of random, scattered hours over such a long period of time, and she wouldn't stand for any of her department heads doing so, either. It wasn't fair to expect someone to be always on call and ready for work for a full month, without a single break.

Only store managers have to do that, she thought with a tinge of wry humor.

But why hadn't Zack made a fuss? Why hadn't he tried to get a change? Was he intending to go straight to Ross to complain?

She didn't think so. From what she'd seen of him so far, he wasn't the sort to hide his feelings or ask someone else to fight his battles. He hadn't hesitated to stand up for his convictions about the darned notebook so why would he have shrunk from arguing about his working hours?

Maybe he was simply further down on his luck than she'd thought. Maybe he really needed the work.

Brandi swallowed hard and tried to remember what the schedule had looked like. It wasn't too bad for the next couple of days, she thought. Not till the

weekend did the scattered, fragmented hours really
start. She'd see how it worked out for a day or two,
and then...

Well, if she had to go to him and back down, it
wouldn't be the first time Brandi Ogilvie had admitted
to making a mistake.

She just didn't relish the thought of facing Zack
with an apology.

CHAPTER THREE

BRANDI leaned on the fence that surrounded Santa's Workshop and watched admiringly as the white-haired man sitting in the big chair encouraged the child in his lap to tug on his long white beard. The child gave it a healthy yank, and Santa yelped in what Brandi thought was only slightly exaggerated discomfort.

The child's eyes widened. "Mommy, it's *real*," he said. "This must be the *real* Santa!"

Now that, Brandi thought, was more like it. Too bad Zack wasn't here to see a qualified professional at work.

Not that she was exactly anxious for him to show up. She hadn't seen Zack in nearly thirty-six hours, since he'd stalked out of the cafeteria yesterday morning. She suspected he was taking care to stay out of her way.

In fact, Brandi wouldn't have been a bit surprised if he hadn't shown up for work today at all, but instead had gone back to see his friend, Ross Clayton. She'd even wasted a little time considering what Ross might have to say about how she'd handled this entire affair, and she'd had to remind herself that her boss was generally a reasonable sort.

Still, she'd ended up sending Dora to the employees' lounge to check the time clock, and only when the secretary came back to report that Zack had indeed clocked in to work his assigned morning shift had Brandi really relaxed. Then she'd devoted herself to the paperwork that had been building up on her desk for the last week. She'd spent the whole morning and much of the afternoon in her office, and it was only as the early winter darkness was closing in that she finally pushed her papers aside and went to make her regular tour of the store.

She watched as Santa tipped his face down to look at a child over the top of his half glasses. The glasses were a perfect finishing touch, and the lenses were real—she'd made it a point to notice in the man's employment interview.

"Now that's a switch," a low, rich voice said beside her. "The admiring look on your face, I mean."

She wheeled around to face Zack. "What are you doing here?" She could have bitten off the tip of her tongue the second the words were out; why should it be any particular concern of hers if he wanted to hang around Santa's Workshop and observe?

The corner of Zack's mouth quirked, but there was little humor in the expression. "I'm just coming off duty, after a half hour in the chair while this guy had his dinner. Since it was your idea, I expected you'd at least remember."

Brandi had forgotten. Why hadn't she been smart enough to keep a copy of that ridiculous schedule she'd given him? Because it was so very ridiculous, she reminded herself, that she hadn't foreseen any possibility it would ever go into effect—that was why.

Zack must have just come from the small dressing room concealed within the shell of Santa's Workshop, for he was wearing street clothes. Brandi had gotten so used to seeing him in the red velvet suit and the white beard that she was startled by his gray trousers and matching cashmere sweater, and more so by his chiseled profile. He looked tired, and there was no hint of a dimple.

Brandi found herself wondering about that dimple. Had it been to the left of his mouth, or the right? She couldn't quite remember. Not that it mattered, of course; she didn't care if she ever saw it again. And it was no concern of hers whether Zack Forrest smiled or not.

"He's good," Zack said. He nodded toward the Santa.

Brandi was surprised that he'd volunteered so much. "Of course he is. That's why I hired him."

"Careful—you don't want the kids to hear that."

She was annoyed with herself for the slip. "Thanks for the reminder," she said sweetly. "I'll be more careful now, so don't feel you have to stick around to keep me in check."

Zack didn't seem to notice the saccharine tone. "Where do you think I'd be going?"

"You surely don't expect me to believe you've actually pitched a tent in the parking lot. I assumed you were on your way home. If you've finished work—"

"But I haven't. I'm off for two hours, then I have another hour on duty just before the store closes."

"But I thought, since you weren't in uniform..."

"I assumed you wouldn't like the idea of an extra Santa wandering around the store."

"No, I wouldn't."

"And since I have a tendency to get claustrophobic, I don't relish the thought of sitting in the dressing room. It's pretty tiny, you know. So that means changing my clothes every time I come off duty."

Brandi bit her lip and debated how to confess that she really hadn't intended it to work out that way.

But before she could find the words, Zack added, "I must admit my Christmas shopping is coming along well, though. I've been killing time by looking over the merchandise, and I've almost taken care of my whole list. What about you? Are you off duty now?"

"No—I'm just making my regular rounds. I try to walk through every department in the store at least twice a day."

One of Zack's dark eyebrows lifted quizzically. "Is this your first trip, or have you been avoiding Toyland today?"

"I haven't been avoiding anything. It's a critical time of year, and I've been very busy in my office." Brandi didn't owe him any explanations, of course, but the question made her feel a little uneasy. *Was* that one of the reasons she'd kept herself so fully occupied all day?

"I'm glad you explained," Zack said earnestly. "You see, I thought it might have something to do with not wanting to run into me."

Brandi's uneasiness flared into full-fledged annoyance. Zack had no cause to indulge in that sort of speculation, and she'd better put a stop to it right away. But keep it light, she warned herself. "Why on earth wouldn't I want to see you?"

Zack started to smile. "You do, then? Well, that's reassuring. It makes my life worthwhile, to know that you've been looking forward to seeing me again after all."

Brandi winced. She'd walked right into that one.

Zack was merciless. "In fact, since we're both

planning to stroll through the store right now, we can do it together. Won't that be fun? Which direction are you heading?''

Whichever way she indicated, he'd no doubt adapt his plans to trail along just to annoy her. Not that he wasn't already doing a good job of that—if there was a contest for irritating the boss, he could be named employee of the month.

''I'm not planning to stroll, exactly,'' she said. ''I'm in a hurry, so—''

''Are you anxious to get done and go home after all?''

''Not particularly. I'll be here till closing time—I usually am this time of year. But I have other things to do. So, since I'd hate to rush you and keep you from looking around to your heart's content—''

Zack leaned against a pillar and folded his arms across his chest. ''I suppose your Christmas shopping is all done?'' he challenged.

''That's right.''

''You don't even need to look for one little thing to finish out your list?'' He whistled admiringly. ''You know, I'd convinced myself that someone who's got such a case of glooms about the holiday would put off shopping till the last possible moment. But you are a wonder of efficiency, Brandi.''

''Well, I'm glad the question entertained you, but—''

''I wonder how I could have been so wrong about you. Unless... Yes, I've got it. I'll bet you're giving everyone on your list Tyler-Royale gift certificates.''

He was dead right, as a matter of fact, and that made Brandi nervous. How had he guessed that? ''So

what if I am? There's nothing wrong with gift certificates.''

''I suppose not,'' Zack said. He didn't sound as if
he believed it. ''One easy stop at the customer service
desk and you're done. Everybody gets what they
want, Tyler-Royale rings up the sales, and you've
even cut back on after-Christmas returns and ex-
changes. What a perfectly thoughtful solution for everybody!''

''You don't need to make it sound like a breach of
good manners.'' Brandi stepped away from the fence.
''It's been nice talking to you, Zack, but since we're
not going the same direction...'' She started walking
down the broad aisle toward housewares.

Zack fell into step beside her. ''Why *are* you so
anti-Christmas? I'd really like to know. If you hate
the pressure of retail sales at this time of year, there
are other jobs, you know.''

''I hope I won't always be at this level, so that I
won't always have to deal with Christmas panic. But
in the meantime, I live for my job the other eleven
months of the year, and I've learned to simply endure
Christmas. It equals out.''

''The job is what you live for?'' There was an incredulous note in his voice.

''What's so amazing? I have other interests, you
know, but this season of the year there's no time for
them. The job has to come first. Or don't you think
any woman should be more interested in a mere job
than in other things?'' Brandi's voice was tart.

''I wouldn't dare tell all women what to do. I just
meant, if that's the case, there's obviously no Mr.
Ogilvie after all.''

It wasn't a question, and yet, since it was pointless

to evade such a direct statement, Brandi answered. "No, there isn't."

"Has there ever been?"

She stopped beside a towering stack of small appliances—mixers, toasters, blenders. "I beg your pardon?"

"I just asked—"

"I know what you asked. My personal history is none of your affair."

Zack shrugged. "All right. Whatever you say." He picked up a box. "Do you think my sister would like a vegetable steamer?"

"Since I don't know your sister, I haven't the foggiest." Brandi's voice was curt.

Zack didn't seem to take offense. "I've already bought her one, you see, but now that I think it over, it just doesn't seem right." His eyes lighted up. "Or maybe I'll just give it to you—you're the sort to appreciate a really practical gift. Well, I'll have plenty of time to think about it before I decide. I've still got more than an hour to kill before I have to go back to work."

That reminded Brandi of the damned schedule. The only thing she really remembered about it was that as the days went on the hours got worse. That meant this had been one of the milder days, even though the work shifts he'd described had sounded bad enough to send most employees into fits. She was going to have to back down, and the sooner she did so, the less painful it would be.

She took a deep breath. "Look, Zack...if you want to simplify that schedule I gave you, it's fine with me. We don't really need a Santa during the dinner break, and it's a nuisance for you to sit around and wait in order to do half an hour's work.''

He didn't nod, or smile, or frown. He didn't do anything at all.

His lack of reaction puzzled Brandi. ''Or for the last hour we're open, either,'' she went on hurriedly. ''We don't need to offer a Santa then.''

Zack still gave no indication that he'd even heard her, but she knew he must have.

She tried to make a joke of it. ''All good little kids are home in bed by that time anyway. So if you'd like to call it a day right now—''

''You're cutting my hours?''

''I'm trying to give you a break!''

Zack shook his head slightly, as if he was disappointed in her. Or perhaps he simply couldn't believe his ears. ''Oh, no, Brandi. I wouldn't dream of asking for special treatment. You assigned me certain blocks of time to work, and I'm not complaining.''

Brandi blinked in astonishment. ''All right,'' she snapped. ''If that's the way you want it, go right ahead.''

Zack smiled, and his dimple flashed for just an instant. ''After all, you're not asking me for anything so out of the ordinary. I'm sure you'll be here every single hour that I am. Won't you?''

The dimple was in his left cheek. Brandi wanted to growl at herself for noticing.

She could feel the change of pace in the store as closing time approached. Even though she was still in her office, out of sight of the sales floors, she could almost hear the beeping of cash registers being cleared, of computers humming to a halt, of lights clicking off.

Brandi signed the last of a stack of letters and put them aside for Dora to mail in the morning. Then she took off her white carnation—a bit bedraggled now, after twelve hours pinned to her lapel—and dropped it into the wastebasket beside her desk.

The rest of the executive offices were dark, though in the employees' lounge next door several workers were putting on coats and boots for the journey home.

The store itself was never really dark; light was the best security measure. But the sales floors looked different with the banks of brilliant display lighting shut off. And the store sounded different, too. For one thing, the Christmas music, which was so cheerfully relentless all day, had at last died into blessed silence.

The escalators had already been shut off. Brandi walked down slowly, running a practiced eye over the entire floor. Outside Toyland, she spotted a red suit; Zack was leaning on the fence by Santa's Worship, talking to a group of kids. And what they were still doing in the store after closing time was anyone's guess. The kids were what had drawn her attention, she told herself. She certainly hadn't been looking for Zack.

A uniformed security guard called her name, and Brandi met him in electronics, where he was checking the display cases to be sure they were locked. The Doberman by his side perked his ears and looked her over with interest. Brandi kept a respectful distance; the dog was securely leashed, but it would take only a nudge to his harness and a word from the guard to turn him into a vicious machine.

"The head of mall security warned me they had a

strange-looking guy hanging around the parking lot earlier tonight,'' the guard said. ''They're suggesting all employees leave by the main entrances. Santa said he'd walk you to your car.''

''That's not necessary. Be sure you tell everybody.''

He nodded. ''I posted a sign on the employee exit.''

Zack had shooed the kids toward the entrance, but he was still leaning on the fence, watching as Brandi approached. ''Ready to go?'' he said.

''You needn't bother, Zack.''

''Don't flatter yourself. It's no bother at all, because I'm going that way myself.''

''How gracious of you,'' Brandi murmured. ''Still, you must want to change clothes before you go.''

''Again? No, thanks. When I take off the suit this time, I'm getting straight into a hot shower.''

Why that comment should make her face grow warm was beyond Brandi's understanding. It was a perfectly straightforward statement, nothing more. ''Well, don't let me keep you from it.''

''The only thing that's slowing me down is the fact that we're standing here talking,'' he pointed out.

That was true enough, so Brandi started for the entrance. But she murmured, ''Can't you take a hint?''

''Of course I can. That wasn't exactly a hint you issued, that was a sledgehammer.''

The metal-mesh gate was already closed, except for a gap just wide enough for her to slip through. ''I can get myself across the parking lot to my car, you know. We have these little episodes from time to time, and it never amounts to anything.''

"But if you don't get to your car, and they find your body tomorrow…"

"You think the authorities will suspect you?"

"Of course they won't," he said promptly. "There must be dozens of people who'll fall under suspicion first. I just hate to think who Ross would replace you with."

"Thanks for keeping my ego cut down to size."

"You're quite welcome."

The grand concourse of the mall was quiet; the usual hurly-burly was reduced to the click of heels here and there and the quiet splash of the fountain. They crossed to the main door, and Zack held it open. Snowflakes swirled in on a blast of air, which sent chills up Brandi's spine.

Sealed in the artificial cocoon of the building all day, Brandi hadn't given a thought to the weather. "I didn't even know it was snowing. What a nuisance."

Zack bowed deeply. "My pleasure, madam. Half an inch of snow, delivered sometime this week, I believe you said?"

Brandi glared at him. "If you think you're getting credit for this because a couple of days ago I happened to say a little snow would help sales… Don't you have a coat?"

"I left it in my car."

"Not one of your brighter moves, I'd say."

"Oh, this suit's surprisingly warm. That's one of the things I've been meaning to talk to you about, by the way. Do you suppose we could turn down the heat around Santa's Workshop? Or the lights, at least? It's a little steamy."

Brandi shrugged. "Maybe if you weren't wearing so much fur…"

Zack brushed a few snowflakes off his white-fur lapel. "You mean this? It's fake. Kids might be allergic to the real stuff."

"I should have known."

"Besides, I'm not the only one who's uncomfortable with the temperatures up there."

"Oh? Have you polled the other Santas? I suppose next you'll try to organize them into a union and picket if you don't get what you want."

"Not a bad idea. I'll have to start making my list of demands. Where's your car?"

Brandi waved a hand toward the farthest row of the parking lot. "Sorry it's so far, but it was your idea to come out here."

"I'm not complaining."

But he must be cold, Brandi thought. Snow had already frosted his velvet cap, and a few flakes had caught in his eyelashes. She hadn't realized before how long and dark they were. She really ought to send him back to the mall, or directly to his car, instead of letting him walk on with her and get colder.

Right. She'd probably have just as much success at that as with anything else she'd tried to make him stop doing.

"I wasn't just talking about the Santas anyway," Zack went on. "The kids are uncomfortable, too. Most of them have their coats on, you know. In fact, a cooler temperature in the whole store might be more popular with shoppers."

"Why don't you start asking them? You can put that notebook to some good use for a change. Just write me a report in a couple of weeks and I'll take it under consideration."

But Zack didn't seem to hear.

Brandi followed his gaze. Twenty yards away, a woman and a small child were walking hand in hand toward a parked car. At least, the woman was walking; the child—perhaps six or seven years old—was hanging back, staring at Zack and saying two words over and over. "Santa Claus...Santa Claus!"

The woman frowned a little and shook her head. "Peggy, no. I told you we only came to look at the Christmas lights."

"But if I can just talk to Santa Claus—"

"What would you like to tell me?" Zack called.

"Zack," Brandi said under her breath. "Isn't this covered in the rules? The mother doesn't want you. And a Tyler-Royale Santa doesn't go marching up to kids. He waits to be approached."

"I'm not working for you at the moment, Brandi. Remember?"

Before she could protest, he was gone. His long stride ate up the distance despite the slick snow underfoot, and before Brandi could catch up he'd crouched down beside the child. "Are you going to come sit on Santa's lap tomorrow and tell me what you'd like for Christmas?"

"No," the child said. It was hardly more than a whisper.

"Why not?" Zack asked gently. "Surely you're not scared of me. I'm nothing to be scared of."

The woman said, "You can't give my daughter what she wants for Christmas, sir."

There was a note of pain in her voice—and a veneer of dignity—that made Brandi look more carefully at the pair. The child's winter coat was obviously not new and was much too big for her. The woman's was rather threadbare, and neither of them was wearing boots. But there was a pink ribbon carefully tied in the child's hair, and the mother's back was very straight.

Zack didn't move; he was still at the child's eye level as he glanced up at her mother. His voice was somber. "Maybe not," he said gently. "Some things are tough even for Santa." He slid a gentle arm around the child's shoulders. "But I'll certainly try. Why don't you tell me anyway, Peggy, just in case?"

The child sent a swift look up at her mother, then hid her face against his soft velvet sleeve. But her voice was clear. "I want you to bring a job for my mommy."

Brandi's heart squeezed painfully.

The woman looked down at her shoes. Brandi noticed that the toes were wet through. "I made the mistake of telling Peggy there won't be a Christmas at our house this year because I don't have a job. It's all she's thought of since. I'm sorry she's bothered you with it." The quiet dignity in her voice made Brandi ache even more.

Zack seemed to be utterly speechless.

He ought to have known better than that, Brandi thought. Now he'd gotten himself into a prize jam, with his big ideas about how easy it was to play Santa Claus. "That," she said under her breath, "is why we have rules."

Zack looked up at her innocently, as if he hadn't heard a word. "Brandi, didn't you say you needed floor clerks?"

"I may have. But—"

The woman interrupted. "Please. Don't trouble yourselves any further. Peggy, come along." She tugged the child gently toward the car.

Brandi scowled at Zack. Then she took one more good look at the woman and said, "Wait!" She reached into her handbag for a business card and a pen, and wrote across the top of the card, *Please do your best to find a position for...* "Ma'am? What's your name?"

The woman told her, with obvious reluctance. "Theresa Howard."

Brandi jotted the name on the card and handed it over. "Bring this to the third floor of Tyler-Royale tomorrow, and ask to see the personnel director."

The woman's eyes widened as she read the card. "Oh, Miss Ogilvie..."

For an instant, Brandi was afraid the woman was going to kiss her hand. "It will probably just be for the season," she said hastily. "But it will help."

Zack didn't say a word. They stood together in the snow until Theresa Howard and her daughter reached their car, and then started walking toward the far side of the parking lot again.

Brandi finally broke the silence. "There's no need to thank me for making you look good, Zack." She didn't look at him.

"I wasn't exactly planning to."

"Oh, you weren't?" Brandi stopped and faced him squarely, her hands on her hips. "How dare you put me in that position?"

"I didn't put you in any position. I just asked a question."

"You embarrassed me."

"Maybe I did. I'll admit I intended to. But I certainly didn't force you to hire her."

Brandi glared at him. "Well, at least you realize that much, so don't get any crazy ideas for the future.

I do happen to need floor help, and Mrs. Howard looked like a good possibility. But that doesn't mean I'm going to start rescuing you if you make a habit of this."

"Of course you won't," Zack said.

Brandi thought he sounded just a little too agreeable, and she shot a suspicious stare at him. He looked perfectly innocent.

"That kind of situation is why you need training," she pointed out. "Which is what I tried to tell you the first day, when you insisted this was such an easy job. The very idea of promising a child something without any idea of what she's going to ask—don't you even realize the damage you could do?"

"I didn't promise the child anything except that I'd try," Zack argued. "I certainly didn't tell her I could give her whatever she wanted."

Brandi thought it over and decided reluctantly that perhaps he was right—technically, at least. Still, he hadn't exactly used good sense.

He'd walked on, and she had to scramble a little in the snow to catch up. "You ought to know better than to plunge in like that and meddle, Zack. The mother clearly didn't want you to interfere."

Zack stopped walking and looked down at her. In the yellowish glare of the lights, his suit had an orange cast, and his eyes were darker than she'd ever seen them before.

"You know what I think?" His voice was light, almost careless—but there was an edge to it that made Brandi uneasy. "I suspect you're really not a person at all, *Ms.* Ogilvie. You're an alien. Or a machine. That's it—you're a robot. Unfeeling and inexhaustible. And I know just the way to prove it."

Before Brandi could do more than blink in surprise, he'd swooped on her. He seized her shoulders and pulled her against him so fast and so tightly that the air was forced out of her lungs with a whoosh. She tried to push away from him, and looked up into his face to protest. But even if she'd had the breath to speak, she wouldn't have been able to, for his mouth came down on hers in a forceful, demanding kiss.

Brandi stopped fighting. She intended to stay still for a few seconds, to allow him to think she'd capitulated, though she was really waiting for a chance to break free. If he relaxed his hold for just an instant... But his arms were like iron around her, and his mouth on hers was taut and fierce and searing.

And infinitely more exciting than anything she had ever experienced before. The beard he wore was soft as silk against her skin, and he tasted of coffee and citrus, and of something incredibly sweet....

Slowly, the anger seemed to drain out of him, and his kiss gentled and softened. At the same time, it became more terrifying—for as the element of force vanished, Brandi felt herself responding to his caress. Her lips softened to welcome him, and she pressed herself to him almost against her will.

Eventually he stopped kissing her, eased her head down on his shoulder, and laid his cheek against her hair. Brandi didn't want to admit that it was probably a good thing he hadn't let go of her; her knees were too weak to support her.

Still, after an episode like that, she could hardly stand there in the man's arms and not make an effort to assert herself. "I'll accept your apology now, Zack." Her voice shook, despite her best efforts.

"Will you?" He sounded a little odd, too, as if he

couldn't quite get his breath. "Then of course I'll apologize. My way."

His hand cupped her chin, and turned her face very gently up to his. This kiss started out differently—soft and easy and tender—but it didn't stay that way, and by the time he'd finished, Brandi's heart was pounding at a threatening rate, and her breath was coming in sharp gasps.

Zack held her just a little way from him, to look down at her. Unable to face him, Brandi let her head droop.

"I must admit," he said huskily, "you sure don't kiss like a robot."

Slowly he released her, keeping a hand on her shoulder for a moment till she was able to steady herself. Brandi took a step toward her car and stumbled over something in the snow at her feet. She was too rattled even to think what it could be, till Zack bent to pick up the handbag she'd dropped. He brushed the snow off the leather and gave it back to her silently. Then he took her arm so she wouldn't trip again, and started toward her car.

The silence that surrounded them was complete, as if they were caught in a bubble, shut off from the outside world. There should have been traffic noises, and sirens, and voices. But Brandi could hear nothing save the beat of her heart and the whisper of their footsteps in the snow.

"What would you have done if I hadn't bailed you out?" she said.

For a few steps she thought Zack hadn't heard her. "Is that why you hired her?" he said. His voice sounded as if it came from a distance. "To bail me out?"

"Of course not. I told you, I need floor help." She didn't look at him. Instead she fumbled for her car keys.

Zack took them and unlocked the door. "Why do you want me to think you're heartless?"

Brandi slid into the driver's seat. She'd have closed the door, but Zack—absentmindedly, no doubt—was standing in the way. "I don't see that I have a lot to do with forming your opinions," she said. "And I must say it wasn't very nice of you to look so terribly astonished because I found her a job."

Suddenly Zack smiled, and the lights were back in his eyes, dancing wickedly. "I was only startled that you didn't crush her for calling you Miss instead of Ms."

"Go home," Brandi said tartly. "You're going to freeze to death."

"Yeah," Zack mused. "Good idea. I'm going to have a hot shower. Then I'm going to open a cold beer and put my feet up and think about everything I learned today." He leaned into the car and drew a fingertip down her cheek. "And I do mean *everything*."

CHAPTER FOUR

THE snow was falling harder by the time Brandi reached her apartment complex, and her car slid a little as she tried to maneuver it into a parking spot. At the rate the flakes were coming down, they'd have a lot more than a half inch on the ground by morning. So much for Zack claiming credit for giving Brandi her Christmas wish...

"I am not going to think about him," she muttered as she closed the door of her apartment behind her. She was off duty now; she'd simply forget about Tyler-Royale's problems till morning. And, after all, Zack was a store problem.

He certainly wasn't a *personal* one.

Brandi kicked off her wet shoes and flipped through the mail—three bills, a letter from a friend, and a catalog of exotic Christmas candies and nuts, which she dropped straight into the nearest wastebasket. Then she went along the hall to her bedroom to change clothes. As soon as she'd traded her suit for jeans and a sweater and put on her warmest wool socks, she could feel the tension of the day begin to drain out of her.

She took her hair down from the tight French braid and brushed it till it gleamed. Then she dropped her gold button earrings into her jewelry case and tugged the diamond cluster from the ring finger of her left hand.

"Is there a Mr. Ogilvie?" Zack Forrest had asked

yesterday. Brandi could still hear the rich undercurrents of his voice echoing through her mind and making her feel warm and cold all at the same time.

It was a question Brandi hadn't expected. She'd been wearing this ring for two years now, and it had been a long time since anyone had actually questioned her about its meaning. Many people seemed to think it was a wedding ring, but that she didn't make a big thing of it because she preferred to keep her private life to herself. And as long as they didn't come straight out and ask, Brandi had never felt obliged to confide the truth.

She had never gone to any particular trouble to promote the illusion that she was married. The ring had been a reward to herself when she'd successfully completed her management training course and been assigned a store of her own, and it had never occurred to her that some people might think it resembled a wedding ring. Brandi didn't think it did; the center stone was much larger than the other gems, with a narrow band of diamonds below it and a sort of starburst above, and it had always looked to Brandi like the dinner ring it was.

But it was funny how suggestible people were. To some of them, any ring worn on the left hand must stand for a relationship. And when Brandi consistently came alone to company functions, never appeared anywhere with a date, and didn't invite anyone to her home—well, maybe it wasn't unreasonable for her employees to assume she was married, but her husband was some kind of hermit.

Brandi didn't mind. A woman's life was a whole lot less complicated when no one worried about her single status or tried to match her up with the right man. That was particularly true for a woman at management level, one who spent most of her waking hours involved with her career. It was dangerous for such a woman to date a man who worked for her—and where else was she likely to run into one, when she had so little time for pursuits outside her profession?

Not that Brandi had bothered to think that argument all the way through, because it held no importance for her. She had no interest in adding a man to her life. A relationship only complicated things; she'd learned that lesson long ago.

So why had she reacted so strongly to Zack Forrest tonight?

Just asking the question brought back tinges of the breathless, achy, almost dizzy feeling that had swept over her as he kissed her tonight in the parking lot. She told herself that her reaction was easily explained; the man had practically assaulted her, so it was no wonder she'd felt breathless and achy and dizzy.

But she couldn't quite explain why she'd eventually kissed him back. Why she'd clung to him. Why she hadn't given him the sock in the jaw that he deserved.

A tinge of loneliness, that was all, she decided. No matter how happy she was with her life—and most of the time she was quite satisfied—still, she was alone a great deal of the time. At the store she was surrounded by people, but apart from Casey Amos, Brandi had been careful not to make those people her friends. A manager had to keep a little distance from her employees in order to be effective.

And at home... Sometimes, she admitted, her own

footsteps sounded loud in the quiet apartment, and sometimes it was a temptation to talk to herself just to hear a voice.

So perhaps it was no wonder that tonight, once Zack had stopped trying to prove his point, she'd gotten caught up in the moment. One thing she had to admit—the man certainly knew how to kiss.

But it wasn't going to happen again. Now that she was aware and on her guard—

The doorbell rang, and Brandi sighed and went to answer it. If it was Zack, she decided, she'd kick him in the kneecap and slam the door in his face.

But it wasn't Zack; her visitors were three pre-adolescent girls selling holiday garlands to raise money for their school club. "We took orders back in October," one of them explained, "but you weren't at home. Now we've got an extra garland, and we thought you might like to buy it. Since you don't seem to have any other Christmas decorations…"

Brandi said, "I don't have decorations because I don't want them, and I don't want a garland, either. Look, I admire your efforts, and I'll happily make a donation to your club, but the garland would be wasted on me. So give it to someone who'll get some good out of it, all right?" She wrote a check and closed the door with relief. At least that had been easily dealt with. If it had been Zack, on the other hand…

And just why had she jumped to the conclusion it might be Zack at her door? That made no sense at all. If the man had anything else to say, he'd surely have said it in the parking lot. Only an idiot would even dream that he might follow her home. By now he was enjoying his shower, or perhaps he'd progressed as far as the cold beer.

"And whatever he might be doing," Brandi said, "it certainly holds no fascination for me!"

It wasn't as if she wanted him around, that was sure.

The snowy streets slowed her down the next morning, and the regular monthly meeting of the store's employee association had already started when Brandi came in. Every chair and sofa in the second-floor furniture department was lined with employees. Many were ready for work when the store opened in an hour; others were in casual clothes because they were scheduled for the evening shift or had the day off. Brandi was still amazed, when she saw them all together, at how many people it took to run a store the size of Tyler-Royale.

Today's crowd was smaller than usual, however. The snow had continued through the night, and traffic was a mess. That, plus the longer-than-normal hours they'd all been putting in, had probably kept some of the off-duty employees from making the effort to attend so early in the morning. And the flu continued to be a worry; yesterday they'd had a dozen employees call in sick. Brandi wondered what the report would look like today.

She didn't realize she was looking for Zack till she found him, and then—when he met her gaze and smiled at her—she could have kicked herself. But in fact, it would have been hard to miss him; he was ready for work, and the red suit he wore, contrasted with the big, dark green wing chair he'd chosen, seemed to cry out for attention.

This morning his white Santa beard lay on his knee. Brandi wondered if he'd left it off because there would be no children here, or because it made his face itch. It was funny that she'd hardly noticed the beard last night, except for that sensation of silky smoothness as he kissed her....

And that, she told herself, is quite enough of that. She had far better things to think about than what had happened last night.

She didn't smile back at him. Zack made a show of pulling up his sleeve to check his watch, and he shook his head sorrowfully at her for being late.

Brandi scowled at him, leaned against a pillar at the side of the room, and tried to pretend Zack Forrest didn't exist. But it took effort to focus her attention on Casey Amos, who stood in the center of the room as she conducted the meeting, and a few minutes later Brandi found her gaze drifting toward Zack once more.

He caught her eye and pantomimed an invitation for her to come over.

Brandi suspected he intended to invite her to sit on the arm of his chair. Wouldn't that look cozy, she thought, and shook her head. Then she moved to the back of the room and leaned against a big armoire.

Casey said, "Those of you who want to take part in the employee gift exchange should put your names in the box in the lounge by next Monday."

One of the customer service representatives hurried in, looking a little frazzled. Zack waved her over and stood up, offering his chair.

"On Tuesday," Casey went on, "everyone who's put in a name will draw one out, and the exchange will be at the party on the following Sunday night."

Zack looked around the room, then lazily headed for Brandi's armoire.

Brandi's heartbeat speeded up just a little in anticipation of being close to him once more. Don't be silly, she told herself. What happened last night had been an aberration, born of mutual irritation and frustration, and it was over. She shouldn't be having any feelings about him at all.

Casey didn't appear to have her mind completely on what she was doing. Her gaze seemed to shift from Brandi to Zack, and then back to Brandi once more.

Her interest didn't necessarily mean anything, Brandi thought. That red suit was hard to ignore, and it must look to Casey as if the man was walking out of the meeting. Even with her eyes fixed on Casey, Brandi couldn't quite avoid seeing Zack at the edge of her peripheral vision, coming steadily closer. No wonder Casey was looking at him.

"Five-dollar limit, just like last year," Casey went on, and glanced at the sheaf of notes in her hand. "The party will be downstairs in the atrium, with music by…"

Brandi tuned her out. The annual Christmas party was just one more nuisance in an already over-busy season, in her opinion. She wouldn't go at all except that it would hurt her employees' feelings if she didn't show up.

Zack appeared beside her. "Avoiding me?" he said softly.

He looked very comfortable, with his arms folded and his shoulder against the door of the armoire, right next to Brandi.

"I beg your pardon?"

"You heard me. You're avoiding me."

"Of course I'm not."

"Then why didn't you come over and sit down? I'm a gentleman. I'd have given you my chair. Or are you so firm a feminist that you wouldn't take it?"

"I'm only an honorary member of the employee association, so I try to stay in the background."

"Is that so? Don't you believe in clubs, either?"

"It's not a club, Zack. Since technically I don't work for the store itself but for the corporation that owns the chain, I'm really not eligible to belong to the employee association. But they invited me to join anyway."

He grinned. "I'll bet that made your day—being asked to join the play group."

Brandi tried to ignore him. It was difficult, he was close enough that the barest hint of his cologne—very light, very appealing—tickled her nose.

"Or did you think I might kiss you again?" Zack murmured. "Was that what scared you off? Let me assure you, I wouldn't."

"I should certainly hope not."

"Not in public, at any rate. In private, on the other hand, you could probably tempt me."

Brandi's jaw dropped and she turned to face him directly. "Touch me again," she warned, "and you'll be out on your ear—Ross Clayton's friend or not. Got that straight, Forrest?"

Zack didn't turn a hair. "I'll try to keep it in mind." He settled both shoulders against the armoire and looked out over the room. He was so close that Brandi could feel the heat of his body, but she knew if she moved, he'd understand perfectly well why she'd done so, and he'd be amused. And Brandi was

just stubborn enough to refuse to give him the satisfaction.

She put her chin up, folded her arms in imitation
of his pose, and turned her attention back to Casey
Amos. Why in heaven's name wasn't the woman
moving the meeting along? she wondered. They
didn't have all day. Despite the snow, there'd be customers arriving in a few minutes. But there stood
Casey staring at her....

Brandi swallowed hard and tried to imagine what
that exchange had looked like from across the room.
The only good news she could think of was that they
were at the back of the room, so only Casey had been
in a position to see much. At least, she hoped everyone else had kept their backs turned.

Casey cleared her throat and flipped to the next
page of her notes. "We're going to need more vol-
unteers than usual to help with the Wishing Tree.
We've had six families register in the first week of
the program, but then Pat Emerson got the flu and
things have come to a screeching halt."

Brandi frowned. Pat was ill? That must have happened just yesterday, or surely she'd have heard it
before now.

"What's the Wishing Tree?" Zack asked under his
breath.

Brandi would have liked to ignore him, but that
would no doubt be just about as effective as pretending an impacted wisdom tooth didn't hurt. "You've
noticed the Christmas trees in the atrium?"

"They're a little hard to overlook. A dozen of
them, each ten feet tall—"

"Most of them are just to set the mood for the store
and show off special merchandise. But one is the

Wishing Tree. Families who can't afford clothes and toys and special things for Christmas ask for what they'd like to have, and the wishes are hung on the tree. Then customers or employees pick out the person they'd like to shop for and buy the gifts.''

Zack frowned. ''You just let people walk in and hang their wishes on the tree? You've never struck me as such a trusting sort before, Brandi.''

''Of course there are restrictions. In the first place, there aren't any names on the trees, just ages and sizes, and the customer service department takes charge of the gifts and delivers them to the right people. They also make sure the family is genuinely in need. People have to be registered with a charitable organization before they're eligible for the Wishing Tree. That's what Pat Emerson was doing before she got sick—coordinating all those details.''

''Who's going to do it now?''

''I don't know.'' Brandi was racking her brain, without success. ''Pat will be hard to replace. It takes a special kind of person to do that job—warm and insightful and empathetic, without being a pushover.''

Zack shrugged. ''Sounds like a management sort of problem to me.''

''Management? If you're implying that I should take it over, Zack, let me assure you—''

''That you haven't the qualifications? I'm not surprised you'd say that. You might not actually be a robot, but—''

''What I haven't got is the time,'' Brandi pointed out.

Casey went on, ''At least one person in every department should try to stay familiar with the needs listed on the tree in order to help shoppers. And if anyone can volunteer to fill in for Pat till she's back in shape, I'd love to stick around after the meeting and talk to you.''

Zack raised a hand to draw Casey's attention.

''It takes a lot of time,'' Brandi warned. ''Pat devoted herself to that project.''

''Time I've got plenty of. Since I have to be here anyway, waiting around for my various shifts, I might as well be doing something constructive.''

Brandi bit her tongue to keep from reminding him that she had offered to amend his working hours. ''I should also warn you,'' she went on, ''that Pat—''

Zack looked down at her, his eyes wide and looking even darker than usual, and interrupted. ''Are you trying to stop me from doing a good deed, Ms. Ogilvie? It's bad enough that you're a Scrooge yourself, but to stand in someone else's way...''

Brandi gritted her teeth.

Zack raised his voice. ''I'll volunteer.''

Casey peered at him. ''Hey, that's great. Stick around after the meeting—I'll get Pat's files, and Ms. Ogilvie will fill you in on the details.'' She turned to the next order of business.

Brandi looked straight ahead and waited.

A full minute went by before Zack said with deceptive gentleness, ''What exactly did she mean, you'll fill me in on the details?''

''Pat was coordinating the program, but I'm in charge of the Wishing Tree. It's not just a store project, it's a corporate one—there are Wishing Trees through the whole chain.''

''I'm going to be working directly with you?''

The look on his face, Brandi thought, almost made up for the certain irritation of having to work with

him for the next week or two, till Pat was back to full
capacity. "I tried to tell you before you committed
yourself," she said sweetly. "But of course it
wouldn't have made a difference to you, would it?
Since it's all in a good cause, I mean."

The meeting was finally over just minutes before the
store opened, and employees rushed off in all directions. Brandi waited till the confusion had eased before she tried to catch Casey. "How long has Pat been
ill?"

"Several days. Don't look at me like that, Brandi.
I only heard it myself this morning, or I'd have told
you. She had a couple of regular days off, and she
thought she'd be over the flu in time to come back
as scheduled."

"That's going to create a major problem with the
Wishing Tree."

"Oh, I don't know. I imagine your Santa can handle anything he puts his mind to." Casey looked up
at Zack and smiled. "It's the hole in my department
I'm not sure I can fill—Pat's my best saleswoman."
She put a hand on Zack's sleeve. "Let me give you
just the highlights on the responsibilities. It's not difficult, really, once you get the hang of it, and I'm sure
Brandi will—"

Just then, the clerk from Salon Elegance who had
taken care of Brandi's mustard-stained blouse came
up to her and held out a Tyler-Royale bag, and Brandi
couldn't hear what Casey was saying about her. It was
probably just as well; Brandi suspected she wouldn't
have liked the program Casey was mapping out for
her.

"Sorry, Ms. Ogilvie," the clerk said. "The cleaners did the best they could, but you can see they weren't very successful.''

Brandi pulled the blouse out of the bag. It was perfectly pressed and neatly folded, but on the front was still an unmistakable blotchy yellow stain.

She thanked the clerk for trying, then crumpled the blouse into the bag and tucked it under her arm. But Casey had finished her instructions by that time, and Zack was fiddling with his long white beard, getting it anchored just right before he went over to Santa's Workshop.

''Was that a favorite blouse?'' he asked. ''It looks like it had a bath in mustard.''

''It did, as a matter of fact,'' Brandi said. ''And since you were the cause of its ruin, I'm tempted to take the price of it out of your pay. So if you're wise—''

''Me?'' Zack sounded shocked. ''How could I have caused that?''

''It happened the first time you showed up here, when my secretary paged me to come and talk to you, so technically you're responsible.''

''Technically?'' Zack started to smile. ''Now why doesn't it surprise me at all that you'd think that way?''

The long white beard hid the dimple in his cheek, but Brandi knew precisely where it was. Suddenly she found herself wanting to slip a fingertip under the edge of the soft, fluffy whiskers and touch that tiny hidden spot. And then she wanted to tug the beard away so the dimple wasn't hidden anymore, so she could kiss it…kiss him…once more.

The desire was so strong, so sudden, and so irrational that she was having trouble breathing. What's happening to you, Brandi Ogilvie? she asked herself. You've lost your mind entirely, that's what!

"Don't you think you'd better get to work?" Her voice was a bit sharp.

"Yes, ma'am," Zack murmured. "Or I won't have enough of a paycheck for you to dock."

Brandi didn't watch him walk away. She didn't have to; she knew without even looking that he was in no apparent hurry. The public address system came to life with a crackle, followed by the opening note of "Jingle Bells." The mercilessly cheery sound was enough to push Brandi over the brink.

She squared her shoulders and turned to Casey. "By the way, would you kindly stop calling him *my* Santa?"

Casey's eyebrows soared. "Well, he does seem to be sticking rather close to you, don't you think?"

Brandi gave it up. Further protest would only call more attention to the situation than she wanted, and she'd already said more than her ordinary good sense would have allowed her to.

"I'd better get downstairs," Casey murmured. "Unless the snow keeps people away, I'm going to need six arms today."

"I might have a new employee for you."

"Joy," Casey said without enthusiasm. "Just what I need—someone to train."

"It'll make your time go faster," Brandi said with mock sympathy. "I'll tell the personnel director to send her down to you if she shows up."

"*If*? You mean you haven't actually hired her?"

"Not yet. It's a long story."

"I wish I had time to listen to it," Casey admitted. She started to walk away.

"Wait a minute," Brandi said. "Where'd you get that button?"

Casey fingered her lapel, where a small plastic-covered badge nestled discreetly against the white carnation that marked her as a department manager. "You mean this one?"

"Of course I mean that one."

Casey cupped a protective hand around the button so Brandi couldn't see it clearly. "Zack gave it to me this morning."

"I should have known Zack would be behind this. What's it about anyway?"

"You mean you haven't approved it? As cozy as the two of you have been—"

"Cozy?" Brandi's voice would have turned anti-freeze to slush. "Give it here."

"Come on, Brandi, it's just a fun little gimmick."

"You know political buttons and protest ribbons and all those sorts of personal statements are forbidden in this store."

"This is hardly a political announcement, and you can't have my button. If you want one, go ask Zack—I'm sure he'll give you one. You just have to promise you'll do something nice for someone every day till Christmas, and he'll make you an official Santa's Friend, too. Look, I've really got to run—we wouldn't want to lose sales because the department's not open, would we?" She was gone—still wearing the button—before Brandi could object.

Brandi stalked across the second floor to Santa's Workshop. There were no children in line; nevertheless she firmly set the "Santa's Feeding His Reindeer" sign in place and closed the gate just in case someone came along before she'd finished with her errant Santa.

Zack had propped one elbow on the arm of the big chair and stretched his long legs out as if he was admiring the high polish on the toes of his boots. As she approached, he rolled his eyes and stood up. "Ms. Ogilvie," he said in a tone of long-suffering patience, "at this rate, the reindeer are going to be too fat to fly."

"Then we'll make venison sausage of them and you can ride the subway and the El on Christmas Eve," Brandi snapped.

Zack sighed. "You know, I have this instinctive feeling you're unhappy with me. What is it now?"

"You mean there's more going on than just the buttons?"

"You're unhappy about the buttons?" He sounded incredulous.

"Not the buttons themselves. It's a cute gag. But you can't just start that kind of gimmick without consulting me. There's a policy in the chain that no employee can wear political or religious jewelry or buttons—"

Zack's eyebrows almost disappeared under the white fur band of his velvet cap. "So which category do you put Santa's Friends in?"

"It's the principle of the thing, Zack! If one kind of personal statement is allowed, where do you draw the line? What about black arm bands? Protest signs?"

"Has anyone ever told you you're a little intense, Brandi?" He shook his head as if in confusion. "And here I thought you were upset because I rearranged Toyland last night."

Brandi was speechless. "You did *what*?"

"Only a couple of the game displays. I got bored with shopping, you see, so I was just looking at the toys. Some of the shelves were too crowded, and it was hard to get one box out of the stack. I just moved them around so—"

"That's it," Brandi said. "You're done. You're fired."

Zack looked at her for a few seconds in silence. "Over a few buttons?"

"No. I'm terminating you because you're meddling in areas that are none of your concern. You were hired to be a Santa, not the manager of this store."

Zack pulled what looked like a television remote control out of the capacious pocket of his jacket.

"What's that?" Brandi asked.

"A cellular phone. You know, you can use it anywhere. It comes in very handy when Santa needs to consult the main data banks at the North Pole."

"Funny. What are you doing?"

"Well, I don't need to ask the elves whether you've been nice or naughty this year. I can draw my own conclusions. So I'm going to call Ross so you can tell him yourself why I don't seem to be working out." He punched a string of numbers and held the phone out to her.

"Dammit, Zack—"

The phone's buzz gave way to silence, and then to Ross Clayton's voice. It didn't surprise Brandi that there was a private number that rang directly into Ross Clayton's downtown office, bypassing switchboards and secretaries, but it startled her that Zack had it. Brandi had never been offered that kind of access; all her calls to the CEO took the standard route.

She glared at Zack, and then at the phone. He continued to silently hold it out to her, and eventually she took it. "Ross? It's Brandi Ogilvie."

"I'm glad you called. I've been wanting to talk to you."

"Have you?"

"Yes. Zack tells me he's thrilled with the cooperation he's getting from the whole store, especially you. From what I hear, things must be working out great."

Zack was looking at her with wide-eyed innocence, as if he could hear the entire conversation.

Ross went on, "Of course I could see that for myself when I was in the store last night."

"You were here?" Brandi's voice was little more than a gasp. "When? You didn't stop in the office."

"Oh, it was the middle of the evening. You'd probably been at home for hours."

Last evening, she thought. Before closing time. Before that kiss in the parking lot.

"Kelly and I brought the kids over to visit Santa. Not Zack, of course—they'd have been onto him in a second—so we waited till the next one came on duty. But afterward he was telling me how much he's enjoying himself."

"I'll bet he told you all this while he was rearranging the displays in Toyland," Brandi said dryly, and waited for the reaction. Surely Ross wouldn't condone this takeover, no matter how good a friend Zack seemed to be.

"As a matter of fact, yes—that was what he was doing. It looked pretty good when he was done. The department manager seemed to like the new look, too.''

Brandi's head was swimming.

''And the Santa's Friend buttons are cute. Which reminds me, I haven't done my good deed for the day yet. So what's on your mind? Surely you're not canceling out of the party now.''

''The Christmas party? No,'' Brandi said weakly. ''I'll be there.''

''Good. I know Whitney's looking forward to seeing you. In fact, I think you're the main reason she's coming this year. What can I do for you, Brandi?''

''I was just...'' She hesitated. ''I called to tell you Zack's the most...innovative employee I've had in some time.''

Ross laughed heartily. ''Now that doesn't surprise me. Take good care of him, and keep in touch, all right? I'll see you Saturday night.''

''Sure.'' She didn't meet Zack's eyes as she handed the phone back to him.

He punched the cutoff button and dropped the phone into his pocket without a comment.

Brandi gathered her dignity. ''I may have acted a little too hastily.''

Zack looked astounded. ''*You*, Ms. Ogilvie?''

''Don't rub it in, Forrest.''

''So that means I still have a job?''

''If I were you, I wouldn't take on any long-term debts,'' Brandi snapped. ''But for the moment—yes, you still have a job.'' She stalked toward the gate and set the sign aside.

''Oh, Brandi,'' Zack called.

She didn't turn around. ''What is it now?''

"Did I hear you say you're going to the Claytons' Christmas party Saturday night?"

"Yes. Why?"

"So am I," Zack said easily. "How would you like to go with me?"

CHAPTER FIVE

BRANDI considered picking up the ''Santa's Feeding His Reindeer'' sign and hitting Zack over the head with it. She settled for saying, as evenly as she could manage, ''No, thank you.''

''Parties like that are a lot more fun when you have a date,'' he pointed out.

''I happen to already *have* a date,'' she snapped. Her arrangement with Whitney Townsend might not be quite the kind of date Zack was thinking of, but in Brandi's opinion it was just as important—and more enjoyable, too.

Zack didn't answer. That made Brandi nervous, and finally, unable to control her curiosity, she turned around to face him. He was looking at her with what appeared to be amazement.

Brandi was annoyed. ''You don't need to look astonished about it.''

''I'm not astonished. I'm merely overwhelmed by disappointment.'' He didn't sound particularly discouraged, though. He went on blithely, ''Well, that'll teach me to ask earlier. About this Wishing Tree business...''

''What about it?''

''I'll be off duty most of the afternoon. Shall we have lunch and you can tell me all about it?''

''I expect to be very busy this afternoon.'' If the tone of her voice didn't freeze him out, she thought, nothing would.

It didn't. "How about later, then? I'll do my dinnertime stint and we can spend the evening on the Wishing Tree."

"I hardly think it will take all evening."

Zack grinned. "Oh, in that case," he said, "we can use the rest of the time to get to know each other. Won't that be fun?"

Brandi finished analyzing November's sales figures and signed the final report for Dora to fax to the main offices downtown in the morning. It was well past six, and Dora would have gone home by now.

Or perhaps she wouldn't wait for morning and her secretary—almost every department in the store was running slightly ahead of her projections, and that was the kind of news Brandi always liked to share.

She was surprised at the time. It seemed she'd been occupied with the sales reports for no more than an hour, but the whole afternoon had sped by while she worked. And there hadn't been a word from Zack. Maybe he'd had to be on duty at Santa's Workshop later than he expected. Or maybe he'd decided they didn't need this little heart-to-heart chat after all. Wishful thinking, she chided herself.

Brandi was startled to find Dora still at her desk, which was covered with the advertising layouts that would run in the next few weeks. Brandi checked her watch again to be sure she hadn't misread the time. "What are you still doing here, Dora?"

"You told me not to interrupt you this afternoon," Dora said comfortably.

"For heaven's sake, I didn't mean you couldn't go home when you were finished with your work!"

"But I'm not finished. Besides, your Santa—"

Brandi frowned a little.

Very smoothly, Dora went on, "I mean, Mr. Forrest was in. I told him I had orders not to disturb you, and he waited for a while."

"And then he just went away? You amaze me."

"He said he'd be in Toyland where he could do something constructive while he waited."

"I suppose that means he's rearranging the whole department."

"He didn't say what he intended to do. At any rate, I was afraid if I left he'd sneak back up here and barge in on you, so I stayed. The advertising slicks needed sorting anyway."

"Thanks, Dora. I don't deserve such loyalty." Brandi handed over the sales report. "Would you fax this downtown? And then just leave the rest of the advertising—tomorrow's soon enough to finish it."

She took the escalator down to the second floor. The store wasn't crowded; the snowstorm was over, but the aftereffects were still keeping many people at home, just as she'd predicted. Till the streets were completely cleared, Christmas shopping would suffer. At least the season was still only halfway along; this kind of storm just a few days before the holiday could cripple the store's bottom line.

Her favorite Santa, the one with the half glasses, was holding court by the Workshop, and Brandi paused for a moment to admire him in action. It wasn't that Zack was out of place in that chair, exactly; he did just fine—far better, she had to admit, than she'd originally hoped for. But she'd prided herself for years on perfect Santas like this one. He looked so at ease, so natural, so comfortable in the big chair....

Except he wasn't sitting in the regular Santa chair, but in a dark green wing one—the chair Zack had been occupying this morning up in the furniture department during the employee meeting, and then had given up to the woman who'd come in late. Brandi didn't want to think about how he'd managed to talk the department manager into letting him requisition it. Or maybe he'd just moved it over to Toyland without anyone's approval....

Santa looked up from the child in his lap and called, "Thanks, Ms. Ogilvie! It was very thoughtful of you to change the chairs. I really appreciate a comfortable seat—you know, those packs of toys are heavy, and I have to take care of my back." He turned his attention once more to the child.

Brandi didn't bother to tell him she'd had nothing to do with the chair. She just waved and went on into Toyland.

She almost tripped over Zack; he was siting cross-legged in the middle of an aisle with a couple of youngsters, and they'd spread the pieces of a train layout all over the floor. The kids were assembling the wooden track while Zack took the engines and cars out of the box.

Brandi leaned against a case full of fashion dolls. "Zack, what are you doing?"

He looked up. "Demonstrating the flexibility and creativity of this particular model of train kit."

"It looks to me as if you're playing."

"Well, yes," Zack admitted.

"I thought so."

"That's part of what makes this a very special toy, you understand. It not only captures the imagination of children and releases their creative side, it intrigues adults, as well.''

Brandi ignored the nods of the man and woman—obviously the children's parents—who were standing nearby. ''You're sure you're not just talking about *some* adults?''

''If you're implying I'm a case of arrested development—''

''Well, I don't see a lot of men your age sitting on the floor playing with wooden trains. Is this the height of your ambition, Zack?''

''Of course not.'' The track was assembled; Zack set the train down on it and leaned back against the nearest display case while the kids took over. ''I hope someday I'll be sitting on the floor playing with trains with my own kids.''

Suddenly Brandi could almost see that picture. A towering Christmas tree loaded with lights, a pile of packages, a train spread out on the floor, a couple of pajama-clad youngsters—and Zack.

Brandi shook her head in amazement. The man was hypnotic; she didn't even like Christmas, but he could still evoke in her mind an image straight out of Norman Rockwell. She could almost smell the turkey cooking.

She was annoyed with herself, and so her tone was sharp. ''I thought you said you wanted to take care of the Wishing Tree business tonight.''

''You'll have to pardon me for keeping you waiting.'' He didn't sound in the least sorry. ''Of course, the dragon on your office doorstep left me kicking my heels for half an hour without even telling you I was there—but I'm sure you can explain to me how that's different.''

"Dora's not a dragon. She just knew I was very busy this afternoon."

"Right." Zack stood up. "I'll be with you in a minute. Let me check with the department manager first."

"Why?"

"To make sure he can do without me. It's not terribly busy just now, but he's short a couple of clerks tonight—the flu got them. In the meantime, why don't you go get your coat?"

"What for?"

"Because I'm taking you out for a sandwich or something."

Brandi started to protest, but she realized abruptly that she was hungry. Still, there was something uncomfortable about going out with him. "Let's just go to the tearoom."

Zack shook his head. "Now that you've broken your self-imposed isolation, everyone in the store probably wants to talk to you."

"And you want me all to yourself?" Brandi's voice was saccharine. "How charming!"

Zack's eyebrows lifted slightly. "It's not that. I just don't care to risk you being paged. You might spray mustard all over me this time, and I'm particularly fond of this sweater."

Brandi could understand that sentiment; today he was wearing hunter green cashmere.

Before she could open her mouth to argue, however, he'd vanished toward the cash register, and by the time he returned she'd thought better of her insistence on the tearoom. It was handy, yes—but the last thing she needed was for another dozen employees to see them together and draw their own conclusions. Besides, though Tyler-Royale food was good, during this season she seldom had time to go anywhere else, and she knew the menus of both the tearoom and the cafeteria by heart. So she went meekly back to her office to get her coat and boots, and met Zack by the employee exit.

The parking lot had been plowed, and the snow that remained underfoot was polished smooth by traffic. But in areas where the snow lay as nature had intended, the crystals caught the lights and sparkled as if a generous hand had scattered diamonds across the soft-sculptured drifts.

"My car or yours?" she asked outside the employee exit.

"Mine's no doubt closer." He showed her to a dark sedan not far from the store.

The car was covered with snow, so Brandi couldn't tell much about it. But she looked thoughtfully at the distinctive trademark embossed into the leather seats, and listened to the soft purr of the engine coming to life. "You know, Zack, when Ross asked me to hire you, he said you'd been having some tough times lately."

"Oh, I have." His voice was emphatic. "Yes. Very tough."

"Obviously he didn't mean financially."

"What makes you think that?"

"I'm not an idiot, Zack. That Santa suit of yours is velvet, and the boots are top-grain leather—"

"Rented," Zack said succinctly.

"You're carrying a cellular phone. That's not an inexpensive toy."

He shrugged. "I'd have to buy my way out of the service contract, and that would cost as much as using it the rest of the year. I'm very careful not to exceed the amount of time my contract allows, though, so I don't have to pay extra.''

"I'll bet you are. And you're driving a very nice car.''

"It's the darnedest thing, but I can't afford to sell it.''

"Oh, really?''

"I'm serious. You know how tough it is to get the full price out of a new car. Once you drive it off the lot, it drops ten percent in value just like that.'' He snapped his fingers. "So I might as well keep it for a little while.''

"Till it's repossessed?'' Brandi said dryly.

"If it comes to that. After all, if I sold it I couldn't clear enough to buy something else, and then how would I get around?''

"You could always use the reindeer. What are you really, Zack? A corporate spy?''

"Brandi, don't you think if Ross wanted to plant a spy in your store he could have hidden me better than this?''

"I wasn't thinking of Ross.''

Zack grinned. "Now that's a unique point of view. Would it make you happier if I started wearing a trench coat and dark glasses and slinking around behind displays?''

"So you're admitting it?''

"I'm not admitting anything.''

"Well, if you're just a Santa, I'm—'' She stopped. A half-formed suspicion stirred to life in the back of her mind, but she couldn't quite put her finger on it. Until she could think it all out, there wasn't much point in pursuing the matter. And in the meantime she was still thoroughly stuck with the man.

"As long as we're speaking of Ross," Zack went on, "are you sure you won't reconsider and go to the party with me Saturday?"

"I thought this was a corporate party," Brandi pointed out. "Last year nobody below assistant manager status was invited."

"I know. Sounds deadly dull, doesn't it—all those assistant managers drinking champagne and buttering people up?"

"So the Claytons are planning to enliven the party by including you?"

"Well, not just me, I'm sure," Zack said modestly. "A few friends here and there. You haven't answered my question, you know."

"I don't believe in breaking a date because another one comes along."

"Even if it's a better one?"

"Now that's a matter of opinion, isn't it?"

She expected he'd take offense, but he didn't seem to. "Italian food all right?"

"It's fine with me."

A couple of miles from the mall, Zack parked the car beside a restaurant and came around to open Brandi's door. "You know," he said, "I've been thinking."

"That sounds dangerous," Brandi said under her breath.

"Well, it was quiet all day. Not many kids, so I had a lot of time on my hands, even while I was occupying Santa's chair."

"Speaking of Santa's chair, Zack—"

"I know, if there's any wear on it you'll take it out of my paycheck."

"That wasn't what I meant."

"It wasn't?"

"No. I haven't sat in Santa's chair, so how would I know it's uncomfortable?"

"Didn't I tell you it was?"

"Well, maybe you did, but you've told me so many things I never know when to take you seriously. I just wish you wouldn't go off on these tangents without checking with me first. You've already got Casey starting to question policy."

"Maybe that's a good thing, if she's going to be managing a store of her own next year."

"I don't want to get into an argument with you about details, all right? The point is, I can't have every stock boy and salesclerk setting their own rules, but with you as a stunning example, I'm apt to have mutiny in the ranks by Christmas."

"Is that all that's bothering you?"

"*All*? Don't you think that's enough?"

"Well, maybe you've got a point," he conceded. "In that case—"

The hostess greeted Zack by name and showed them to a table with a checked cloth and enormous red napkins. The menus were huge, too, and seemed to list every conceivable combination of pasta and sauce. Brandi glanced at hers and put it aside. "You were saying?"

Zack looked at her over the top of his menu. "I knew you were decisive, Brandi, but really—"

"The only thing I've decided is that I'm not going to read the whole menu. Since you obviously come here often, you can choose."

"And that way you can concentrate on me," Zack mused. "What a perfectly charming—"

Brandi interrupted. "Just make it something that doesn't take hours to cook. Now I believe you were going to agree to some terms concerning your job?"

Zack held up a hand as if he was taking an oath. "I'll check out anything important with you before I do it."

Brandi supposed she'd have to be satisfied with that, inadequate as it was. What was his definition of important anyway? "All right. Now we can talk about the Wishing Tree."

"Just a minute. I want to tell you about my idea first."

Brandi looked at him a little doubtfully. "Zack—"

"You said not two minutes ago that you wanted me to consult you before I did anything else," Zack reminded her.

That does it, Brandi thought. I'm caught in my own trap. "What now?"

"Have you considered keeping the store open extremely late one night a week till Christmas, so parents can leave the kids at home and come to do their Santa shopping in peace?"

Brandi frowned. "Can't they just get a sitter during normal hours?"

"Not as easily as they can once the kids are in bed. Besides, the kids are apt to know where they've gone, and there are boxes and bags to hide when they get back. If it's the dead of night and the little ones are asleep, it's much easier to sneak the packages in and keep the Santa myth intact."

"How do you know so much about kids?" Brandi

challenged. "If you don't have any of your own yet—"

"Oh, there are a dozen or so who have adopted me as their favorite honorary uncle." He ordered manicotti for both of them and a bottle of red wine, and leaned across the table to drape Brandi's napkin solicitously across her lap.

"And that's why you thought being a Santa would fill in an awkward spot in your life?"

"I suppose that's what brought it to mind. What do you think? Shall we organize Parents' Night Out?"

"Aren't you going to have enough to do with your job and the Wishing Tree?"

"What's to do? A little advertising, a few signs in Toyland..."

"A few employees who are disgruntled at having to work even crazier hours."

"I don't think that will be a problem. I've talked to several, and most of them think it's a good idea."

"And I suppose you've already mentioned it to Ross, too."

"Well, yes. I didn't think it would hurt."

Brandi sighed. So much for checking things out before he acted! "Go ahead, then—ask the manager of Toyland and see what he thinks. But you're only authorized to proceed if he wants to, and if you can get the mall management to agree to let us break the rule about normal business hours. Understand that, Zack?"

"Absolutely," he said airily. "And while we're on the subject, what about a special night for senior citizens to shop? I bet they'd like not being knocked over by the regular shoppers. We could organize buses to go around and pick them up—''

''One thing at a time, Forrest. What are you doing anyway? Maneuvering for a job in public relations?''

''Now that's a thought.''

''Well, take my advice and don't settle for a single store. With all your ideas, you could keep the whole chain hopping.''

''Thank you.''

''I didn't intend it as a compliment.''

The waiter brought their wine. Zack tasted it and nodded, and the waiter filled their glasses and silently went away.

Brandi swirled her wine and sipped. ''Take those crazy buttons, for instance...''

''What about them?''

''Where did you get the things anyway?''

''The notions department made up a thousand for me. They did a good job, didn't they?'' He reached in his pocket. ''I've got an extra if you'd like it.''

''No, thanks.''

He tipped his head to one side and studied her.

''You don't think I'm capable of doing a good deed a day, do you?'' Brandi challenged.

''I'd sure like to watch you try.''

''Well, that's got nothing to do with it. There's a corporate policy that forbids wearing that kind of thing, and until it's lifted, I feel I have to abide by it—even if I end up blinking at violations by every member of my staff.''

''Ross has a button.''

''I know. He told me. That's different, because Ross makes the rules.''

''The idea seems to be working anyway. I just

started handing the buttons out yesterday, and I think the store feels more cordial already. Everybody likes being Santa's friend, you see. I think that good feeling could transfer into the Wishing Tree program, too.'' He leaned forward confidingly. ''We could end up with the biggest Wishing Tree program in the chain.''

''It's not a competition, Zack.''

''Pity. So tell me what I've let myself in for.''

''Mostly a whole lot of paperwork and detail. The family comes in to talk to you. You check with the agencies to be sure they're really needy.''

Zack frowned. ''I can't imagine someone applying for charity if they don't need it.''

''Then you'd be surprised.''

''But their pride—''

''Exactly. The people who need help the worst are the ones who are too proud to ask for it.''

''Like Theresa Howard,'' Zack said.

Brandi nodded and made a mental note to check with Casey Amos and the personnel director tomorrow about whether the woman had come in. ''On the other hand, there are some who are out to get anything that's available. Pat used to spot-check some of the families whose stories sounded a little fishy— she'd go drive by the address and be sure the pieces all fit together.''

''And did they?''

''Not always. But don't go on a crusade. The majority are legitimate. It's basically pretty simple. The family makes a list of their needs, and you'll fill out a star for each person and put it on the tree, with age and clothing sizes and likes and dislikes, so the person who chooses that star to shop for has some ideas. Then as the wishes are filled, the customer service department will let you know, and you'll pack things up and deliver them.''

Zack shrugged. ''You're right. It sounds pretty easy.''

''I said *simple*, not *easy*. There are always snags. Gifts don't come in at a nice, steady pace, and sometimes one member of a family is passed over altogether. There's a fund provided by the store, so you can go shopping to fill in all the gaps.''

Zack didn't look enthusiastic at the prospect.

The longer Brandi thought about it, though, the happier she was that he'd taken over the Wishing Tree. If he gave the project the attention it needed, he wouldn't have time to annoy her. ''Just think,'' she consoled him, ''all that time you've spent wandering around the store looking at the merchandise won't be wasted after all. I'm sure *somebody* would like that steamer you bought for your sister.''

The manicotti was perfectly cooked but literally too hot to eat, so they dawdled over dinner, and it was midevening before they got back to the mall. ''Are you going into the store or home?'' Zack asked.

Brandi yawned. ''Home, I think. After a couple of glasses of wine I probably wouldn't get much done in the office anyway.''

Zack eyed her in mock disappointment. ''I'm shocked at you, Ms. Ogilvie. *I* have to go back to work. And you were late this morning, too. Maybe I should report you to Ross.''

''Go ahead. You'll no doubt find him at home.''

Zack parked his car next to hers. ''Meaning that he doesn't work sixteen-hour days? That's a good question, you know. If the CEO doesn't have to, why do you?''

"Because he's the CEO, and I'm not. He's already at the top and I'm still climbing. Sit still, Zack—don't bother to come around and help me out."

Her protest came too late, though; he was already out of the car. She'd parked in the farthest corner again, and the lights were dimmer here. Zack seemed to loom over her as he had last night—right before he'd kissed her. He was awfully close. Brandi wondered if he was thinking of doing it again, and told herself that the odd little ripple in her nerves was anxiety.

"Thanks for dinner," she said quickly, as she slipped her key into the door lock. "I still think you should have let me pay for it, though, since it was store business."

"That's okay. You can take me out for lobster someday, and I promise not to protest." But he smiled as he said it.

She couldn't close her door because he was standing in the way, almost leaning over her as if he was inspecting the equipment—or her. "And you said *my* car's nice," he murmured.

Brandi almost laughed in relief. "If you think I'm going to get into that argument, you're crazy." She turned the key in the ignition. The only sound was an ominous clicking from somewhere in the engine. "What the—" She tried again.

"Your battery's dead, so you might as well give it up." Zack put a fingertip on the switch that controlled the headlights and gently pushed; the switch clicked off.

Brandi groaned. "The sun was just coming up

when I got to work this morning, and I must have left the lights on. What an idiotic thing to do!''

''No, it's not. But why don't you use the setting that automatically turns the headlights off?''

''Because I don't trust it to work,'' she admitted.

Zack didn't laugh; she gave him credit for that. But even in the dim glow of the parking-lot lights, she could see the gleam of humor in his eyes.

''All right,'' she said irritably, ''so I'm a fool, too.''

''I didn't say that, Brandi.''

''Well, you don't have to stick around. Though I would appreciate it if you'd pull out your magic little telephone and call a wrecker for me.''

Zack shook his head. ''I would, but—''

''I know, you've used up all your free time.''

''It wouldn't do any good to jump-start the engine unless you plan to drive around for an hour or two to recharge the battery. Otherwise, it'll be dead again by morning.''

''Oh. I hadn't thought of that.''

''Besides, do you really want to sit here in the cold and wait? The wrecker guys are probably hours behind on their calls, with the snow. You'd be better off to leave it till tomorrow.''

Brandi had to admit he was right. ''In that case, Santa's Friend, how about doing your good deed for the day?''

''And take you home? I'd love to, but I'm supposed to go on duty in fifteen minutes, and I'm afraid if I don't turn up for my last half hour of work the boss will fire me.''

''Zack—'' She waved a hand at the thinly populated parking lot. ''Skip it. Nobody's there anyway.''

"Certainly. But may I have that in writing?" Brandi stuck her tongue out at him. Zack grinned and helped her into his car again. "Did you lock your car?" he asked.

"You think someone's going to hot-wire that vehicle and drive it off if I didn't? Of course I did, Zack—I've lived in this city all my life. I always lock doors."

"And turn off headlights?" But the smile that tugged at the corner of his mouth made it a teasing comment, not a tormenting one, and Brandi was surprised to find herself feeling almost warm because of it. Warm, and a little confused. What was happening to her anyway?

She gave him directions to her apartment complex, and when they arrived she unfastened her seat belt and let him help her out of the car. "Would you like a cup of coffee, Zack? Nothing fancy—I haven't been to the supermarket in days—but..."

It was the least she could do. He'd bailed her out of a jam after all. It was only friendly to offer him a hot drink. He'd probably turn her down anyway; he'd be anxious to get home, too.

Zack smiled and said, "I'd like that."

Brandi swallowed hard. It wasn't fair, she thought. All the man had done was smile, and the odd, breathless ache she'd felt this morning—when she'd been assaulted by that sudden, idiotic urge to kiss the dimple in his cheek—swept over her once more.

She found herself wondering what he'd have done if she actually acted on that kooky impulse. Not that she had any intention of finding out, she assured herself. A cup of coffee, a little polite conversation, and he'd be out the door.

Just outside her apartment was a visitor, obviously waiting for the bell to be answered. As they approached, the girl swung around to face them, and Brandi recognized her as one of the three who had been selling garlands the night before. Her arms were full of evergreens.

"Oh, you're finally home," she said with obvious relief. "I've got your garland, you see."

Brandi frowned. "I thought I told you to give it to someone who wanted it."

"But I can't. My mother got really annoyed with me, and said I couldn't sell things to people and then not deliver them. So here." She thrust the sharp-scented greenery into Brandi's arms and hurried away.

"Well, isn't that a switch," Brandi muttered. "All I tried to do was make a donation, and now I'm stuck with this thing." The bundle was huge and prickly; she shifted it gingerly and tried to reach her key. "And I do mean *stuck*. Do you want a garland?"

"No, but I'll hold it for you." Zack rescued her from the evergreens. "Can't you use it?"

"I don't decorate for Christmas."

"Not at all? Don't you celebrate it, either?"

"Of course I celebrate, in my own style. I'll collapse and rest up from the rush and get recharged for the next one—the after-Christmas sales and returns."

Zack frowned. "That doesn't sound like much of a celebration. Don't you have a family?"

"Not really. My mother died when I was eighteen."

"That's a tough time to lose a parent."

She nodded curtly and went on. "My dad's in

California. They divorced when I was little, and he's got a second family."

"So you don't feel you fit in?" Zack's tone was gentle.

His conclusion was true, but Brandi didn't feel like admitting it. The last thing she needed was well-meaning sympathy. "It's got nothing to do with that. I can't go dashing off halfway across the country in the midst of my busiest season for the sake of carving up a turkey."

"So you stay home and have a bologna sandwich by yourself."

"Something like that." She wasn't about to get drawn into a discussion of her habits. "Just dump the garland anywhere."

"What are you going to do with it?"

"I'll put it out with the garbage if I can't find anyone who wants it. Maybe some of your Wishing Tree people would like to have it. Coffee or hot chocolate? I think I have some of that powdered mix."

"Coffee's fine." He was still standing in the center of her living room, the garland in his arms, looking around. "It's a shame, you know. You've got a perfect place for a tree, right by the balcony doors so the neighbors can enjoy it, too."

He had to raise his voice, since Brandi had gone on to the kitchen. She put the kettle on and called back, "That's it, you see. On the rare occasions I'm in the mood to look at a Christmas tree, I just step onto the balcony and enjoy everyone else's. No fuss, no muss, no dropped needles..."

Zack didn't answer, and Brandi busied herself finding a tray—since she didn't entertain often, she had to look for it—and setting it up. "I don't have any fresh cream," she warned.

"I don't use it, remember? You know what you need to get you into the Christmas spirit? A couple of kids."

Brandi choked. "Oh, no. Never." She stepped around the corner and almost dropped the tray. Most of the garland was now draped neatly over the mantel; Zack was arranging the last few feet. And the gas log in the fireplace was burning brightly. "Make yourself at home," she said dryly.

"Thanks. Why no kids?"

"They're altogether too much responsibility."

Zack tipped his head to one side. "Were you a difficult kid?"

Brandi was puzzled at the question. "No more than most, I suppose. But it's a different world these days. People who aren't willing to be at home with their kids shouldn't have them in the first place."

"And you aren't willing?"

"Not particularly. I could hardly quit—I have enough to do making a living for myself as it is, without taking on a couple of people who'd need college educations one day. Besides, I told you I love my job."

"To say nothing of your ambitions for the future."

"That's right. Zack, the garland's kind of cute, but—"

He hadn't paused as they talked, and the last bit of greenery seemed to nestle down around the mantel as if it belonged there. "Doesn't that give the whole place a festive air?" He came to take the tray out of her hands and set it on the wicker trunk in front of the couch. "I didn't mean permanent kids anyway."

"You mean I could be sort of an adopted aunt to someone else's? I don't know any kids all that well. Besides, I don't seem to have the knack for getting along with them, and it's dead sure I don't have the time to learn it, even if I wanted to."

Zack didn't answer. He sat quietly, cradling his coffee cup in one hand, staring at the fire.

Brandi wondered what he was thinking, and the suspicion she'd felt earlier in the evening stirred to life again. But this time, as if her subconscious mind had spent the intervening time chewing on the problem, it was not just a half-formed hunch but much more.

She'd asked if he was a spy, and without pausing to consider, Zack had made a joke about Ross. Was it her imagination, or had there been something almost Freudian about how fast that answer had come? Did it mean he was working not for some rival of Tyler-Royale's, but for Ross Clayton himself?

He'd even had that very private telephone number, she reminded herself.

Brandi stirred sugar into her coffee and leaned back in her corner of the couch. "Ross has always had a troubleshooter he can call on," she said almost dreamily. "Someone who can go into any of the stores and diagnose and fix problems."

Zack's eyebrows rose. "What brought that up, Brandi?"

She didn't answer the question. "A few years back it was Whitney Townsend, but now she's settled in Kansas City. At the moment there doesn't seem to be a troubleshooter, because when San Antonio got into some minor difficulty a few weeks ago, Whitney went down to sort it out."

"I don't quite—"

"Or maybe there is a troubleshooter—but for some reason Ross doesn't want anyone to know just now who's doing the job. So he sent Whitney to take care of the small problem, and held the real troubleshooter in reserve for the big one."

Zack shrugged as if he was willing to humor her by playing along. "Secrecy could be an advantage for Ross at times, I'm sure."

"Exactly." Her fingers were trembling. "And that's what made me start to wonder tonight about what you're really doing here. You're certainly not an ordinary Santa, Zack, so what are you? Are you Ross's troubleshooter? And if that *is* what's going on—then why are you here? What's wrong with my store? And why didn't I realize there was a problem before the head office did?"

CHAPTER SIX

THEN Brandi held her breath. Was her suspicion the truth? Was the trouble Ross had spoken of that first day not Zack's personal problem at all, but something wrong with the store?

And if it was, would Zack admit it?

The suspicion had been building in her mind all evening, and so quietly that Brandi had been unable to put her finger on it. Her misgivings had started when he'd showed her to his car—or maybe long before that, when she'd first noticed the quality of his Santa suit—and had finally burst forth in full flower.

The trouble was, even though the theory was her own, Brandi couldn't quite make herself believe she'd hit on the right answer. She couldn't imagine how she could be oblivious to a problem large enough to cause that kind of response; even now, she couldn't begin to think of anything going on in the store that would upset anyone in the head office.

But there was something strange going on—and she could find no other combination of circumstances that made sense. Zack's explanation of why he was still using his cellular phone despite a financial downturn might hold water—but the easy dismissal of his expensive car didn't.

"You may have to run that one past me again." Zack sounded as if she'd hit him solidly right in the diaphragm.

As if he was startled, Brandi thought. But was he

surprised at the accusation because it was false, or because he'd been discovered?

He went on, "Ross wouldn't go behind your back like that, would he?"

"He has before," Brandi said. "Not with me, exactly. I mean other managers, in other circumstances. Whitney Townsend's told me some tales about investigating a store without telling the manager."

"How could you be unaware of a problem so bad that Ross would go into overdrive about it?"

Brandi's eyelids were stinging. She shut her eyes to try to keep the tears from showing. She was a professional woman, and she didn't cry about business matters; what had come over her anyway? "I don't know," she mumbled. "I don't know."

The silence was oppressive.

Zack hadn't really answered her question, she realized, and she found herself wishing that she hadn't said anything at all. If it was true, she wasn't helping the situation by blubbering about it like a baby. And if it wasn't true, she'd simply made a fool of herself.

Zack slid closer. She could feel the warmth of his body next to her even before he slipped a hand under her chin and raised her face to his. "Brandi, look at me."

She had to make a great effort to open her eyes.

Zack's voice was husky. "Nothing like that is going on. The troubles I'm dealing with are my own."

Her unshed tears made his face look blurry, but despite that fact, Brandi thought he had never looked better. "You're telling the truth, Zack?" she whispered.

"I swear it. From everything I can see, the store is doing beautifully, and you..." He paused, and said something under his breath that Brandi didn't quite catch. Then he bent his head to very deliberately kiss a tear from her eyelashes. "And you are beautiful, too," he whispered, and his mouth claimed hers.

Already emotionally off balance because of her fears, Brandi reacted to his kiss almost as she would have if she'd stepped off a cliff. She was dizzy, and her stomach had an all-gone feeling as if she'd looked down and found nothing but air beneath her feet. Her breath came in painful gasps, and she clutched at Zack.

He eased her back against the couch, but that didn't seem to help, for each kiss increased her dizziness. The only thing she could depend on was the strength of Zack's arms holding her, cradling her, keeping her safe. He was the one remaining solid object in a world gone suddenly topsy-turvy, and so she pressed against him and kissed him back, until suddenly she didn't care if she fell all the way to the center of the earth, so long as he was with her. Her ears were ringing already—had she fallen so far?—but she hardly noticed.

Zack pulled back a little. Brandi murmured a protest and tried to draw him down into her arms once more, but he resisted.

Brandi frowned a bit. Her senses came flooding back, and she realized the telephone was ringing. How had she gotten so frazzled that she hadn't even heard it? And what did Zack think of her preoccupation—for obviously *he* hadn't been so carried away that he'd missed it.

She was still a little light-headed, and she had to clutch at the door frame to steady herself as she went into the kitchen to answer the phone.

She recognized the voice; it belonged to one of the security guards at the store, and he sounded tense. "Ms. Ogilvie? There's been a little trouble down here. It's over now, but I thought I should call you anyway."

Brandi shook off her giddy feeling. "What happened?" Midway through the guard's explanation, she cut him off. "I'll be there as soon as I can."

Zack was standing in the center of the carpet when she came back into the living room. Had he heard the conversation, Brandi wondered, or was he on his feet because he intended to leave just as soon as possible?

While she wasn't naive enough to think Zack hadn't enjoyed that kiss, the whole situation *was* a little awkward. She'd kissed the man as if she was starving—as if she expected never to have another chance to be held and caressed. She wondered if he thought she'd thrown herself at him; she couldn't blame him if he did.

Her voice was a little tense. "I hate to ask for another favor, Zack, but can you take me back to the store?"

He reached for the coat he'd draped across the back of a chair. "Trouble?"

"Remember the weird guy the security guard warned us about?"

"You mean the one who was hanging around the parking lot last night?"

Brandi was momentarily distracted. Had it really only been last night that Zack had walked her to her car—and kissed her? She pushed the memory to the back of her mind. "Tonight he tried to hold up the clerk at the perfume counter just inside the main door from the mall. She reached for the panic button instead of the cash, and he gave her a shove and ran.'' She slid her arms into the coat he was holding for her. "I should have been there.''

Zack gave her shoulders a sympathetic squeeze. "And just what do you think you'd have been able to do about it?''

"That's beside the point. It's my store, and my job." She flipped her hair over her coat collar, and the gleaming auburn mass hit him squarely in the face. "Sorry. I didn't mean to swat you with my hair.''

Zack shook his head a little, as if the blow—light as it was—had stunned him. "A robbery—right in the mall?''

Brandi nodded. "Crazy, isn't it? He'd have to run a hundred yards down the mall to get outside.''

"Or else cut across the store to the parking-lot exits.''

"Yes—but either way, he might run into any number of security people before he got out of the building and away.''

"Did they get him?''

"I guess not," Brandi said reluctantly. "By the time the clerk could stop screaming and tell anyone what had happened, the guy was long gone.''

"Then maybe he wasn't so crazy after all.''

Brandi settled into the passenger seat and nibbled at her thumbnail. "Fortunately the clerk wasn't badly hurt—just shook up and maybe bruised a bit. You know, I've always felt we were safe from that sort of thing, just because there are seventy stores and hundreds of people around all the time, and it would be so difficult for a robber to get away.''

"Maybe this kook isn't smart enough to think about things like that."

Brandi shivered. "If you're trying to make me feel better, Zack, you're not getting the job done. I'd rather think a would-be robber would be smart enough to think through the consequences, because if he isn't, anything might happen." She lapsed into silence, which lasted till they arrived at the mall.

Closing time had passed, so Zack ignored the no-parking signs and pulled up in the fire lane beside the mall entrance nearest the Tyler-Royale store. Just a few yards away were three police cars, lights flashing.

"Zack," Brandi said slowly as they crossed the sidewalk to the mall entrance. "About what I said earlier—I'm sorry I accused you of being involved in some kind of plot."

Zack silently held the door for her.

Brandi went on. "I must have sounded absolutely paranoid. When something threatens this store, or even appears to…well, I go a little crazy, I'm afraid."

"Brandi—"

The tone of his voice scared her; he sounded almost somber. Brandi hoped he didn't intend to discuss the kiss they'd shared, and how it fit into the pattern of her behavior. She couldn't look straight at him. "This isn't the time or the place for a chat, Zack. So can we just forget it happened? Please?" She didn't wait for an answer.

Inside the Tyler-Royale store, a knot of people was gathered around the perfume and cosmetics counter nearest the atrium entrance. The still-shaken employee was sitting on a tall stool, twisting a handkerchief in her fingers and talking to two policemen. She didn't even see Brandi.

The security guard came hurrying up. "I'm sorry if I woke you, Ms. Ogilvie, but I thought—"

"You didn't, John. I'm glad you called."

"Oh? You sure sounded funny, like you'd just dozed off." The man glanced from her to Zack, who was standing just a step behind her, and suddenly a tinge of red appeared in his face.

Obviously, Brandi thought, he'd gotten the wrong idea. There was no point in trying to correct his impression, though; any kind of protest would sound fishy. She said crisply, "Where's the Doberman?"

"In his kennel. I thought with all the cops around, we didn't need the confusion of a dog just now."

"You're sure you won't need him?"

The guard nodded. "The guy's long gone. Lots of people saw him go, but they didn't realize what was happening in time to stop him."

"Of course." Brandi turned to Zack. "This is obviously going to take a while. You don't need to wait around."

"How would you get home if I left?"

"Someone will give me a ride. Or I'll take a cab."

The perfume clerk heard her and turned around. She looked pale and shaken, and when Brandi patted her shoulder, she burst into tears.

Brandi put both arms around the woman. "It's all right," she whispered. "You did just fine."

"But Ms. Ogilvie," the woman wailed, "the policeman says I should just have given the robber the money!"

Brandi shot a look of acute dislike at the nearest cop. No doubt he was right; no amount of money was worth the risk of a life. But now was hardly the time to suggest to a shaken woman that she'd done precisely the wrong thing. "Well, it's done now," Brandi said soothingly. "And you did the very best you could. When you're finished with the interviews, we'll make sure you get home, and you can take as much time off as you need."

The policeman said gruffly, "I'm finished. She should probably be checked out at a hospital, though." After the employee had gone, leaning on a co-worker's arm, he turned back to Brandi and folded his arms across his chest. "Worried about the money, are you? Well, he didn't get any, so I guess in your view she handled it exactly right."

"Of course she didn't," Brandi snapped. "But did you really think you'd make her sleep better tonight by pointing out she could have gotten killed because of the way she handled it?"

Zack moved a little closer. "Brandi..."

Brandi bit her lip. She didn't look at Zack, but at the policeman. "I'm sorry. Look, if you want to come back and teach all my employees the proper response, I'd be glad to have you. But scaring her a little more tonight isn't going to help anything."

She thought she saw, from the corner of her eye, a smile tugging at Zack's lips.

The police looked for another half hour to be certain the would-be robber hadn't left any fingerprints or dropped any belongings, but finally they finished up, and Brandi was free to go. The store was quiet by then. She could hear the soft click of the Doberman's toenails against the hard-surfaced floors as the guard made his regular rounds. Brandi yawned as she said good-night, and wondered how long it would take for a cab to show up.

But Zack hadn't gone after all. He was sitting quietly on a carpeted display cube at the far side of the atrium, and when Brandi came toward him he stood up and slid a hand under her elbow.

The warm support was welcome, but Brandi wasn't in the mood to talk. Zack seemed content with the silence, as well. It wasn't until they were almost back at her apartment complex that he said, "You're a thoroughly confusing creature, Brandi."

She was puzzled. "I don't know what you mean."

Zack didn't answer. Instead he said, "You'll be all right alone?"

It didn't sound like a question, but a statement. Obviously, Brandi thought, whether she'd invited him or not, he didn't intend to come in. Well, that was all right with her; it was late, and she was drained.

Still, she couldn't help but wonder what his reasons were. Was he simply tired himself? It would be no wonder; he'd had a long day, too. Was he being sensitive to her exhaustion? Or was he still wary of what had happened between them earlier this evening?

"I'll be fine," she said. "After all, I'm not the one who got held up."

He parked the car and helped her out. "You don't depend on anybody but yourself, do you, Brandi?"

She shrugged. "Who else am I supposed to depend on?"

He didn't answer that, and he didn't make any other move to touch her. He leaned against the passenger door and watched till she was safely inside the building.

Despite the central heating in her apartment, Brandi felt cold. That was the aftermath of shock, no doubt, from the evening's events. Tyler-Royale had its share of shoplifters. The main office had discovered an em-

bezzler once, and now and then a store was burglar-
ized. But so far as Brandi knew, this was the first
time any of the stores had actually been robbed during
business hours.

It was no wonder she was still feeling stunned. But
was the robbery the only reason she was upset? Was
she still suffering the aftereffects of that kiss, as well?
Things had come very close to getting out of control.
What would have happened if the security guard
hadn't interrupted?

Nothing, she told herself. She certainly knew better
than to allow it.

She warmed her hands over the fireplace. She'd
been in such a hurry to get to the store that neither
of them had remembered to turn the gas log off. Fortunately Zack had put the fire screen in place, so there
had been no danger.

The sharp scent of evergreen seemed to float from
the garland atop the mantel and fill the room. Zack
had done a good job of arranging it; nevertheless the
greenery was a little bare. Brandi knew exactly what
would make it look right—some twinkling lights
twisted through the branches and a scattering of small,
bright-colored ornaments. Then the barest dusting of
spray snow on the end of the needles, with some glit-
ter for emphasis, and the garland would be perfect.

Not that she would do any of those things. There
wasn't any point to it when she was scarcely ever
home.

Zack had said this evening that she needed a couple
of kids to get her into the Christmas spirit. Well, she
didn't know about getting into the spirit—it seemed
to her that having a couple of little people around for

the holidays was likely to do nothing but increase her level of exhaustion.

The mental image she'd created in Toyland this evening, as she watched Zack playing with the kids and the train, sprang unbidden to her mind once more. In fact, if she closed her eyes halfway she could almost *see* that scene. A decorated tree stood beside the patio doors where he'd said it should go, and the train went round and round the track as two children in fuzzy sleepers knelt to watch. She couldn't see their faces, but they weren't very old.

Once, she had assumed she'd have children one day. It wasn't something she'd thought a great deal about; she'd never been around children much, and she had no great longing for them. But kids were part of the package of life—when the time was right, there would be a man and a marriage, and ultimately, a family.

And up to a point, things had followed the pattern. There had been a man; there had very nearly been a marriage. Thank heaven, she thought, that it hadn't come to that, for Jason didn't really want a wife, he wanted a caretaker.

Zack had observed tonight that she depended only on herself. Brandi could have told him, if she'd wanted to, how she'd learned that lesson not once but over and over. First from her father, who'd seldom shown interest in her after the divorce. Then her mother had died, and—unfair though it was to blame her for that—Brandi had felt abandoned once more. And, finally and most cruelly, there was Jason, who said he admired her independence, but meant only that he appreciated the freedom it offered him to be untroubled and irresponsible.

But she hadn't told Zack any of that, and she wouldn't. Sharing so much with someone she barely knew would be asking for another kind of hurt, and Brandi had learned the hard way not to allow herself that kind of weakness. She didn't need anyone to confide in anyway. She was used to depending only on herself. That she knew how to do.

The apartment was so quiet she could hear her own heartbeat. So quiet that she was tempted to talk to herself just to hear a voice.

Maybe she should get a cat to keep her company. Talking to an animal was nothing like talking to herself. Nobody would think she was crazy if she talked to a pet.

And having a cat around would certainly be less troublesome than dealing with a man. Particularly, she thought, with her sense of humor restored, a man like Zack Forrest!

Brandi was running late. Saturdays were always busy at the store, and this afternoon she'd had to deal with a series of unhappy customers who wanted to talk to the manager. Then the personnel manager had come in to complain that Zack was sending half his Wishing Tree clients upstairs to apply for jobs. And after that, she'd stopped to visit the perfume clerk to see how she was getting along after the robbery attempt.

As a result, Brandi was still feeling a little frazzled when she turned her car over to the valet in front of Ross Clayton's lakeshore mansion, and her palms were just a little damp as she started up the long walk to the immense carved front door.

Under the circumstances, she'd rather be almost

anywhere than here tonight. If it wasn't for Whitney Townsend's order to attend, she'd probably have found a last-minute excuse.

Brandi had never been particularly fond of business events that masqueraded as parties. It seemed such a waste of time to get dressed up to go out with the same people one saw regularly through the course of the job. If people were going to talk about their work anyway, she thought, why not just put them in a boardroom and let them get on with it? And if they weren't going to talk business, why were they bothering to get together in the first place? The only thing all these people had in common was Tyler-Royale.

No—*most* of these people had only the stores in common, she corrected herself. There was Zack, of course, and whatever other friends the Claytons had decided to include tonight to liven things up. Though even Zack had ties to the store...

Suspicion flickered once more at the back of her mind, and resolutely Brandi extinguished it. He had reassured her that her store was in no danger, and she had no reason to disbelieve him.

She might not even see Zack tonight anyway. She'd be busy with Whitney Townsend. Besides, there were so many Tyler-Royale executives that it was quite possible to circulate all evening and still not see every single one of them.

Every leaded-glass window in the Claytons' Tudor Revival mansion was aglow. Standing guard at each side of the walk were huge evergreens, crusted with snow and golden lights, which were reflected from the snow-covered grass.

Before Brandi reached the house, another car pulled up; she recognized the manager of the San

Francisco store and paused on the sidewalk to let him and his wife catch up. She'd done part of her training in the San Francisco store, but she hadn't seen much of the couple since.

The night was cold and still; her breath hung in a cloud, and the manager's wife scolded her for waiting outside.

Brandi smiled and kissed her cheek. "I'm used to this kind of weather. And I wanted to say hello before we got into the crush inside." It was true; the fact that she didn't particularly want to walk into the party alone had little to do with it.

Why should she be feeling sensitive about that anyway? Certainly the crowd wasn't going to pause and hush to admire her new black velvet dress. All the Tyler-Royale people were used to Brandi appearing by herself; they'd hardly even notice.

But Zack would. And even though she'd told the truth about having a date, if he saw her coming in alone, he'd have good reason to wonder.

Not that he'd be looking, she reminded herself. So it was silly to go to any extra effort for his sake.

Just inside the massive carved oak front door, Ross Clayton and his wife were greeting their guests. Brandi hung back to let the San Francisco couple go ahead of her, but within a minute Ross took Brandi's hand and murmured, "Now who wins the honors for getting you to show up here tonight, I wonder?"

Brandi let her eyes widen just a little. "What on earth do you mean? Ross, you know I'd never miss a Tyler-Royale event unless I had overwhelming reason."

Ross chuckled. "I know. It's just our bad luck that you always seem to have overwhelming reason. Why not this time, that's what I'd like to know. Which reminds me, you've been awfully quiet all the way around for the past couple of days. How are things in Oak Park?''

Brandi shrugged. "Hectic, but what else is new? Have you ever considered moving the company Christmas parties to July? It would be a whole lot easier to fit them into everyone's schedules.''

"You mean you'd actually like to fit them into yours? You amaze me.''

Brandi bit her lip.

He smiled a little. "It's not a bad idea, actually. I'll consider it. You know, Brandi, that's one of your strengths. You always have a different way of looking at things.''

"Thanks,'' Brandi said crisply. "At least I think that was a compliment.''

Ross laughed. "Is Zack still working out so well?''

Brandi's eyes came to rest on the velvet lapel of Ross Clayton's tuxedo, where one of Zack's buttons proclaimed that he was Santa's Friend. "Depends. Do you want reassurance, or the truth?''

"Ouch. Maybe we should talk—''

Ross's wife interrupted. "Don't you think that's enough business, darling? You did promise me you'd lay off tonight and let everyone have a good time.'' She offered her cheek to Brandi. "We're using the guest room at the top of the stairs for the ladies' coats. The maid will take yours up if you'd like.''

The San Francisco couple had already handed over their coats and moved off into the throng, and the guests who had followed Brandi in showed every sign of monopolizing Ross for the next ten minutes at least.

"Thanks," Brandi said, "but I'll go and comb my hair, too." That way, when she came back down, it wouldn't be like walking into the party alone. It was silly, she knew—all her life she'd been walking into parties by herself, so why should it bother her tonight?

She slowly climbed the massive staircase. From one of the lower steps, she had a good view of the big formal living room, and she paused to look over the crowd. She told herself she was trying to spot Whitney, but she was terribly aware that there was no sign of Zack, either. That should be no surprise, she decided; there were more guests here tonight than Brandi had seen at any other Tyler-Royale party she'd ever attended.

There were several women in the guest room, chatting as they fussed with their makeup, and the air was heavy with cologne and hair spray. Brandi laid her coat on the bed, ran a quick comb through her auburn curls, and left. It was better to take the chance of being considered rude then to risk a full-fledged sneezing fit by sticking around for another minute.

But even such a short stay in the overfragrant room had made her eyes water, and Brandi paused in a little alcove in the hallway, leaning against the paneling and trying to blot the moisture away with the edge of a lace-trimmed handkerchief.

Party noises drifted up the open stairs. From the room she'd just left came a woman's voice and an answering laugh. And from down the hall came a peal of childish giggles.

The Claytons' kids, she thought. No doubt their parents thought they were safety tucked away for the night. Brandi took a step toward the sound and then stopped; it was none of her business after all. Probably the children were with a sitter or a nanny anyway. She didn't know much about kids, but surely these were too young to be left on their own with their parents so busy.

A door opened, sending light streaming into the dimly lit hallway, and a small girl, perhaps three years old, appeared. She was holding the hem of her pink flannel nightgown up with both hands, and her chubby knees pumped as she ran down the hallway toward Brandi.

A man followed. The dim lights and the moisture in Brandi's eyes prevented her from seeing him clearly, but he looked incredibly tall compared to the child, and one of his steps corresponded to half a dozen of hers. Before the little girl had covered more than a couple of yards, he'd caught up with her, bent, and tossed her over one shoulder.

The child squealed happily.

"Shush, Kathleen," the man said, "or we'll have your mother up here and nobody will have any more fun."

His voice was rich and warm, and—despite the warning—loaded with good humor. At least, Brandi thought, this little scene explained why Ross had thought Zack would make a good Santa Claus.

She stepped out of the shadowed alcove. "Hello, Zack. Having a bit of trouble?"

"You might say," he answered. "The little varmint gave my bow tie a good yank and then ran."

Brandi took a good look at him. His dark trousers looked just a little rumpled, he wore no jacket over his stiffly pleated formal white shirt, and the ends of his tie dangled loose. She thought he looked wonderful.

The child giggled and grabbed for the tie again. "I got you, Uncle Zack! Didn't I?"

Uncle Zack? He'd mentioned a sister. Was it possible she was Ross Clayton's wife? And how did that all fit together?

"And now I've got you, nuisance." Zack shifted the child to a more comfortable position.

"Uncle Zack?" Brandi asked. "I didn't know you were related."

"I'm not—it's purely an honorary title." He studied Brandi's face. "Is something wrong?"

"No. Why?"

"You look as if you've been crying."

"Oh." She shook her head and tucked her handkerchief into her tiny black evening bag. "It's just all the scents in the cloakroom. I have to be careful at the store, as well. Too much perfume in the air and I'm a mess."

"That's good. I thought it might be something serious."

The child squirmed to get down, and effortlessly Zack rotated the little body into a firmer hold so she couldn't escape.

"You're obviously no amateur at this sort of thing," Brandi said. "Though I must say you don't look like a baby-sitter."

"Oh, after you turned me down for the party I figured I might as well be useful. These affairs are so deadly dull. Come and join us if you like."

His words were casual, but the way he looked at Brandi was anything but. Ever so slowly, his gaze roved over her, from the loose cloud of auburn curls, over the sleek black velvet of her dress to her high-heeled pumps, and back to her face again.

Brandi felt herself growing warm, and she had to force herself to stand still. He had warned her the day they met, she remembered, that sometime he'd give her a good looking-over. She supposed this was it.

"We were halfway through a game when Kathleen attacked me," Zack went on, "so I'd better finish or I'll have a mutiny from her big brother. Coming?"

Brandi hesitated. "I don't think so. I don't know anything about kids."

He smiled a little. "How do you think people learn?"

"Anyway," Brandi remembered with relief, "someone's waiting for me."

Zack's gaze skimmed her body once more. "Yes," he mused. "And getting impatient, no doubt. I can understand why they would be."

His voice was very slightly husky, and its effect on Brandi was like silk rubbing softly against her skin, creating an electrical charge that fluttered her pulse and did funny things to her breathing.

She retreated toward the stairs, trying her best to look dignified. She wasn't sure she succeeded.

CHAPTER SEVEN

BRANDI reached the bottom of the stairs before she realized she hadn't even been looking for Whitney. Instead, she'd been basking in the memory of Zack with the little girl in his arms.

The child had been charming. And Zack hadn't exactly been hard on the eyes, either, Brandi had to admit. Despite his slightly rumpled appearance—or perhaps because of it—he had a personal magnetism that she'd bet few of the other men at this party did. Zack looked better in half a tuxedo than most men did in the whole thing, and there was something heartwarming about a guy who ignored his dress-up clothes in order to play with a couple of kids—

Brandi shook her head in rueful disbelief. What was happening to her, for heaven's sake? She was suddenly discovering a romantic streak she'd never dreamed she possessed! What was it about kids anyway? It wasn't that she had anything against them—in fact, she'd hardly been around any kids since her own childhood days—but she'd never been one to coo over babies or be charmed by tiny tots. So why should she suddenly find Zack's Father Goose act appealing?

She tried to focus her attention on the swirl of guests. Surely by now Whitney would be here, and once busy with her friend, Brandi would forget all about Zack.

The party had grown even larger in the few minutes

Brandi had been upstairs. More guests were streaming in, and she had trouble making her way through the entrance hall and into the living room. Standing near the enormous, glittering Christmas tree in a bay window was a group of executives; they waved her over, but Brandi smiled and shook her head, and went on looking for Whitney.

The massive doors between the main rooms had been thrown open, and waiters were circulating with trays of drinks and hors d'oeuvres. Brandi took a glass of champagne and wandered toward the dining room.

But her progress was slow; several times she was interrupted by people who exclaimed over how well she looked and how long it had been since they'd seen her. They made such a big deal of it that Brandi began to feel guilty. Just how long *had* it been since she'd attended one of these parties anyway?

She'd just spotted Whitney, at the far side of the dining room, when the manager of the Minneapolis store buttonholed her to ask how she was planning to handle the new bookkeeping system that the head office was putting into place. It took twenty minutes to dislodge him, and by then the cocktail hour was over and people were starting to drift out of the room.

Brandi was just looking around for her friend again when Whitney appeared beside her, tall and sleek in pure white silk and a neckline that outdid every other woman in the room.

"*There* you are," Whitney announced with relief. "I was beginning to think you'd stood me up after all."

"I wouldn't dare," Brandi admitted, and gave her a hug. "You look wonderful!"

The man beside Whitney gave a little snort. Whitney turned to him with a stunning smile. "You've already made it clear what you think of the neckline, Max, so no further editorial comment is necessary. You remember Max, don't you, Brandi?"

"Of course." Brandi extended a hand to Whitney's husband.

Whitney glanced around the room. "I suppose we'd better move toward the pool—that's where dinner is being served." She eyed Brandi. "It's very polite of you not to wrinkle your nose. When I first heard about it, I couldn't help telling Ross he had to be kidding."

"Well...it is a beautiful pool. But—"

"Not anymore. His newest innovation is a portable dance floor that sort of hangs over the water. Can you imagine?" But Whitney seemed only half-interested; her gaze was moving steadily across the room. "Drat the man, where *is* he? I saw him just a minute ago."

"You mean Ross? He was in the front hall when I came down from the cloakroom, but that was at least half an hour ago."

"Why would I want Ross?"

Brandi's heart gave an odd little leap. "Then who are you searching for?"

Whitney said sweetly, "Don't look at me like that, darling. I'm not matchmaking."

"Of course you're not. You've got far better sense than that." But Brandi's breath was doing odd little things, nevertheless.

"Not that I wouldn't, if I thought it might do some good," Whitney admitted. "But in this case I'm completely innocent. The new manager of the Seattle store is here, and it's his first corporate party, so I thought it would be nice to make him feel at home.''

It wasn't Zack, then. And come to think of it, why should Brandi have jumped to the conclusion that he was the one Whitney meant? Zack could hardly be the only unattached male in a crowd like this. Who was to say Whitney even knew him? In fact, Brandi was sure she'd mentioned Whitney's name the other night, and Zack hadn't reacted at all.

None of which explained the twinge of disappointment she felt—which of course was an utterly ridiculous reaction. ''It's sweet of you to look out for him.''

''So's he,'' Whitney murmured. ''Sweet, I mean. Not that I'd expect you to notice that on your own. We may as well go on. He'll catch up with us sooner or later, as the seating's all arranged.''

The pool occupied a much newer wing of the house. The high-arched ceiling and glass walls allowed the space to act as a conservatory, as well, and huge green plants softened the sharp angles and hard surfaces. Tonight, since the snow-covered lawns outside were lit as brightly as the interior, the glass almost vanished and the pool wing seemed to be an island of tropical warmth floating freely in a sea of winter.

Tables for four were set up all around the perimeter of the room, and a band's equipment was ready in a corner. It took a close eye to recognize the pool in the center of the room, covered as it was by a hardwood dance floor, elevated a step above the surrounding area.

''It looks pretty solid,'' Brandi said.

"Well, that's one thing in its favor," Whitney murmured. "If it hadn't, I wouldn't have set foot on it."

A dark-clad arm slid around Whitney's waist, and she gave a little crow of surprise as Zack kissed her cheek.

Brandi was startled. Zack in half a tux had been impressive enough, but the complete picture was stunning. She'd known from the first time she met him that he looked wonderful in black, but she hadn't dreamed of this magnificence. He certainly didn't look as if he'd been roughhousing with a couple of children within the last hour.

He wasn't paying any attention to Brandi, but looked instead at Whitney as if she was the focus of all his dreams. "Lovely dress, dear," he said. "Of course, I'm surprised Max let you out of the house displaying that neckline."

"Watch what you say, Zack," Max warned. "Or you'll have a whole lot of guys laughing up their sleeves at you when your wife turns up wearing a dress like that."

There was a strange all-gone feeling in the pit of Brandi's stomach. A wife? But he'd asked her to come to this party with him!

Of course, no one had ever told her Zack *wasn't* married. And there was certainly no reason she should be feeling let down over it, Brandi told herself crossly.

"And I will happily help her choose it, too," Whitney said. "Though I'll no doubt be hobbling 'round the store with my walker by the time you get married."

The surge of relief that sang through Brandi's veins

made her feel weak—and then angry. What was happening to her anyway?

"I'll take my chances," Zack murmured. "Our table is right at poolside." He smiled at Brandi and took her hand, holding it between his two. "Isn't that delightful?"

Our table? But hadn't Whitney said just a minute ago that the seating was prearranged? "Hold it," Brandi said. "*He's* the new manager in Seattle?"

Zack looked horrified. "Who told you that?"

"Of course he's not," Whitney said. "And he's not joining us for dinner, either. As a matter of fact, I'm not even going to introduce him to you. Look, Zack, just be a good boy and go away, will you?"

"You don't have to introduce us," Brandi said. "We've already met." The way he was looking at her made the room feel a little too warm all of a sudden. He was still holding her hand, too, but Brandi noticed that fact only when he raised her fingers to his lips.

Whitney looked exasperated. "How?"

Zack said, "I make it a point to get acquainted with every pretty woman at a party." He drew Brandi toward the table and pulled out her chair.

"I know you do." Whitney's voice was dry. "And that's exactly why I wasn't planning to introduce you—I'm not about to give you my seal of approval. Brandi isn't simply a pretty woman at a party. She's worth three of you, Forrest. So go away, will you?"

Zack gave no indication that he'd even heard the order.

Brandi decided it was nice to know that it wasn't just her he ignored in order to do as he pleased. It was some relief to find that Zack could be as immovable as the Rock of Gibraltar where others were concerned, too.

He seated Brandi with a flourish and moved around the table to hold Whitney's chair, as well. Whitney glared at him; he simply pointed at the tiny name cards that adorned each place. She read them, and finally sighed and sat down. "Is there nothing you won't descend to, Zack?" she asked. "I thought rearranging place cards was too low even for you, but…"

He looked innocent. "I never touched them."

"Then you bribed somebody who did," Whitney muttered. "It's the same thing."

"Oh, you really wouldn't have liked the Seattle person. He's too agreeable—he'd have bored you stiff before you'd eaten your appetizer."

"Well, there's certainly no danger of that with you, is there?" Whitney said sweetly. "How did you two meet anyway?"

"Zack's the newest Santa at my store," Brandi said.

"*Zack*?" Whitney sounded horrified.

"Didn't Ross tell you?" Zack asked.

"Don't tell me it was his idea," Whitney said firmly.

Brandi murmured, "It certainly wasn't mine."

Max leaned forward. "We haven't had a chance to talk to Ross. We just got in a half hour before the party."

A uniformed waiter brought their appetizers, huge, succulent shrimp marinated in a vinaigrette dressing.

After the waiter was gone, Zack added thoughtfully, "Ross probably didn't mention it because he felt bad for me. This is just to tide me over some troubled times, you understand.''

"No doubt you'll get back on your feet eventually," Whitney said.

"Oh, I'm sure of it."

"I can't wait to see this," Whitney said.

"What? Getting back on my feet, or playing Santa? You can catch the late performance tonight, if you like—I'm scheduled to work the last hour the store's open." Zack glanced at his watch. "You'll help me keep an eye on the time, won't you, Brandi?"

"That's a crazy schedule," Whitney said.

"I'm not complaining."

"You'd better not be," Brandi said softly, "because you chose it yourself."

"You were very firm about the idea of my setting my own hours."

"I also told you I was willing to negotiate that schedule, Zack."

He smiled. "Does that mean you'd rather I stayed here tonight instead of going back to the store? That's wonderful, Brandi, because it was going to make a terrible dent in the party for both of us if I had to leave."

Whitney looked as if the shrimp she'd just bitten into tasted sour, but she didn't say anything.

Brandi studied her with puzzlement. She'd known Whitney Townsend for several years, ever since Brandi had started her management training course under Whitney's supervision, but she'd never seen the woman at a loss for words before.

"It's a fascinating job," Zack went on airily. "I'm getting quite attached to it. There's no predicting it, you see. One minute I'm getting smeared with chocolate-covered kisses, and the next I'm defending the whole idea of Santa Claus to a kid who's really too old to be sitting on anyone's knee. Yesterday I not only rescued a lost child, but I stanched a bloody nose after two kids got in an argument about whose turn it was. I felt immensely valuable.''

Brandi frowned. ''I didn't see a report on that.''

''What? The bloody nose? It was no big deal. They stopped the fight themselves as soon as they remembered Santa was watching.''

''Anytime a customer needs medical attention, I should be notified, Zack.''

''The situation didn't require medical attention so much as comfort. It was a very minor bloody nose.''

''Still—''

''You know, Brandi, it wouldn't hurt if you'd learn to delegate some authority.''

Zack's tone was mild, but the reprimand stung a bit anyway. Brandi was annoyed not only at the remark but at her reaction to it—why should she be feeling sensitive over his criticism? It was her store, and her responsibility, and he had no business criticizing her.

And he ought to have notified her; the policy handbook he'd been given stated very clearly that any time a customer needed medical attention, no matter how minor the situation appeared, the matter was to be brought to management's attention. Minor ailments could become big ones, and the store could end up being held responsible, especially if there was no proof of what had actually been done for the customer.

Didn't Zack understand that rules weren't simply made for the fun of it, but for good reason? Just a couple of days ago he'd agreed to consult her on important matters—but already he was taking things into his own hands again.

"Too bad it's such seasonal work," Whitney was saying. "You could make a career of it."

"That's a thought. Maybe I could play St. Valentine next, and then a leprechaun. And I'm sure there's an opening for the Easter Bunny. The costume might be a little uncomfortable, though—all that heavy fur."

The band had begun to play by the time they finished their appetizers, and Max leaned across to Brandi and asked her to dance. There was nothing Brandi wanted less right then, but good manners forbade her to refuse.

The music was slow and easy, and she could look over Max's shoulder and see the two at the table deep in conversation. "I wonder what they're talking about," she said finally.

"Probably not the Easter Bunny. Beyond that, I haven't a clue."

Ross Clayton appeared beside them. "May I cut in, Max?"

Brandi waited till Max was out of hearing, and said, "What kind of hold has Zack Forrest got on you, Ross?"

"You mean like blackmail material?" Ross was obviously amused. "Why? What's he been telling you?"

"Nothing much. That's part of the problem." Brandi stopped herself just in time; it wasn't exactly prudent to complain to the boss about a difficulty she ought to be able to solve herself. "How well do you know this guy, Ross?"

"Pretty well. Don't worry—he's a bit of a free spirit, but perfectly harmless."

Brandi looked up at him through narrowed eyes. "I'm charmed to hear it," she murmured, and wondered what her personnel director would have said about that. Sending the Wishing Tree clients upstairs for job interviews was another thing she'd have to bring up the next time she got a chance to talk to Mr. Free Spirit in private; he apparently thought he was running an employment agency. "He seems to be enjoying the Wishing Tree, at any rate."

"I think he'd like to be more involved," Ross went on.

"Oh, don't worry about that." Brandi's voice dripped irony. "He does just fine at minding other people's business."

Zack tapped Ross's shoulder. "Something tells me I'm being discussed," he murmured. "Ross, did Brandi tell you the manager of Toyland wants me to replace him when he retires after Christmas? No? I didn't think she would." He slid an arm around Brandi just as the music changed to a soft, slow, romantic beat, and drew her close.

"I didn't tell him because I didn't know it." Brandi missed a step, and Zack's arm tightened a little more.

She was feeling a little light-headed, but she wasn't sure if it was because of the intimate way he was holding her or the announcement he'd made. The idea of having Zack around on a more or less permanent basis was enough to make any store manager lose her grip, that was sure.

She lifted her chin. It was uncomfortable to look straight at him when he was holding her so close.

"The only thing he's said to me is that you're running him off his feet with special orders for oddball toys."

"I know. He's extremely proud of me. The increased volume alone—"

"Oh, really? I thought he sounded plenty worried. It'll be wonderful if everything comes in, of course— but what if it doesn't, Zack? We're going to have a lot of unhappy parents and infuriated kids."

"So that means we shouldn't try? I didn't make promises, you know."

Brandi shook her head. "Sometimes it doesn't matter how carefully you say it, customers still think you've promised. Maybe I'll just put you in charge of complaints, and then you'll have to deal with the mess you've made."

"Do you always assume it's going to be a mess, Brandi?" His voice was easy, almost casual.

The question startled her a bit. "Of course not. The store would never get anywhere if I had that attitude. We'd never try anything new."

"So your hesitation only applies to me?"

"You must admit you're a bit more challenging than the average employee, Zack."

He didn't smile as she'd expected he would. A moment later, he said, "Can we leave business for another day and just enjoy the party?"

Brandi shrugged. "I'm enjoying myself as it is." She was a bit surprised to find that she was telling the exact truth, and also a little concerned that Zack might think she meant it was his presence that pleased her so much. "I mean—"

"Are you happy, Brandi?"

Happy? That was an odd question. "If you mean does the blood sing joyfully in my veins every single minute of my life, no. But I'm content. I like my job—''

"Is that all you want? All you need? Are you satisfied to be just content?"

"I have goals, of course," she said a bit stiffly. "But you said you didn't want to talk about business. What do you mean anyway? Not many people are all that wildly happy, you know. Simply being content isn't a bad thing at all."

"It's not enough for me. I want the world—all the wild swings and the breathless joy and the overwhelming ecstasy there is to be had."

Brandi shook her head. "Sounds uncomfortable."

"At least it's never boring."

"Just because something's consistent doesn't make it boring, Zack."

He was silent, as if he was thinking that over.

Brandi decided the conversation had gotten a bit too serious. Why was it that talking about happiness could be so depressing anyway? "By the way, what did you do to the man from Seattle?"

He smiled. "Nothing much. I simply introduced him to the sultry lady clothing buyer from Atlanta."

"Was that before or after you switched the place cards?"

"I'm wounded, Brandi. I didn't do that—he did."

"At your suggestion?"

"Well, I did tell him where everyone was sitting," Zack admitted. "Don't take it personally, though— she really is very attractive, and he hadn't caught so much as a glimpse of you at that point."

"I'm surprised, if she's such a stunner, that you didn't reserve her for yourself," Brandi said sweetly.

Zack slanted a look down at her and smiled, and

Brandi's heart seemed to turn over. She couldn't look away, and for an instant, her body felt numb and completely out of her control. She stumbled, and Zack drew her closer still. She could feel his breath stirring the hair at her temple, and the warmth of his hand seemed to melt the black velvet at her waist. She wanted to stretch up on her toes and kiss that delightful dimple in his cheek, and then close her eyes and let her head droop against his shoulder and forget the party in order to lose herself completely in him.

She had to use the last bit of common sense she possessed to tear her gaze from his face and turn her head away. She realized gratefully that the waiter had returned to their table with their entrées.

Zack had seen, too. "Mighty inconvenient timing," he murmured as he guided her to the edge of the floor.

Brandi pretended not to hear, but her pulse was thumping madly. What had he been thinking just then? she wondered. And if they hadn't been in the middle of a crowded room, what might he have done?

As they sat down once more, Whitney studied them with an impartial, level gaze. It wasn't an unfriendly look, just an appraising one. Still, it made Brandi a bit nervous, and she tried to laugh as she said, "You usually look at things that way when you're considering damage control."

Whitney didn't answer. Instead she said, "I hear you had some excitement at the store the other night."

"You mean our robber?" Brandi tried a bit of her prime rib; it was so tender that the weight of the knife was almost enough to cut it. "I suppose next we'll have to start combat training for all employees."

"It's got to be a fluke," Whitney said.

"Would you want to take a chance?"

Zack said, "How's the employee doing?"

"Incredibly well, from what I can see." Brandi put her fork down. "I went to visit her this afternoon, and she insisted she'll be back to work tomorrow."

"So soon?"

"Don't look at me that way, Zack. I suggested she take a few extra days off, but she thinks the longer she stays away the more difficult it will be to come back, and it's hard to argue with that logic."

"Especially when you're short of help," Zack murmured.

"Exactly." It was the perfect opening to mention his habit of sending prospective employees up to personnel. "And as long as we're on the subject of employees, Zack..."

"Yes?"

Brandi thought better of it. That kind of discussion was far better held in private, and it seemed she'd lost any desire to delve into business tonight. "Never mind. We can talk about it later."

Zack smiled, and the talk moved on to other things. As soon as they'd finished dinner, he drew her back onto the dance floor. The band was playing a series of slow, soft, dreamy numbers, and Brandi had no idea what time it was when Zack shifted his hold on her in order to check his wristwatch.

"You don't have to do your last shift," she murmured.

Zack's voice was soft and lazy. "You *are* having a good time, aren't you? The store's been closed for hours. It's almost midnight."

"Really?" She was vaguely surprised that it didn't

bother her much. "Are you afraid I'll turn into a pumpkin when the clock strikes twelve?"

"Do you usually?" He didn't wait for an answer. "The kids were planning to drive their baby-sitter nuts by trying to stay awake all night, and I told them I'd peek in at the stroke of midnight to find out how the slumber party's going. Want to come?"

She didn't even hesitate. "All right."

The room he'd come from much earlier that evening was quiet and shadowed now, the only light falling from a night-light on a desk in the corner. It was obviously a boy's room; he was curled up in the top bunk, under a coverlet decorated with cowboys. In the bottom bunk, surrounded by a couple of dozen dolls and stuffed toys, was the little girl Brandi had seen earlier. Her rosy cheeks were flushed, and her cheek was pillowed on the fat tummy of a furry panda bear. She'd kicked off her frilly quilt.

Zack tucked it back around her. "Baby-sitter one, kids zero," he murmured. "I didn't think they'd make it to midnight."

Brandi studied the softness in his face. "You're very attached to them, aren't you?"

"They're very special kids." He gave a last pat to the cowboy quilt and drew Brandi back into the hallway. In the quiet little nook at the top of the stairs he stopped and turned her to face him.

Almost automatically, Brandi put her hands on his chest—to keep a little distance between them, she thought. Or, perhaps, so she could feel his warmth and the strong beat of his heart through her palms.

Even in the dim light, the diamond cluster on her left hand sparkled. Zack caught her hand and turned it to watch the stones at play. Then he said quietly,

"Allow me," and slid the ring from her finger. Brandi started to protest, but she hadn't finished forming the words when he slid it into place on her right hand instead. "That's much better," he murmured, and kissed the bare spot at the base of her engagement finger.

Brandi had never realized that was such a sensual spot. She gasped a little, and Zack let go of her hands and drew her into his arms.

In the space of an instant, Brandi considered all the reasons she shouldn't let him do this. Then she dismissed them. She relaxed into his embrace and raised her hands to cup his face and draw him down to her.

This was very different from the other times he'd kissed her. This time he seemed almost hungry, as if only she could satisfy the needs he felt, and the sensation rocked Brandi to her bones.

She didn't know how long he kissed her, only that it seemed forever and still wasn't long enough. When Zack raised his head, his voice was almost hoarse. "I need to talk to you. But this isn't the time or the place."

She couldn't speak; her throat had closed up. She shook her head, meaning to agree that this was hardly the best choice for a heart-to-heart discussion, but before she could do more, they heard footsteps coming up the stairs, and they moved apart just in time.

"There you are, Zack," said a jovial voice. Brandi didn't recognize the man; he must be one of the Claytons' friends, not a Tyler-Royale executive. "How are you enjoying the toy business? I wanted to ask you—"

Zack made an impatient gesture, as if to cut him short. Brandi knew exactly what he was feeling; she would have little patience right now with another discussion of bookkeeping systems. What she needed was a few minutes by herself to clear her head. "Excuse me," she murmured.

"I'll wait for you downstairs," Zack said, and Brandi slipped away for a moment to the cloakroom.

Whitney was seated at the dressing table, tipping her lashes with mascara. She looked at Brandi in the mirror, and her eyes narrowed slightly.

As if, Brandi thought guiltily, she can see the kisses still burning on my lips.

Whitney replenished her mascara wand and leaned closer to the mirror. "I should probably bite my tongue off rather than say this," she murmured, "but watch out for Zack."

Brandi didn't look at her; she dug through her bag in search of a lipstick. "Why? Don't you like him?"

"Of course I like him. Everyone likes him; he's perfectly charming, just as most love-'em-and-leave-'em guys are. But you never know what's he's up to. This whole Santa episode makes no sense whatever."

Brandi carefully outlined her lips. As casually as she could, as if it didn't matter, she said, "I thought maybe he was really working for Ross as the new troubleshooter or something."

Whitney gave a genteel little snort. "I doubt you'd ever catch Zack doing anything that responsible." She snapped the catch of her handbag. "Watch out, Brandi." She left the room without waiting for an answer.

For a couple of minutes, Brandi was alone in the cloakroom, but then it began to fill once more. The laughter and heavy mix of perfumes made her head start to ache, and she went back out to the hallway.

Zack had already gone down to the party; the shadowed little nook at the top of the stairs was empty. Brandi paused for a second at the top of the steps, trying to regain her mental balance, when she heard a voice from the room across the hall from the cloakroom.

It was Whitney's voice, low and urgent, with a hard edge that made the hairs at the nape of Brandi's neck rise.

"What's going on, Ross?" Whitney said. "Zack wouldn't tell me the reasons, but I've mentored Brandi for years, and I have a right to know. Why have you planted Zack in that store?"

CHAPTER EIGHT

BRANDI'S hand closed on the newel post with a grip so tight it should have hurt, but she was too stunned to notice.

Just two nights ago she'd asked Zack if he'd been sent to investigate her store, and he'd denied it. He'd said straight out that the problems he was dealing with had nothing to do with the store, or with her. His troubles were his own, he'd said; the store was performing beautifully....

At least, that was what he'd seemed to say. And then he'd kissed her so intensely and thoroughly that Brandi had stopped thinking about her suspicions. She wondered now if that was why he'd kissed her—because it was the simplest way to distract her from an inconvenient line of thought. It had been a very effective move, if so.

But Zack had been lying. Or perhaps he had told the literal truth, but phrased his words so carefully that she'd missed the underlying reality. It didn't make any difference, really, which it was—the intent had been to deceive.

Or was it possible instead that Whitney was simply wrong?

Brandi seized on that explanation with relief. It was easier to dismiss Whitney's intuition and business experience than to believe Zack had lied to her. Whitney's judgment was at fault, that was the problem. For some reason Brandi didn't understand, Whitney had taken a dislike to Zack, and she was willing to believe the worst of him.

Now it all made sense.

Brandi had actually taken the first step on her way downstairs when Ross said quietly, "I have my reasons, Whitney. And I'm not able to discuss them with you at this point."

The words hit Brandi with the force of a pile driver. Then Whitney's suspicions, and her own, were the truth.

Zack had lied.

Before she could recover her balance, Brandi heard the creak of a hinge as the bedroom door started to open. Ross and Whitney were coming out.

Brandi couldn't risk meeting them just now. She was in no shape to confront her boss and ask for an explanation—not on a matter of this much importance. And she was not up to seeing concern and perhaps pity in her friend's eyes, either.

But she couldn't just run downstairs. She couldn't brave meeting Zack at this moment; she didn't have enough self-control for that. She would need a chance to sort out her thoughts before she did anything at all.

Without making a conscious decision, Brandi fled back to the cloakroom and extracted her coat from the pile on the bed. She waited a couple of minutes, giving Ross and Whitney a chance to return to the party, and then tried to make herself invisible as she slipped down the stairs. If she could just get outside before anyone noticed...

But luck wasn't with her. She was almost at the front door when Ross called, "Brandi! You're leaving already?"

She turned, keeping her head down and drawing

her shoulders up till the high collar of her coat hid a good part of her face. "It's been a lovely party," she said, "but I'm sure you'll forgive me for ducking out. I've got another long day tomorrow." Her voice was huskier than she'd have liked, but she hoped he wouldn't notice. He didn't argue, and she nodded a goodbye and went outside.

The temperature seemed to have dropped like a rock during the hours she'd been inside—or perhaps it was just that shock and fear had made her more sensitive to the cold. As Brandi stood on the curb and waited for the valet to bring her car, she tried not to look over her shoulder. With any luck at all, Zack would still be waiting for her in the party rooms, unaware that she was running away.

Which was, she freely admitted, exactly what she was doing.

I need to talk to you, he'd said. Brandi wondered what he'd been planning to tell her. Would he confess? And if so, what sort of explanation would he have for why he had lied to her before?

Maybe tomorrow she could listen to him. Right now, she'd probably start screaming.

She could see her breath, but by the time the valet returned with her car, Brandi had stopped feeling the cold. No amount of chill in the air could match the frigid brittleness deep inside her.

Even the long drive across the city with the car's heater running full blast didn't warm her up. Once inside her apartment, she lit the gas fire with shaking fingers, and huddled in front of it.

Just a couple of hours ago she had been happier than she had been in years, so happy that all sense of time had vanished in the enjoyment of Zack's company, of the warm security of his arms around her, of the delicious sense that the world was a saner place when she was with him.

But he had lied to her, and now all the freedom, the enjoyment, the hope that she had thought he represented were gone.

Only once before in her life had she felt this confused, this upset, this frozen. Once before she had given her trust, and she had been betrayed.

But that time, she had believed that she had known the man she trusted. As it turned out, she'd been wrong, and the disillusionment she'd suffered had kept her from making the same mistake for years afterward. In fact, she'd thought the memory of her pain would keep her from repeating that particular error forever.

But it hadn't. In fact, this mistake was worse, if anything. She had never allowed herself to believe that she knew Zack at all—but still she had allowed herself to trust in him, to believe that he was different, special. The kind of man she could truly care about.

Brandi sat beside the fire, listening to the soft hiss and crackle of the flame, smelling the sharp pine fragrance of the garland Zack had so carefully fitted over the mantel two nights ago, and staring at the diamond-cluster ring that he had moved from her left hand to her right. It had been such a romantic gesture—such a touching, world-shaking signal that he was serious about her.

Oh, he was serious all right, she reflected. Serious about deceiving her.

She tugged the ring loose and put it back on the hand where it belonged. The hand where it would stay.

*   *   *

Brandi was in the store early the next day, though she had to admit that her almost-sleepless night had left her with less than her usual concentration.

She normally enjoyed Sunday mornings. The quiet hour before the employees started to come in was a perfect opportunity to walk through every department, undistracted by customer problems or employee concerns. On her normal walk-throughs, she was watching her people as much as the store itself. On Sundays she could concentrate on the merchandise, keeping a sharp eye out for displays that looked tired, mannequins that sagged, stacks that had been pushed out of line. It was tiny details like these that made Tyler-Royale stand out among other department stores, and Brandi was determined her store was going to be the cream of the crop.

But today it took effort to focus on the job. The store was too quiet, and her mind kept slipping back to the party the night before. Surprisingly, though, it wasn't only the abrupt end of the evening that seemed imprinted on her mind, but the earlier fun. Even the night before, with the pain still fresh and raw, whenever she had managed to close her eyes it hadn't been the shock at the top of the stairs she remembered, but the hypnotic rhythm of dancing with Zack....

And that kind of thinking, she told herself, was going to get her precisely nowhere.

She pulled her mind back to the task at hand. They were halfway through the Christmas season, and the biggest shopping days of the year were still to come. Did the store have enough stock in the areas that were selling best? Was there an excess of certain merchandise? If so, perhaps it should be marked down to speed its sale, or perhaps offered to other stores in the chain where the demand might be heavier.

The computer in her office would give her the numbers, of course, but Brandi had long ago learned to put more faith in her instinct than in statistics.

She paid particular attention to Toyland, since it was the busiest single department at this time of year. The stock was starting to drop, she noted, but so far there seemed no shortages anywhere. Extra supplies of toys and games were no longer stacked clear to the ceiling, but the regular shelves were still full and inviting.

She wondered which displays Zack was responsible for rearranging. He'd said something about games, hadn't he? There was a pile of board games laid out in an eye-catching pattern at the end of an aisle.

Not that it mattered, she told herself, and went on to electronics and housewares before she could dwell on the subject of Zack.

Before Brandi was quite finished with her tour, employees were coming in. The lights came up, the Christmas carols began to play, and soon the great doors opened and the first wave of customers poured in. Sundays during the Christmas season were always busy, but this was a particularly hectic day. Shopping urges that had been pent up by the week's snowstorm seemed to have been released in a frenzy.

Every department seemed to be overrun, and Brandi found herself pitching in on the floor, greeting customers in the atrium entrance, directing them to the merchandise they wanted, even ringing up sales for a while in the ladies' active-wear department, when Casey Amos and her new trainee—the woman

Zack had discovered in the parking lot the night of the snowstorm—got behind.

Theresa Howard was apologetic. ''I'm sorry I'm so slow, Ms. Ogilvie,'' she said. ''Sometimes I think I'm all thumbs and I'll never learn this job.''

Brandi smiled. ''Casey and I have trained a lot of people,'' she reassured the woman. ''You're doing just fine.''

Finally the pressure let up. She showed Theresa Howard how to greet three customers at a time and still make each of them feel valuable, and then retreated to the executive floor, where the paperwork she'd intended to do before the store opened still waited.

But as she passed the customer service department, just down the hall from her office, Brandi saw that the two representatives were being run off their feet settling problems and wrapping packages. There was not only a line waiting for help, but a woman who wanted to apply for Wishing Tree assistance. Brandi took her off to a corner and went to work.

Where was Zack when she needed him? she thought irritably. There wasn't time to check the schedule to see if he was due to come in today—but she rather thought he was. She seemed to remember that the kooky schedule she'd arranged hadn't given him a single day off. Though, since she *had* told him last night that the schedule was more flexible than it implied, perhaps he'd decided to go back to setting his own hours.

Or maybe he didn't intend to come in to work at all. Maybe Whitney's question to Ross had tipped a balance somehow, and now that the secret was at least partially out, there was no further point in having Zack play his role.

Brandi wondered for the thousandth time what had happened last night after she'd left the party, and how long Zack had waited for her.

The client said hesitantly, "Excuse me?" and Brandi pulled herself away from the fascination of imagining the look on Zack's face when he realized she wasn't coming back.

"I really appreciate this, you know," the client said. "It's—well, it's the only way we'd have a Christmas, through the generosity of other people." Her voice was thick with emotion.

Brandi smiled sympathetically, but she didn't answer; she knew how close the woman was to tears. Instead she said gently, "What about you? Now that we've got the kids' lists made, what would you like?"

The woman shook her head. "Oh—nothing. The best gift for me will be if people care a little about my kids."

Brandi looked down at the form she had just finished filling out, and her eyes began to prickle uncontrollably. It was such a simple list—warm jeans and boots for a couple of little boys, and a snowsuit and a baby doll for a three-year old. "You'll get everything on your list," she said firmly.

A sudden tingle in the back of her neck warned her that Zack was somewhere around. She sneaked a look through her lashes and spotted him near the door of the employees' lounge. He was leaning against the wall and watching her.

Brandi found herself feeling hot and cold all over, and all at the same time. She tried not to look at him

again, but it was impossible to keep her gaze from
straying in his direction.

No Santa suit today. He was still dressed for the
street, in a black leather jacket and jeans. His garb
was the most casual she'd seen him wear, and it made
him look tougher somehow—as if he no longer
needed to project a sophisticated veneer.

The client thanked her, gave Brandi's hand a fierce
squeeze, and left.

Brandi stacked the papers she'd filled out in a
folder, fussing till she had them lined up just right.
She didn't see Zack leave the lounge area and come
toward her. She didn't have to; she could feel his
closeness as easily as if she'd suddenly sprouted radar
antennae.

He didn't take the chair across from her where the
client had sat, but leaned against the table beside her
instead, his hip almost brushing her arm. ''Now
who's making rash promises?'' he said.

She tried to keep things casual. ''It wasn't rash. I'll
take care of it myself. You needn't even put those
stars on the tree.''

''Shopping and everything? You amaze me,
Brandi.''

She could feel his warmth, but there was no place
to move. Her chair was already against the wall, and
the dominating position he'd assumed not only
blocked her from slipping past him but made her feel
tiny and helpless.

Though Brandi wasn't about to admit that; no one
was going to bully her simply by sitting on the edge
of a table and looking down his nose. ''The manager
of the supermarket down at the other end of the mall
offered to fix food baskets for our Wishing Tree peo-

ple," she said. "You might want to go talk to him about it."

Zack nodded. He didn't speak, and he didn't move.

"I suppose you'd like to look over the application?" Brandi held out the folder. "I hope I did it to your standards."

Zack didn't reach for the paperwork. He folded his arms across his chest instead and looked down at her. She followed his gaze; he was looking at the diamond cluster on her left hand, and there was a shuttered wariness in his eyes that she'd never seen before.

She put the folder down. "Don't look at me like that, please. You know, I wouldn't have objected if you'd wanted to take over that job—it is your department after all."

"You were obviously almost finished." His voice had a rough edge. "Besides, I didn't want to take the chance that you'd scream and run if I approached you too suddenly."

"What?" Brandi was honestly at a loss.

"You didn't seem to want to talk to me last night," he reminded her.

"Well, I certainly wouldn't scream and run here."

"Oh, that's right." There was an edge of irony in his tone. "We're in the store now, and all the rules are different."

She watched him warily. He sounded angry—no, it was more than that. There was a tinge of bitterness in his voice, and that made Brandi furious. Did he honestly expect that he could lie to her and get away with it forever?

She was aware that the crush at the customer service counter had abated, leaving the clerks free to observe. She should probably take him back to her office and close the door and have it out.

Before she could suggest it, though, Zack said softly, "Why did you run away last night?"

She couldn't deny it, for it was true, she had run. But she wasn't going to let him put her on the defensive. "I don't owe you any explanations, Zack."

"What the hell does that mean? Of course you owe me an explanation! How do you think I felt when I discovered you'd slipped out without even telling me?"

"Guilty, maybe?" Brandi guessed.

There was a flicker in his eyes, as if the jab had struck deep into his soul. His voice grew softer, but it was no less resolute. "I told you I needed to talk to you, and you promptly vanished. Were you afraid to hear what I had to say, so you ran?"

"Maybe I just wasn't ready to listen to another round of lies just then."

"Lies?" The softness had vanished. "Dammit, Brandi—"

"Oh, come off it, Zack! The innocent act might still be convincing if I hadn't heard Ross telling Whitney last night that he planted you in my store."

"He said *what*?" Zack sounded astonished.

"She asked him why he'd put you in this store," Brandi said impatiently, "and he said he wasn't at liberty to tell her. Now correct me if I'm wrong, Zack, but a few days ago I asked you the same question, and you denied it—right?"

He shook his head a little, more in confusion than denial. "You asked me if I was Ross's troubleshooter, and I said no, I'm not. Which is the absolute truth."

"Oh, I beg your pardon! Perhaps I got the details a little askew, but—"

"I'm not here because of Ross, Brandi."

"Oh, really?" Her voice dripped sarcasm. "I suppose I imagined him telling me to hire you?"

"I mean, he suggested this particular store. But playing Santa was my idea."

"Well, maybe you should tell me what this is all about!" She didn't realize how shrill she sounded until she noticed both of the customer service representatives watching her intently, mouths ajar.

"I tried last night," Zack said. "You wouldn't listen."

Maybe he had intended to tell her, she thought wearily. She'd have to give him the benefit of the doubt on that question. "Well, I'm all ears now."

Zack glanced over his shoulder at the customer service representatives. "You and a lot of other people," he said dryly. "Perhaps we could go into your office?"

They were in Dora's alcove when the manager of Toyland came bursting out of the elevator. "Ms. Ogilvie!" he called. "There you are! I've been trying to find you."

Brandi paused. "What is it?"

"Not now," Zack said through gritted teeth. "Can't you, just once, let the store go to hell?"

She glared at him. "When I've got an undercover agent standing right here? Of course not!"

"And Zack," the department manager said with relief. "Man, am I glad to see you." He seized Zack's arm with both hands.

"If you're short a clerk, I'm sorry," Zack began. "But—"

The manager shook his head. "It's a whole lot worse than that. This afternoon's Santa came in to work all right, but he's in the dressing room now— as sick as anyone I've ever seen."

"The flu?" Brandi asked.

"Sure looks like it. He's far too sick to do his job—he'd expose every kid in the store to this bug. But there's a line from here to the moon waiting to talk to Santa. Zack, you'll help me out, won't you? I've got to have a Santa!"

Zack didn't answer.

Brandi looked up at him. His gaze was dark and steady and watchful, as if he was asking a silent question.

But there could be only one answer; the needs of the store came first. "I'll have to ask you to pitch in," she said levelly. "We'll talk later, Zack."

"You can bet on that." There was a steel thread underlying his voice.

Brandi put her chin up. "Believe me, I'm as eager as you are to get this sorted out. But in the meantime, look on the positive side. You'll have all afternoon to get your story straight!"

Brandi made it a point to be highly visible for the rest of the business day. Zack was not going to be able to accuse her of hiding away in her office. Besides, though she wouldn't have admitted it to him, she couldn't have settled down to her regular work if her life had depended on it.

Her mind was going a million miles a minute, trying to anticipate his explanation—but she couldn't think of any that made sense.

If he *wasn't* in the store because of Ross...but Ross had said quite plainly...

Give it up, Brandi, she told herself finally. She'd simply have to wait till she heard his side of it and make her judgment then.

She got caught up in a crowd on the escalator and her white carnation was smashed. She was in the employees' lounge, digging through the refrigerator for a replacement, when a couple of clerks came in to put their names into the jar for the Christmas gift exchange. "You're going to be in it this year, aren't you, Ms. Ogilvie?" one of them asked. "It's just good fun."

Brandi shook her head, but after the clerks were gone she pinned her flower in place and thought of what the Wishing Tree client had said—about how the best gift would be knowing that people cared.

Maybe she should take part, she thought. It was such a simple little thing. And it was Christmas after all—the time for caring.

Before she had a chance to argue herself out of it, she'd written her name on one of the little cards Casey Amos had left beside the jar and dropped it in.

She walked through Toyland several times during the afternoon, watching the line inching past Santa's Workshop, and happened to be there for the big stir of the day, when a couple brought in their infant quadruplets, dressed in identical red velvet suits, for their first visit with Santa.

"Makes quite a picture, doesn't it?" a bystander asked Brandi, chuckling at the sight. "Santa's got his hands full, holding all four of 'em at once."

She nodded and leaned against the fence to watch. The babies were three months old, their mother told her, and for a moment Brandi lost herself in sheer enjoyment not only of their antics but the way Zack handled them. The babies wriggled, made faces, and yanked at his beard; Zack watched them with a tenderness in his face that tugged at Brandi's heart.

Then he looked up and caught her eye, and the tenderness faded, to be replaced with something that looked more like a challenge—and Brandi stepped away from the fence and almost tripped over her own feet in her eagerness to be away.

Last night he had held her and kissed her, and he had seemed to say that he had serious feelings about her. For why would a man move a ring from her left hand, unless he intended to make room for a more important one?

But today…today he had looked at her almost with scorn.

Closing time approached, and the crowds began to thin. Brandi waited beside the perfume counter nearest the main entrance till a customer turned away with a bag full of fragrances.

The clerk was back at work as she had promised. Brandi thought she looked a little shaky, as if she wasn't quite over her shock. That would be no surprise, she thought, and wondered if she should have refused permission to let the woman come back just yet.

But the clerk greeted her with a wide smile. "It's good to be back," she said. "I wondered if I'd have the jitters all day, but it hasn't been bad at all. Of course, it's been busy, and that helps."

The clerk turned away to help a customer, a long-haired young woman wearing faded jeans and a canvas vest, its pockets stuffed with odds and ends. "I'd like an ounce of Sensually Meghan," she said, and pulled a credit card out of her back pocket.

Brandi's eyebrows went up just a fraction of an inch. The woman didn't look like the Sensually Meghan type—that particular scent cost three hundred dollars an ounce these days. It was just another example demonstrating that customers couldn't be judged by appearance. She made a mental note to mention the incident at the next full staff meeting as encouragement to her employees not to jump to conclusions based on a customer's clothes.

The clerk was processing the charge when the customer asked, "How long does it usually take after closing for all the people to clear out of the mall?"

Brandi's sixth sense started to quiver. "On Sundays, not long," she said. "Why?"

The woman smiled at her. "It is an odd question, isn't it? We work for an advertising agency." She gestured toward the main entrance, where two men with video cameras waited. "We'll be shooting footage for ads for the mall."

Brandi relaxed. Really, she thought, since the robbery attempt, I'm starting to get paranoid.

"We don't want our equipment to get in the way," the young woman went on, "but frankly, we're not wild about working Sunday nights, either, so if we time it just perfectly we can shoot and get out and not annoy anyone."

"I think I'd get started setting up," Brandi advised. "If you're off to the side of the main doors, no one will trample you."

"Hey, thanks." The customer stuck her expensive perfume carelessly into a pocket and headed for the entrance.

''You just never know, do you?'' the clerk said.

The public address system crackled to life and announced that the store was now closed, and the clerk began to clear the cash register. Brandi dug out her keys and went to shut the big metal gates that barricaded the Tyler-Royale store from the rest of the mall.

She stopped the gate just short of full closure to allow procrastinating shoppers an exit, and watched the camera crew setting up their tripods and lights just outside the store.

But her mind wasn't on them, but on the coming confrontation with Zack.

Thinking of him seemed to have the power to conjure him up, for just a couple of minutes after the closing announcement she saw him coming down the now-stationary escalator. He was still wearing his Santa suit.

''I'd have waited for you to change,'' she said as he came up to her.

''Then I will. I saw you hovering down here as if you were ready to run, and I thought perhaps—''

He broke off as a scream sliced through the air.

Brandi looked around frantically. The only thing she was certain of was that the sound hadn't originated anywhere inside Tyler-Royale. Sound echoed oddly in the huge open mall, however, and the scream could have come from a hundred places.

Just outside the gate, a member of the camera crew said, ''What the—''

Another scream sounded, and a man erupted from the cookie and snack shop next door to Tyler-Royale and started down the length of the mall at a dead run. Under his arm was what looked like a brown paper bag.

The perfume clerk gasped, "That's the guy who tried to rob me!"

Zack shot one look at the clerk, pushed Brandi out of his way, and took off after the robber.

Propelled by the push, Brandi collided with the metal gate and grabbed the rods to keep herself upright. She was shrieking something; she thought it was his name.

Time seemed to stretch out in slow motion as she clung to the gate and watched the chase. Ever so slowly, stride by stride, Zack gained on the man with the bag, till with one final lunge he slammed a shoulder into the robber's back, and the two of them went down together onto the hard tile floor.

As they rolled, Brandi saw the flash of metal in the robber's hand. Was he holding a knife? A gun?

In her terror for Zack, she screamed again. It was a useless warning for him, but a blinding revelation for her.

As the two man grappled for the weapon, Brandi knew, with the terrible clarity that sometimes comes with shock, that it didn't matter to her what Zack had done, or who he was, or why he was in her store. Or even whether he had lied to her after all.

That was all unimportant, less than nothing beside the fact that somehow, while she wasn't even looking—much less protecting herself—Zack Forrest had crept into her heart.

Last night she had been hurt by the discovery that she had let herself trust him despite her lack of knowledge of what he really was. Now that discovery paled beside the blinding realization that this was not only a man she could care about if the circumstances worked out just right, but the one and only man she loved.

CHAPTER NINE

THE struggle in the mall could only have lasted for a minute or two, but to Brandi it seemed to go on for years. Where were the mall security guards? she wanted to scream. What good did it do to have people on the staff if they weren't there when they were needed?

Finally, the guards converged on the pair in the hall. Two of them sat on the robber; another helped Zack stand up. Logic told Brandi he wasn't hurt after all, for the first thing he did was to dust off his red velvet suit.

Nevertheless, she was still shaking minutes later when the camera crew came triumphantly down the corridor. She hadn't even noticed they were gone, and she paid little attention to the video cassette the young woman in the canvas vest was waving over her head.

"What a piece of action!" she was saying. "We'll be on the news on every station in greater Chicago. Santa Claus busts a robber, and we've got it on tape!" She grinned at Brandi. "What can you tell me about your Santa—besides that he's in great shape under the velvet suit?"

Brandi noticed with almost clinical detachment that each of her fingertips was quivering to a different rhythm. "Not much," she said. "His name's Zack Forrest, and he's a temporary employee, just for the season. That's all I really can—"

"Zack Forrest?"

Something about the woman's tone made Brandi's eyes narrow in suspicion. "That's what I said, yes."

"You mean the toycoon?"

"What did you call him?"

"*Toycoon.* It's the nickname Wall Street gave him last spring when he bought Intellitoys. You know, the educational-toy maker."

The little oxygen still in Brandi's lungs rushed out with a whoosh. *How's the toy business?* one of their fellow guests had asked Zack last night. Brandi had thought the guest meant the Santa job.... Zack owned a toy company?

"We were shooting an ad for one of their new products last week," the young woman went on, "and I did my research. I wonder what he's up to? Why's he playing Santa anyway?"

From the corner of her eye, Brandi glimpsed a red suit, and she turned around to get a better look.

Zack's hair was ruffled, and his fake beard hung askew. He'd lost his velvet cap in the fracas, and he sounded as if he was still a little breathless. "I'm just doing my volunteer stint for the children," he said, and smiled at the woman who held the videotape.

Brandi was torn between the desire to fling her arms around him and kiss the dimple in his cheek in gratitude that he was safe, or slap him across the face as hard as she could for taking a foolish risk.

"Perhaps I'm being immodest to ask," Zack went on, "but am I the star of that videotape you're waving around?"

The young woman grinned. "Yeah. You can watch yourself on TV tonight—I bet every station in the city will want this. Maybe even the networks."

"Ah," Zack said knowingly. "Doing a little moon-lighting, are you?"

"Anything wrong with that?" A defensive note crept into the woman's voice. "There's no clause in my contract with the advertising agency that forbids me to make a little money on the side."

"Of course there's nothing wrong with a little en-lightened capitalism," Zack soothed. "Though, as long as the tape's for sale…" He reached for his wal-let. "How much do you think they'll pay? And how many stations are there?"

The woman told him, and then looked at him in-credulously while Zack counted a series of bills into her hand.

"There," he said. "And a little extra for good mea-sure. You've turned a profit, and this way you don't even have to mess around making copies for all the stations." The videotape vanished into a capacious pocket of the red velvet suit, and Zack looked around with a smile. "I think you might want to reschedule your regular business, though. It looks as if the mall will be tied up for a while tonight."

In the meantime, Brandi saw, the police had arrived in force. She watched while they cordoned off the snack shop and the videotape crew packed up their equipment and left.

Only then did she speak, still without looking at Zack. "What are you planning to do with the video-tape?"

"Haven't decided. But it was obviously a once-in-a-lifetime opportunity, so I thought I'd better grab it while I could."

"You could always show it at parties. I'm sure it would be a hit."

"Now that's a thought," Zack said agreeably. "People who don't know that's the most incompetent robber in the Western hemisphere would think I looked like a hero."

Brandi nodded. Her voice was perfectly calm. "That was a sizable amount of money you just handed over for someone who implied a few days ago that he couldn't quite keep up with the payments on his car."

Zack had the grace to look ashamed of himself.

Brandi didn't wait for an answer. She looked straight at him, and fury hardened her voice. "Dammit, Zack, why didn't you tell me who you are? Or what you do? Why the big secret?"

His tone was even and perfectly calm. "Because I didn't want to advertise the fact that Intellitoys is in big trouble."

She shook her head more in confusion than disagreement. It seemed such an inadequate reason.

A burly policeman came up to them. "Uh...Santa. We'll need a statement from you, sir."

For a moment Zack ignored him; he was watching Brandi. Finally he sighed and said, "I'll be back as soon as I can, Brandi."

"I'll be in my office."

It was more than an hour before he tapped perfunctorily on the door and came in. He'd taken the time to change clothes, she saw, and he was once more wearing the jeans and leather jacket he'd had on when they'd started this conversation earlier in the afternoon.

It felt to Brandi as if that had been a very long time ago. Back then, she'd known only that he had the power to hurt her. But she hadn't understood how deep that power ran, or how devastating the hurt could be. She hadn't yet realized that she loved him, and she hadn't begun to conceive of the deception he'd practiced.

Now she felt as if he'd torn her heart from her chest without bothering with anesthesia.

She'd been trying to concentrate on a supplier's catalog with little success. She put it down when Zack came in, but she didn't say a word.

Neither did Zack; he pulled a chair around and straddled it, his arms crossed on the back. Brandi wasn't surprised that he felt as if he needed a shield.

For a full minute it seemed as if they might sit that way forever. Silent as the confrontation was, however, the air between them seemed to sizzle.

When Zack finally spoke, it was almost as if he was picking up in the middle of a conversation. "Intellitoys' advance orders for the Christmas season were reasonable," he said quietly. "Not good, but acceptable. But as the holiday got closer, we started getting cancellations from stores because merchandise they already had on hand wasn't selling. And soon a fair performance was turning into a disaster. We could absorb a single season of low sales, even a Christmas season, but there was a larger problem—nobody seemed to know why the sales were down. And unless a company knows why it's not selling merchandise, next year is apt to be nothing but worse."

Brandi fidgeted with a paper clip. She couldn't argue with that logic as far as it went. She just didn't understand what it was supposed to have to do with her.

"It was apparent to anyone with eyes that the marketing firm we were using didn't have a clue," Zack went on. "They kept saying it was just a cyclical drop that would correct itself with time, but we haven't got that kind of time to play with. The company could be dead and buried by the time they'd admit they might be wrong."

Brandi knew the helpless feeling he must have suffered—knowing action was required, but not knowing which direction to move.

"So I fired them," Zack said. "It was an impulsive decision, I admit, but it left me no worse off than I was before."

Brandi didn't intend to rescue him, but she couldn't help but agree with that philosophy. "Bad information is worse than having none at all."

Zack smiled approvingly, as if she were a particularly bright student. "Very true. But firing the marketers didn't solve the problem, either—we still had to somehow find out what was going wrong. Why did kids suddenly not seem to want our products, and why had parents lost interest, as well?"

"So you decided to become a Santa?" Brandi shifted restlessly in her chair. "Pardon me for questioning your judgment, Zack, but there's more than one marketing firm in the world. Couldn't you just hire another one and use focus groups? Get a bunch of kids and parents into a room and ask them what they like? Putting on a red suit and a beard is just about the silliest—"

"Oh, is it really? Focus groups are no more honest than statistics, you know—it's not at all hard to skew the results, even with the best of intentions. I figured I'd ask the real authorities—the kids themselves, and the parents. And how better to get their honest feelings than to sit in Santa's chair?"

"It's not what you'd call a scientific sample."

"Scientific samples take time, which I haven't got. Right now, I don't need analysis, I need a gut reaction of what's wrong. Which, I might add, I started getting the first day I was out there."

"With a notebook," Brandi reflected.

"You'd better believe I was taking notes. I didn't want to forget a single comment because that's a good way to be led astray, too. It's easy to remember only what you want to."

"And you think you've got the answers?"

"No—but I know which direction we need to go." There was confidence in his voice.

Brandi sighed. There wasn't much point in arguing with him; Zack was convinced he'd taken the right course. In any case, it didn't matter, because his reasons for starting this masquerade weren't really important. "So why didn't you tell me what you were up to?" she asked softly.

He shook his head as if in disbelief of her innocence. "The stock-market wizards would have been on me like the sharks they are. With the first drop of blood, those guys go into a feeding frenzy. That in turn would have very nasty effects on my stockholders' confidence level."

"No doubt, but—"

"What would you think if the president of the biggest manufacturer of light bulbs in this country showed up at the corner drugstore demonstrating them, and asking people why they suddenly seemed to prefer other brands to his?"

Brandi shook her head. "No. You're telling me why you didn't want it known, and I understand all the reasons. But that's not what I asked, Zack. Why didn't you tell *me*?"

He seemed to be staring at his feet. "It was important that I be just an ordinary Santa," he said. "A working stiff with no stake in the answers I got. People are amazingly adaptable at telling a survey taker what they think he wants to hear. If I stood out in any way, it would affect what I was trying to accomplish."

As if this unlikely Santa hadn't stood out from the beginning, Brandi thought wryly. "And just what did you think I was apt to do? Call a press conference and announce your little project?"

"I didn't know you, Brandi," he said softly. "How could I possible have had the answer to that question?"

And what about later, she wanted to ask. What about after he'd had a chance to get to know her?

But too many of the possible answers to that question scared her. She didn't think she could stand to sit there, loving him as she did, and listen as he told her that he still didn't trust her to keep his secrets— at least, not enough to volunteer them without being forced.

And so she didn't ask.

"It was safer if you didn't know," Zack went on. "No one could get information out of you if you didn't know it in the first place."

The gentle note in his voice made her want to hit him; the desire was even stronger than it had been a couple of hours ago, right after that crazy stunt he'd pulled.

"Ross thought it was better if nobody knew. That way there couldn't be a slipup."

Brandi swallowed hard. "So Ross didn't trust me, either?"

"It's not that, Brandi. Honestly, it's not. But Ross is a major stockholder in Intellitoys, and if it got out that he was worried about the company…"

There was no need to finish that sentence. Once Wall Street got hold of that information, there would be nothing left of Intellitoys but splinters.

"Or, for that matter," Zack went on, "if the other toy companies that Tyler-Royale deals with discovered that Ross was favoring my business over theirs by using his stores as a laboratory, they'd be unhappy."

That was an understatement. Brandi knew from long experience what suppliers could be like if they thought someone else was getting an unfair break. She shivered.

"I see you understand the problem," Zack said. "Even Tyler-Royale's board of directors might well have had a collective fit. Maybe Ross was wrong to keep you out of the loop, Brandi—"

"*Maybe*? Didn't it occur to either of you that if I knew, it might keep me from saying something I shouldn't?"

"Yes. But you must admit, right or not, Ross had good reason for asking me to stay under wraps."

Brandi thought it over, and finally nodded. She still thought Ross and Zack had been wrong, but she didn't have to agree in order to understand.

But somehow, she thought, she was never going to feel quite the same about Ross Clayton again. And as for Zack…well, she'd have to think about that one for a good long time.

"So that's why Ross wouldn't tell Whitney what was going on," she mused.

"If he thought you didn't need to know," Zack said reasonably, "why would he be willing to tell Whitney?"

She couldn't argue with the logic of that, either, but it made her furious that she couldn't find a flaw in his reasoning.

Zack's voice was soft. "I wanted to tell you, Brandi, when you asked me about the troubleshooter and whether the store was in trouble. But it wasn't altogether up to me. You understand, don't you, that it was Ross's secret as much as mine? I couldn't spill it without warning him."

And that, Brandi thought wearily, told her exactly where she ranked, didn't it? Well down toward the bottom of his list.

Suddenly the office felt stuffy, as if they'd used up all the oxygen, and she felt an almost overpowering need to get out of the store and into the fresh cold air.

"Goodness knows I understand putting business first," Brandi said crisply. "In fact, it's nice to know that you have enough sense to do that—at least when it's *your* business that's concerned." She knew she sounded a bit catty, and she didn't care. "I think we've covered everything, don't you?" She stood up and came around the corner of the desk. It was the most obvious dismissal she could imagine.

Zack put a hand out toward her.

She took a half step back, well out of his reach. "Or is there something else you'd like to tell me, Zack?"

For a moment, his eyes looked cloudy, as if he was

staring into the distance at something she couldn't see. Then his dark gaze focused once more on her face. "No."

"Then I suppose the only thing left is to agree on an explanation of why you're suddenly not playing Santa anymore."

Zack didn't move. "Why?"

"To avoid any uncomfortable questions, of course. Would you rather I say you've had a job offer you couldn't turn down, or that illness in the family called you away? Either way, I could imply you've gone out of state. Or maybe that's not far enough. How about out of the country?"

"I'm not planning to quit now, Brandi."

"You certainly can't keep on."

"Why not? I'm not finished. I told you I've got direction now, but not answers. Ross agreed with me that you'd have to know, but there's no need to bring anyone else into it."

"Wouldn't you be better off finishing your research somewhere else?"

Zack looked up at her for a long moment. His eyes had narrowed, and they looked darker than she'd ever seen them before. "You really want me to leave, don't you? Why, Brandi? Is it because I'm some kind of threat to your peace of mind?"

"A threat? To me? That's a joke." To her own ears, Brandi's voice lacked conviction. "But if you insist, stay. Goodness knows, I don't want to take chances with my career by making Ross mad at me."

Zack didn't seem to hear her. "You haven't answered my question yet about why you didn't stick around and listen to me last night."

She shrugged. "The delay doesn't seem to have

made much difference. Or isn't this what you were planning to tell me?''

He hesitated, and then said quietly, ''Not exactly.''

He no doubt meant he'd had an edited version in mind till he'd been caught out and had to tell the whole story. Well, that didn't surprise her. ''If you'll excuse me, Zack, I still have work to do.'' She sat down behind her desk again and picked up the catalog she'd been holding when he came in. She couldn't even remember what she'd been looking at.

He stood and slid the chair into position across from her. ''Then I'll see you tomorrow.''

Only if I don't see you first, Brandi thought.

If she'd had more energy, Brandi would have pulled the pine garland down from the mantel, shredded it needle by needle, and flung it like confetti over the rail of her apartment balcony to mulch the garden below.

If the fireplace had been real instead of merely a gas log, she'd have stuffed the garland in and set a match to it, and sent the whole thing up in one explosive puff of resin.

But perhaps it was just as well that she didn't; demolishing the garland might have been cathartic, but Brandi knew the memories it represented would not be so easily destroyed. As long as she lived, she would remember the night Zack had so carefully draped the greenery—and then kissed her, to cover up...not an outright lie, perhaps, but certainly a half truth.

Part of the trouble was that she truly understood the position he'd been in. He'd given his word in a matter of business, and an honorable man didn't go back on that. She understood that Zack had been caught in a situation where he couldn't—technically—do anything at all. He couldn't tell her the truth without first warning Ross, but he couldn't tell her anything else without lying, at least by implication.

The same thing had happened to her on occasion, and she'd handled it the same way. So how could she blame him for doing what he'd had to do?

But her heart still told her that if he had cared about her…

Stop tormenting yourself this way, she told herself. Loving wasn't always reciprocal—hadn't she learned even that much from Jason?

She'd cared desperately about him, that was sure. After it was over and the pain had receded, she'd realized that perhaps her desperation had been even stronger than her caring. She'd lost her mother not long before, and she'd needed someone to make her feel valuable, connected to the world. Jason had been quite happy to fulfil that role—as long as it was convenient, and as long as Brandi had required nothing more serious of him.

But Zack was different, and she'd known it at some level all along—even while she'd thought that the experience with Jason would keep her safe. Even when she'd thought Zack was just another careless, happy-go-lucky young man out for a good time with little thought for the future, somewhere deep inside her heart she'd recognized how different he was.

Jason would never have challenged her decisions, her orders, as Zack had; it would have been too much trouble. Jason had never fussed about the hours she worked, for it gave him time to tinker with his novel;

Zack had seemed worried about her. Jason had often told her how proud he was of her independence; he would never have cared for her as tenderly as Zack had—taking her home, walking her to her car, making sure she wasn't alone at the party.

Jason had been a cardboard figurine. Only after he was gone from her life did Brandi realize how little she had known him, and how much of the man she thought she'd loved had been constructed from her own imaginative longings.

But Zack…Zack was a living, breathing, three-dimensional man. Sometimes difficult, often opinionated, always challenging.

But always lovable. That would never change.

On Tuesday, her secretary came into Brandi's office with a computer printout and a worried expression. "You know how we open a charge account automatically for every new employee?" she began.

Brandi nodded impatiently. "What about it, Dora?"

"We've got a new hire who's charged almost up to the limit."

Brandi put out a hand for the printout. "One of Zack's finds from the Wishing Tree project, no doubt?"

"No. It's Zack himself."

What a way to hide out, Brandi thought. For a man who said he wanted no special treatment—nothing that would distinguish him from the ordinary employee—Zack was hardly fading into the wallpaper. Of course, Zack could create a storm in a teacup and probably never realize it. He was so supremely confident of himself that he thought everyone else was just as self-assured.

But she wasn't going to get caught up in thinking about his attributes today, she reminded herself.

She ran an eye down the list. Most of the charges were on the small side, but there were a lot of them. No wonder Dora's attention had been drawn to this; what was the man thinking of?

Brandi sighed. "I'll talk to him. In the meantime, I don't think you need to worry about it."

Dora looked doubtful, but she didn't argue. Brandi went back to work, but the printout on the corner of her desk seemed to be looking at her, and finally she couldn't stand it for another minute. She'd managed to avoid him since Sunday, but she would have to seek him out now.

It was the dinner hour, so he was apt to be down in Santa's Workshop, filling in during the break. She picked up the printout and took the escalator to the second floor.

The crowd was small tonight; in fact, just one man in a trench coat and a couple of small children were inside the fence that surrounded Santa's Workshop. The man was chatting with Zack while the kids climbed all over him.

She set the "Santa's Feeding His Reindeer" sign in place and closed the gate. Zack looked up as if her presence was magnetic, and Brandi felt her heartbeat flutter a little under his steady gaze.

The man in the trench coat turned, and only then did Brandi realize it was Ross Clayton. "Hi, Brandi. Is it time for Zack's dinner?"

"No. I just needed to talk to him a minute."

Ross grinned. "I'll get my angels out of the way,

then. I'll give you a call this week, Brandi. There are a couple of things we need to talk about.''

She nodded. No doubt Zack had told him how upset she was. Well, that was all right; she still had a few things to say to Ross about this whole affair, and the sooner the air was cleared, the better.

Zack slid the little girl off his knee and stood up. The child took two steps toward Brandi. ''I remember you,'' she announced. ''You were at the party.''

Brandi nodded. ''You have a very good memory, Kathleen.''

The child nodded without self-consciousness. ''Uncle Zack said maybe we could see you again and help put up your Christmas tree. Then he said he didn't think so after all. Why not?''

Brandi shot a glance at him. What had he been planning anyway?

Before Brandi could answer, Kathleen's brother, with the arrogance of a couple of extra years, announced, ''Because it's too late, dummy. Everybody's got their Christmas trees up by now.''

''Don't call your sister a dummy,'' Ross said.

''Even if she is?''

Ross gave Brandi a crooked grin. ''See all the fun you're missing by not having kids?''

It was a teasing comment, of course, but Brandi watched them till they were out of sight. She felt lonely, as if she'd thrown away something she hadn't even looked at yet—and only now realized that it was too late to change her mind.

Uncle Zack said maybe we could see you again and help put up your Christmas tree...

Brandi closed her eyes and remembered her brief vision of a track set up under a decorated tree, with a couple of children watching blissfully as a train went round and round, and Zack—

Stop it, she told herself. Just stop it.

"I thought Ross didn't want them to see you in costume," she said.

"Oh, they overheard some talk about my new job, so he thought it would be better for them to see me in the role than use their imaginations."

"They seemed to take it well."

"Maybe it's the fact that I've been trying toys out on them for months, so it seems an appropriate job for me to have."

"I see." She stuck her hands in her pockets; her fingertips brushed the folded computer printout and reminded her of why she'd come downstairs. "I need to warn you that you've just about exhausted your credit limit. If you need an increase, I'm afraid you'll have to convince the credit manager that you have resources beyond what we're paying you." There was a faintly ironic note in her voice.

Zack ignored it. "That's all right. I didn't feel I should profit financially from this little experience, so I've been buying some extras for the Wishing Tree. I'll just turn over my paycheck to pay the bills, and we'll be square."

Brandi nodded. "All right." The public address system crackled to life, and Dora asked her to come to the office. Great timing, Brandi thought; she couldn't have planned it better if she'd tried. "I'll see you later, then."

She hadn't quite met his eyes the whole time she'd been standing there, and she didn't intend to. It would be not only too painful, but too revealing. But as she turned to leave, he said her name, and the note of longing in his voice sabotaged all her intentions.

"I've missed you," Zack said huskily.

Brandi couldn't deny the ring of truth in his voice. And she could see desire in his eyes. He wanted to kiss her, and every cell in her body knew it and was recalling precisely how it had felt to be in his arms, to be held and caressed and kissed till nothing mattered but him....

"I thought maybe we had something special," Zack said.

Brandi swallowed hard. "Not without some trust."

He nodded. "I was wrong not to tell you."

"You certainly were."

"I'm sorry."

Every nerve was tingling. Was he really saying what she thought he might be—what she hoped he was telling her—that these few days of separation had made him realize, as she had, that he cared? *I thought maybe we had something special*, he'd said. Was it possible there was a second chance after all?

The last remaining fragment of common sense reminded her that this wasn't exactly a private spot for a conversation, much less anything more. Zack certainly couldn't kiss her right outside Santa's Workshop, in full view of every kid and parent in Toyland. Could he?

She couldn't help it; the urge to sway toward him was an irresistible one.

At the gate, a child cried, "But there's Santa! He's not gone after all!" and sanity returned with a snap.

"Later," Zack said.

Brandi nodded and hurried away. He hadn't even touched her, but her skin was tingling as if electrical jolts were running through her. Later, she thought dreamily, when the store was closed and the kids were gone, they could explore what he'd meant. What they meant to each other.

In the alcove outside Brandi's office, Dora looked relieved to see her. "I was starting to fret that you hadn't heard the page," she said. "Mrs. Townsend's on the telephone for you. She said she'd hold as long as it took, but—"

Brandi had forgotten all about Dora's summons. Feeling guilty, she hurried into her office and grabbed the phone. "Whitney? I'm sorry I took so long."

"Don't fret about it. I'd have waited forever."

There was a tense, almost harsh edge to Whitney's voice that scared Brandi. "What's going on?"

"I found out what Zack's up to."

Brandi relaxed. She turned her chair around, propped her heels on the corner of her desk, and considered how much to tell Whitney. She wouldn't volunteer that Intellitoys was in trouble, of course—but how much did Whitney already know?

Thank heaven Zack had told her everything, she thought. If he hadn't, she might have said the wrong thing just now and destroyed his plans—and maybe even his business.

"A little extra market research," Brandi said airily. "Finding out what kids want for Christmas. I know all about it."

"Oh, that much was obvious." Whitney's voice dripped impatience. "Good heavens, before he bought the company he was asking all the kids he ran into for their opinion of Intellitoys, so of course a stint as Santa would be right up his alley. But there's more, Brandi."

She means the drop in sales, Brandi told herself. But she couldn't quite make herself believe it. There was a black hole of dread in the pit of her stomach.

"I asked Ross last weekend why he'd planted Zack in your store," Whitney said, "and he wouldn't tell me."

Brandi didn't mean to admit to anything at all, but before she could stop herself she said, "I know." Her voice was little more than a croak.

"What did you say? Anyway, he wouldn't tell me right then. He was keeping his mouth shut because he knew I'd do exactly what I'm doing right now— I'd call you up and warn you. But now that he's made up his mind..."

Brandi's palms were damp. "*Warn* me? About what?" She could hardly force the words past the lump in her throat. Then there was something wrong! What disaster was about to descend on her?

Surely, she thought, she ought to *know*. Simply admitting that she didn't have the vaguest idea what was going on was tantamount to confessing that she wasn't fit to manage a store!

"Ross is going to offer you the job as his troubleshooter."

For a moment, Brandi thought she couldn't possibly have heard correctly. That wasn't a disaster; that was a promotion beyond even her craziest dreams.

She said, "I never in my life considered that."

"Well, think it over before you jump," Whitney said dryly. "Don't let yourself be awestruck into taking it. It's not all that great a job, aside from the fact that it puts you straight on the fast track to the head office."

Brandi shook her head a little. "Is that what you're

warning me about—that the job has its disadvantages?''

''Not entirely.'' Whitney sighed. ''In fact, that's not it at all, and this isn't going to be easy. Ross knows you're a good manager, but the next step up is a big one, and he wasn't so sure you were ready for it. So he sent Zack out there to do a little undercover work to see whether you had the right qualities to move up to the next level. Watch out for Zack, Brandi. He's there to spy on you.''

CHAPTER TEN

BRANDI'S brain felt frozen. *Is there anything else you'd like to tell me*, she'd asked him. And Zack had said no, there wasn't.

Of course not, Brandi thought. He wouldn't *like* to tell her that his main reason for being in her store was to spy on her. Accidentally, she'd phrased the question so he could answer it with total truthfulness and still not be honest. He must have loved that!

"I'm terribly sorry to do this to you," Whitney said. "It's a rough blow, but perhaps it's better that you know it now. I could tell just from seeing you with Zack that you'd gone head over heels where he's concerned—"

"Head over heels? Don't be silly." Brandi's voice was a little shrill.

"Listen, kid, don't try to fool me. I know you too well. I just wish I'd found this out earlier."

"That makes two of us," Brandi admitted wearily. There was an instant of sympathetic silence, and Brandi, fearful of what Whitney might say next, hastily changed the subject. "There's something I don't understand about all this. How could I possibly be Ross's troubleshooter? I could hardly go under cover because everybody in the chain knows me."

"They know your name, but your habit of avoiding corporate parties works to your advantage. Not all that many people would recognize you on sight. Besides, troubleshooters don't stay anonymous for long,

435

Brandi. About fifteen minutes after the job's offered, the grapevine starts spreading the word. You think everyone in the whole chain didn't know me?''

''I always thought—''

''And don't overestimate the amount of secret work that's to be done. Most of the time it's pretty straight-forward. It's not an easy job, though—it wears people out and burns them up, and it doesn't take long for travel to lose its glamor. I held that job for almost three years, and I think my record stands to this day. But if that's what you want...''

Brandi considered the warning in Whitney's voice. But there really was only one answer she could give when the question was asked; this promotion was what she had worked for and dreamed of. It was an-other important step up the ladder to ultimate success. She had earned it, and she deserved to enjoy it. It was impossible to consider turning down such a plum.

''It's what I've always wanted,'' Brandi said qui-etly.

''Then you have my very best wishes, my friend. But at least think it over before you jump.''

Brandi thanked her and put down the telephone. She should be feeling wildly elated, she told herself. All her hard work had finally landed her on the fast track to the top of the corporation. Someday she might even sit in the office that was Ross Clayton's now, as the head of the whole chain.

When the shock wore off, she told herself, she'd be happy about her promotion. But just now, her head was spinning with fury and disappointment and sad-ness.

By the time Brandi came out of her office, Dora had gone; the lights were still on in the alcove, but

the computer was hooded and her desk was neat.
Down on the second floor, the Santa with the half
glasses had returned from his dinner and taken his
place in the big green wing chair outside the
Workshop. Beneath his white whiskers, his face still
looked a little pale from his bout with the flu, and
Brandi wondered if she should send him home despite
the doctor's release that said he was fit to return to
work.

He greeted her with a smile, however, and a hearty
Santa chuckle. "If you're looking for your young
man, Ms. Ogilvie, he's back in the dressing room."

Your young man. The words fed the flames of
Brandi's irritation. Did everyone in the store think
that she was helplessly in love with Zack Forrest?
Even Zack? Had he, perhaps, fed that rumor on purpose? Maybe it was even part of his effort to predict
how she'd handle the stress of the new job!

She might not be able to wipe him out of her heart
as easily as she'd like, but she could certainly put a
stop to this nonsense. She could make it clear to
everyone that they were not, and were never likely to
be, a couple.

Brandi stalked around behind Santa's Workshop to
the dressing-room entrance and, without pausing to
think, yanked the door open.

Zack was standing with his back to her, tucking in
the tail of his long-sleeved shirt. He half turned and
grinned at her. "Hi, there. Is it my imagination, or
are you a little impatient to get out of the store tonight?"

"I need to talk to you."

His eyebrows rose a little at her tone. "Give me a
minute to put my shoes on," he said. "I'd invite you

in, but as you can see, there's hardly room for both of us.''

He was right. Santa's Workshop was a masterpiece of illusion. The interior was much smaller than the structure looked from the outside, and a closet and dressing table took up the majority of the dressing room's space. The ceiling was scarcely high enough to clear Zack's head.

Next Christmas, Brandi thought, they really ought to make it larger. But of course, next Christmas it wouldn't be her concern.

"Something wrong?" Zack inquired.

He actually sounded as if he didn't have a suspicion, and Brandi's exasperation rose another notch. She leaned against the door frame and folded her arms across her chest. "You know, Zack," she said, trying to keep her voice light, "I can't make up my mind whether to thank you for my promotion or throw you bodily out of my store for lying to me."

His eyes narrowed, but he didn't say anything.

"Of course it wouldn't be prudent to fire you now, would it?" Brandi mused. "So I guess I'll settle for thanking you for the recommendation you obviously gave me."

"I didn't have anything to do with your promotion, Brandi."

She hardly heard the denial because of the accompanying admission—that there was to be a promotion, and Zack quite obviously knew it. If he hadn't, he'd have said something else altogether. "Nothing at all?"

Zack shook his head. "It was Ross's decision. I didn't make any recommendation."

Brandi's voice was deceptively gentle. "You

know, Zack, if you'd tell me the moon was shining, I'd go and check it out before I'd believe you.''

He flushed a little, as if he felt ashamed.

''You've lied to me at every turn, and even when you've told the truth, it turned out to be a lie, too. You're a master of careful phrasing, aren't you? How dare you sit there in my office and say *there's nothing else I'd like to tell you*!''

''Brandi—''

She considered, for an instant, that it wasn't wise to say all this, that it would be better to keep her feelings inside and never let him see. But hurt and fury and disappointment welled up in her like an oil gusher, and once the surface calm had cracked, there was no stopping the flow.

''I suppose you believe the end justifies the means, Zack? Well, no matter how thrilled I am with my promotion, I think the way you conducted yourself is a disgrace. I can't ask you never to set foot in this store again, but I can promise that any further conversation between us will be limited to business. And I thank heaven it's only ten more days till Christmas, so you can get out of that ridiculous Santa suit and go back to playing with toys yourself. Have I made myself perfectly clear?''

''Oh, yes.'' Zack's voice had a hard edge to it. ''And considering the circumstances, I can't imagine wanting to talk to you about anything. Will a handwritten resignation letter do, or shall I go over to electronics and type one?''

''Unless you're planning to give it to Ross, don't bother,'' Brandi snapped. ''You've certainly never answered to me, and I wouldn't want you to pretend to start now!''

She turned on her heel and stalked off across Toyland.

At least that was all over, she told herself when she reached the safety of her office. It was finished. She didn't have to be concerned about Zack anymore, and she could relax and enjoy the challenge of her new promotion.

As soon as her head stopped aching.

The week edged by, and Brandi didn't hear from Ross. There wasn't even a phone call, much less an offer of a promotion.

After a couple of days of silence, she considered the possibility that Whitney's information might have been wrong. But she soon dismissed the idea. Zack had known about the promotion offer, too. It was real—or at least it had been at the time.

Of course, it was quite possible that after her explosion Zack had reconsidered his recommendation. He might well have gone back to Ross to report that Brandi Ogilvie was an uncontrollable maniac, unfit even for the position she already had, and completely unsuitable for anything higher.

Brandi thought that over and decided she didn't care. If the price of telling Zack exactly what she thought of him turned out to be the sacrifice of a job, then she was willing to accept the loss. At least she'd been honest. She could live without the job, and there would be another promotion someday—one she didn't owe to Zack Forrest.

In the meantime, she split her days between the store and the Wishing Tree. Someone had to take over, since Zack had walked away and Pat Emerson's flu was proving to be worse than the average case.

Actually, however, Zack hadn't quite walked away. He'd left a telephone message for her the day after he left the store, asking her to let him know if he was still needed to finish up the Wishing Tree. Brandi had asked Dora to call and tell him no.

She was surprised to find that she really enjoyed working on the Wishing Tree. Sorting through the requests, matching up the gifts that customers brought in, and making sure that every person on the tree was remembered was a detailed and time-consuming task, but it absorbed her attention in a way nothing else seemed to. Sometimes it hurt, though; every time Brandi looked at an application that displayed Zack's signature approving it, she felt as if she'd been stabbed anew.

To escape the paperwork, she started shopping for the family she'd adopted—the one she'd signed up on that Sunday afternoon when she'd first challenged Zack for the truth. Warm clothes for the children were easy enough, but shopping for the mother was difficult—what did one buy a woman whose only request had been for her children? And toys gave her a problem, too. She wasn't sure what to buy for boys.

More than once she found herself wishing that Zack was still around to ask. When that happened, she gritted her teeth and plunged back into work again.

She was in ladies' active wear one afternoon, looking at a casual slacks-and-sweater set and wondering if she could guess the size the woman wore, when Theresa Howard finished with another customer and came up to Brandi.

"That's a nice combination," Theresa said.

Brandi held up the sweater. "Do I hear a little hesitation in your voice?"

"Oh, no. But is it for you? I think the blues would show off your gorgeous hair better than pink would. May I show you?"

Brandi laughed. "Very tactful," she complimented. "You're obviously taking to this job. Actually, this is a gift."

Theresa relaxed. "Oh, in that case..." She was ringing up the sale when she added, "If you need help delivering all the Wishing Tree stuff, I'd be happy to volunteer. I'm still trying to get on my feet financially, so I can't donate much money, but I'd like to give something back, and I thought perhaps if I helped with deliveries..."

"I *will* need help, thank you." Brandi picked up the neatly bagged sweater and slacks. "I believe I mentioned right at the outset that this was probably just a seasonal job, Theresa?"

"Yes, ma'am. And I understand that, I really—"

Brandi interrupted. "I've been talking with Miss Amos about your performance, and we've agreed that you can consider this position permanent."

Theresa's eyes filled with tears. "Oh, Ms. Ogilvie..."

"Unless, of course, you leave it to move up," Brandi added hastily, before she could start crying herself. "And don't thank me, because you've earned it."

Besides, she thought as she walked away, tucking the bag under her arm, if there was anyone who deserved Theresa Howard's thanks, it was Zack.

That reminded her of the snowy night in the parking lot and the first time Zack had kissed her, and she had to bite her lip hard to drown out the pain in her heart.

When she returned to her office, Ross Clayton rose from the chair beside Dora's desk. "Finishing up your shopping?" he asked cheerfully.

Brandi stared at him in surprise. It had been days since Whitney had told her of the promotion, since her confrontation with Zack. What was Ross doing here now? "This is the last of it," she admitted, and ushered him into her office. She put the bag on the corner of her desk, so she wouldn't forget to wrap it to match the rest of the toys and clothes she'd bought for her Wishing Tree family, and sat down.

"I'm sorry it's taken me so long to get back to you," Ross said. He pulled up a chair across from her. "I've been out of town, sorting out some trouble in the Phoenix store. That's a good deal of what I wanted to chat with you about. I need someone to do that job for me."

Brandi's head was swimming. Did this mean the job offer was still good? But after the way she'd yelled at Zack...

Ross said, "You've talked to Whitney, no doubt?" Brandi nodded, and he smiled. "I knew I could count on her to pass the word along. What about it, Brandi? Are you interested in being my troubleshooter?"

Brandi looked down at her hands. Of course I'm interested, she thought. This was what she'd worked for since the very first week she'd been a salesclerk, when she'd set her sights on a much higher goal. She was going to have a career, not a job that simply let her get by....

"I think you're ideally qualified," Ross went on, "because you're not only experienced at the store level, but you're bright and you're a creative problem solver. But I won't sugarcoat this offer—it wouldn't be fair. This isn't an easy or a popular job."

"I've always liked challenges, and I've never worried about being popular." But Brandi's voice sounded odd to her own ears, as if it belonged to someone else.

Ross leaned back in his chair as if confident that he had his answer. "The thing that convinced me, you know, was when you sniffed Zack out. There was no reason to think his being here had anything to do with you—but you knew it. That's exactly the kind of sixth sense I'm looking for."

Brandi didn't think it was necessary to tell him that that hadn't been her managerial instincts at work, but an awareness of an entirely different sort. *My nose for trouble*, she told herself, aware that wasn't quite true, either.

"I can't legally ask you whether you plan to stay single," Ross went on, "but I must warn you that this kind of job is terribly hard on families and friendships."

Brandi closed her eyes, and once more let an image wash over her, of two small children and a train and a Christmas tree…and Zack. The scene was faded now, as if it was a photograph that had been left out in the sun, but it still had the power to move her.

"You can plan to be on the road up to six weeks at a time," Ross said, "and away from home about fifty weeks of the year. If you want to try it, I would like to have a commitment from you for two years in this job. After that, we'll talk about what you want to do next. Maybe move through the district managers' positions, getting to know the whole chain."

She took a deep breath and wondered why she wasn't happier. Certainly he was not making the job sound like a plum, but that was no surprise; Ross wasn't the kind to hide the disadvantages of whatever he offered. Brandi had known about the difficulties of the job anyway, so why was she reacting now as if they were insuperable? Why did she have this nagging feeling, now that the plum lay within her reach, that she really didn't want it after all?

She was being stupid, she told herself. Zack would never be a part of her life. The children she had once visualized so clearly were nothing more than a wispy dream. She was free as a cloud, responsible only to herself. And *for* herself. Certainly for the sake of her future, it would be wise to take the promotion. And yet...

Her gaze fell on the blue-and-silver paisley bag that lay on the corner of her desk. She wanted to take the necessary time to wrap that package as beautifully as she could. She wanted to be there to watch as it was opened, and perhaps to get to know that woman better.

She wanted to watch Theresa Howard grow in confidence, move up in the department, maybe eventually take it over after Casey Amos left.

She couldn't do those things if she took the job Ross offered, for she would not be able to stay in one place long enough to nurture a friendship. Not as the troubleshooter. And probably not afterward, either, if she had to move around the country in order to continue up the corporate ladder.

Perhaps she wasn't as free as she'd believed. Perhaps her treasured independence had truly been self-imposed isolation instead.

A year or two ago, she wouldn't have given a second thought to leaving everything and everyone behind for a new challenge. Now, without even realizing it, she had grown roots here.

"If you'd like a chance to think it over before giving me an answer..." Ross began.

Brandi shook her head, almost automatically. "No. I can answer you now." She wet her lips and said, "Thanks, Ross, but I'm happy where I am."

He was obviously startled. "Perhaps I shouldn't have hit you with this in the midst of the busiest season. Take a while to think, Brandi. After Christmas is over and things settle down a bit, you may change your mind."

"It won't make a difference," she warned.

He studied her thoughtfully for a moment, and then his eyes began to sparkle. "I see. My wife and Whitney both said there was something cooking between you and Zack—"

Brandi said steadily, "This has nothing to do with Zack. It's just what's best for me."

Ross gave her a knowing grin.

Obviously he didn't understand, Brandi thought. But then, she hadn't expected him to.

The employee party was always held on the last Sunday before Christmas, starting just after the store closed. There had been a an air or excitement all afternoon; Brandi caught the drifts of enthusiasm as she walked through the store shortly before closing time. She even caught herself humming a snatch of "Jingle Bells" once.

She wasn't precisely happy, of course. She thought it would probably be a long time before the ache in her heart receded enough to be ignored, and she didn't even dream of a day when she might altogether forget the twin agonies of loving Zack and discovering his lies.

But there were increasing stretches of time when she was content, for she was certain the decision to stay at the store was the right one.

She'd done as Ross asked; she'd spent many hours thinking about the job he'd offered. Sometimes, in the darkest hours of the night, she'd found herself thinking that perhaps she *should* take it. In the trouble-shooter's post she could get away from almost everything and make a fresh start.

But that was the problem, Brandi concluded. The things she *could* leave behind, she didn't particularly want to. And the memory of Zack—the one thing she'd have liked to forget—would accompany her no matter where she went or what she did.

By the time she got downstairs to the party, the store was officially closed, the caterers had set up the long buffet tables in the atrium, and stacks of brightly wrapped packages of all sizes were appearing under the largest of the Christmas trees.

Brandi slid the package she'd brought into the nearest stack as discreetly as she could. As she turned away from the tree, she ran headlong into Casey Amos, who hunched protectively over the packages she carried. Her eyes widened when she saw Brandi.

Brandi shook a playful finger at her. "You look guilty," she chided. "I'll bet you took an extralong coffee break this afternoon to wrap those, didn't you? Shame."

Casey swallowed hard. "You want some shrimp?"

she said weakly. "Let me get rid of these and I'll join you."

The caterer's table was a masterpiece, loaded with simple food beautifully arranged to tempt the palate. Brandi picked up a plate and pulled a giant boiled shrimp off a lettuce-wrapped stand.

From the corner of her eye, she caught a glimpse of a red velvet suit, and her heart seemed to do a somersault. Don't be silly, she thought. In the first place, Zack couldn't possibly be attending the employees' party, because he wasn't an employee anymore. In the second place, he certainly wouldn't be wearing a Santa suit.

Very deliberately, she turned around to prove to herself that the suspicion was only a figment of her imagination, and discovered that she'd been half-right. The Santa she'd seen was the one with the half glasses, who hadn't bothered to change clothes after his shift.

Zack wasn't wearing red velvet.

He was standing at the entrance. His black-and-white patterned sweater seemed to Brandi's eyes to swirl like an optical illusion, and she thought for a moment that she was going to faint.

She had convinced herself that she was better, that the agony was receding, that someday soon she would forget him. Now she knew how foolish she had been. She had been hiding from the pain, but seeing him again brought it all bubbling up like an acid bath. And she had to admit that she would never be all right, that she would never forget, and that she missed him more than she had thought it possible to long for another human being.

She had thought she loved Jason, and time had

salved the wound. But this was different. This was forever.

Beside her, Casey Amos heaved a long sigh, as if she'd made up her mind about something desperate. "I'd better confess."

"What?" Brandi said tersely. "That you invited Zack?"

"Is he here?" Casey looked over her shoulder, only half-interested. "No, it's not that. I hope you won't hate me, but I put your name in the gift exchange drawing."

"Is that all?"

"I thought it was too bad for you not to be included. But it hit me when I saw you putting a package into the pile a minute ago that you'll be the only employee to get two gifts tonight."

A couple of weeks ago Brandi would have been a bit annoyed at being dragged into something she had no interest in. As it was, she thought the mix-up was mildly funny; she'd probably be teased for a day or two and then the event would be forgotten. "Don't worry about it, Casey. I just hope you got something nice for the person whose name I'm supposed to have drawn in return." Her gaze drifted toward Zack once more; he'd moved toward the Christmas tree.

Across the serving table, Theresa Howard turned pale and dropped a shrimp. "I put your name in, too," she whispered. "Casey said something about your being left out, and I thought…"

The humor of the situation—and the rightness of the decision she'd made—struck Brandi sharply, and she started to laugh uncontrollably. "What a party," she managed to say finally. "I wouldn't have missed this for the world!"

Even if Zack *was* there, for he stayed at the fringes of the crowd. Brandi had started to relax, thinking that he was as intent on avoiding her as she was on staying out of his way, when they abruptly came face-to-face at the portable bar.

"How's business?" Brandi asked, trying to keep her voice light. She squeezed the twist of lime into her club soda and wiped her fingertips on a napkin.

"Busy. We're reorganizing produce lines, repackaging some toys in smaller units...nothing earthshaking in itself, but I hope it will have an impact well before next Christmas season."

"I'm sure it will." She didn't look directly at him. "I'm happy you found what was wrong."

For a moment, she thought he wasn't going to answer. Then he said softly, "And I'm happy you're getting the job you want."

Before Brandi could tell him any differently, he'd walked away. Not that it mattered, she thought. But the ache in the pit of her stomach—the nagging pain that had been her constant companion since the day she'd found out he'd spied on her—intensified.

The gift exchange proceeded with more than usual hilarity; Brandi's three packages got exactly the reaction she'd expected. Then a fourth was delivered, and she laughingly demanded, "All right. I know about Casey and Theresa, but who else has been setting me up?" Too late, she looked across the circle at Zack. He, too, had thought she was a Scrooge who needed a dose of Christmas spirit....

Dora sheepishly raised a hand, and also the manager of Toyland, who said, "I thought it would be sad if you weren't included on your last

Christmas—'' He caught himself too late and clapped a hand over his mouth.

Brandi sighed. Obviously Whitney had been right about the corporate grapevine. Too bad the gossips hadn't picked up on the latest installment. ''No, I'm not terminally ill,'' she said over the speculative whispers. ''And no matter what rumor says, I'm not leaving to take another job, either.'' She looked down at the stack of gifts in her lap. They were small things, even silly things, but the thought that had gone into them meant a great deal to her. ''I'm happy here—with my friends.'' It was mostly true, she told herself. She was as happy as she could be just now.

The party ended early, since they were going into the final and most wearing week of the season. Zack left among the first group, walking out with Theresa Howard. Brandi tried not to notice. She stayed till the caterers had cleaned up the last scrap of turkey, and then she locked the employee exit behind her and went home.

Another ordeal survived, she told herself. It would get easier with time, though she could no longer fool herself that the pain would end entirely someday.

She made a hollow in the garland on the mantel so she could set up one of her gifts there—a ceramic statuette of a winking Santa—and she was just setting him in place when the doorbell rang. Through the peephole, she recognized Zack, and with resignation she opened the door.

''I'm glad you didn't pretend not to be home,'' he said. ''I'd have looked pretty silly climbing up the drainpipe and over the balcony rail.''

Brandi didn't invite him in, but leaned against the jamb with the door open only a few inches. ''I can't see why that would be necessary. If you left something at the party, you can get it at the store tomorrow. I'm not going back tonight."

Zack shook his head. "That's not why I'm here. Didn't Ross come through with the job offer?"

"Why not ask him? I suppose you're worried because you recommended me and I didn't live up to expectations."

Zack looked exasperated. "Look, must we have this conversation with my foot in the door?"

"I didn't invite you here."

"Brandi, I don't blame you for being angry with me. And I'm not justifying what I did. But I'd like to have a chance to explain it—so you'll know I didn't do it for fun, or without thinking it through."

Brandi shrugged and moved back from the door. "I suppose I have nothing to lose by listening."

She purposely didn't offer him a cup of coffee, and she didn't sit down. Zack didn't seem to notice; he moved around her living room with the nervous energy of a caged panther, stopping for a moment to look at the ceramic Santa on the mantel. Brandi had forgotten that, or she'd have left him standing in the hall.

"Ross and I have been friends since college days," Zack began. "In fact, we met in the dean's office—both of us were close to being thrown out of school because of a little too much high-spirited fun. Ever since then, we've pitched in to help each other when trouble's brewing, so of course when I started getting bad news about my Christmas sales, I called Ross."

Brandi decided to hurry things along. "And he thought it would be a good idea to kill two birds with one stone by sending you to spy on me."

Zack winced. "He didn't, Brandi. All he asked of me was an opinion about how well you'd be suited to the job he was thinking of offering you."

"That's what I called it," Brandi said softly. "Spying."

"No. He was just asking for another point of view—it's the kind of thing I've done myself a thousand times, with Ross and with others. He knew you were good, you see—that was never in doubt. But he questioned whether you were flexible enough for the fast changes and the constant shifts that a troubleshooter faces every day. All he wanted was an opinion. The decision would be his, no matter what I thought."

She shrugged. That must be what he meant when he said he hadn't actually made a recommendation. It ended up being the same thing.

"It seemed a very small favor," Zack said softly, "compared to the one he was doing for me, so I agreed. I didn't realize then—how could I, Brandi?— that it wasn't just Ross's employee I'd be looking at." Zack was looking very steadily at her. "I had no idea that I was going to meet a very special woman here."

Brandi swallowed hard. *A very special woman.* It wasn't all she wanted; in fact, it wasn't really very much at all, but she would treasure those words forever. It was half a minute—an achingly long silence—before she regained her balance enough to say coolly, "That's touching, Zack. But once that possibility occurred to you, didn't you think about backing out of your promise and telling me what was going on?"

"Yes—but don't forget that by the time I realized I needed to tell you the truth, I was in pretty deep. I warned Ross the night of the party that I was going to tell you the whole thing—my reasons for masquerading as Santa, the troubleshooter job..."

Brandi's body went absolutely still. He had intended to confess the whole lot?

"And I tried," Zack went on softly, "but you ran away rather than listen to me. The next day, when you found out about Intellitoys, you didn't even try to understand that there might have been a reason for not telling you right away. You didn't ask questions. You just attacked."

I was hurt, she wanted to say. I was aching with love for you, and you didn't even seem to care that I might have liked to know what was going on! "I suppose that's why you didn't make a recommendation to Ross, because I'd conducted myself so badly. Why didn't you just tell him I'd be a terrible troubleshooter?"

She thought for a moment he wasn't going to answer. Then he said quietly, "Because I thought you'd make a damned good one."

A very special woman... She felt as if he'd snatched away the fragment of joy that comment had held for her; obviously he'd meant it professionally, not personally, after all. She ought to have known that from the beginning.

"Even after that I wanted to confess it all," Zack said, "and at least be square with you, whatever else happened. But don't you see, Brandi? If I told you what Ross was considering, and you changed your behavior in the least—as you'd be bound to do, it's only human—he would never have offered you the job. I was caught in my own trap."

She nodded a little.

"So I told Ross I couldn't make a recommendation, that I was too personally interested in you to have a valid opinion."

"And he believed that?" Brandi's voice was dry. Then she remembered what Ross had said about his wife's suspicions, and Whitney's. Maybe Ross *had* believed it.

"Any reason he shouldn't?" Zack sounded a little annoyed. "Just because you can't stand having me around—"

Brandi's heart seemed to give a sudden jolt and stop beating altogether. "What did you say?"

"Look, you've made it obvious how you feel, Brandi. Your career comes first, and I respect that. I don't have much choice about it, do I?" He zipped his leather jacket. "All right, I've said what I came to say. At least you know I didn't lie to you for the sheer enjoyment of it, so I won't bother you anymore."

As he brushed past her, Brandi's hand grasped his sleeve. The contact seemed to burn her fingers, and Zack stopped as if he'd run into an electrical field.

Brandi stared up at him, willing him to stay, knowing that if he left she would always regret letting him go. Her fingers tightened.

Slowly his hand closed over hers and tugged it loose. But instead of letting her go, he cradled her fingers on his, and ever so slowly raised her hand to his face.

She let her fingers curve around his jaw, savoring the warmth of him and the faintest prickle of his beard. If she could never touch him again, she thought, she would treasure this moment, this memory. She smiled just a little, and her eyes misted, and so she couldn't see clearly what emotion was in his face as he pulled her tightly against him.

He kissed her as if he couldn't deny himself, and his hunger woke a passion in her that was deeper than anything Brandi had ever felt before. This is where I belong, she thought, and burrowed against him as if she was trying to make herself a part of his body.

Eventually he stopped kissing her and simply cradled her close, his cheek against her hair. "Dammit, Brandi," he said unsteadily, "you're not my kind of woman."

Slowly, sanity dawned. Brandi tried to pull away from him, embarrassed at her own uninhibited behavior.

But Zack wouldn't let her go. "I've always made it a point to steer clear of high-powered career types."

"Love 'em and leave 'em," she said coolly, remembering what Whitney had said.

"No," Zack corrected. "Have fun, but don't get serious. And I planned to do the same with you. But it just didn't work, you see." A note of bitter humor crept into his voice. "I came here tonight to confess—so I might as well tell it all, right? I didn't realize right away why you affected me so. I thought for days that I was always on edge around you because I didn't like you at all."

"Gee, thanks." The crack in Brandi's voice robbed the comment of irony.

"The night you asked me if I was Ross's troubleshooter... You were so vulnerable, so helpless, so open, and I began to think that you might be what I'd been looking for all these years. It was almost a heretical thought—that my idea of the perfect woman had been so far from the reality. But then at the party,

I saw you with the kids—and I couldn't help but think that you wanted that, too. I guess it was wishful thinking, wasn't it?''

Brandi's throat was tight with pain and unshed tears.

"I was going to propose to you that night," Zack said softly. "And then—if you accepted me—I planned to throw myself at your feet and tell you the truth."

She'd asked him what he was going to tell her that night, and he'd dodged the question instead of answering—and so she'd assumed he'd intended to share only a version of the truth. How could she have been so blind?

"But you wouldn't stick around to listen. The only thing I could think was that you knew what I wanted to say—and you didn't want to have to turn me down, so it was easier to run away than to hear me out."

Brandi put her hand to her temple, where a vein throbbed.

"I knew then I'd read you wrong after all, that your career was more important than I could ever be. And I loved you so much I wanted you to have what you wanted—even if it wasn't me." He kissed her hair gently, and set her aside. "It isn't too late, I'm sure. I'll talk to Ross—"

Brandi had to clear her throat twice before she could say, "He offered me the job. I turned it down, Zack."

He stood as if turned to stone. "What?"

"Why do you think I blew up at you like that? I didn't do it on purpose, exactly, but I thought if I exploded at you, you'd tell Ross I shouldn't get the job."

"You *wanted* that to happen?"

"I didn't reason it out ahead of time. But yes, I think I did."

"Why don't you want the job?" He sounded as if he'd been hit a solid blow just beneath the ribs.

Brandi didn't look at him. She picked out a spot on the front of his jacket instead and stared at it. "A long time ago, I thought I was in love," she said slowly. "He was a charming man, but he liked things easy—so when he found a woman who had family money, he dumped me. And I decided never to let anyone get that close to me again. Especially not the happy-go-lucky sort who didn't worry about where the next car payment was coming from—"

"And who'd take a temporary job as Santa Claus to make ends meet? I think I begin to see."

She nodded. "I wasn't looking for a man at all, but even if I had been, you were so obviously not what I wanted that it never occurred to me to be wary of you. But before I realized what had happened, you'd crept into my heart—and made me want to feel again, and to give, and to be close to people...."

Zack drew her tightly against him once more. He kissed her temple, and the pain went away. But there was still a knot in her stomach. "I love you. But I don't know, Zack," she said on a rising note of panic. "I'm scared. Kids are so important to you. What if I can't be a good mother? I'm not exactly promising parent material!"

He smiled down at her. "If you weren't," he said softly, "it would never occur to you to ask the question. We'll wait till you're ready, that's all. And if you're never ready, I can live with that—as long as I have you."

Slowly, the knot eased. "You scare me to death sometimes," she confessed, "but I've never been as alive as when I'm with you."

"Can you forgive me for not being completely truthful with you?"

Brandi nodded. "Now I can. Now that I understand why."

He kissed her again; it was as much a promise as a caress. "If you still want the job, Brandi, we'll make it work somehow."

She considered the question, and shook her head. "My career is important to me, Zack. But it's not all-important anymore."

Zack's hands slid slowly down her back, drawing her even closer against him. "And what *is* all-important?"

Brandi looked up into his eyes, and the last whisper of doubt disappeared. This was right, and real, and forever. "You are," she confessed. "And you always will be—my unlikely Santa."

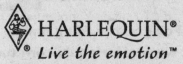

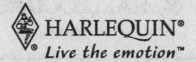

Forrester Square

LEGACIES . LIES . LOVE .

**This brand-new *Forrester Square* story
promises passion, glamour
and riveting secrets!**

Coming in January…

WORD OF HONOR

by
bestselling Harlequin Intrigue® author

DANI SINCLAIR

Hannah Richards is shocked to discover that
the son she gave up at birth is now living with
his natural father, Jack McKay. Ten years ago
Jack had not exactly been father material—
now he was raising their son.
Was a family reunion in their future?

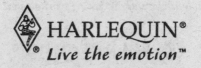

HARLEQUIN®
® *Live the emotion*™